Ann McIntosh was born in the frozen north for a numbe resides in sunny central Flor. She's a proud mama to three grown children, loves tea, crafting, animals—except reptiles!— bacon and the ocean. She believes in the power of romance to heal, inspire and provide hope in our complex world.

Becca McKay worked as a nurse in the NHS for several years before becoming a librarian, when she discovered the joy Mills & Boon books brought to readers. As an avid reader and writer, becoming a published author has been a lifelong ambition of hers, and she's delighted to be writing for the Mills & Boon Medical series. Becca lives in the North of England with her family and an assortment of animals. On the rare occasions she's not writing, you'll find her with her nose in a book or her head in the clouds.

Also by Ann McIntosh

Christmas Miracle on Their Doorstep
Twin Babies to Reunite Them
The Vet's Caribbean Fling

Boston Christmas Miracles miniseries

The Nurse's Holiday Swap

Nurse's Twin Pregnancy Surprise
is **Becca McKay**'s debut title.

Look out for more books from Becca McKay.
Coming soon!

Discover more at millsandboon.co.uk.

CELEBRITY VET'S SECOND CHANCE

ANN McINTOSH

NURSE'S TWIN PREGNANCY SURPRISE

BECCA McKAY

MILLS & BOON

First published in Great Britain 2025
by Mills & Boon, an imprint of HarperCollins*Publishers* Ltd,
1 London Bridge Street, London, SE1 9GF

www.harpercollins.co.uk

HarperCollins*Publishers* Macken House, 39/40 Mayor Street Upper,
Dublin 1, D01 C9W8, Ireland

ISBN: 978-0-263-32501-0

03/25

CELEBRITY VET'S SECOND CHANCE

ANN McINTOSH

MILLS & BOON

For my partners in crime,
Traci Douglass and Amy Ruttan.

Thanks for keeping me somewhat sane!

CHAPTER ONE

DR. JONAH BEAUMONT blinked against the grittiness in his eyes, his body aching as though he'd already worked for eight hours, although it was only nine thirty in the morning.

Besides the clinic being short-staffed and extra busy, getting out of bed to tend to a sick patient only to have the animal die on you was always a draining experience.

At least, it was for him.

Pushing the memory aside, he finished bandaging the irate duck's foot and, over the angry squawks of Jennifer Mulligan's pet mallard Hofstetter, said, "You're gonna have to isolate this baby, keep him confined and out of the water till the wound heals. Bumblefoot can become serious if it doesn't completely heal."

"He won't like that," Jennifer replied, struggling to hold the wriggling Hofstetter still. "He's used to being in charge of the flock. There'll be a mighty fuss going on all day, with him trying to boss them around from in the pen."

Jonah chuckled. "I feel for you, especially when it comes time to rebandage this foot. He doesn't much like this part of the proceedings, any more than he liked me cutting out the abscess."

Jennifer snorted. "I'll get Fen to hold him while I do it. She's the only one he'll allow to do whatever she likes with him."

Jonah straightened and peeled off his gloves. "That little girl of yours is a natural with the animals. I've never seen anything like it."

"She's already decided she wants to be a vet when she grows up," Jennifer said, shaking her head as she maneuvered the still squawking Hofstetter into a pet carrier. "Bruce and I are trying to figure out how to afford it."

"Tell her she needs to keep her nose to the grindstone at school, and when she's a little older, as long as I'm still around, she can come here as an intern after school and on the weekends. That'll go a long way toward helping her get scholarships and grants."

Jennifer's smile lit up her face and made the exhaustion weighing on Jonah lift a little.

"I'll tell her," Jennifer said. Then her smile faded. "I heard about Marnie Rutherford's mare dying this morning. What a blow that must have been to her." She hesitated a beat, then added, "And to you."

And, just like that, the weight of the world seemed to drop back onto his shoulders and, with it, that pervasive sense that no matter how hard he tried, he could never do or be enough.

"Yeah," he replied, turning away to toss the gloves into the garbage. He used the excuse of grabbing a wet wipe to keep his back to Jennifer. "She was devastated. Unfortunately, there was nothing I could do."

Behind him, he heard Jennifer pick up the carrier, and he turned to face her once more, knowing his expression wouldn't betray his real feelings. He'd had years to perfect hiding them, since his clients needed to have complete confidence in his abilities, even when he didn't.

"Torsion is like that a lot, isn't it? Quick to come on, and quick to kill."

Jennifer spoke matter-of-factly—a farmer to the core, who understood all too well the vagaries of animal husbandry. Jonah was opening the door for her and pondering how to respond to her statement when the waiting room suddenly erupted in a cacophony of barks, shouts, squeals and bleats.

With a muttered, "Excuse me," Jonah slipped past Jennifer in the corridor and ran toward the door leading to the waiting area. Throwing it open, he was in time to see a tall, dark-haired stranger put Geoffry the billy goat into a professional-looking horn hold, while his owner, old Mrs. Kimball, fluttered around ineffectually. Geoffry, not being used to such masterful treatment, seemed too shocked to do anything but stay still.

Something about the back view of the man holding the goat sparked a rush of awareness in Jonah, but he wasn't sure whether it was familiarity or something completely different. Instinct had him turn his attention, instead, to the rest of the people in the waiting room, most of whom were hanging on to their upset and anxious pets for dear life. Yet, there was also excitement on more than one face, and there'd been a smattering of applause too.

"Oh, Geoffry." Samantha, one of the vet techs, brushed past Jonah in the doorway and crossed the room to take the goat's harness. "Mrs. Kimball, we always ask you to leave Geoffry outside until it's time for Dr. Beaumont to see him. He's such a spicy guy. And he doesn't like dogs."

"That's not true," Mrs. Kimball replied. "He gets on fine with Mic and Mac at home. I'm sure that doggy must have growled at him."

Considering the dog in question had somehow wedged itself under its owner's chair despite being at least a hundred pounds, Jonah somehow doubted that statement.

The German shepherd mix looked frankly terrified.

Samantha couldn't get through the door with him standing there, so Jonah stepped back to let them pass as the goat wrangler walked away from him toward the reception desk. There was a brief shuffling of people— Sam, Geoffry and Mrs. Kimball going into the corridor, the patient Jennifer with her carrier leaving—and then the door swung shut, leaving Jonah still standing there, a little breathless and somehow confused.

Must be the lack of sleep.

But rather than go back to the examination room to see his next patient, he found himself circling over to behind the reception desk, wanting to see the strange man's face.

Hear his voice.

"Hi," the receptionist, Laura, said, while Jonah hung back out of sight behind the dividing wall, waiting to hear their interaction. She was fairly new, so if Jonah was caught spying on her, he could legitimately say he was evaluating her skills with the clients. "Thanks so much for jumping in like that. We really appreciate it."

"No problem," the man replied, amusement clear in his tone. The hair on Jonah's arms and back of his neck lifted, leaving a tingling sensation behind that made him shiver. "That poor dog didn't know what to do with itself, and the goat clearly runs the show, wherever he is."

Laura giggled, and someone else nearby called out, "You got it, man. Geoffry's a beast."

"So, what can we do for you today?" Laura asked.

"Well, I'm here in town on business, and saw your sign. I'm a vet too, and wondered if by chance your Dr. J. Beaumont is the same person I went to college with. Dr. Jonah Beaumont?"

Unable to restrain his curiosity a moment more, Jonah took the two steps necessary to get to the front desk and stood behind Laura, drawing the attention of the man standing in front of her.

Their eyes met, and Jonah's heart did a weird little stutter step before starting to pound way harder than was appropriate for the moment.

Neither of them spoke for the space of a couple of seconds, although it somehow seemed to stretch on for an eternity, during which time Jonah took in the man in front of him.

His first thought was, *expensive*.

It wasn't often you saw someone dressed that way in small-town Butler's Run. Although not much of a clotheshorse himself, Jonah knew enough to ascertain that the casual outfit—which fit to perfection—hadn't been bought in a chain store. The leather jacket alone probably cost more than all the clothes in his closet at home. And while it was paired with jeans and a flannel shirt, he'd bet both garments had designer labels in them as well.

All this he took in with a sweeping glance, down then

up, just as aviator sunglasses were being lifted to reveal the other man's face.

It was sharp, almost vulpine. Ruddy, with high cheekbones, a narrow nose that flared slightly at the end, and a cheeky, full-lipped smile. His thick dark hair fell to his shoulders and could have seemed effeminate except that the man himself exuded masculinity and sex appeal.

The consummate Latin lover come to life, with a dash of what looked like Hollywood flair added in.

But it was the eyes that brought back the sharpest memories. Light brown, almost coppery, and gleaming with good humor. Jonah remembered wanting to see them turn his way, again and again, although even when they did it was never in the way he wanted them to.

Jonah forcibly squashed that thought, and the rush of arousal that came with it.

Instead, he forced himself to remember how nice and kind the man across the desk had been to him. And also, that he'd always been so far out of Jonah's league it sometimes felt impossible they existed in the same universe, much less the same world.

"I can't believe it." Jonah finally found his voice and was amazed when it sounded fairly normal, although there was a definite edge of surprise—or shock—to it. "Rob Sandoval? What the heck are you doing here in Butler's Run?"

Rob couldn't help grinning across the reception desk at Jonah Beaumont, who looked almost the same as he had ten years before, which was the last time they'd seen each other.

About three inches shorter than Rob's six feet one inch, Jonah was broad-shouldered and barrel-chested, stocky but obviously still muscular. His scrub top hung down over a taut belly and clung to bulging biceps. There was definitely a touch of silver in his short black hair, and a few more creases in his chocolate-dark skin, especially at the corners of his mouth and eyes. But that full-lipped mouth still smiled in the same restrained way, and the deep-set eyes, with their heavy lids, gave his face a sleepy, sexy look, in contrast to what Rob remembered as a sharp intellect.

Behind him he could hear the murmuring of the people in the waiting room, and the receptionist was looking from him to the card he'd handed her, back and forth, as though trying to figure something out.

It made him grin a little wider.

Small towns, no matter where in the world they were, were all the same. Almost everybody knew everybody else's business, and what they didn't know, they'd nose out or make up.

He'd had enough experience since starting the video shorts and documentaries to realize someone would recognize him when he'd walked into the clinic. Even in the most remote corners of the States, at least one person had known about his alter ego, Vet Vic, who traveled around revealing the secret lives of animals.

Clearly there were a few Vet Vic fans in the waiting area, and they were probably waiting for him to admit to who he was.

But, instead of answering Jonah's question about why

he was there, Rob couldn't resist leaving them all hanging, just a little.

"Why would you say it like that, as though Butler's Run was in the middle of the Kalahari or something?"

Jonah's lips twisted slightly, the surprise fading to be replaced by rueful amusement.

Or was it annoyance?

"It might as well be. Butler's Run, South Carolina, isn't on the beaten path like, say, New York City, is it?"

"Thank the good Lord for that," drawled one of the clients, bringing a wave of laughter and murmurs of agreement.

"True," Rob replied, then glanced over his shoulder at the crowded waiting area. "Listen, I can see you're busy. I'll be here for a few weeks. Want to get some lunch and catch up?"

Jonah rubbed the back of his neck as he nodded. "Sure. I'd love to catch up. And normally lunch would be good, but we're short-staffed today, and I might end up working through it."

"Why not ask Vet Vic to help you out?" called someone from behind him, making Rob mentally shake his head. "If he's not filming today."

Whoever it was obviously just couldn't take the suspense anymore.

"Vet Vic?" Jonah's forehead creased with obvious confusion. "Filming?"

"I knew it!" The receptionist bounced in her seat. "I've watched all your videos. They're great."

"Where you been, Doc? Didn't you hear they were coming to do a piece on the Marsh Tacky?"

"Haven't you seen any of this guy's documentaries?"

"Vet Vic is the bomb."

Rob held up his hand, cutting through the overlapping chatter and hubbub. While there was a dawning of understanding in Jonah's expression, the tumult couldn't be allowed to continue. Turning so he could see the waiting room, he scanned it, making eye contact with most of the clients there.

"Come on, guys. Give Doc Beaumont a break, will you? He can't just have some strange vet come in and start working on his patients. There are liability issues."

"Oh, forget about all that legal claptrap," a woman with pink hair said. "Anyone here gonna sue if something happens?"

The resulting negative response was seemingly universal, but Rob shook his head.

"I'm not putting Jonah in that position."

"He's got interns and stuff working for him all the time. How would it be any different?"

Clearly the pink-haired lady was determined not to give up without a fight, and Rob hoped there were no emergencies in the back, waiting for Jonah's attention. The entire situation was getting completely out of hand. The best thing he could do was leave, before it went any further.

And when he turned back to the desk to apologize and tell Jonah goodbye, there was that expression again—the one he couldn't decide was amusement or irritation. But, to his surprise, before he could speak, Jonah's face smoothed of all emotion, and he said, "If you're free, I really could use an extra pair of hands today. I have two vet techs and my intern out sick."

Rob searched the other man's face, trying to figure out if he was just pandering to the clients' demands, but there was no reading him.

He hesitated for a moment, not wanting to cause a disruption to the running of the clinic. And yet, the opportunity was too good to pass up.

"You're sure?" he asked, and got a nod in return. "Well, then, can you lend me some scrubs?"

A ridiculous cheer went up from the waiting clients, and Rob glimpsed Jonah's mouth twist again as he turned away from the desk.

CHAPTER TWO

THE ENTIRE SITUATION felt completely surreal to Jonah, and, as he went to open the door to let Rob into the surgery area, he vaguely wondered if he'd fallen asleep and was dreaming.

He'd heard about the documentary featuring the Carolina Marsh Tacky equine breed and "Vet Vic," the celebrity veterinarian set to star in it, but hadn't really paid much attention. Never in a million years would he have thought Vet Vic and Roberto Sandoval would turn out to be one and the same person.

Nor would he have suspected that easygoing and down-to-earth Rob would have turned into what looked like a movie star—sleek, polished and overawing.

As they met in the doorway, he was ill prepared for Rob's handshake turning into one of those up-close-and-personal bro hugs.

Just the sensation of having Rob's body collide with his made his entire being tighten and tingle, even though their clasped hands were between them.

"Man, it's good to see you after all these years." Rob's eyes seemed to gleam with sincerity, but Jonah couldn't figure out why.

After all, they hadn't been very close friends back

then. Not only had Jonah been a year behind Rob in college, but for the most part Rob had hung out with a far cooler group than Jonah.

And it sure looked like they would still be moving in very different circles now.

Jonah had never felt more provincial than he did standing beside this elegantly put-together man.

"Provincial" had been one of the worst things his grandmother could call anyone, and it made Jonah want to wince to know it applied to him in this situation.

"It's good to see you too," he replied, carefully extricating himself from Rob's iron grip but retaining the sensation of hard muscles and the scents of leather, cologne and something deeply male. It made him have to swallow to clear the sudden constriction in his throat. "Come on back to my office and let me see if I can find you some scrubs. My shirts would fit you, but you're too tall for the pants."

"I can always work in my jeans," Rob replied, following Jonah down the corridor. "And I'm pretty sure your shirt will hang on me like a curtain. You're pretty ripped."

Silly to feel a glow of pride, hearing the other man describe him that way, and Jonah hid it with a deprecating, "I'm trying to stave off the middle age spread I hear so much about."

Rob's chuckle washed over him like warm honey, reminding Jonah just how much he'd liked that rich sound in the past.

"I've been lucky so far," Rob replied. "But I have to watch it too. Obesity runs in my mother's family, and who knows what the gene lottery has in store for me going forward."

As he opened the door to his office, Jonah gave Rob a skeptical glance.

"I doubt you'll have a problem with that. You look pretty much the same as I remember you from college."

Rob said, "Knock wood," and rapped his knuckles on the door as he went through, making Eunice lift up her head and give a tentative *woof*.

"It's okay, girl." The elderly golden retriever's tail beat a tattoo on her bed at the sound of Jonah's voice, but she also kept her milky gaze fixed on Rob, uncertain about the stranger.

"Oh, hi there, sweetheart." Rob's voice dropped low and silky, and Eunice reacted to it pretty much the way Jonah wanted to, by wagging her tail even harder and grinning as only a golden could. Rob moved forward to crouch and offer the dog his hand to sniff. "What's your name?"

"This is Eunice." After giving the dog a quick scratch behind her ear, Jonah went to the cupboard behind his desk to rummage for some scrubs. "She's thirteen now, so she spends most of her day snoozing in here while I work."

"Wow. She's doing well for her age. You've taken really good care of her."

Eunice actually deigned to get up, so as to cuddle close to Rob and try to lick his face. He was playfully fending her off, but Eunice was suddenly determined, in a puppyish way Jonah hadn't seen her display for months.

"Well, my mom made sure of that, until she passed a year ago." A pang of sadness made his chest clench,

but he was so used to it now, Jonah rode right through it.
"Eunice was so depressed after Mom died, I wasn't sure
she'd make it, but here she is."

Not wanting to see the sympathy he was sure would
be in Rob's eyes, he'd addressed the last of his words to
Eunice who, hearing his tone, turned her wiggly, happy
attention to him. He bent to accept her licks and snuffles.

"I'm sorry to hear about your mom."

They were crouched on either side of Eunice, who was
going back and forth between them, and Jonah reluctantly
met Rob's gaze. There was sympathy there, for sure, but
also understanding that, somehow, made it bearable.

Jonah found himself giving the other man a half
smile—something he'd never have thought himself capable of when talking about his mother at this stage.

"Thanks. She was ill for a long time though. Multi-
ple sclerosis. And she was dreading the end stages, you
know? So, when she died, I was sad, but just for myself.
Not for her. She didn't want to live like that."

Rob's eyes were like liquid bronze, soft and kind, and
Jonah wanted to look away but couldn't.

"Family is everything, right? And the worst part of
any loved one having a degenerative disease is watching
the progression and knowing there's nothing you can do
to stop it. The sense of impotence, when all you want to
do is take it all away."

That cut way too close to the bone. Overwhelmed,
Jonah rose and held out the scrub top toward Rob. If he
allowed himself to think about it, to even agree to the oh-
so-true statement, he thought he might cry. Which was
ridiculous. He hadn't cried since his mother's funeral.

"Here you go. And let me go see if I can find you some longer pants from the storage closet."

Rob rose too, smiling again, but with a rueful tilt to his lips.

"Don't bother. Even if my jeans get filthy, it wouldn't be the first time I've had to double-wash my clothes. Nothing like being called out to a large animal birth when you're not really prepared for it."

That made Jonah snort in agreement, but he was already at the door.

"I'll just be a minute. No use getting your fancy clothes dirty."

As he rummaged for an appropriate pair of scrub pants, he ruefully admitted to himself how snarky he'd sounded, but he'd been unable to help it. Having to accept Rob's help—even when he knew he really needed it—just made him feel even more of a failure on an already hard day.

Besides, where did the other man get off, looking so damned prosperous and gorgeous?

Stupid. Coming into a small town like Butler's Run dressed like he was walking the red carpet.

Stewing on those sour thoughts helped take his mind off how attractive he found Rob.

Still. After ten years.

That had been a nonstarter back then, and no doubt would be one again.

When he got back to the office, Rob had taken off his jacket and hung it up on a hook by the door. After taking the scrub pants from Jonah, he cocked an eyebrow.

"Should I change in here?"

Jonah froze, forgot how to breathe, realized he'd probably have a heart attack if Rob undressed in front of him and quickly said, "There's a bathroom just down the hall. Left outside, then the first right."

The sound Rob made sounded suspiciously like a snicker, but since he was heading for the door Jonah couldn't see his face to be sure. Heat flared in his chest and up into his cheeks, and he rounded his desk to flop into his chair, relieved to have a few minutes to himself to get his bearings.

Then he realized he had a chance to do a little clandestine research, and pulled his phone out of his pocket. Quickly plugging in *Vet Vic*, he was surprised by the plethora of videos that came up—some free, some on streaming services. Clearly Rob had been busy at it for quite a while.

And all the places he'd traveled to while doing it! All over the States, and even into Canada and Mexico. There was no mistaking the harsh spurt of jealously that burned bitter in Jonah's heart as he glanced down the list of programs.

Now that was a life. Not this truncated, stagnant existence he was living.

The only way to grow and to understand the world is to travel through it, his grandmother always said. *It makes you complete in ways nothing else can.*

Jonah felt stuck, unfulfilled and, yes, incomplete.

But not for too much longer, he promised himself again.

Not that he regretted having postponed his dreams. To do that would also be to regret the time spent taking care of his mom, and that had been a true privilege. As Rob had said, in the final analysis, family was everything. Besides, although it was never quite enough for his own satisfaction, he'd done some good work here in Butler's Run.

He was still scrolling through the list of videos when Rob came back into the office and tossed his clothes over the back of a chair. Jonah couldn't help noticing how the scrub top stretched tight across his shoulders, and his thighs filled out the pants with little room left over.

The slender young man he remembered had definitely filled out some, and in the best possible way.

Dragging his thoughts away from checking Rob out physically was a lot harder than he wanted it to be, so when he spoke, his words came out harsher than necessary.

"So, what's with the whole Vet Vic thing?"

Rob paused in the act of putting his hair back at his nape with a band and sent Jonah a startled look, no doubt because of the tone of the question.

"I'll give you the short version now, and the long when we have more time. My sister Beeta was in film school and about to graduate in 2019. Since she was planning a career in animal photography and videography, she asked me to help her make a short film. I agreed, and it grew from there."

The envy Jonah felt intensified, but he suppressed it, not wanting to bark at the other man again. After a deep breath, he admitted, "That sounds amazing."

Rob shrugged and gave a grimace. "It's not as exciting as it might look. Long days, sometimes out in the middle of nowhere. Constant travel from one place to the next. It all takes a toll, after a while."

Sounded like heaven to a man who'd hardly left his small town for more than a couple of days a year, and hadn't had a chance to go anywhere much, but Jonah bit his tongue. No need to let Rob know just how pathetic and insular his life had been since they last saw each other.

Rising, he bookmarked the Vet Vic page on his phone and said, "Let's get going, before the clients start rioting out there."

"I'm yours to command," Rob replied, sketching the kind of exaggerated bow seen only in cheesy movies.

Jonah chuckled, but deep inside, that irrepressible, lusty part of his psyche that he usually kept buckled down tight took notice—and wished he meant that literally.

There were a bunch of things Jonah would love to command Rob Sandoval to do, none of which had anything to do with veterinary medicine!

Rob was a great believer in fate and synchronicity, and could only think that Beeta getting the opportunity to come to Butler's Run fell straight into those categories.

He'd told his sister he was finished with the whole video and documentary thing, but she'd gotten a request to do a piece on the Carolina Marsh Tacky equine breed and asked him to reconsider.

"The contract specifies you participate, since you're the face of the series so far," she'd said. "I doubt they'd agree to have someone else take your place."

"Did you tell them beforehand that I wouldn't be available?" he'd asked, and he knew from the way Beeta refused to meet his eyes that she hadn't.

"Not really," she admitted, finally looking straight at him. "After all, we've been in this together from the beginning. How was I to know you'd suddenly decide you don't want to do it anymore?"

She'd known, since he'd been saying it for a while, but Rob didn't bother to argue the point with her. Beeta knew he had a hard time saying no to her, and they both knew she was taking full advantage of that fact in this instance.

Their collaboration had been financially lucrative for both of them, but Rob was tired—bone tired—of the constant moving around. The rootlessness and loneliness of traveling, of never being in one place for any length of time. Even when he'd had a chance to go home to LA, his apartment felt barren and sad.

Plus, there was her insistence that he always look like he'd stepped out of a fashion magazine when in public. That part of it he particularly hated. Especially like here, in a rural setting, when he'd fit in far better if he'd been wearing the clothes he did when he went back to visit his parents on the ranch.

He'd stuck out like a sore thumb, and Jonah's little digs about his appearance hadn't gone unnoticed. He was trying to avoid reacting, but it had been hard.

After all, if he hadn't seen Jonah's name mentioned in the briefing the Marsh Tacky folks had sent, he'd definitely have refused to come. It was as though he were being sent a sign.

He'd been so discontented with his life, and seeing Jonah's name had taken him back to a simpler time. One where he was charting his own course, rather than following someone else's, where he could just be himself, and not this mythical person, Vet Vic.

"Just this last one," he'd told Beeta firmly. "Then I'm done, for real. You've made the name for yourself you needed to get your career on a solid footing, and it's time for me to go back to my life."

"I have," she'd replied, but from her tone and earnest expression he'd known he was still in for an argument. "Producers and investors know I'm the brains behind the innovative camera work, but you're the one everybody recognizes in the streets. We have such a good thing going, I can't believe you want to give it up. What are you going to do? Go back to clinical work?"

That's exactly what Rob wanted to do, although Beeta had looked skeptical when he said so.

They may be brother and sister, and share a love of animals and the outdoors, but beyond that, they were completely different.

Beeta had always been independent, with itchy feet and the kind of driving personality that sometimes had her butting heads with others—from their parents to strangers on the street. Rob, however, liked a quieter, more laid-back life, which made him more cautious. Beeta would jump into things with both feet and fight her way through whatever came next, but Rob found that kind of lifestyle too stressful.

Think first, act later was his mantra.

Rob looked around as he followed Jonah down the corridor, toward the back of the clinic. There were three exam rooms coming off the hallway, and another door marked as storage. Ahead of them he could see a general exam and treatment area, with tables, an X-ray room and two glass enclosed operating rooms.

People were bustling around, smiling at and greeting Jonah, and giving Rob the once-over. Everything was neat, and clean, and looked like heaven to him.

This was what he'd been craving over the last eighteen months, and lucky Jonah Beaumont had it all. A place to call his own, surrounded by people he knew, serving the needs of animal owners he was familiar with.

The longing that swamped him was almost crushing. His life had been anything but stable over the last four years, and he craved the security of having a home again, wherever it might end up being.

"Hey, y'all," Jonah called out. "Come on over here a second." As they gathered around, Rob noticed two of the techs nudging each other and sending sideways glances his way. When everyone had closed in on where they were standing and fallen silent, Jonah said, "This is Dr. Rob Sandoval—a friend of mine from vet school. He's agreed to help us out today, since we're short-staffed. He'll be working alongside me, kinda as a vet tech, since he's not listed on our insurance, so don't be asking him to operate on any animals, okay?"

There was a smattering of laughter, and a round of introductions, starting with the associate vet, Dr. Inez Nguyen, all the way down to a timid-looking teenager, who mumbled his greeting toward the ground.

But it was that same youth, Alan, who asked, "You're Vet Vic, aren't you?"

"Yeah, I am." No call to pretend otherwise. "But only when I'm being filmed. Otherwise, you can call me Rob."

"Okay, Dr. Rob."

Alan still hadn't looked up at him, but Rob smiled at the youngster anyway, and didn't object to the more formal name.

"Oh," Jonah added. "Somewhere around here is Gilligan, our office cat. Where is he, Alan?"

"In the hospital, Dr. J.," Alan replied. "Making his rounds."

"His rounds?" Rob looked from one face to the other, wondering if they were messing with him.

"Yeah." It was Alan who answered, giving him a brief glance, before his gaze dropped once again. "He likes to visit the animals. Seems to make them feel a bit better."

"Sounds like a solid member of the team," Rob said, delighted at the mental image of the cat going from cage to cage, offering comfort to other sick animals.

"He is."

"All right, y'all. Let's get back to work," Jonah called. "Sam, you work with Dr. Nguyen on Geoffry—I think he's in for a parasite check—and Dr. Rob and I will deal with whoever's next on the list."

The packed waiting room should have alerted Rob to the pace of the clinic, but he was still surprised by the number of patients they saw that morning. And the variety of animals.

"You have a lot of exotic animals coming through here," he remarked to Jonah while they sat in his office during a brief break, munching on muffins someone had brought in. "I've never treated an Egyptian uromastyx, even in the clinic in LA."

Jonah gave a little shrug, which included a sexy little tilt of his head that Rob couldn't help noticing, although he knew it wasn't smart to be thinking about the other man that way. So far Jonah's reaction to him was less than welcoming, and Rob was smart enough to take a hint.

Wasn't he?

"I've seen a lot more exotic animals being kept as pets since the pandemic," Jonah replied. "I don't know if people had more time to search for interesting animals or what, but I've had more unusual reptiles, rodents and mammals in the last four years than I'd seen any time before."

"Bet some of those textbooks from college came in handy," Rob teased, wanting to see Jonah smile.

He was rewarded when the other man laughed outright.

"Some of them had to be replaced. They fell apart. And then, one night I fell asleep before taking Eunice out for her walk, and she peed on the last of them." He shook his head. "I couldn't be mad at her. It was my fault."

They were on their way back to see their next patient when the receptionist came barreling down the hallway, a frantic look on her face.

"I just got a call about a dog that—I'm not sure—I think they said it got stung by wasps?"

"Calm down," Jonah said, putting his hands on her shoulders. Poor girl looked as though she was about to burst into tears. "Take a deep breath. What did the owner say, and where are they?"

After following his instructions and inhaling a massive lungful of air, the young woman said, "I couldn't understand all of it. Someone was shouting in the background. But I know I heard something about wasps and the dog's tongue being swollen. They're on their way in to the clinic."

"I'll go out and meet them," Rob said and, without waiting for a response, strode down the corridor toward the front of the clinic.

"Hey, Vet Vic," called one of the men in the waiting area. "Are we going to get to see the doctor anytime soon?"

"I'm sure Dr. Nguyen will be with you in a moment," he said, not breaking stride as he headed to the front door. "We have an emergency coming in any second."

There were a few murmurs, but no one complained. At least not that Rob heard before he went out the door. They'd probably expect the same diligence if the injured animal coming in were theirs.

Going out the front door, he paused to scan the parking lot and driveway leading to the clinic, but there was no one there. So, leaning a shoulder against the wall, he took a deep breath of the warm spring air. Set back from the road, and surrounded by what he figured was at least an acre and a half of land, the clinic gave the impression of being in the middle of nowhere, even though it was right off the main thoroughfare. At the corners of the front of the building were two peach trees in glorious bloom. The pink blossoms exuded their delicate honey-almond scent, which, with the odor of freshly cut grass, merged into an almost intoxicating mix.

Rob took another deep breath and felt more alive and happier than he had for a long time.

Then he shook his head and smiled.

Jonah Beaumont.

He'd had a massive crush on Jonah back in vet school, but there'd been a distancing bubble around the other man, and Rob was unwilling to do anything to try and breach it. For a while he wasn't even sure Jonah was gay, since he'd kept himself firmly to himself. Ironically, it was only at the end of one semester, when he'd seen Jonah at a club dancing with another man, that he'd been sure.

But thereafter, although he'd flirted shamelessly with Jonah, there'd been little reaction. Then, before he could work up the courage to openly approach him, Jonah was gone.

Now, working alongside the other man, Rob had realized just how good a vet Jonah was. Not just in the way he handled and treated the animals, but in the way he connected with the owners too.

He wasn't overly jovial, but he was the epitome of politeness, patience and gentleness. When he smiled or laughed, he lit up the entire room. And more than once Rob had found himself fixating on Jonah's wide-palmed hands, whether while he was examining an animal or gesticulating while he spoke.

Rob found himself rubbing his left arm, where goose bumps had suddenly appeared, despite the sultry air.

He couldn't help wondering what those hands would feel like running over his body, finding all the most sensitive places, making him lose himself in sheer pleasure.

With a grunt and a shake of his head, Rob pulled himself back from those thoughts.

Yes, he was attracted to Jonah, but no, he wouldn't pursue him.

He was already wondering if coming here had been a mistake, a misguided rush of nostalgia that had kept him on the same track he'd been so determined to get off of. Whether it had actually been born of his fear that he'd never get his life back to where he wanted it to be. Or fear of the unknown, after so many years of being towed along by the freight train of Beeta's ambition.

Was there actually a placc for him, somewhere?

And if so, where?

The craving for stability was visceral, and almost always top of his mind. Jonah had what Rob wanted, which begged the question: was that what Rob was really attracted to, rather than the man himself?

He needed to figure that out, rather than just concentrate on the desire he felt in Jonah's presence.

Just then a pickup came careening off the road into the driveway, and he waved it up to the front door, moving to meet it as it screeched to a halt.

No more time for daydreaming, no matter how sweet the fantasy may be.

CHAPTER THREE

THE DOG, A ROTTWEILER or Rottie mix, jumped out of the back of the truck, but staggered when it hit the ground. Rob could see the dog couldn't close his mouth, and when he got a front view of its face, he realized the tongue was so swollen it looked like a huge pink sponge.

The woman was sobbing as she got out of the passenger side, and the male driver looked like he was on the verge of a breakdown, literally spinning one way then the other, rather than bringing the dog in.

"Will he try to bite if I pick him up?" Rob asked, taking the leash from the owner's hand.

"I was trying to get rid of—"

"Hang on," Rob interjected, realizing they were too frantic to be of much use just then. "Let's get him inside, and then you can tell Dr. Beaumont what happened."

Taking a chance, hoping the dog wouldn't struggle much, he bent and picked him up, grunting at the sheer weight of the animal.

"Get the door," he ordered, as he moved as quickly as possible to the building. "And don't forget to turn off your truck."

The woman ran ahead and held the clinic door open for Rob. Thankfully, the dog put up no resistance to being carried, and as he hurried through the waiting area, he heard the murmurs of the other clients.

"Have you brought your dog here before?" he asked the woman, who was opening the door leading to the exam rooms.

"Yes," she answered, tearfully.

"What's his name, and yours?"

"He's Bear, and I'm Maggie Cole. My husband is Chad."

"Laura," he called as he hurried past. "Please pull Bear Cole's file. His owners are Maggie and Chad Cole. Bring it back ASAP."

Jonah was hurrying down the hall toward them, and Rob heard the door from the waiting area bang open behind him too. No doubt Chad Cole rushing to catch up.

"What happened to Bear?" Jonah asked, turning to keep up with Rob and listening for the answer over his shoulder. He bent slightly, so as to visually examine the dog's mouth, as Chad replied.

"There was a wasp's nest on the shed soffit, and I decided to get rid of it. When I knocked it off, Bear grabbed it and ran off. By the time I found him, he was chewing on it."

"Did you use pesticide to get rid of the wasps?"

Rob couldn't stop himself from asking the question, even before Jonah could, and he sent the other man an apologetic glance as he put the dog on the table. Jonah didn't seem to notice or care though as he stuck his stethoscope into his ears.

"No. I never use pesticides on the farm. We're organic growers. I burned them out."

That, at least, was a relief. Bad enough to be dealing with the venom from the grubs still in the nest. If there was also a pesticide involved, it would make the situation that much more perilous.

Rob was already at the drug cupboard when Jonah said, "Epinephrine. And bring the oxygen. His breathing is labored."

Rob grabbed the medication Jonah asked for, as well as antihistamine, and took both back to the table.

Poor Bear was lying there, his eyes wide and pitiful, and after Rob handed Jonah the epinephrine and antihistamine, he stood by the dog's head and encircled its neck with one arm.

"You're going to be okay, Bear," he crooned, wanting to keep the dog calm while Jonah injected the epinephrine into the muscle on his flank.

"This is to help him breathe easier, and get his blood pressure where it needs to be," Jonah explained to Maggie and Chad, as he gave Bear the shot. "And I'm going to administer an antihistamine and a steroid injection. Those'll work over time to help him recover."

One of the vet techs brought the oxygen apparatus, and Rob took the mask and placed it in front of Bear's nose, while the tech got the flow going. The animal's breathing was still labored, no doubt obstructed by the massive tongue. If it didn't start to shrink soon, they would have to intubate or, worst-case scenario, do a tracheotomy.

"There isn't much more we can do right now. I want to keep him here for a while, to monitor him. We'll call once we have an update," Jonah said to Maggie and Chad.

"Oh, but can't we stay with him?"

Maggie's eyes were filled with tears, but Jonah shook his head. Softly, he replied, "I'm afraid we just don't have the space for you to be back here for any length of time. We'd have to be working around you, and that wouldn't be safe for any of us. Don't worry," he added, putting an arm around her shoulders and his hand on Chad's arm. "We'll take good care of him and let y'all know as soon as there are any changes." Turning to Rob, he asked, "Do you mind keeping an eye on Bear for a while?"

"Not at all." Jonah probably wanted the clients out of the room, in case they had to intubate or insert the tracheostomy tube. With the couple already so upset, that would be extra traumatic for them.

"But you'll check on him too, won't you?" Chad asked Jonah, his lack of confidence in Rob's abilities as clear as if he'd voiced them.

"I will," he replied, then added, "But this is Dr. Rob Sandoval. He's a vet too, so Bear is having the best possible care he can right now, even if I'm with another patient."

"Oh." Maggie's eyes widened in surprise. "I hadn't heard that you brought in another vet."

"It's a long story," Jonah replied, easing both the Coles toward the door. "But I'm sure you'll hear all about it very soon."

And, as they walked away, Rob couldn't help silently chuckling to himself.

Yep. Small-town life summed up right there.

Jonah tried to go on with his day as though nothing untoward was happening, and thought he was doing a pretty good job—despite the way his pulse leaped each time he exited an exam room and glimpsed Rob keeping vigil at Bear's side.

There was something intensely appealing about the way the other man stroked the dog's fur and whispered into his ear. Plus, Gilligan, the black cat, was perched on Rob's lap, his face on the edge of the examination table, close to Bear's. He might be there to offer his version of care, but Rob was also stroking his back at the same time, so Gilligan was getting something in return too.

It took a while for Bear's breathing to even out and for there to be a visible reduction in the size of his tongue, but Jonah was able to call Maggie and let her know the dog seemed to be out of the woods.

"We're gonna keep your baby here for a while longer," he said when she asked if she could come and pick Bear up. "But unless there's a deterioration in his condition this afternoon, you can come and get him before six, when the clinic closes."

Like a trout caught on the end fishing line, Jonah found himself drawn back to Rob's side, although there was no need for him to be there.

"Hey," Rob said, giving Jonah one of his cheeky smiles. "He's doing a lot better. O-sat is good, and he can almost close his mouth, although he hasn't gotten control of his tongue back yet. Respiration is smooth, heart rate within normal parameters too."

"I told Maggie she could come get him before the clinic closes, unless there's a change for the worse. Looks like he's out of the woods now though."

Rob stroked the dog's head and got a gooey, love-struck glance from the Rottie mix.

Jonah shivered, thinking he'd probably do the same if Rob Sandoval touched him that way.

Dragging his mind away from the abyss it seemed determined to stand on the edge of, Jonah turned back toward the exam rooms, then paused. Facing Rob once more, he said, "I think he'd be okay in a kennel now, with periodic checks. You must be hungry. Why don't you go get something to eat?"

It was already after two thirty, and the clinic was finally slowing down, but with Bear's emergency neither of them had had time to get food since having muffins earlier.

"I'm okay," Rob said, getting up off the stool he'd been sitting on and stretching. Jonah looked away quickly on seeing the scrub top rising, revealing a strip of what appeared to be a most delectable belly. "What about you? You haven't eaten either."

Jonah shrugged, ridiculously touched that the other man was concerned for his welfare, even in such a small way. The people around him were kind and considerate, and more like family, but they seemed to believe he was more than capable of looking after himself.

"I'm used to working through lunch. Even if you're not starving, there are some snacks in my desk if you want to take a breather and have some."

"Keep an eye on this guy for me a moment," Rob said, gesturing to Bear, "while I get a kennel ready for him. And why don't we have an early dinner together, when the clinic closes? I just heard from my sister, and there's some issues she has to deal with before we can start film-ing, so I'm free both tonight and probably tomorrow. If you need help again, I'm available."

Oh, he needed help all right, but not at the clinic…

Someone needed to give him a quick rap over the head so he'd stop lusting after Rob and keep his mind on busi-ness.

He should refuse. Make some excuse not to go or to have Rob back the next day. Spending the day with Rob had been both pleasure and torture. The other man's easy-going character, sly humor and obvious care for the ani-mals threatened the tight control Jonah kept on his needs and desires.

Rob Sandoval, in short, confused the heck out of his world, and Jonah didn't like it.

Or he liked it too much.

Hard to know which, when his brain seemed deter-mined to drop down into his shorts whenever the other man was around!

Hopefully, after a short while, Rob and his sister would be gone, and Jonah could get back to normal.

Boring ol' normal sounded both good and horrible right now. Considering how badly he wanted some ad-venture in his life, you'd think he'd be glad of this sud-den turn of events, but this wasn't the kind of excitement he'd expected.

Yet, even as the thoughts barreled through his mind, he heard himself say, "Sure. Sounds good. And I'll be glad of the help tomorrow too."

"Awesome." Rob's smile set Jonah's heart thumping

again. "How about Lonie's Café? I noticed it on the way through town earlier."

Jonah only just stopped himself from grimacing. Lonie, proprietor of the café, was his aunt, favorite relative and the one person in the world who could read him like a book. Sometimes like a kid's picture book, at that.

"We could go there," he said, trying to find a way out of what felt like a situation he wasn't ready to face. "Or we could drive fifteen minutes up the road and go somewhere nicer."

Rob lifted Bear off the table like the dog weighed nothing at all, and Jonah saw the way the muscles in his back flexed with the action. Mesmerized, he hardly heard the other man's words.

"Is the food at Lonie's not good?"

Now Rob was bending to slide Bear into the low kennel, and Jonah tried to force his gaze away. But there was no escaping the allure of Rob's lean, toned body in motion.

"My life wouldn't be worth a hill of beans if I said it wasn't," he answered, his mouth on autopilot as he tried to get himself under control. "It's my aunt's restaurant."

Rising, Rob looked over at him, that impish smile playing around his lips, his eyes gleaming with amusement.

"So, you don't want me meeting your aunt? Is that why you're reluctant to go there?"

"It's not… I just…" What was it about this man that reduced him to a blithering idiot? Worse, he'd hit the damn nail on the head too, which was completely unfair. Jonah allowed annoyance to overcome attraction and, in an act of sheer self-preservation, came up with what seemed to him a completely reasonable excuse. "I eat there all the time. Kinda thought it might be nice to get out of town instead."

Rob's amusement didn't abate, and one eyebrow jumped, as if querying the veracity of Jonah's words.

"Next time," he said, his voice dropping a little, as if not wanting to be overheard. Which was silly, since they happened to be the only ones in the room. "Tonight, I'd like to see more of the town. And meet your Aunt Lonie."

There was an undercurrent in his words, impossible to ignore or pretend not to hear. It gave them a kind of heated intimacy that made Jonah want to run, or to hide.

Or to grab Rob and kiss him until they both exploded into flames.

Scared, aroused, confused, Jonah turned on his heel and headed for his office, saying, "Whatever. Just let me know when you're ready to go."

It sounded rude. He knew it did, but he couldn't make himself feel ashamed.

As he dropped into his desk chair, leaned his head back and closed his eyes, Jonah wondered why it felt as though his world, which had previously been staid, boring and way too settled, was all cattywampus.

Rob Sandoval.

Something about that man turned Jonah inside out.

Always had.

He'd had the hots for Rob back in vet school, but Jonah had been determined to keep his eyes on the future he dreamed about. Traveling and treating animals around the world. Learning about different cultures, while saving endangered species. He couldn't afford to be distracted by anything, or anyone—not even a man with the most alluring eyes he'd ever seen, and a mouth made for loving.

So he'd made it a point to not take Rob's flirtations seriously, or even really acknowledge them.

"You can only control your life if you control your emotions and urges," his grandmother had told him when he was a young teen. "That ability is what truly separates humans from animals."

Back then she'd been lecturing him because of a fight he'd gotten into, but he'd somehow known she'd meant it as a life lesson, and he'd taken it to heart.

And it was just as well he had, since it had only been a few more months before he'd had to leave Southern California and move back home. That would have been much harder if he'd been romantically involved with Rob and leaving him behind.

Now the damn man was back in his life, and already making waves, rocking his world in ways both big and small.

Looking way more delectable than he had a right to.

Charming everyone, from staff to clients—including Jonah himself.

And, worse, showing his absolute competence around the clinic.

A little part of Jonah had been hoping Rob had fallen back on the whole Vet Vic thing because he couldn't make it in the competitive world of veterinary medicine, but clearly that wasn't true. He'd not only shown his capabilities, but even preempted Jonah a couple of times with questions and treatments that were completely on point.

Considering how determined Jonah was to always be

in charge, he should resent the way Rob had of quietly taking over, but somehow couldn't.

It was a real conundrum.

Sighing, shaking his head to try and clear it, Jonah tried to think about his plans for the future. Goals that had sustained him for years, and brought him joy, even when his reality was in shambles.

But instead of seeing himself traveling, free to go wherever he wanted, all he could see was Rob smiling. And the yearning that vision created was even stronger than any of his oldest dreams could engender.

CHAPTER FOUR

HAVING HEARD THE dismissal in Jonah's voice, Rob stayed out of his way for the rest of the afternoon, instead offering his services to Inez Nguyen, which were accepted.

"Today was shaping up to be rough until you stepped in," she said, as they took a cat suspected of swallowing a hair tie back to X-ray. "Thank goodness we didn't have any surgeries scheduled, or we'd have had to either cancel them, or one of us vets would have had to work the crowd on our own."

"Is it always this busy?" he asked as he put on the lead apron.

"Not always. But Dr. Beaumont is really popular, and everyone knows if you want the best care, this is where to get it." She gave him a clear-eyed glance. "That's why I'm here, instead of in Charleston with my family. Working with Jonah will be a boost to my reputation."

While he positioned the unhappy feline on the X-ray detector, holding it still, Rob considered what Inez had said.

It was a little strange to think of this relatively small clinic, in a very small town, having the kind of reputation she'd intimated. Not that Rob didn't believe it possible, although he wondered how it had come about.

Jonah had been at the top of his class when they were in college together, so it wasn't surprising to realize he'd become a great vet. How his reputation had grown beyond the borders of his obvious purview was another thing entirely.

"How did you find out about this place?" he asked, trying to sound as though he were making small talk, although curiosity was burning away inside.

"Jonah is known as an equine and exotic animal expert in the state," she replied, squinting at the X-ray, now projected onto the screen in front of her. "Even though he'd deny it, he made a name for himself during the year he spent at the Cricket City Zoo, just outside of Charleston. He's also the official vet for the Carolina Marsh Tacky Association, doing all their genetic testing and everything else. Since taking over this clinic, he's poured himself into it, and people noticed."

Another facet to an already complex character, Rob mused. Coming from a farming community himself, he knew the local vets had to be well-versed in a wide variety of animals, but the breadth of knowledge Jonah obviously had was amazing.

"But you're an all-rounder yourself, aren't you?" Inez asked, giving him another of those piercing glances. "You'd have to be, to host your show."

"Not really," he replied honestly, although he knew Beeta wouldn't like to hear him say so. She was all about his so-called image, constantly saying he had to maintain that air of knowing far more than he actually did, even when off camera. "Remember, I get to do a bunch of research before we film, so I have an unfair advantage. It's not like when someone brings an animal into the clinic presenting with symptoms you've never seen before, and you have to hurry to make a diagnosis."

She nodded thoughtfully, then pointed at the screen.

"What do you think?" Abruptly ending their conversation.

And, thankfully, there was no sign of anything foreign in the cat's digestive tract, so they didn't have to operate.

By six o'clock, when the Coles came to pick up Bear, the Rottie mix was back to normal, although Jonah made sure to tell them to keep an eye on the dog for any residual symptoms.

"You have my cell number," Jonah told them, while Bear danced around, licking everyone within tongue reach, as if delighted to have use of that organ again. "Call if you're at all worried. And next time, keep him inside if you're dealing with wasps. Clearly, he has a taste for the grubs."

"You bet I will," Maggie said, stooping to hug her recalcitrant pet around the neck, and getting a lively face wash in return. "'Cause you know this goofball won't have learned his lesson."

They were the last clients to leave, and the staff wasn't far behind, calling out goodbyes as they went.

Then there was just Jonah, Eunice and Rob left.

"I have to take Eunice home and give her a little walk," Jonah said, still sounding distant. "Want to meet me at Aunt Lonie's?"

"Sure," Rob said, although he'd been about to suggest they ride together. "How long do you need?"

"I'll be there in thirty minutes, God willing and the creek don't rise. By that, I mean as long as Eunice cooperates."

Rob couldn't help chuckling, even though Jonah was already walking toward his truck. And he stood and watched the other man gently lift the aged golden into the back of the vehicle before he turned toward his rental.

Once inside, and after Jonah had driven off with a toot of his horn, Rob sat for a while without starting the vehicle.

It had only been a day, and not an overly eventful one at that, yet it felt as though he'd experienced a seismic shift, and he couldn't figure out why.

Maybe it was just being in a place where he felt at home? At peace?

Where—although he'd grown up a continent away—he had no problem understanding the mindset of the people he'd met?

He refused to consider that it had anything to do with Jonah Beaumont.

Realistically, although Jonah looked almost the same as he had ten years ago, and despite the attraction Rob still felt toward him, they were actually strangers.

His earlier thoughts and questions had stayed with him throughout the rest of the afternoon, and he'd decided it was his overwhelming yearning to once more belong somewhere that was messing with his head.

What a relief it had been to be able to do his job without fanfare or any kind of false adulation. Years of pretending to be someone he wasn't had taken its toll. All he wanted now was peace, quiet and a place to belong.

But he wasn't quite there yet, and he couldn't afford

to allow his libido—or any other emotions—to add additional problems to the mix.

Once he found a place to settle down, all this angst would retreat.

It didn't take him long to drive to Lonie's Café, or to find a spot to park on the main thoroughfare. There were a few cars scattered on the street and in a parking lot farther along the way, but clearly Butler's Run wasn't a happening place on a Wednesday evening.

Lonie's was a long, rectangular room, with well-worn dark wooden floors, round tables and a counter with a brass rail and tall stools along one side. Behind the counter was a pass-through to the kitchen, from which emanated such delicious smells Rob's stomach rumbled, loudly. Thankfully that was covered by the strains of new country coming through hidden speakers.

Three tables were occupied, closer to the back of the room, but Rob chose one overlooking Main Street, wanting to enjoy any people-watching opportunities that may arise. By the time he sat down, the waitress came bustling over.

"Hi, there, honey. Welcome to Lonie's. My name is Carmen, and I'll be your server. Can I get you something to drink?"

"Just water for now, please, Carmen." Rob smiled up at the young woman, taking the menu she held out. "But can I order an appetizer while I wait for my friend to join me? I'm starving, and the food smells are killing me already."

Carmen chuckled, nodding, as if this was nothing unusual. And it probably wasn't. Rob doubted people walking by could resist coming into the restaurant, even if they weren't hungry.

"Give the menu a quick look then," she said. "And I'll get Ms. Lonie started on whatever you want."

"What do you recommend?" Rob asked in return, scanning the beginning of the menu but not being able to make a choice.

"We got in a fresh catch of crayfish today, and Ms. Lonie makes the best crayfish balls you've ever tasted."

"Oh, yeah." Rob's stomach rumbled again, making them both laugh. "I'll definitely have some of those."

"You got it."

As Carmen headed back toward the kitchen, Rob turned his attention to the street outside, his mind going straight back to Jonah Beaumont.

There was a reticence about Jonah that intrigued Rob in a way he couldn't resist. Hidden depths of character he sensed couldn't be readily understood, but would need to be teased out, little by little. Yet, why he wanted so badly to be the person to draw those secrets out, Rob couldn't say.

Sighing, he rubbed the bridge of his nose. He always tried to be honest with himself, which Beeta said was one of his worse habits, since it led to far too much of what she called "navel gazing." His sister was more the action type, eschewing introspection for constant movement. Rob needed to understand himself, at the very least, to be truly comfortable with his own needs and feelings. Understanding other people was a lot harder, but he knew if he could get even an inkling of someone else's motivation, connecting with them became easier.

But he still wasn't sure why, exactly, he wanted a connection with Jonah to begin with. It could be just that Jonah's life in Butler's Run so closely mirrored what he wanted for himself that Rob was drawn to get to know the other man better. Doing so would help him figure out how to build the future Rob wanted, the one Jonah already had.

Yet that didn't ring true either.

Rob already had a pretty good idea of how to get to where he wanted to be. All that was left to be decided, as far as he could tell, was where, exactly, to put down new roots. While there were questions he could ask Jonah about the running of a clinic like his, that wasn't what he was curious about.

No. What he wanted to know was far more personal. Intimate.

Like whether he was involved with anyone, and why he kept such a distance between himself and the people around him.

Or was it just Rob that Jonah kept at arm's length? Now that he thought about it, Jonah had an easy way with his clients and staff, with none of the snark he'd thrown Rob's way.

It was a bit off-putting to think there was something about him that made Jonah act that way.

Both Carmen—with his crayfish balls—and Jonah arrived at about the same time, interrupting Rob's reflections.

"Hey, beautiful," Jonah said to Carmen, bending to kiss her cheek. "I see you've already met Rob."

"Not officially," Carmen said with a grin. "But I knew

who he was. Emma Gorman was in earlier. Told us all about seeing Vet Vic and convincing you to let him help at the clinic."

Jonah's lips twisted, and he exchanged a knowing look with Carmen.

"No doubt."

"Lady with the pink hair?" Rob asked.

"Well, ain't you the smart one?" Carmen said, giggling, while Jonah chuckled too. "How'd you know?"

Shaking his head, Rob replied, "I come from farm country, so I know how small towns work. I never met her, but she was the most vocal one in the waiting room this morning. Seemed like a pretty good guess."

"Will you two stop jaw-jacking and let that man eat his crayfish balls, before they get cold?"

At those words, all three of them at the table turned to watch the diminutive lady marching from the kitchen toward them, with what looked like a ferocious scowl on her face.

She was dressed in a black chef's coat, wearing a small cap and matching pants in a Kente-inspired pattern, and there was no mistaking her air of command. The resemblance between Jonah and his aunt was marked, with both having the same complexions, noses and shape of mouths. But where Jonah's eyes had that sleepy droop, his aunt's were large and wide, and lighter brown than her nephew's impenetrable darkness.

"Uh-oh, Mom's coming," Carmen muttered to Jonah, grinning. "You're in trouble now."

"Nah," he replied, pinching Carmen on her side, as his aunt got to the table and Rob rose to his feet, earning himself a swift glance from the older lady. "Aunt Lonie loves me. I'm her favorite nephew. Isn't that right, Auntie?"

"You're my only nephew," the older woman replied tartly, even as she held her face up for Jonah to kiss her cheek. "And a sassy-pants to boot."

"Sassy-pants." Carmen sing-songed the words through her giggles, earning another pinch from Jonah and a narrow-eyed look from her mother.

"What you standing around for, girlie? Think the customers gonna go back into the kitchen for their own food?"

With one last giggle, Carmen headed off toward the other occupied tables in the restaurant, and Rob found himself the focus of Jonah's aunt's full attention.

"So you're the famous Vet Vic, huh?" Her tone was curious rather than rude, and it made Rob smile.

"Just plain old Rob Sandoval, ma'am," he replied, holding out his hand, which was quickly clasped in her tiny but firm grip. "It's a pleasure to meet you."

"Ooh, and so polite too," she said, giving him a grin and looking about as young as her daughter with it. "We might have to keep you around, just to teach these other young'uns some manners."

"Hey," Jonah said, putting his hands on his hips. "That's not fair. I'm a perfect Southern gentleman."

"Huh." Lonie's grunt spoke volumes, and made Rob have to hold back a laugh. "Rooster today, feather duster tomorrow."

That was too much for Rob, and he couldn't stop his amusement from showing. Bending, he kissed her hand, then said, "Ms. Lonie, you are a gem beyond price. I'll do my best to smarten this fellow up while I'm here, just for you."

"You do that," she said, as she gave his fingers a quick squeeze at the same time that she whisked the menu off the table with her other hand. "Now, sit you down, both of you, and I'll send you out some food. Chef's choice."

"Thank you, ma'am," Rob called as Ms. Lonie marched off toward the kitchen, getting a flap of her hand in reply.

As they sat down across the table from each other, Jonah sighed. "Well, you've got Aunt Lonie's seal of approval."

Rob smiled, not sure why that made him feel so good. "Why'd you say that? We hardly got a chance to chat or get to know each other."

Jonah shook his head, his lips twisting—this time in obvious amusement rather than anything else. "If Aunt Lonie doesn't know you, or can't get a read on you, she waits to see what you order and makes a decision based on that. When she offers to choose for you, it's because she likes you." He grinned. "And it also means she's about to send out enough food to feed the Gamecocks football team, so I hope you're real hungry."

"I definitely am." Unable to resist anymore, Rob cut into one of the crayfish balls. When he put the first piece into his mouth, his eyes all but rolled back in pleasure. When he'd chewed, savored and swallowed, he said, "OMG, I'm so up for anything your aunt wants to feed me."

Glancing up, he found Jonah staring at him in a way that made heat fire down his spine, and had goose bumps rising all over his chest and arms. Those usually sleepy eyes were even more hooded, but his expression was anything but slumberous. Instead, there was an intensity to the concentrated way he kept his gaze trained on Rob's face, and his lips were tense, causing two lines to form on either side of his mouth.

Frozen, Rob could only stare back, their gazes clashing for what felt like forever, but couldn't have been more than a couple of seconds. Then Jonah looked away, breaking the spell holding Rob captive.

Completely frazzled, and now unsure of what exactly just happened, Rob stuffed the other half of the crayfish ball into his mouth to give himself time to calm down.

For a moment—a crazy, lust-inducing moment—he'd thought he'd read longing in Jonah's expression. But, when he looked across the table again, there was no sign of anything like that on Jonah's face anymore.

Maybe he'd imagined it?

But the tingles still tiptoeing up and down his spine seemed to whisper he hadn't.

"Good, huh?"

Jonah's voice was normal, with a hint of amusement, causing Rob to intentionally match his tone.

"Amazing. Here." He pushed the plate to the middle of the table. "Have some."

Jonah reached for one and popped it whole into his mouth.

Rob quickly looked away, not wanting to have his gaze snared by the sight of the other man's mouth.

Libido running amok again. Calm down.

Although the thought was meant to settle him down,

it didn't really help. And he was relieved when his phone rang, giving him a necessary distraction.

"My sister Beeta," he said to Rob. "Forgive me, but I need to take this."

"No problem." Jonah started to get up. "I'll give you some privacy."

"No need," he replied, hitting the button to start the call and gesturing for Jonah to stay where he was. "Hey, Beeta."

But, as he listened to his sister bring him up to date on what was happening with the proposed documentary, Rob almost wished he'd let Jonah get up, or that he'd gotten up and taken the call outside.

He could have used a brief respite from the tension he was experiencing from just being in the other man's presence.

CHAPTER FIVE

JONAH KEPT TRYING to train his gaze elsewhere, but it returned to Rob over and over again.

The sight of Rob eating that first bite had thrown Jonah completely for a loop.

If he'd thought his world felt cattywampus earlier, that was nothing in comparison to what it felt like now. As though he were sitting not on a chair, but in a puddle of shifting, waving sand, threatening to pull him down into a place he both feared and desperately wanted to be.

Looking down at the table where his fingers drummed, seeking to alleviate some of his angst, he couldn't help wondering if, when their eyes met, Rob had felt the same lightning strike of desire. The surge of arousal had damn near incinerated every sensible atom in Jonah's body, making him long to reach across the table and kiss the taste of the food off Rob's lips.

Learn Rob's own special taste.

He'd lusted at first sight before. After all, that was kind of a prerequisite when you'd resigned yourself to one-night stands and occasional booty calls far from home. Traveling to Atlanta, far enough away he'd be pretty sure not to see anyone he knew, meant limited time to spend on making any but the most superficial connections. He hadn't been looking for anything solid or lasting anyway.

At this point in his life, he wasn't even sure if he'd ever want a relationship. Not only would it be another rope to tie him down, but the part of him that had always known there was something lacking within himself constantly whispered he'd be courting disaster to even try.

It wasn't something he'd be able to explain, had someone asked, but even as a child he'd known he somehow wasn't enough. That despite his best efforts, he could never fulfill other people's needs or expectations.

Imagine giving himself over to another, just to be told he was somehow deficient. Not sufficient to make and keep a man he loved happy.

It had even happened once, long ago, and although he'd eventually gotten over it, the thought of going through that again was way too distasteful to be contemplated.

Thankfully, just then Rob finished his call, so Jonah was forced to pull himself out of those torturous thoughts before they went any further.

"Everything all right?" he asked, seeing the thoughtful look on the other man's face.

"The documentary is on hold, at least for another few days. One of the participants lost a mare and wants some time to recover, and the town council is hemming and hawing over the permit we need to film the Easter Marsh Tacky parade. Beeta was assured it would be issued without any problem, but now it's in question."

There. If Jonah needed a reminder of his own shortcomings, he'd been smacked in the face by the mention of Marnie Rutherford's mare. All amorous thoughts and feelings drained away, to be replaced with a wash of cold reality.

No skirting around it though. It wasn't in his nature to hide from difficult truths.

"Marnie had mentioned to me that she'd be participating in the documentary, and she'd planned to have Night Wing feature prominently in the film. Losing her was a tragedy."

"I'm sure it was."

The sincerity in Rob's tone, along with his not asking any probing questions about the mare's death, was somehow exactly the response Jonah needed. A little of the stress released from his shoulders and chest, and he took a sip of water before continuing with the conversation.

"As for the permit, I'd guess the bugbear is Henry Aitkins. He's on the council and also a Tacky aficionado, and he's been complaining about the documentary to anyone who'll listen."

Rob's eyebrows rose questioningly. "Do you know why?"

"He's worried that increasing the Tackys' profile might attract the wrong kinds of breeders. The type that just want to make money off the horses by saying how rare they are, etcetera."

"Ahh."

Rob was leaning forward, his arms crossed on the table, and he nodded. Suddenly, Jonah realized he was mirroring the other man, and that by doing so their faces were very, *very* close together. He could see the tiny lines at the outer edges of Rob's eyes, the way the light played off his cheekbones and the humorous, sexy tilt of his lips in fine detail.

God, he was beautiful.

"I hope y'all are hungry." He'd been so enthralled he hadn't heard the kitchen door open or his aunt approach. Swiftly leaning back in his chair, avoiding Aunt Lonie's gaze, Jonah pretended a great interest in his cutlery.

"Ms. Lonie, whatever that is, it smells divine." Rob's crooning tone drew Jonah's gaze like a gecko to a moth, and once more he was forced to quickly look away from the other man, not wanting anyone—especially Lonie—to notice he was staring.

"And it'll taste that way too," Lonie replied, as she shifted dishes from her tray to the table.

"Mom's not known for her modesty," said Carmen, as she also unloaded a tray of food, until the tabletop was almost covered.

"Course not. I'm known for my cooking," was the swift and tart reply. "We've got some braised short ribs, chicken fried steak, potato and leek mash, collards, fried okra, fresh biscuits and gravy. And make sure you save space for dessert. I have a mixed berry pie that'll knock you into next week."

Rob's warm laughter spiked right through Jonah, leaving him dry-mouthed and wondering if, famished as he was, he'd be able to eat. His stomach was in knots.

"Thank you, Ms. Lonie. I wouldn't mind a quick time travel experience."

That drew amused chuckles from both his aunt and cousin, and Jonah forced himself to join in.

What he really wanted to do was run out the door, before Rob cast more of a spell on him. That, or grab Rob and take him somewhere private, so he could find out if he was the only one feeling this dangerous, delicious pull.

Neither of which was possible just then. Nor advisable.

So, he settled his napkin more firmly on his lap and braved a look up at his aunt.

"Thanks, Auntie."

She nodded, putting a hand on his shoulder and giving him a sly, knowing grin.

"Don't thank me yet. Wait until that man falls in love with the food. It'll make him want to stay around forever."

Crap.

His aunt was always on him to get involved in a relationship. It had been that way since he was in high school and still dating girls. It was only after his grandmother died that he confessed, first to his mom and then to Lonie, he was gay. Neither had cared, but Lonie had her own slant on it.

"Just means you have to find a nice *man* to settle down with, instead," was her sanguine reply. As if she'd always known, but hadn't wanted to broach the subject until he did.

Now he was sure she'd seen through his casual facade to the interest he had in Rob.

That didn't bode well for the next couple of weeks. She'd be all over him like a leisure suit, trying to find out whether there was anything going on, and she'd be disappointed when he told her no.

"I think you're right, ma'am." Rob was piling his plate with food, his smile wide and unfettered. "Can I just move in here? Be your greeter and busboy? I'm a really bad waiter though—found that out in college—so I won't volunteer for that job."

"I'm sure someone can situate you more comfortably," Aunt Lonie replied, squeezing Jonah's shoulder again. "But you come by and see me whenever you want. I'll keep your stomach happy."

Then she and Carmen were gone, leaving Rob and Jonah alone together again.

"Aren't you going to eat?" Rob paused, knife and fork in hand, to give Jonah a concerned look. "You didn't really have anything much today. Aren't you starving?"

"Yeah." Jonah tried for a smile as he started dishing out his own dinner. "I was just lost in thought for a moment."

They ate silently for a while—or silently if you didn't count Rob's sighs and quiet moans of pleasure with each mouthful. Jonah tried not to hear them, but they were completely, utterly distracting.

He wanted to be the one causing those sounds to issue from Rob's throat—drawing them out with touches and kisses and...

Wow! No!

Dragging his brain away from those fantasies, he searched desperately for something innocuous to say.

"You don't seem very upset by your sister's call." Thank goodness for the subliminal brain, which apparently hadn't been fogged over completely by lust. When Rob cocked an eyebrow at him, Jonah elaborated. "Hearing that the documentary is being delayed."

Rob swallowed, took a sip of water, then replied, "I'm

not. Honestly, I didn't even want to do this documentary at all."

"Really?" After all the different videos Rob and his sister had made, what was it that made him not want to do this one? Probably the ridiculous small-town location, Jonah thought. And who could blame him? Butler's Run was the epitome of insignificant, except in the eyes of its inhabitants.

Maybe he shouldn't feel that way about his hometown, but he couldn't help it. There was an entire world out there to explore and experience. Why would anyone want to come here?

"Yeah." Rob met Jonah's gaze, and his expression was suddenly completely serious. "I'd told Beeta I was through with the videos from last year. That I wanted to stop traveling and find a spot to settle down."

"She didn't believe you?"

Rob huffed. Not quite a laugh but a mixture of amusement and annoyance. "She knew I meant it, but she also knew I have a hard time saying no to her, so when this opportunity came up, she took it without consulting me."

Hard to believe that Rob would want to give up a lifestyle Jonah would give his eyeteeth to have, or that the other man would be a pushover for his sister.

Unable to restrain his curiosity, he asked, "Why would you want to give up making the videos? It looks like you've done well with them."

"We have," Rob admitted readily. "I'd have never believed I could make that much money from something like that. But it's not for me, long-term. I need a certain amount of stability in my life, you know? And being on the road for so long that I even had to send my dogs to live with my brother because I was never home doesn't provide that. I want to get back to clinical work and have a place to call my own."

Jonah considered that for a few minutes, thoughtfully chewing a mouthful of steak while he did.

"I guess you've been doing it for a while." Rob had said the videos started in 2019. "But it's still difficult for someone on the outside to understand why you'd give it up. So many people are dying to be internet famous. Or just plain famous."

Rob's lips tightened slightly, and he shook his head.

"Sure, but I was never one of them. I've made good money from it, but it's cost me as well."

"Your dogs?"

"Sure. And a relationship, back in 2020. And a life beyond airports, rental cars and motel rooms, if I'm lucky to be sleeping in one, and not out in the middle of nowhere in a tent. When I finally go home to my apartment, you know what I find? Emptiness. Nothing. Not even a potted plant to give the place a little life. I've moved around so much, there's been no opportunity for meeting anyone and having any kind of meaningful relationship."

The near ferocity in his tone told the story even more broadly than his words. While Jonah was coveting Rob's life, the very experiences he longed for were soul destroying to Rob. Jonah felt a wash of sadness and compassion for the other man.

"I…" He hesitated, wondering whether Rob would appreciate being commiserated with. But he went for it anyway. "I'm sorry it's not working out for you. And that it caused a breakup." Although he couldn't understand why anyone would break up with Rob.

Rob shrugged, but Jonah wasn't fooled. There was still a brooding cast to the other man's face, which told him it still hurt.

"It was during the pandemic." He sighed, slowly spearing a piece of okra but not putting it into his mouth. "The clinic I was working at closed, and Beeta suggested we hit the road and do more videos. Andy—my ex—was an accountant and started working from home, and I think it irked him that I was out and about while he was trapped in the apartment. One day I came home and he was packed and ready to go." His lips quirked. "At least he waited for me to get back and didn't just desert the dogs."

"That sucks." Although Jonah was kind of glad Rob didn't have a significant other in his life just now.

Not that he was planning to make a move on the guy, but it was good to know anyway.

"I'm over it," Rob said, a determined note, and a finality, to the words. He smiled, eyebrows rising. "What about you? Any special someone waiting for you at home?"

"Other than Eunice? No. Frankly, there are only four gay men other than me, that I know of, in this town, and I'm not interested in any of them. Not that I'm looking for a relationship anyway."

"Oh?" Closing his knife and fork, Rob pushed his empty plate aside and gave Jonah an intent stare. "What's wrong with the men here?"

Glad he hadn't homed in on the fact he wasn't looking for a relationship instead, Jonah readily answered, "Gerry's at least eighty, John and Marlon are married, and Tony…" How to explain Tony? Six feet three inches tall, mountain man beard, with a bit of a mean streak. "Tony's just not my type."

Rob had his elbows on the table again, leaning in, giving the conversation a level of intimacy Jonah couldn't help but notice. The hair on his nape prickled, and it took every ounce of control he had not to lean forward too. Get closer to those now copper-colored eyes and quirking, sexy mouth.

"What is your type?"

Rob's voice was low, a murmur. Sinful and inviting.

Was Rob interested in him, sexually?

Jonah's head reeled at the thought, and then he caught himself.

Rob had always been like this—seemingly flirtatious, sexy as sin and twice as tempting—but Jonah reminded himself not to fall into the trap of thinking it was personal. It hadn't been ten years ago when they'd first met, and it definitely wasn't now either.

Swallowing, battling between prevarication and deflection, he decided, instead, to be honest.

"My type is someone far from Butler's Run, who isn't interested in anything more than a night or two of uncomplicated sex."

Rob's eyes widened.

"Damn. Okay."

"Did I surprise you?"

"I don't know why, but you did."

He'd surprised himself too, if he were being honest,

but Jonah wasn't going to admit that to Rob. Normally, he was completely mum on anything to do with his sex life, not wanting to give the town gossips anything to talk about. Maybe it was because Rob wasn't from here and was simply transient that made it easy to talk to him about it.

"In a place this small, it makes sense to keep my… activities…elsewhere," he said, warmth rushing up from his chest at the way Rob was staring at him. "It's not like I can sneeze here and everyone not know."

That made Rob chuckle and nod. "I remember, from when I was a kid. I hated it then—that feeling of always being watched—but I miss it now." He waved a hand, his mouth rueful. "Not the always being watched part, but knowing most everyone around and being a part of a community. In LA I wouldn't recognize most of my neighbors if they walked up and bit me on the nose."

"Sometimes, I think I'd like to be anonymous like that," Jonah admitted. "I felt like that at UC Davis, and it was freeing, to be honest. When I had to leave, it sort of felt like coming back to a cage."

Rob's expression was intent. "Why did you leave anyway? You were acing the coursework, and then, poof, you were gone between one year and the next."

"My mom got sick, and the doctors didn't know how the disease would progress. Although Aunt Lonie was here with her, I wanted to be as close as possible, since we didn't know how long she had, or how much help she'd need. I transferred to a college nearby. Thankfully, although I lost my scholarship, my grandmother had set up a trust for all her grandkids' education, so my tuition was covered."

Rob smiled, a soft tip of the lips. "You're a good son. There are a lot of people who'd make every excuse—including there being other family nearby—to go on with their lives, regardless."

Why that filled him with pride was a question for another time.

"I'm an only child, and it was just the two of us since I was little. I just did what I had to. Not that it made much of a difference."

With a tilt of his head, Rob questioned, "How can you be sure? She lived quite a while after that. Maybe she wouldn't have, without your support."

How to respond to something that goes straight through your heart, lightening it to the point where you feel as if it would float away?

Jonah looked down so Rob wouldn't see how moist his eyes had become, and he was struggling to find a reply when he was saved the effort by Rob's phone dinging. From beneath his lashes, he watched as the other man picked it up and read something on the screen.

"Oops. Beeta's back in town and wants to discuss how to move forward on the project," he said, laying the phone back down before getting to his feet. "I'm going to have to run. Let me go pay for the meal."

As he got up, Jonah replied, "You can try, but I think Aunt Lonie will have something to say about that."

Rob chuckled as he walked away, and Jonah let out a long breath as soon as the other man was out of earshot.

That off-kilter feeling had intensified as the evening

went on, and he was equal parts glad and unhappy to have their time together end. He really needed to get his head on straight when it came to Rob Sandoval. Otherwise, the week or however long the other man would be in Butler's Run would be excruciating.

"He's handsome." Carmen had come over so quietly Jonah hadn't even been aware of her approach. "And charming too."

With a silent sigh, Jonah agreed with his cousin. "He's all that."

"Gay?"

"Yeah, but please don't tell your mom. You know how she gets on my case."

Carmen snorted. "If you think she doesn't already have it sussed out, you don't really know your auntie."

"Ugh." Jonah looked up at Carmen and caught her sympathetic look. "There isn't anything between us. And there can't be."

She shrugged as she piled their empty dishes onto her tray.

"Don't see why not, but you know your business best."

Jonah couldn't help smiling at her. They'd grown up together, and Carmen was the closest thing he had to a sister. Closer than one, maybe, since there wasn't much they didn't talk about together.

"Thanks for that. And if you could just convince Aunt Lonie…"

That earned him another snort. "Fat lot of good that would do, *mon ami*. You know she has a mind of her own, and a stick of dynamite won't change it."

Unfortunately, he was well aware of that fact.

Rob came back just then, two carryout containers in his hand.

"Not only would your aunt not take my money, but she also gave me two pieces of pie for us to take home." He shook his head, grinning, as he handed Jonah one of the cardboard boxes. "How was I to say no to her?"

"You can't," both Carmen and Jonah said at the same time, which reduced them all to laughter.

After saying good-night, Rob left, and Jonah followed right behind, forestalling the grilling he knew his aunt was itching to give him. Getting home, he took Eunice out for a quick ramble, then settled down in his home office with his pie, telling himself he'd look at the pile of bills he needed to get paid within the week.

However, when he turned on his computer, it wasn't to open the accounting software but to go to the channel where some of the Vet Vic videos were available.

Rob Sandoval was stuck in his head, and maybe seeing him over and over on film would begin to inure him to the man's presence.

Yeah. Sure.

And he was so enthralled he didn't even register how delicious the pie was until he was finished and the taste lingered, tantalizing on his tongue. Not unlike the way Rob lingered in his mind.

CHAPTER SIX

THE NEXT MORNING Rob got to the clinic at seven o'clock—earlier than Jonah had suggested, but since he'd been awake since six, he figured he might as well. Besides, unless the clinic was very different from the ones he'd worked at before, there'd be at least one person there, checking on the overnight dogs, beginning the cleaning process and preparing for the day.

So it was no surprise there were three vehicles in the parking lot at the side of the building, one of which was Jonah's truck. Seeing it ignited a spark of excitement deep in Rob's belly that was impossible to ignore.

He'd spent most of the previous night thinking about Jonah—about his complicated personality, his life story and the intense attraction Rob felt toward the other man. There'd been moments when he was sure Jonah felt the same pull toward him, but then a curtain would come down behind those sleepy, sexy eyes and shatter Rob's certainty.

Jonah was a master of concealing his emotions, making Rob want, more than ever, to break through the barriers surrounding the other man.

Sometime in the night he'd realized that all thoughts of keeping his distance were slowly fading into the background. And no matter how many times he tried to remind himself not to get too involved, he couldn't ignore his own interest in Jonah.

He'd been touched by the other man's devotion to his mother, and surprised to hear him confess to seeking sexual encounters away from home. In his head, after spending some time together, Rob had been sure Jonah would have been snatched up by some lucky guy long ago. After all, there was absolutely nothing wrong with the other man, as far as Rob could tell.

He was kind, successful, smart and sexy as hell.

And sure, Butler's Run was a small town, with not much opportunity to meet someone and develop a relationship with them, but this wasn't the nineteenth century. There were so many other ways to meet other people—online dating sites, mixers, even matchmakers—and he couldn't figure out why Jonah hadn't gone any of those routes.

If there ever was a man who deserved a stable and happy home life, it was Jonah. Just seeing him interacting with his aunt and cousin showed the love between the three, and how much he cared about them. He even gave up being a student at a prestigious school to be there for his ill mother. Those natural attributes would translate wonderfully into a more intimate relationship, Rob was sure.

Or was he projecting his own desires onto Jonah?

Maybe he didn't want that kind of closeness, or a life partner. Not everyone did, although Rob couldn't really understand why. Wasn't life better with someone to share it with? Someone to depend on, and who depended on you?

Although it had been so long since he'd been intimate with anyone, Rob wouldn't turn down a night or two of no-strings sex. It wasn't usually his thing, but if Jonah were to offer...

Rob drew himself up and muttered a curse.

That was no way to start the workday. Especially when the subject of his lust was one of the people he'd be working with, closely.

Not as closely as you obviously want, the irrepressible part of his brain whispered, propelling him out of the vehicle.

Hopefully having something to do with his hands would quell this obsession with Jonah.

When he got to the side door, he found it open and stepped inside. Alan was there, as was Jada, one of the other techs.

"Mornin', Dr. Rob." Jada smiled at him as she thrust an armful of towels and drapes into the washer. "You're here early."

"Just thought I could help get things set up," he replied, wiping his feet before starting across the floor. "Do you know what's on the agenda today?"

"Eight surgeries this morning," Alan replied, looking from the list in his hand to the rolling tray beside him, which held a variety of cleaning equipment already in place. "I'm finishing up the dog kennels."

"Is Dr. B in his office?"

"Yep," Jada said. "Go on through."

Rob forced himself to move at a normal pace through

the back part of the clinic, past the overnight hospital cages, X-ray room and surgical suites. Yet, a sense of anticipation made his strides just a little longer, and his heart was racing at the thought of seeing Jonah again.

Outside the office door, he paused to take a deep breath and compose himself. Then he knocked.

"Come."

"Good morning," Rob said, as he walked into the office, receiving a grunt in return from Jonah, who was staring at his computer screen, and little *yip* of welcome from Eunice.

At least one of them was glad to see him, Rob thought, annoyed at himself for being let down by Jonah's lack of enthusiasm. Rather than sit down, he went to stoop beside Eunice and began to make much of the sweet senior.

"How did your meeting with your sister go?"

Apparently Jonah was ready to acknowledge his existence.

"Okay. She was considering whether to stay and battle it out with the council or just call the whole thing off." He wasn't going to admit that he'd argued for giving the project a chance, while Beeta—never the most patient of people—was leaning toward going back to LA. "She finally decided to give it a couple more days, after I gave her a few suggestions on how to frame the project to the town."

Eunice lay back down, so, with a final scratch behind her ear, Rob rose to step over and sit in the chair across the desk from Jonah. Their gazes clashed, but Rob was once more reminded of Jonah's ability to disguise what he was thinking or feeling. While his heart was racing, and he was sure his desire was written all over his face, Jonah's expression could have been carved from stone.

He looked away, feigning interest in a bit of fluff from Eunice, which he picked off his scrub pants.

"I told her to remind them that the Marsh Tacky is still considered critically endangered, and that a closed stud book exists for the breed. Anyone interested in getting involved in breeding them has to go through one of a handful of reputable breeders, and the paperwork has to be in order. Our documentary will definitely emphasize those points, and make it clear that the bloodline of any animal being sold can be checked through the association."

Jonah shook his head, a movement Rob noticed from the corner of his eye, and he forced himself to look at the other man.

"I don't see why that would deter anyone who wants to start breeding them."

"The object isn't so much to deter additional people getting involved with breeding the horses, but to show it's not an easy occupation to get into. It's not like buying any old horse, or horses. It's a carefully overseen process, with a DNA bank and oversight from different associations. Scammers want something easy. And anyone seeing the documentary will go away from it fully informed."

"Hmm…" Jonah leaned back in his chair, his hands clasped at his nape, his gaze drifting across the ceiling. "Okay. That sounds like a valid argument."

"I also suggested that she request you join the shoot."

Jonah's feet hit the floor with a thump.

"Me?" His eyebrows were up almost at his hairline. "Why?"

"Well, my understanding is that you're the foremost expert on the Marsh Tacky, from a veterinary point of view. If you're involved, I think the dissent will fade away."

Jonah didn't say anything for a few long moments, his gaze searching Rob's face. In his expression there was what Rob interpreted as a hint of excitement.

Was what he'd said the day before about fame—how so many people craved it—something he felt, himself?

"What did your sister say to that?" he finally asked, eyelids drooping to hide his gaze, the curtain back in place.

"She thought it was a good idea and told me to ask if you'd be interested."

"Let me think about it," Jonah said, as his computer pinged, and he leaned forward to look at the screen. "In the meantime, knowing I had a slew of surgeries scheduled today, I emailed my insurance company last night and asked about putting you on my policy, temporarily. This is the rep getting back to me to say she checked your credentials, and she's made the insertion, so you're on your own today, as a vet here."

It was exciting and frustrating at the same time. He'd been looking forward to working closely with Jonah again, but it was a good chance to get back into the swing of things.

Besides, Jonah obviously didn't share his eagerness, a fact that irked Rob a lot more than it should.

But he made sure to keep his voice even when he said,

"Great. Inez and I will hold down the fort while you're operating. What do you have on the table?"

Jonah clicked through to a different screen on his computer and said, "Three spays—one of which is a rabbit—two neuters, a canine aural hematoma, a lipoma—that I'm hoping is noninfiltrating—and cystotomy stone removal on a cat that came in yesterday." He frowned slightly, his lips twisting downward. "Those are always tricky, so I explained to the owners that the outcome was no better than fifty-fifty and let them take their baby home to love on her last night, just in case."

"How old is the cat?"

"That's the problem," Jonah replied, pulling on his chin. "It's eight, so not so young anymore. Anesthesia will be tricky, and recovery isn't a given."

"Well, good luck." Rob glanced at his watch and stood up to stretch. "I'm going to go through and make sure I'm completely familiar with where everything is. Don't want to look like a bumbling fool in front of the clients."

"The techs know where everything is, even if you don't."

"Where I used to work, we didn't have techs come in with us all the time when we examined patients, so I'm used to muddling through on my own. It wasn't as fancy as your setup here. But then, we were dealing with pets, not a patient like Geoffry the goat."

He smiled at the other man, hoping for a smile in return, but was disappointed. Jonah was still frowning at his computer screen.

"Yeah. Farm animals definitely need an additional pair of hands."

Feeling dismissed, and put out, Rob grunted in reply and bent to give Eunice one last pat.

After all, he thought as he left the room without another word, it wasn't the golden's fault her owner was being a jerk.

Jonah sat back in his chair and exhaled the breath he felt he'd been holding since Rob walked into the office.

Seeing the other man had had his pulse racing and his body reacting like a teenager.

In fact, he couldn't remember a time when he'd reacted this way—libido out of control, driving him nuts—since his teen years. Since the summer he turned eighteen and had his first romantic encounter.

Remember how that turned out...

The thought should have quashed the arousal racing like lava through his system, but, although it cooled it somewhat, such was Rob's effect on him, it couldn't douse it completely.

With a groan, he rubbed at his face with both hands, trying to force himself back to normality. He had a full schedule ahead. Delicate surgeries that demanded his complete attention. Allowing Rob's presence to shake his cool wasn't an option.

After the other man was gone—*please, Lord, soon*—he'd definitely need a trip to his favorite club in Atlanta. Although he wondered if he'd find anyone able to arouse this kind of desperate interest. Even though he wasn't into relationships, in the past there'd always had to be a higher level of personal interest. Not emotional, but definitely physical.

But no one had ever exerted such a strong pull on him before.

Who could match up to Rob Sandoval?

Eunice groaned, got up and tottered over to lay her head in his lap, looking up at him with her wise, liquid gaze. Grateful for the comfort, he scratched behind her ears the way she liked.

"I wish you could talk, Eunice. I get the feeling you'd have some really great advice to give me. Maybe even be able to tell me what Mom would say, if she were still here."

Eunice's tail swished slowly, and her mouth opened in a grin.

"What do you think I should do—about Rob, and also about his sister's request that I take part in the documentary?"

It was easier to think about the latter, which didn't have the power to upend his life the way the former did.

Having watched the videos the night before, he knew he didn't have the charisma that had made Vet Vic so popular. Rob's easy warmth and charm translated perfectly to the screen, while Jonah knew himself to be far more detached and reticent in character. Yet, it was certainly tempting to get a taste of Rob's world, even though he'd be a mere bit player.

And it was even more tempting to think that, if his participation would sway the council, it would keep Rob around for a bit longer.

Although, if he were in his right mind, he'd want the other man gone ASAP.

Eunice grumbled, gave his hand a lick and wandered back to her bed.

"Yeah," he said, rotating his shoulders and neck to loosen up the muscles. "I guess it is time for me to get to work."

As he made his way to the surgical suite, he forced his brain away from his personal life and onto work. No matter what else was going on around him—or in him—the animals always came first, and he was determined to do the best he could for them.

And he didn't have much time to ruminate as he and his surgical staff went through the cases, starting with Mona the cat's bladder surgery, which thankfully went well. In between two of the spays, he went to check on her and saw Rob rushing two medium-sized puppies into the isolation area.

"What's up?" he asked.

Without stopping, Rob turned a grim face his way to reply, "Parvo. Bad cases."

Following him, Jonah paused at the door to the isolation unit. "Crap. How old?"

"The owner isn't sure. He was told they were eight weeks old, but it's hard to tell. They're pretty undernourished and could be younger. Do you have the CPMA treatment?"

"We do," he replied. "We signed up to be a test site, because of the prevalence of parvovirus in this area."

The new intravenous medication, using monoclonal antibodies, had been approved for the treatment of parvovirus, but it was only for dogs eight weeks old and over. If these pups were too young, they would have to be treated the way they'd always treated infected animals—with fluids to counteract dehydration, medication to combat the symptoms and a whole lot of luck.

"Should I administer it?" Rob asked.

"What do you think?" Jonah asked, wanting to hear Rob's opinion.

"With the virus load, and their otherwise poor condition, I think I'd take the chance on giving them the treatment, since it's available. I doubt they'll survive otherwise."

"Go for it," he replied, somehow trusting the other man's judgment. "Jada knows where it is."

But there was no time to stop and ask anything more, as Cliff, who was administering the anesthetic for the surgeries, called out to say the next patient was down and ready.

It was late in the afternoon before Jonah finished up the last surgery, because they'd also had an emergency come in, and he'd had to put the dog with a severely lacerated paw into the rotation. When he'd paused for lunch, there'd been no sign of Rob, and he'd avoided asking about him. The staff might not have thought anything of it if he had, but he had formulated the idea in the back of his head that he needed to wean himself off the other man.

That way, when he left, it wouldn't be so much of a wrench.

But, as the end of the day was drawing close and Jonah was checking on his surgical patients, he casually asked Cliff, "Hey, have you seen Dr. Rob?"

"He just finished up with his last patient, and I saw him heading to isolation."

Checking on the parvo pups, no doubt.

Jonah hesitated, vacillating, and then, with a sigh of resignation, went that way. It was, after all, his clinic. His name on the board outside. The patients were his, no matter who else was looking after them.

When he opened the door, he saw Rob sitting on the floor, leaning toward the cage where one of the puppies lay, gently stroking the small inert form with his gloved forefinger. Just his posture alone showed his concern.

"Any improvement?"

Rob looked up and gave a little shrug.

"I think so, but that might just be wishful thinking. They're on fluids, anti-nausea and pain meds, and I gave them a dose of antibiotics and a wormer. But they were in such poor condition when they got here, I think they came out of one of those damned puppy mills, from what the owner said."

Jonah moved into the room, letting the door close behind him. Then he lowered himself to sit beside Rob. The puppies were fluffy and looked to be some type of toy breed, although it was hard to say which one. Both were on drips to try to keep them hydrated, since the vomiting and diarrhea associated with parvovirus would cause dehydration and potential organ failure. The mono-clonal antibody treatment was supposed to help prevent that though.

"What did the owner say?"

"That he saw an ad on the internet, saying the breeder had shih tzu pups for sale. When he expressed inter-est, the seller told him to meet them at a gas station, rather than having him come to their home. The pups looked bright and lively, and he fell in love with them and bought both."

"Yeah, that does sound sketchy." Jonah reached into his pocket and took out a pair of gloves. After putting them on, he opened the second cage and reached in to pick up the other pup. It was heartbreakingly thin beneath its fluffy coat, and hardly reacted at all to being lifted. After closely examining it, he added, "I don't think this one is a shih tzu at all. Looks like a mix."

"I agree," Rob said with a frown. "I told the owner that, and he was so disappointed. But he also told me that he hopes they pull through, because he's gotten attached. Apparently, his wife passed away not long ago, and he got the dogs for company and, as he put it, a reason to get out of bed in the morning. He named them Milo and Ovaltine."

Jonah grunted, not knowing what to say to that. Eventually, he came up with, "Well, you're doing the best you can for them." Placing the puppy back in the cage, Jonah added, "It's time to close this place up. Most of the staff is probably already gone."

Rob nodded but didn't move. "If it's okay with you, I'm gonna stay here a while. Keep an eye on these two. Lock up, and I'll call you when I'm ready to leave, if that'll work?"

"Sure. If that's what you want."

"Yes. I won't stay long."

But as he got up to go to the door, Jonah looked back at Rob and had a feeling the other man planned to stay the entire night, nursing the puppies.

It was just the kind of dedication and caring he'd expect from him.

And damn him for being so appealing in this nonsexual, lovely way.

CHAPTER SEVEN

ROB STOOD UP and stretched, trying to get the feeling back in his leg. A glance at his watch showed it was just past six. Beeta had been texting him, asking where he was. She planned to go to dinner with her assistant and assistant cameraman over in Hilton Head and wondered if he wanted to come. Of course, he'd refused the invitation, although his belly reminded him he hadn't eaten since lunch. He wanted to be here in case he needed to adjust the puppies' meds, and just in case the worst should happen despite them being given what had been called a "miracle" treatment for the virus.

Although the circumstances weren't ideal, there was a certain feeling of rightness being here, taking care of the babies. It had been so long since he'd been invested in the well-being of specific animals. It felt like coming home to be able to devote his time and energy to these pups.

They were both sleeping, their respiration was even and the little hearts were still beating away, albeit a bit too fast for his liking, but he felt confident enough in their condition to take a little break. Although one of the vet techs had brought him a cushion before they left, so he wasn't sitting directly on the concrete floor, he needed to move a bit. And a bathroom break wouldn't be a bad idea either.

Walking to the bathroom, it occurred to him just how comforting it was to be back in his own milieu, rather than in Beeta's world of camera angles and close-up shots. If he'd needed a sign that his intention to leave that all behind was right, he'd certainly got it.

He needed the ebb and flow of real life around him. The sense of community and commitment he felt existed in places like Butler's Run. Even his crazy desire for Jonah made sense in that light, since, if anything could come of his longing it would—in a perfect world—create the ideal life.

Partnership with a man as devoted to animals as he was, in a town that could give him the peace and stability he craved after his crazy life on the road.

The fact that it probably wouldn't happen didn't really matter. He'd enjoy these sensations and the feeling of doing something worthwhile for as long as it lasted. Besides, there was also the excitement of truly *feeling* again. Of longing for connection, both emotional and physical, with Jonah.

It brought him alive in a way he hadn't been for a long, long time. And what was so terrible about that?

As he was coming out of the restroom, he heard the sound of the outside door rattling and, startled, stood stock-still for a moment. Walking as quietly as possible, he slipped back into the examination area at the back of the clinic and peered around the corner, toward the side door.

It was Jonah, backing in through the door, juggling a box, his keys and Eunice's leash.

"Hey," he said, moving forward to give the other man a hand. "What are you doing back here?"

Jonah shrugged, surrendering the box and turning back to close and lock the door he'd just come through.

"I couldn't leave you to starve to death," he said. "So I went by the café and got some food. It was that or pizza."

"Either one would work, but your aunt's cooking can't be beat. I really appreciate it."

Warmed by the other man's concern, Rob rested his hand on Jonah's arm and drew in a breath as his palm made contact with Jonah's skin. Heat bloomed in his chest and seemed to jump through his entire body, just from that simple touch.

He could have sworn Jonah was affected too, as he stood frozen in place, his gaze trained down to the point of connection between them. Then he looked up, and, for an instant, Rob saw the flare of desire in Jonah's eyes, and his heart leaped.

At that moment, more than anything else in the world, he wanted to kiss Jonah silly. Make that spark turn into an inferno that would disintegrate the other man's habitual reticence and every other barrier that there could be between them.

Jonah moved away so suddenly Rob was left with his hand still in the air.

"Let's take the food through to the office," he said over his shoulder, walking in that direction. "How are those babies doing?"

For an instant Rob couldn't find his voice because of

the mix of desire and disappointment racketing around in his body. Taking a deep breath, he cleared his throat and started after Jonah, replying, "They're still hanging in there."

"That's what I like to hear."

He was already shifting stuff off his desk by the time Rob made it into the office. Putting the box down on a clear corner, Rob stood for a moment, undecided.

Should he make his interest known to Jonah, or leave it alone?

Normally, he tended to be cautious in his personal life, waiting to see how things developed before exposing his own feelings, but with Jonah there was a strange kind of urgency goading him to act. Maybe it was because of the time constraints? Knowing he wouldn't be around for very long made it seem imperative to admit his feelings. Yet, even with that excuse, it had only been two days since they'd come back into each other's lives. Way too soon to be reacting this way, right?

Jonah looked at him, raising his eyebrows.

"You gonna sit down or what? Don't let Aunt Lonie's food get cold."

Rob dropped into the chair in front of the desk, pushing aside the thoughts twisting through his head. It was really only then that the scent of the food made its way into his consciousness, and he groaned.

"Wow, that smells fantastic. What is it?"

"Hoppin' John, shrimp and grits, fried okra and chicken bog." He paused as he was pulling out containers from the box and shook his head. "Aunt Lonie never feeds me like this. She really likes you."

Rob chuckled, half rising from his seat to peer into the containers. "I'm thankful for her liking, believe me. But you have to explain what Hoppin' John and chicken bog are, since I've never heard of them."

"Apparently she's trying to woo you with all the traditional South Carolina favorites," Jonah said, handing Rob a large plate with high sides—almost like a combination plate and bowl—and a fork. "Hoppin' John is this one here." He spooned some of the rice mixture into Rob's plate. "Rice, peas, bacon, deliciousness."

Rob's mouth was already watering from the smell, and he wasted no time in taking a bite. The sound that rose in his throat when the flavors burst to life on his tongue was unintentionally sensual, but completely appropriate.

"Oh, sweet merciful father," he said when he'd swallowed. "That's downright sinful, it's so good."

"Try the rest," Jonah said, his lips twitching into a smile. "It's all amazing. But save space for berry cobbler."

"At this rate, I'm going to have to buy a new wardrobe. I can feel my belly growing, just from looking at this feast."

The food had done the trick to dissipate any lingering discomfort between them, and they chatted casually during the rest of the meal, when their mouths weren't full.

"Inez said you worked at a zoo nearby?" Rob asked Jonah. "What was that like?"

"It was amazing," he replied, and there was no mistaking the enthusiasm in his voice. "That's what I'd wanted to do, from the beginning," he continued, helping himself to more grits. "I'd planned to go off to Africa, or Asia, and work with sanctuaries or zoos. Kill two birds with one stone—get to travel and to work with the animals."

It was clear that he'd given up that dream to take care of his mother, and once more Rob was moved by his dedication to family.

"I'm actually thinking of resurrecting that dream," Jonah said. "Now that Mom's gone, there's nothing holding me here, except for Eunice." At the sound of her name, the dog's tail beat a brief tattoo against the floor, but the golden didn't open her eyes. "Once she's..."

His voice trailed off, and Rob nodded, not needing him to finish.

"But what will you do with this place? Seems to me a lot of people around here rely on you to take care of their animals."

"I'll sell it. Hopefully I can find someone capable to buy it, and the clients will be taken care of."

Rob didn't even think it through—the words just popped out of his mouth. "I'll buy it."

Jonah was glad he'd finished what he was eating, because he was so surprised by Rob's pronouncement that he inhaled a huge gulp of air and would have choked if he'd had food in his mouth.

For a long moment he just stared across at the other man, trying to decide whether he meant what he'd said or not. There was no hint of amusement on Rob's face. In fact, he looked excited, eyes gleaming and lips turned up in an enthusiastic smile.

"You're kidding me," he finally said. "Why on earth would you want to do that?"

"It would be perfect," Rob replied, the words almost tripping over each other with his obvious excitement. "I've been looking for a place to call home, and I think this could be it. Of course, I've only been here two days, but what I've seen and experienced so far makes me feel at home."

As Jonah sat there, still in shock, Rob got up to stride back and forth across the office floor, eyes unfocused, as though envisioning the future and speaking it into being.

"I know it sounds crazy—"

"It does," he agreed.

"And impulsive—"

"For sure."

Rob paused, sending him a look that he didn't know how to interpret. "But from what you said, you're not quite ready to sell, so there's time to figure things out."

Leaning back in his chair, completely flummoxed, Jonah said slowly, "Are you actually serious?"

"Completely," Rob replied, back to striding across the floor. "We could start out with me coming on board as an associate, so you can figure out if I'm the right fit. Then, if you wanted, we could discuss my investing into the clinic." He grinned. "You have a lot more expertise with exotic animals, and you can bring me up to speed on how to treat them. Plus, I'd have the benefit of your reputation to help me keep the clinic going after you leave."

Suddenly he paused, both in his pacing and his monologue, and Jonah found himself the focus of a penetrating stare.

"That is, if you decide to leave at all."

Mouth dry, Jonah swallowed before replying, "I plan to."

"But, if you don't, we'd have to have a provision in the agreement to cover that eventuality." He'd been near the door, but now walked slowly closer. "We'd have to come to some arrangement about whether we could still work together."

Rob had stopped at the side of the desk, and Jonah noticed how bright his eyes were, as though behind the bronze depths a lamp had been lit. They were dazzling, hypnotic, their sparkling intensity creating a bubble that encompassed the two men and had Jonah's heart racing. He couldn't break free, even if he'd wanted to.

"Why wouldn't we be able to?" Why did his voice sound so faint, barely rumbling out of his throat?

"Because I'm attracted to you," Rob replied, equally quietly, tightening that intimate bubble even more. Drawing Jonah in, as if a cord stretched between them had shortened, creating a searing drag on his body. "If anything happens between us—of an intimate nature—that would muddy the waters. Considerably."

"I…"

Shock and a rush of intense arousal rendered Jonah mute, and he couldn't even think of what to say. He was lost in those brilliant eyes, the moments stretching on to what felt like eternity, as he absorbed the realization that Rob too felt the magnetic pull between them.

That he wasn't alone in the need.

The wanting.

His head was swimming with thoughts, questions, images, but he couldn't articulate any of them. He just sat there, frozen with surprise.

It was Rob who finally broke the spell, turning away abruptly with what sounded like a muttered curse.

"I need to check on Milo and Ovaltine."

He threw the words over his shoulder when he was already halfway to the door, and before Jonah could say anything, he was gone.

Still stunned, Jonah didn't move, although the sharp snap of the door closing made him jump.

Rob was attracted to him…

That thought racketed through his head, ping-ponging back and forth, trailed by others both collateral and random.

I thought it was just me…

He wants to buy the clinic…

What would it be like…?

Images of what it might be like to hold Rob, kiss him, make love with him invaded his mind, and he lost his ability to breathe.

I couldn't…

Yet, there was no mistaking the rush of heat that fired down his spine and straight into his groin.

Then one thought overrode all the others and drew him up short.

Why did Rob leave so abruptly?

You'd think he'd want to talk things through a little…

Probably because you sat there gawking at him like a largemouth bass gasping on the riverbank…

Galvanized by the realization he'd made no real re-action to anything Rob had said, probably sending the wrong message entirely, he sprang to his feet and headed to the isolation area.

Rob was back on the floor by the cage, using his stethoscope to listen to one of the pup's chests.

When he straightened and removed the earpieces, Jonah asked, "How are they doing?"

Easier to start there than to reopen the can of worms Rob had thrown at him.

Or maybe that should be cans, in the plural, even though there was one bigger than the others.

"They're holding their own, but I'm not terribly optimistic, despite the CPMA treatment," Rob replied, and Jonah appreciated the honesty, and the hint of sadness in Rob's tone. "I think it's going to be a long road for them, if they make it through the night."

"You're not planning to stay here with them all night, are you?"

He felt a little hypocritical asking the question that way. There'd been a number of nights when he'd slept in the clinic to monitor a patient.

"I haven't decided yet." Rob glanced up, then immediately looked back at the pups. "Would that be a problem?"

Jonah found himself shaking his head, although he really wanted Rob to go home and get some rest.

"No, but I can stay instead."

Rob shrugged. "It's no problem. They're my patients, so I'll stay. You go on home."

Besides that one glance, he'd kept his gaze lowered, and Jonah was suffused by the need to have him look up. Hopefully he could gauge what was going through his head by his expression.

He gathered his courage.

"Listen. You've thrown a lot of…ideas at me today."

That brought Rob's head up, and Jonah found himself on the receiving end of a narrow-eyed stare. It almost dried up the words on his tongue, but he found the strength to forge ahead. "The documentary. Your interest in buying the clinic..."

That was as far as he could go, whatever nerve he'd dredged up deserting him again.

Rob's lips twitched into a shadow of a smile.

"Not to mention suggesting that I want to sleep with you," he said, amusement and regret somehow both coming through in his voice and expressive face. "I'm usually more cautious about getting intimate with anyone," he confessed. "But I've been thinking about it since the moment I saw you, and it just...came out."

Would this man ever stop surprising him? Jonah was beginning to think not.

"It's okay," he muttered, not sure what else to say just then, mired in the kind of deep confusion he'd never experienced before.

"And it was ridiculous of me too," Rob continued, his voice a little bitter. "Considering you've been giving me the cold shoulder most of the day, it was stupid of me to think you might be interested in me in that way."

That rocked Jonah back on his heels, and he heard himself say, "No. No, it wasn't." Rob's eyes darkened, until all that was left was a ring of what looked like fire around his dilated pupils, and Jonah stepped back instinctively, knowing that if he didn't, he'd be lost. Fear and desire were at war within him, and, this time, fear won. "I… I just need time to think," he croaked, before turning around and fleeing.

Running from the intensity of his own desires.

CHAPTER EIGHT

EVEN AFTER JONAH left the clinic, Rob's stress level stayed high, and he couldn't stop going over and over the conversation they'd had.

Jonah's obvious shock and hesitancy on hearing his confession, coupled with the other man's seeming admission that he too felt the attraction between them, had thrown him into a tailspin.

He wasn't normally so aggressive or forward. In fact, most of his relationships had been forged after the other man had made the first move. Rob could flirt with the best of them, but when it came to actually taking things to the next level, he tended to hang back, let the other person be vulnerable first.

Vulnerability.

That tended to be a hard one for him.

When he'd first started dating, there'd been some rejection involved. He'd assumed the other person was as into him as he was interested in them, and had been crushed when they turned out to only want sex—or not want him at all. And he'd never been the kind to give of himself—physically or emotionally—in a casual way. He was all or nothing.

Which made his approach to Jonah that much more unusual.

Sure, there'd been flashes, moments when he'd thought he'd seen an equal attraction in Jonah, but they'd been fleeting. Plus, he'd sensed a very real resistance from Jonah, as though even if he were interested in Rob, he didn't want to be.

Even hearing that Jonah only got involved in short-term, informal couplings or one-night stands should have been a turnoff, but actually wasn't.

Instead, it made him want to be the man who changed his attitude. Who made him want to keep coming back for more and more. Maybe never want to leave.

Which was another problem, since leaving Butler's Run was exactly what Jonah seemed determined to do. From what he'd said, only an aging golden retriever kept him from riding off into the sunset on a search for adventure.

They could simply switch places—Rob taking over Jonah's life and giving him his—and ostensibly they'd both be happy.

But Rob knew he wouldn't be happy. At least, not if that were to happen right now.

There really was unfinished business between them. At least in Rob's mind.

He'd never felt this way about anyone before—more than attracted, almost obsessed—and it was uncharted territory.

With a sigh, he checked on the puppies one more time, adjusting their drips, and set an alarm for three hours' time. Making his way to the staff lounge where there

was an old couch, he found that Jonah had put out a pillow and a light blanket, and the concern warmed him.
After toeing off his shoes, he stretched out and threw
the cover over his legs. He knew he should try to doze,
but he was still wired from his conversation with Jonah,
so he opened his reading app on his phone and tried to
concentrate on the thriller he'd been reading.

When his phone rang, his heart stumbled, until he realized it was Beeta.

He'd hoped it was Jonah, wanting to talk.

"Hey," he said, after clicking through to the call.
"What's up?"

"That's what I'm calling to find out. I went by your
room and you weren't there. Where are you?"

Beeta's rapid-fire questioning made him shake his
head. Anyone listening to them would think she was the
older sibling.

"I'm at the clinic still. We had a pair of puppies come
in with parvovirus. I'm monitoring them overnight."

"Are you getting paid for that?" While he wouldn't
classify her as only concerned with money, she was a
staunch advocate for everyone getting paid for whatever
work they put in.

"That wasn't the arrangement, B, and I'm okay with
it. No one asked me to stay. It was my decision."

The sound she made was one of irritation, but thankfully she didn't pursue that line of conversation. Instead,
she asked, "Did your friend decide whether he wants to
be a part of the documentary or not?"

"I'll find out in the morning." He'd completely forgotten about the documentary, with everything else going on. "He has a lot on his mind right now."

Probably the understatement of the decade, but the truth, nonetheless.

"At this point, I'm not sure I'm even going to bother with it."

"The documentary?"

"Yeah. They had us come all this way, assuring us everything was set, and now it's just one big hassle and delay. I'm fed up."

"At least give the council a chance to change their minds. As you said, we've come all this way…" And he definitely wasn't ready to leave.

She snorted, impatience fairly rolling off the sound. "I'm not going hat in hand. We were invited to be here, and they're being ridiculous. Even if they agree to allow us to film the Easter parade, I might still decide not to do the film. Then we can get back to civilization quicker than we planned."

Rob experienced an irrational annoyance at her characterization of Butler's Run as somehow outside the realm of civilization. For all her love of the outdoors, having lived in LA for years Beeta could be a snob about small towns, but her tone still irked him.

"You can leave," he said, deciding on the spur of the moment to break the news to her this way, rather than face-to-face, as he'd initially planned to. "But I'll be staying a while longer."

That silenced Beeta for a few seconds, but not for long.

"What do you mean? Why? What would you be staying for?"

"I like it here," he said, evenly, just as Gilligan the cat wandered into the lounge and, without a pause, jumped onto the blanket over his legs.

"What's there to like?" Beeta couldn't contain her astonishment.

Jonah Beaumont.

But he kept that thought to himself.

"You know I've been looking for the right place to settle down—"

"You can't be serious. Besides, they already have a vet here. You'd compete with your friend?"

As though a part of the conversation, Gilligan found a comfortable spot and sat blinking at Rob, for all the world as if he were offering support.

"No. Jonah is thinking about selling his practice, and I'm thinking about buying it."

Once more, Beeta was reduced to silence. Gilligan climbed up onto Rob's chest and lay down, head butting him once, obviously demanding pets. When Rob obliged, the black cat started making biscuits on his shoulder.

"You're nuts," Beeta said frankly. "I think after two months you'll be climbing the walls because of the sameness. Moving here, after living in LA? Preposterous!"

It was on the tip of his tongue to remind her he'd only moved to LA because of her, but he bit that organ instead. He'd never come right out and said that to her, although both of them knew it was true. While he was off at school on his parents' dime, Beeta had been doing hard graft in coffee shops and retail stores, just to make enough money to live and go to college.

It hadn't been fair, and the guilt he'd felt had caused

him to want to help her in whichever way he could. Well, he'd done that, and now it was time to get on with his life, but he didn't feel like having a long, protracted discussion with her about his plans.

"Maybe," he said, just to placate her. "But I'm going to give it a shot anyway."

"Good luck with it." She always retreated to sarcasm when unsure or hurt. "This place is as bad as Johnstown, and we both know how bad *that* was."

And he didn't bother to remind her that he actually liked the small town near where they grew up.

That would have just gotten her more riled up.

Gilligan headbutted him again, as though he'd read Rob's mind and agreed with him.

Jonah took Eunice out for her late evening walk, glad that it was a warm evening. The old dog suffered terribly with arthritis during the colder months, even with regular treatment for her joints and hip dysplasia. As the golden shuffled her way from bush to bush, Jonah looked back on the day just gone.

Had it only been one day? It felt longer, as though too much had happened and his brain couldn't reconcile the timeline being so short.

His head was also still spinning with the questions and concerns Rob had brought into his life. That man had definitely turned his world upside down.

"Be logical, Jonah," he said aloud, making Eunice lift her head and look at him with enquiring eyes. When he ruffled her ears, she went back to her nature investigations.

Yes. It made sense to cut through the noise and look

at each of the issues separately. Logically. And do it in a logical order—easiest to hardest.

Hardest...

Just thinking that word made him snort, since he'd been in what felt like an almost constant state of erection since Rob came back into his life. The truncated laugh seemed to annoy Eunice, and she woofed at him in reprimand.

She liked her late-night strolls to be done in silence so she could hear the wind blowing and the wildlife noises. Being more than a little deaf meant any comments from Jonah were unwelcome.

"Sorry," he said, rubbing his hand down her back. "Just my juvenile sense of humor."

So, the easiest question was whether to participate in the documentary or not. On the plus side it might raise his professional profile, so that when he started looking for new opportunities, he had something extra to offer. Yet, that wasn't really enough of a reason to do it.

Did he really want or need a facsimile of the internet fame Rob enjoyed, and yet seemed to dislike, if not despise?

No.

And Rob wasn't terribly keen on doing this doc anyway.

Doing this doc...

This time he was able to keep his laughter to himself so as not to disturb Eunice, even though it rose like a hysterical bubble into his throat. But the double entendre almost made him abandon his train of thought and consider that Rob had, indeed, expressed a desire to do this particular doc.

Stop it, Jonah. You're acting like a teenager.

Dragging his mind out of the gutter, he brought it back on task.

Realistically, he had no idea whether his involvement would weigh the scale one way or another with the town council. But the bottom line was that Rob had asked for his help, and, no matter what else was happening between them, he owed the other man for stepping in at the clinic.

So, that was settled. He'd tell Rob that he'd be in the documentary.

Next was the suggestion he might want to eventually buy the practice.

It really should be a no-brainer. Rob had the credentials to be an asset to the clinic, and intimated he had the funds to buy it as well.

So why was Jonah hesitating there too? He should be firing off emails to his lawyer for advice, and figuring out exactly how to go about it, if Rob really was serious.

Because it's Rob, and I'm burning inside for him. And if we sleep together, it'll complicate things. And if we don't, I might just spontaneously combust.

That about summed it up, and made him realize he couldn't avoid the biggest of the questions: whether to make good on his near confession to Rob that he was attracted to him too and see where that all led.

Eunice had reached the end of her self-allotted distance and stood for a moment, looking up into the sky, before turning back toward the house. Jonah turned too and, for the first time in a long time, found himself really looking at his home.

He'd grown up here, after his father's far too early demise, which had brought him and his mother back to Butler's Run from Virginia, where his dad had been stationed.

Suddenly, he remembered the fear he'd felt on seeing the house, and his grandmother, for the first time. The car coming up the long driveway—the house was on five acres, he'd later learn, and set back far from the road—the big old oaks on either side seeming to reach out to grab at them. Then the elderly woman opening the door before they even got there.

Gran had been medium height and ramrod straight, salt-and-pepper hair pulled back into the neatest bun you'd ever see. Although she was stocky, there was nothing matronly about her. No one would expect Matilda Hawthorne to bake them cookies, or make a fuss if they fell. A pillar of the nearby Baptist church, where her own maternal grandfather had been a preacher, she was upright and forthright. And to him, just then, terrifying.

Even at just six years old, he'd recognized his mother's trepidation, and now realized he'd absorbed it from her.

She's a dragon, Lonie. And she'll consume us if we move back there. Besides, she said she didn't want to have anything to do with me after I married Sam against her wishes.

He'd heard them talking in the kitchen—Mom and Aunt Lonie—just a few months before. Although he was supposed to be in bed, how could he sleep when his auntie, who he adored, was visiting?

You can't stay here alone, by yourself, Myra. Even with Sam's death benefit, how're you going to make ends meet? You need people around you that you can count on.

Jonah had almost stepped into the room then, ready to shout that Momma wasn't alone. She had him, and could count on him too. He'd be good and take care of her, the way Daddy said he should whenever he left to go on deployment.

You take care of your momma while I'm away, you hear?

I will, Daddy.

And he had, hadn't he? He never gave her any trouble, although sometimes feelings he didn't understand boiled and boiled inside him, making him want to hit someone or something. Anyone. Anything. But he held all that inside, because he didn't want to make Mom cry any more than she already did.

So, he was ready to stand up to Aunt Lonie. Tell her to go away and leave them alone…

You're right, Lonie. I can't stay here alone…

It was the first time he'd realized he didn't count. Not really.

That he wasn't enough, couldn't be enough for the people he wanted to please the most.

Time and again he'd read between the lines of what others said and realized there must be something lacking in him—something that created emotional distance between him and those around him.

His mother, grandmother, even Aunt Lonie and Carmen.

It wasn't that he couldn't love, or wasn't prepared to

make an effort for those he loved, but somehow that love and effort seemed insufficient.

And there, right there, was why he hesitated about getting involved with Rob.

Now though, he had to consider how he'd feel if he weren't enough for Rob. If the other man found him somehow deficient as a partner, either in work or in bed. Or both.

But you don't plan to stick around, do you? You'll be leaving. So, why make this into a federal case? Things don't work out, you sell up and move on. No harm, no foul.

It was only when Eunice gave a sigh and sat down that Jonah realized he'd been standing in the darkness of the night, unmoving, for what the dog probably thought was an unconscionable amount of time.

"Sorry, girl. Come on, let's go home."

But the house, although well-lit and infinitely familiar, suddenly seemed more like a jail than a home. Solitary confinement awaiting.

If you didn't count the four-legged companion slowly shuffling beside him along the path.

"You are more than enough for me, Eunice," he heard himself say, as if she'd understand him and needed the approbation. "You're the goodest girl ever, and I love you."

Funny how easy it was to love an animal, and both tell and show them so, and how hard it was to open himself up to another human being…

CHAPTER NINE

AFTER A RESTLESS NIGHT, when he was back and forth keeping an eye on the puppies, Rob was just about to head back to the hotel to shower and change when Jonah got to work.

He didn't look any better rested than Rob felt.

"How're the babies?" Jonah asked, first thing.

"Made it through the night," Rob answered, stifling a yawn. "Still not out of the woods, but I'm a little bit more hopeful about them."

"Good. You go on and get outta here. Go get some rest." Rob was about to object, but Jonah held up his hand. "I know you probably dozed a bit, but that's not enough. Get some sleep and come in this afternoon, if you feel up to it. We can manage the workload, and although I'm sure you'd be okay working with little sleep, I'd prefer you be well rested."

Rob couldn't help grinning at the other man's workmanlike tone.

"Yes, boss." And he threw in a salute for good measure.

Jonah snorted, but his lips twitched into a smile nonetheless.

"Don't be a smart-ass."

"Can't help it," he replied, feeling somehow buoyed by the interaction. "Ask Beeta. She'll tell you."

"Oh, which reminds me… Tell your sister I'll take part in the documentary."

Rob felt his grin widen.

"Great. I'll let her know, but I have to warn you, she's pretty fed up with the whole thing at this point. Even if they give her permission to film the parade and horse show, she might decide to not go ahead with the shoot."

Jonah nodded slowly, his gaze fathomless.

"Don't make no never mind. If she decides to stay and film, I'm in. What about you?"

Genuinely confused, Rob asked, "What do you mean?"

Jonah cocked his head to one side, his habitual poker face firmly in place.

"If she decides not to do the film and leaves, are you going too?"

Surprised that he would even ask that, Rob stared at the other man, trying to figure out if he was serious. After their conversation last night, he'd have thought he'd know the answer to that question was a resounding no. Maybe he thought Rob had been joking, or had changed his mind? Did he really think he was that fickle or flaky?

Or was it some unwarranted lack of self-confidence making Jonah believe Rob didn't really want him, the way he'd said he did?

Unable to decide, and aware of other people moving around the clinic, all he could do was slowly—ever so slowly—shake his head.

"No, Jonah. I'm not going anywhere. Not until you and I get some stuff sorted out."

Something flashed behind those sleepy eyes but was quickly masked as Jonah gestured Rob toward his office, and Rob fell into step beside him to walk down the corridor.

"What will I have to do, if she goes ahead?" The change of subject wasn't lost on Rob, but he let it pass without comment.

"Once Beeta firms up the shoot, I'll go over the process with you," he told Jonah. "She goes for a conversational style of dialogue, so there's no script. All the excitement is provided by her camera angles and shots."

"Really?" Jonah asked, as he opened his office door. "What you do seemed pretty exciting to me."

"You watched some of the videos?" He knew Jonah hadn't known about the docs before he'd come to town. Which meant he'd somehow, over the past couple of days, made time to check them out.

The thought gave Rob a pleasant jolt.

Jonah just shrugged, not making eye contact. "A few. They were interesting. Everyone had made such a fuss, I wanted to see for myself what all the hoopla was about."

Although he was obviously trying to sound casual, there was a defensive note to his voice that made Rob smile. He coughed to hide it and inadvertently made himself yawn.

"You're beat," Jonah said, giving him a stern glance. "Get outta here. I'll keep an eye on your babies. I'll see you when I see you."

"Not before I give my girlfriend some love," he replied, already stooping down beside Eunice's bed and ruffling the fur around her neck. "Right, girl? How dare he suggest I just ignore you?"

Eunice just sat there, taking his affection like the queen she was, and offering a small kiss as her official acceptance of his tribute.

But Jonah was right, Rob knew. He was exhausted. So, with a last hug, he let Eunice go and stood up.

"Okay, I'm outta here, as ordered." It amused him to hear the way he'd unconsciously mimicked Jonah's Southern intonation. "I'll see you later."

"Yes, sir," came the answer, but, just as he'd gotten to the door, Jonah continued, "And if you're up for it, let's do dinner this evening, to discuss some of the other issues."

Rob froze with his hand on the knob, his heart suddenly pounding at a frantic pace. But when he turned to look at Jonah, the other man was seemingly focused on his computer screen.

Ironic, really, that Jonah had made the suggestion. During the long night just past, Rob had made the decision to bring up neither the purchase of the practice nor his physical interest in Jonah again. He'd seen the tension in Jonah and didn't want to exacerbate it.

"I'm guessing the venue won't be Lonie's?"

Jonah's gaze flicked up for an instant before those lazy, sexy eyelids drooped again, shielding the expression in his eyes.

"No. I have somewhere else in mind."

"Okay. Just let me know what time."

"Uh-huh."

Taking that as a dismissal, Rob exited the office, but he couldn't hold back a grin. And he was still smiling as he dialed Beeta's number to tell her that Jonah had agreed to do the documentary.

And the feeling of anticipation that had fired through him when he'd heard Jonah say he wanted to talk about "other issues" stayed with him, keeping him awake, tossing and turning, until exhaustion dragged him down into sleep.

A spring thunderstorm rolled in, bringing heavy rains and the threat of flooding. Although the weather people had been predicting it for the last couple of days, they'd underestimated the severity of it. The clinic had a slew of canceled appointments that afternoon, which turned out to be a good thing when, after a particularly violent clap of thunder, the lights went out. When they didn't come back on after ten minutes, Jonah called the power company and was told a substation had been damaged by lightning.

As for when it would be repaired and the power would come back on, they couldn't say.

"I'm sorry, folks," Jonah told the few people waiting before explaining what he'd been told. "We're going to have to reschedule. Until I know when the power's coming back on, I'm going to use the generator to keep the hospital area running. But please, wait until the lightning's moved off before you leave."

"Yeah," Tom Kingston said. "No use leaving 'cause of the dark and getting all lit up out there."

Jonah was still chuckling as he made his way to the back of the clinic to tell the staff to get ready to go home, once the storm eased up.

"There aren't a lot of animals in the hospital," he replied to Alan, when the youngster asked if he should stay to feed the animals as usual later in the afternoon. "I'm gonna hang around, so I'll do it."

When the worst of the lightning passed, the clients left, followed not too long after by the staff. Jonah put on a raincoat and trotted out to the shed where the generator was housed and got it going. At some point it would be nice to upgrade to an automatic unit, he thought, as he sprinted back to the clinic building, trying avoid the next shower, which he could see coming in the distance. But maybe it would be easier to let the next owner take care of that, if they wanted to.

After all, when he'd bought into the practice initially, Doc Harding didn't even have a generator in place. Jonah had only been able to convince the old guy to install one after they'd been shut down for close to a week after a hurricane passed through.

He was hanging up his raincoat when he heard the front door open and Rob call out.

"Back here," he said, wishing his heart wouldn't start galloping like a colt seeing pasture for the first time every time the darn man was close by.

"What's going on?" Rob was damp, his shirt sticking to his chest, so that when he raised his hands to slick the droplets of water off his hair, every muscle was delineated.

Jonah looked away, but the image seemed seared onto his retinas.

"Storm knocked out a substation, so I closed for the day." He moved to the sink to wash his hands, keeping

Rob out of his line of sight. "Even though the generator can run most of the clinic, I don't want to overtax it by using anything like the X-ray machine, or the autoclave. Besides, it's a blessing in disguise for the staff, you know? They've been putting in extra hours to keep up, without complaint, and it'll do 'em good to get some unexpected time off."

Rob moved toward the isolation area, asking, "How're the babies?"

"They're still with us. Lethargic, and not interested in food, so still on the drip. I did get them to take a little oral rehydration though."

"I'll call and update the owner," he said, as he disappeared to look in on his babies.

"He called earlier, and I spoke to him. Told him we'd give him a call tomorrow morning to update again."

"Oh, great." His voice floated out from the other room. "Hey, did someone clean these babies up?"

"Yep. Alan is as obsessed with them as you are. He wouldn't leave until he'd made sure they were clean and comfortable. Insisted on trying them with a little more rehydration fluid too."

"He's a really reliable worker. Do you think he'll go to school to become a tech?"

Jonah pondered that for a second and then shrugged, forgetting that Rob couldn't see him.

"I don't know. He has time to figure it out. He's successful here because everyone knows and understands his quirks are caused by his Asperger's. His mother tends to be a bit…overprotective. It's going to be up to Alan to decide whether he wants to go on to college or not."

"That's one of the benefits of growing up in a small town where everyone knows you." Rob's voice came from almost right behind him, making Jonah stiffen. "Even though it can be a pain too, when you need some understanding you're more likely to get it."

"Hmm." He didn't have a reply; he was too busy concentrating on not looking at the other man. Every inch of skin on his back was prickling with awareness, heat traveling through nerve endings to make his entire body feel supersensitive.

"Did you like growing up here?"

Jonah moved away as slowly as he could, although it was the last thing he wanted to do.

If he didn't, he wouldn't be able to carry on a coherent conversation. Even so, Rob's scent, warm and fresh, seemed to follow him.

Busying himself with collecting some soiled drapes from a receptacle, he replied, "Not at first, but it grew on me, over time."

Rob had moved to another receptacle and was gathering up the bag there. "You weren't born here?"

"Nope. I was born in Virginia. Mom and I moved back here after Daddy died. I was six, and terrified of my grandmother, who I'd never met before."

"Wow. You were six before you met her?"

"Yeah. Apparently, she didn't approve of my mom marrying my father. Grandma came from a pretty affluent background—you know, Black cotillion, mainstay of society, that type of thing—and Daddy was from the other side of the tracks. She'd raised Mom to follow in her footsteps. Even sent her to France to a finishing school.

So when Mom met Daddy at college—just a guy there on scholarship—and decided to marry him, Grandma disowned her."

"Wow. That's hardcore."

"You know it." They both shook their heads in disbelief, as Jonah went on, "When Daddy died, Mom was going to stay in Virginia, although it was too expensive for her to make ends meet. Then Aunt Lonie came and told her Grandma was offering her the opportunity to come back here. I think she was reluctant to come back…" Once more the conversation overheard so very long ago came back to him, and he snorted. "Actually, I know she didn't really want to come back. She called Grandma a dragon."

They were moving side by side toward the mudroom, where the washer and dryer were located, but both paused in unison just outside the door. Jonah knew Rob was looking at him, and he turned so they were face-to-face, but separated by the bags of laundry.

"So, how bad did she turn out to be?"

There was true concern on Rob's face, as though he dreaded hearing what was going to come next, but Jonah shook his head, wishing his hands were free so he could touch the other man.

"Not bad, at all. I don't think Mom would have stayed if Grandma had been abusive in any way, no matter how badly off we were financially. Grandma was tough, stern and strict, but we got along okay. She was even the one who fostered my interest in animals."

There was no mistaking the relief that crossed Rob's expression.

"I'm glad to hear that."

"Mothers and daughters are a different dynamic than grandmothers and grandkids, I think. Mom and Grandma still bucked heads occasionally over the years, but by then it was more of a generational gap than the old arguments."

Realizing they were just standing there with the laundry in their hands, Jonah moved ahead of Rob into the mudroom and dropped the bag on the ground.

"She was old-fashioned, and old-school in a lot of ways. You kept your private business to yourself and presented a respectable, God-fearing front to the world, no matter what was going on behind the scenes."

Rob looked up from where he was loading the machine, his gaze searching.

"I'm guessing your being gay didn't go over so well with her. Did that cause a rift?"

Jonah leaned a hip against the dryer and tried to smile, although it felt stiff and false on his face.

"It might sound cowardly, but I waited until she'd passed to come out. She had cancer, and didn't have much longer to live by the time I'd sorted my sexuality out in my head, you know? I knew how she'd feel about it, from things that she'd said about gay people, that there was something fundamentally wrong with them. She was so old-school, and I just didn't want to disappoint or hurt her."

Rob straightened and reached for the detergent.

"I don't think it's cowardly at all. In fact, it's kind of loving, in a way. Why potentially make her worry about you, and cause her last days to be unhappy?" A flash of what looked like pain crossed his face, as he continued,

"That was my plan too, with my *abuela*, and I've always wished it had worked out, but it didn't."

"What happened?"

Rob didn't answer immediately, just measured the soap into the machine and closed the lid with a snap. Then he turned to face Jonah, and he was frowning. That was such an unusual occurrence, Jonah found himself focusing on the conversation with even greater attention.

"I got outed, by a guy at school." He shook his head, gaze taking on a distant look, as though seeing it all over again. "It was my own fault. Other kids said they thought he was gay, I thought he was flirting with me, and I'd had a crush on him for a while. So, I took the chance and tried to kiss him."

"Uh-oh."

"Yeah." Now a small, rueful smile replaced the frown. "That led to a fight, which had us ending up in the principal's office, where it all came out—including me—in front of my parents."

Despite the other man's smile, which wasn't that convincing anyway, Jonah ached for the young Rob, caught up in such a situation.

"How did your parents take it?"

He shrugged slightly, tilting his head from side to side. "My parents are decent people, and even if they'd been tempted to disown me, they didn't. Papa, in particular, had some trouble with it, but eventually he got over it. But my *abuela*… Nah, man, she was horrified. Was sure I was going to hell, praying over me, crying, the whole nine yards. That made me so sad, and angry."

"I'm sorry, man. That's terrible."

"Don't feel bad," he replied, that crooked smile tipping his lips again. "It was a long time ago, and I didn't mention it for sympathy, just to let you know that I completely understand how you felt about not telling your grandmother you were gay."

"Thanks for that," Jonah replied, meaning it sincerely. He'd secretly viewed his actions back then just as he'd told Rob—as cowardice. But now, having heard Rob's perspective and the outcome of his story, maybe someday he could put it to rest without that burden of guilt.

His grandmother really would have been unhappy, knowing her grandson was gay. Thank goodness neither his mother nor Aunt Lonie had seemed to care. That had been a blessing.

Rob brushed his hands together, as though to dislodge the last of their conversation.

"What else do you have to do around here? You might as well make use of me while you have me."

"Sure. I made a list of things I was planning to do this afternoon, once I decided to close the clinic. It's kinda nice to be able to do them at a more leisurely pace, rather than have to fit them in between patients. If you could fill the autoclave, that would be great. When the power comes back on, I'll start it."

"You got it, boss," he replied with one of his salutes, which always made Jonah want to laugh.

And Jonah found himself still smiling as he went about cleaning and inventorying the clinic, listening to Rob whistling in the distance, just happy to have the other man there.

CHAPTER TEN

JONAH WAS IN his office, trying to sort through the paperwork on his desk, when Rob stuck his head around the door to say, "Beeta's on her way here."

"Did she say what happened at the meeting?"

Rob came closer, shaking his head, a thoughtful expression on his face.

"Nope, and I can't figure out what that means. It could be that she's planning to go ahead and wants to discuss the schedule with both of us, or that she wants to tell us face-to-face it's not happening."

The slow *thump-thump-thump* of Eunice's tail on the floor drew Rob like a magnet as usual, but this time he simply sat on the floor, cross-legged, so as to be able to drape an arm across her neck to pat her.

"Which one seems more likely to you?"

"Probably…she's pulling the plug. She sounded pretty fed up when she called."

Jonah's heart skipped a beat. Although Rob had said he was going to stay whether the documentary got made or not, Jonah wasn't sure he believed him. Even though he was right there, sitting on the floor petting Eunice, the thought of him somehow remaining a part of their lives in Butler's Run seemed absurd.

"And, what about you?"

Rob looked up at him, not smiling but with eyes gleaming coppery, and something about his expression hinted at amusement.

"What about me? I already told you I'm not going until we sort some things out, and you've told me you need time to think. So, I'm staying."

"How long?"

Now the amusement faded, leaving Rob's expression watchful.

"I don't know. How long do you need to think about everything?"

Jonah didn't answer, whatever he was contemplating replying fading away at the look in Rob's eyes—questioning, impatient.

Longing.

Was that longing for him, or for the fantasy small-town life Rob seemed determined to have?

Before either of them could say anything more, there was a banging on the front door, which made Eunice bark and struggle to get up.

"I'll get it," Jonah said, while Rob tried to calm the dog down.

Thankful for the reprieve, he hurried through the waiting area to unlock the door for the woman standing outside.

"Hi," she said, as he opened the door for her. "Thanks."

"You must be Beeta," he said, as he relocked the door behind her. The resemblance to Rob was marked—especially the eyes, although hers were a little darker. "I'm Jonah."

"Nice to finally meet you." Beeta smiled and stuck out her hand. "I met your Aunt Lonie this afternoon. If I didn't know better, I'd think she was planning to adopt that lunkhead of a brother of mine. She couldn't stop talking about him."

Jonah laughed, amused and yet wondering just what else Lonie might have said.

"Come on through to the office."

He noticed her looking around as they walked, pausing to glance into the reception area and through an open door into one of the examination rooms. No doubt trying to figure out what it was, exactly, her brother was thinking of getting himself into.

But she didn't ask any questions, or fill the silence with small talk. Instead, she strode alongside him with quick, long steps.

When Jonah stepped back to allow her to go through the office door ahead of him, she shot him a cheeky, sideways smile that reminded him so much of Rob, his breath hitched.

"Hey, sis. Forgive me for not getting up, but my girlfriend and I are having a moment."

"Hello, sweetie," Beeta said, going straight toward Eunice and offering a hand for sniffing. "You should be more careful about the company you keep. Nice girls like you don't need guys like this."

"Says you. Eunice knows I love her, and that's all there is to say about it."

"I'd have thought she'd have better taste," Beeta rebutted, as she bent to kiss the top of Rob's head. Then she tossed her bag onto a chair and sank down beside her brother on the floor, despite her chic ensemble. "What a day…"

Jonah retook his seat behind the desk, watching the byplay between the siblings. There was a high level of familiarity and comfort between them. Clearly, they knew each other extremely well.

"So, what's the verdict?"

Beeta scrunched up her nose. "The council agreed to a permit, of sorts. But it's so restrictive, I'd have a hell of a time getting any decent shots. I guess the person who didn't want the documentary made at all went around and convinced a bunch of people to sign a petition saying they didn't want their likeness, home or business in the film. Honoring their requests would hamstring me."

"Calling it off then?"

Beeta blew out a long breath and reached across Rob to pat Eunice.

"Yeah, I'm done. I told the Marsh Tacky folks, and they're upset but that can't be helped. I'm sending Gary and Lena home, then going to head up to Charleston for a few days before I go back to LA." She leaned back to give Rob an intent look. "What about you? Want to come to Charleston with me?"

"Nope." At Rob's reply, Jonah found himself releasing a breath he hadn't even realized he'd been holding. "I'm going to stick around here, like I told you."

Beeta suddenly turned her head to look straight at Jonah, and something about the quality of that look made him wonder what she was thinking.

"Well, if you change your mind, I won't be leaving until tomorrow." Looking from Rob to Jonah and back again, she added, "Why don't the three of us have dinner together this evening? I'd like to get to know Jonah a little better."

"Nope," Rob said again, giving his sister a smile that didn't quite seem to reach his eyes. "We already made plans to discuss the potential of my getting further involved with the practice, and since you've changed the timeline, that talk is even more important."

His answer seemed to shock Beeta, who stared at Rob for a few long seconds, before abruptly getting up.

"Well, okay, then." There was a sour note to her voice, although she too smiled. "I'll be heading back to the hotel to pack and let the rest of the team know what's happening." She looked at Jonah then, and shook her head slightly. "If I don't see you again before I leave, it was nice meeting you."

Rob got up too.

"I'll walk you out."

Between the headshake and her abrupt departure, Jonah was left once more wondering what she was thinking. Clearly, she was annoyed about Rob refusing to go to dinner or to Charleston with her, which made him recall that Rob had said his sister knew he had a hard time refusing her anything.

What had made him take such a hard line with her this time?

Maybe he didn't want Jonah spending time with his sister for some reason?

His cell phone rang just then, breaking him out of his reverie, and a glance showed it was Marnie Rutherford.

With his heart in throat—hoping she wasn't calling to say another of her horses was ill—Jonah answered.

"Hi, Jonah," Marnie said when he'd answered. "Sorry to bother you, but I'm here in town and saw a young woman with a kitten she said she'd found outside her workplace. It looks to be in a pretty bad way, so I sent her to your clinic. She should be there any minute."

"Okay." His sense of relief was immediate, and he didn't bother to tell Marnie that the clinic was closed. He'd gladly do whatever he could for the kitten. "I'll look out for her."

"Thanks. Appreciate it. Talk to you soon."

Getting up, he moved down the hallway toward the front of the clinic, realizing as he got closer that Rob and Beeta were obviously still there, talking. The door to the waiting area was open and the voices carried through to him clearly.

"I know you, Rob. You'll get bored in a couple of months and that'll be that, unless you've already locked yourself into something you can't get out of. How on earth can you even think you'll be happy here after living in LA? That's nuts."

"Maybe you don't really understand—"

Jonah came through the door, making sure to make as much noise as possible, to let them know he was there. He already felt bad about hearing what he had, but it had been unavoidable.

"I have a client coming in," he said, not breaking stride as he went past the siblings, who were standing in the middle of the waiting area.

"I thought you were closed?" Beeta said, her aggression evident.

"Doesn't matter," said Rob, before Jonah could reply. "If Jonah's willing to see the patient, that's his business."

"The person who sent her didn't know we were closed, and I don't mind taking a look at the kitten she found."

But he was feeling a little guilty about potentially causing a rift between Rob and his sister. They seemed so close, and Rob had said family was everything.

As he got to the front door, he saw a car driving up to the building. After unlocking the door, he stepped outside, allowing it to swing closed behind him and giving Rob and Beeta some privacy.

The woman who got out of the car was a stranger, and he watched as she walked toward him, a small box in her hands.

"Hi," she said, as she got within earshot. "Are you Dr. Beaumont?"

"Yes. I hear you found a little baby outside your work and it needs some help?"

"Yes," she said, shifting the box to under one arm so she could shake his hand, adding, "Amanda Parr," by way of introduction. "I found him just under my car. And when I went to pick him up, he hardly moved. I don't know what's going on with him."

"Come on in," he said, taking the box from her and looking into it. A ginger kitten, lying unmoving on a towel, looked back at him with dull eyes.

Just as they got to the door, it was pushed open from inside, and Beeta stepped out.

"What you got there, Jonah?" she asked, pausing to

peer into the box. "Aww, just a baby. Make him better, okay?"

"I'll do my best," he replied, as he moved into the clinic, glad to see she seemed to be in a better mood.

With a wave, she let the door close behind them, and Rob was there peering into the box as he walked alongside Jonah.

"Tiny guy," was his only comment.

"Yeah. Can you take him into exam room one, while I go get my computer?"

"Sure."

Rob took the box from him, and Jonah headed for his office. While he gathered up his computer, Jonah thought back to what he'd heard Beeta say to Rob about his getting bored and not staying in Butler's Run.

It made perfect sense to him. In fact, he'd thought the same thing many times.

Butler's Run on a permanent basis after living in LA and traveling all over the country?

Ridiculous.

It was then the realization suddenly hit Jonah. He'd been tying himself up into knots over Rob, worried about the ramifications of getting involved with him professionally and personally, while the person who knew him best had already realized nothing would come of any of it. If Beeta was so sure that Rob wouldn't stick around, then there was nothing to worry about.

They could work together for a while, sleep together for a while, and then Rob would change his mind about settling down in Butler's Run and that would be that.

Sure, Jonah would have to find a new purchaser for the clinic, but he'd cross that creek when he came to it.

In the meantime, he could take a chance on enjoying the other man.

Why look a gift horse in the mouth?

CHAPTER ELEVEN

THANKFULLY THE POWER came back on before they were ready to leave the clinic after five thirty, and Rob asked Jonah where he wanted to meet up for dinner.

"The restaurant is east of here, closer to my house than the hotel," Jonah replied. "So why don't you drive over to my place, and we'll drive there together?"

"Sure," he replied, both surprised and pleased, since he'd wondered about Jonah's home and was curious to see it.

After getting directions, he headed back to the hotel to change out of his scrubs and into more appropriate clothing.

Although, standing in front of the hotel closet, he wondered what that was, exactly. It wasn't a date; should he dress as though it were? Certainly he wanted to make a good impression on Jonah, show the other man his best side, so to speak. Yet, he didn't want to look as though he was trying too hard either. None of the LA styling that he'd had to wear in the past seemed right.

Finally, aware of time ticking away, he went with a black Henley and jeans, his favorite black boots and a turquoise pendant on a leather thong—a gift from his mother the previous Christmas. Hair loose, or back? Laughing at himself, he left the thick strands loose, but out of habit tucked a hair tie into his pocket.

Wallet, watch and a last look in the mirror, and he was out the door.

But before he closed it behind himself, he hurried back inside to spritz himself with cologne.

Nothing wrong with smelling nice!

Getting into the car, he acknowledged his anxiety about the evening ahead. Not even Beeta could understand how much this opportunity meant to him. Or, more accurately, she refused to believe he was serious, because it didn't suit her own agenda. At the end of their conversation earlier, she'd admitted as much.

"I can't imagine not having you close by," she'd finally said. "Not after all we've done together. You can open a clinic in LA, or nearby. Be closer to the family. Also," she'd added, as if unable to stop herself, "we can keep doing some videos together. Not all the time, like we have been, but every now and then."

Normally he appreciated her focused determination, her wish to keep her favorite brother close by, but not today.

Today it felt intrusive and overbearing.

Rob sighed, taking a hand off the wheel to rub at the back of his neck where an ache had settled.

Not that he totally blamed her for being concerned. Everything had happened so quickly, he sometimes wondered what had gotten into him too. But, on the other hand, he was an adult. Her older brother, to boot. The one who'd always looked out for her as best he could, while also letting her live her life the way she wanted.

Couldn't she at least acknowledge he had the right to do the same?

He'd been following the directions on his GPS, and now realized he must be close to his destination. Taking the indicated left turn, he found himself on a gravel road lined with old oak trees dripping with Spanish moss. It was only as he drove around a curve that he realized it wasn't a road, but a driveway leading to a large white two-story house.

Just as he was wondering if he'd made a wrong turn, the front door opened, and Jonah stepped out onto the wraparound porch.

"Good grief," Rob muttered, still taking in the old-world charm of the building. As soon as he got out, he called to Jonah, "This is where you live?"

With amusement in his voice, Jonah called back, "Yep. Like it?"

"It's amazing. Kinda big for just you and Eunice though, isn't it? Unless you have an entire family stashed in there somewhere."

"Nope. Just us two." They met at the bottom of the stairs and stood side by side, looking up at the facade. "It's a family place, so although I use maybe four rooms total, I can't bring myself to sell it."

"I'd beat you myself if you ever tried to. She's a grand Southern lady."

He turned his head just in time to see Jonah smile at him, and something about that curl of his lips made Rob's heart skip a beat.

"I'm too hungry to give you the tour now, but maybe when we get back?"

"I'd like that," he replied, wondering if he was imagining a shift in Jonah's demeanor. A lifting of his usual reticence. He seemed more relaxed.

"Great. Let me just lock up and we'll be on our way."

The drive to the restaurant took about fifteen minutes, and during that time, they spoke casually about the clinic and the untimely demise of Beeta's project.

"She's artistically spoiled," Rob said. "She's so used to getting her way, or doing her own thing, she doesn't like being given boundaries on her work. Hopefully she'll eventually get over herself, or she'll be butting heads with clients going forward."

Jonah sent him a sideways glance and seemed to hesitate for a moment before saying, "You once said you have a hard time saying no to her. Is there a reason, other than she's your sister?"

The question took him by surprise, but, after a moment, he didn't see any reason not to be honest.

"Yeah, there is. Beeta is the youngest—there are four of us—and closest to me in age. We've always been tight. And she's the only one my father refused to help with college. For some reason he decided that being a videographer was a ridiculous career path, and Beeta, being Beeta, got angry and left home right after graduating high school. She was in LA, working, trying to get through school when I graduated, so I moved there to help her finish."

"This might be a rude question, but why?"

Confused, Rob asked, "Why what?"

"Why did you think it was your job to help her through school?"

Rob felt a spurt of annoyance but swallowed it. After all, to an outsider it would be a reasonable question.

"You know how expensive UC Davis is, and I was only on partial scholarship. My parents shelled out a lot of money to help me get through vet school, while Beeta was struggling alone. Why wouldn't I want to help her out when I could? She's my sister."

"I guess," Jonah said. "But I have to say I admire you for putting your sister's needs ahead of your own ambitions—unless, of course, LA was your idea of a great place to live?"

"It wasn't and isn't." He hadn't meant to sound so emphatic, but he couldn't help the forceful way the words came out. "I've always wanted to live in a more rural setting, not having to budget an extra hour or two just to get from one place to the next, and deal with people who seem to have their heads in the clouds most of the time."

Jonah put on his indicator and turned into a parking lot that was about half-full of vehicles. When he'd parked, he turned off the ignition and turned in his seat to face Rob as he was reaching for the door handle. He was smiling and, beneath those sleepy lids, his eyes were glittering.

"Well, here you'll still have to drive a ways to get out to some of the farms, and unfortunately you can't cure stupid, which exists everywhere. But for the most part the people are down-to-earth, so we've got LA beat in that respect."

He'd spoken quietly, intimately, and although the words were humorous—even prosaic—Rob felt as if the temperature in the vehicle had gone up by twenty degrees. Unable to stop staring at Jonah's mouth, the urge to lean forward and capture those smiling lips with his own was almost overwhelming.

The distance between them narrowed, narrowed, until he could feel each rush of Jonah's exhales across his face, smell the mint on his breath, mixed with the warm scent of his cologne.

Heart hammering, Rob held his breath, about to close those last few inches…

Jonah inhaled sharply and popped the door handle, opening his door.

"Let's go get something to eat. I'm starving."

Squashing his disappointment, Rob replied, "Me too."

And he didn't try to hide the irony, which made Jonah send him a laughing look from those sexy, heavy-lidded eyes.

Inside, they were taken to a table overlooking a salt marsh inlet, which was bathed in the last orange and rose tinges of the setting sun, with boats parked along a small dock. The vista was gorgeous and calming, and Rob allowed the lingering sexual tension to dissipate.

He'd made the decision not to push Jonah, and he'd stick to that, no matter how crazy the other man made him.

Instead of sitting across the table from Rob, Jonah chose the seat next to him, probably so he too could enjoy the view.

Once they'd placed their drink orders, Jonah got right down to business.

"I've been thinking it over, and I need to contact my business lawyer for advice, but what I propose is that we agree to a trial period where you work at the clinic for a salary. While that's happening, we can get all necessary legal details and contracts sorted out. It'll give us both an opportunity to figure out what, exactly, we want to do and when, long-term."

Was it ridiculous to feel impatient with this cautious approach?

"When you say a trial period, what are you thinking?"

"Two, maybe three months." Before Rob could say anything, he continued, "It'll take at least that long for the lawyer to figure out the legalities anyway. You know how slow they can be."

It felt like talking to Beeta all over again, but Rob knew he was being unfair to Jonah. And selfish too, if he were being honest with himself. Just because he'd made up his mind about what he wanted to do didn't mean that everyone else had to fall into line.

"Okay," he said, albeit reluctantly. "But I have to tell you I won't change my mind about this, unless something completely untoward happens."

Jonah's eyebrows rose at that, but he didn't ask for clarification. Instead, he said, "We can discuss the financial aspect of it more tomorrow. I never discuss money on an empty stomach."

Rob grunted, still annoyed but even more amused by that pronouncement.

The waiter brought their drinks, and they asked for a bit more time to order, since neither had looked at the menu. Once the waiter left the table again, Rob wondered if Jonah would go back to their discussion, but when next he spoke, the other man asked a question that came out of left field.

"What do you like, in bed?"

It was the last thing he'd expected, and the easy, casual way Jonah asked was shocking. No doubt that showed on his face, because Jonah snorted—a truncated laugh that surprised Rob even more.

"Why do you look like a deer caught in an illegal hunter's spotlight?" Jonah asked, amusement rife in his drawled question. "I'm curious. Besides, we're kinda negotiating here, aren't we? I'd like to know what I'm getting into."

It suddenly struck Rob that their past dealings, with Jonah playing his cards so close to his chest, and Rob doing the pursuing, had made him forget what Jonah's love life had been up to this point. He most likely had far more experience with these kinds of situations than Rob did, with a lot more "negotiations" under his belt.

For an instant it made Rob feel off balance. Even a little silly. But then he rallied.

"Afraid I might be into some kinky stuff?" he drawled in return, using the voice he did when he was trying to get a rise out of one of his siblings.

Jonah's lips twisted, and his eyelids drooped.

"Maybe," he said. "Forewarned is forearmed."

Jonah watched the various emotions play across Rob's face and enjoyed the show. Shock morphed to surprise, then faded to a narrow-eyed look of concentration. Jonah didn't look away, but held the other man's intent stare until Rob was the one to drop his eyes.

He'd never seen Rob thrown off balance, and felt something akin to pride that he'd been able to do it. This sexy

Latin man was far too sure of himself, far too smooth to be allowed to always run the show. And to this point, Jonah realized he'd let him do just that.

He wasn't a pushover. Never had been. In fact, he'd always been the one in control of his own affairs—both businesswise and in his private life, such as it was.

But his reactions to Rob—so primitive and visceral— were a warning that he might not be able to control what was happening between them. Not completely anyway.

The best he could do was put the other man on notice that he'd do his utmost not to get in over his head by allowing Rob to set the pace or make all the decisions.

Finally, Rob looked up at him again and smiled one of his sly, cheeky smiles, but his eyes were wary.

"What do you want to know? I've never been asked that before. Usually, I just go with the flow, let things evolve naturally, without too much preplanning."

Jonah tilted his head, wondering what had created that cautious expression.

"Does talking about this make you uncomfortable?" he asked, now surprised at the tenderness he felt. "That wasn't my intention."

Shaking his head, a more natural smile breaking over his face, Rob said, "Not uncomfortable, really. It just feels strange to—how did you put it?—'negotiate' in this way."

"In the scene, I have to be careful not to put myself into situations I'm not prepared for," Jonah explained. "Sometimes men want more than I'm prepared to give, and it can turn dangerous."

Rob's face tightened. "Have you been hurt?"

The harshness of his tone came as a surprise, and Jonah jerked in his seat.

"No. Not recently, and not in the way you think, mainly because I've learned to ask questions up front."

Rob took a sip of his beer, almost as though buying time, his gaze never leaving Jonah's. When he put down the glass, his face was somber.

"Tell me who hurt you, and how, and I'll promise never, ever to do what they did."

Jonah waved his hand, trying to dismiss this strange turn the conversation had taken, even as his heart beat so heavily he could hear it in his ears.

How had this gone from what he'd thought of as a simple exploratory chat to this? And why did it make him almost feel like crying to hear Rob say those words?

"Forget about that," he said, even though a part of him wanted to tell Rob that old story—one he'd never shared with anyone. "It's long gone. Dust in the wind. This is about you. Don't turn it back on me."

Rob shook his head. "One day I'll get it out of you," he said, making it a promise and a threat, all rolled into one.

"But not tonight," Jonah replied, wanting to kiss Rob so badly his face hurt. "Tonight, I just need to know what you like. What you want."

Rob's lips parted, and he started to speak, then stopped, as if rethinking what he'd been about to say. Then he shook his head again, as though in disbelief, and replied, "I like a little excitement in the bedroom, but not BDSM or anything like that. I've experimented some, and had fun, but I've also had completely vanilla relationships and enjoyed them too. If that's what you want, I'm good with it."

Vanilla.

Was he vanilla? Jonah had always sort of thought so, since his need for control made it harder to experiment in many ways. Who could he trust to experiment with? But now, looking across the table at Rob, he couldn't decide.

Around Rob he felt anything but vanilla, which was synonymous with ordinary. Boring.

It was time to find out exactly what he was, and get some relief from this constant thrum of desire.

"I think we'll need to figure out if that's really what I want," he said, his voice coming out like a truck driving over gravel. "How about we get started later?"

And the flare of Rob's gaze, which darkened almost to black in a blink, was all the answer he needed.

CHAPTER TWELVE

THE WAITER CAME back just then, and Rob placed an order for the first entrée that caught his eye, pretty damn sure he wouldn't be able to eat anyway. And even if he could, he doubted he'd taste anything.

He was still reeling from the turn the conversation with Jonah had taken, his emotions ping-ponging between embarrassment and excitement.

It was interesting, and somewhat disconcerting, to know Jonah had had such a varied sex life in comparison to his. Rob wasn't an innocent. Not in the slightest. But obviously Jonah was leagues ahead of him when it came to experience.

Knowing that didn't bother him, and now that they'd had this conversation, he could see the benefit of it. Why stumble forward into intimacy, when just talking it out could save you from making hurtful mistakes?

Pushing everything else aside, he leaned a little closer to Jonah and said, "I want to tell you something. Something you should know about me."

Jonah turned an inquiring look his way, over the rim of his glass, and raised his eyebrows.

"The truth is, I just want to know what will drive you

wild, give you maximum satisfaction. That's where I get the most pleasure."

Jonah's eyes widened, and the flare of desire in them almost incinerated Rob right then and there.

"We'll have to discuss that further," Jonah murmured in that gravelly tone that sent shivers down Rob's spine.

The waiter approached with their meal, and Rob was happy to see he'd apparently ordered a pork chop, mashed potatoes and steamed vegetables. He wasn't a fussy eater, but it was disconcerting to realize he couldn't remember ordering because of the turn the conversation had taken.

After placing their plates in front of them, the waiter hesitated long enough that Rob looked up at him inquiringly.

"Excuse me," the young man said. "But I have to ask. Are you Vet Vic?"

From the corner of his eye, he saw Jonah lift his head to stare at the waiter. Rob feigned confusion, as he asked, "Sorry, who?"

"Oh." The young man's face fell into lines of disappointment. "Never mind. Sorry to bother you."

After he'd walked away, Jonah asked, "Why'd you do that?"

"Couple of reasons," he replied, ignoring his dinner and making sure Jonah was paying attention. "Firstly, with the documentary falling through, and my decision that it would have been my last one, Vet Vic is officially dead."

"Okay." Those sleepy eyes were intent on his, and Rob couldn't help leaning just a little closer.

"Secondly, and most importantly, I'm out with you.

I don't want anyone making a fuss. I just want to enjoy being with you."

Jonah looked away, but Rob noticed the upward tilt of his lips and was happy with that.

After eating in silence for a little while, Jonah once more surprised Rob by going off in a completely different conversational tack. "Did your grandmother ever accept your gayness?"

Rob felt a pang of remembered hurt.

"I don't think so, although she never brought it up. She was a worrier—always had been—and I think it was one more thing she worried about, though she never talked about it after that one time."

"She lived with you?"

It felt good to know Jonah was interested in his life, so Rob was smiling when he replied, "Yes. I never knew my *abuelo*—he died before I was born—but Abuela was there in my first memories. Mama worked alongside Papa on the ranch, and Abuela looked after the house and us. We used to drive her crazy, because she was sure we were going to kill ourselves every time we went outside."

Jonah chuckled. "My grandma was the opposite. She'd take Carmen and me to her friends' farms and let us run wild. I remember trying to ride one of the goats while she stood outside the pen laughing. You'd never think it to look at her, either. She was prim and proper, always dressed to the nines, but said little kids should get messy and have bumps and bruises."

"Meanwhile, my *abuela* was running after us, shouting, 'Put on your shoes!' 'Don't go in the mud!' 'Don't go near the pens with the bulls!' And was freaked out when we didn't listen."

Jonah laughed, and Rob loved the way the sound echoed in his chest. Jonah didn't laugh often enough.

"That must have been hard on both her and you kids too."

"It was, and of course we couldn't understand why she was that way. It was only after I got older that I thought to ask Mama if she knew why Abuela worried so much, and she explained that it was because of the things that happened when she was young. How her father had gambled away what they had, and they ended up living in a tent and working in the fields. Before that the children were going to school, had enough to eat and lived in a house. Then suddenly it was all gone.

"Mama said one of Abuela's brothers died while working, and he was only thirteen at the time. Abuela was lucky to get a job working as a maid, and the woman she worked for encouraged her to keep educating herself whenever she could, giving her books to read. That was also where she met Abuelo, who was visiting the people she worked for. He fell in love with her and insisted she marry him. Although he took good care of her, she never stopped worrying that it would all disappear, or someone would die unexpectedly."

Jonah chewed, a thoughtful expression on his face. But after he swallowed, he didn't comment. Rob wasn't sure whether it was his habitual reticence or something else causing him to not say whatever it was on his mind, and he didn't feel secure enough to ask.

Things were still pretty tenuous between them, in every way.

The moon was rising above the horizon by the time they were finished eating, not full but waxing—a lopsided disc casting silvery light on the water. There was something so peaceful about the scene that Rob exhaled, losing much of the tension tightening his shoulders.

"It's beautiful here," he said. "Now I understand why people rave about the Low Country."

"As beautiful as some of the other places you've been?"

There was both curiosity and a hint of wistfulness in his tone.

"Most places have some particular beauty," Rob replied. "But not every place will speak to my soul the way this one does." It was difficult to find the right words, but he felt as though he needed to try. "From the first moment I drove into town, I knew it was going to become a special place to me."

Jonah chuckled. "You're a romantic."

"Is that an accusation?"

Jonah's eyes were twinkling. "Maybe…"

Rob shook his head in pretend sadness. "Well, I am one, and proud of it. I feel sorry for you if you're not one too."

"I'm a realist," Jonah shot back, grinning. "Practical to a fault, or so I've been told. Aunt Lonie tells me so all the time."

"Hmm… But don't you think your dream to sell everything and travel the world is even a little bit romantic?"

That seemed to surprise Jonah, whose eyebrows lifted.

A thoughtful expression crossed his face, and his gaze grew distant.

Finally, he replied, "Not really romantic. It's not like I plan to just drift around. I want to visit other places to broaden my mind and knowledge base. There are some things you can only learn by experiencing them."

"So, you're viewing it as an intellectual exercise, rather than an adventure?"

Jonah turned in his seat, so as to face Rob completely. The gleam in his eyes had morphed from amusement to something Rob thought almost fanatical.

"Every other member of my family has traveled extensively or lived in other places. It was something my grandmother, and her father's family, believed in, implicitly. My great-grandfather made his money at sea and explored much of South America. My grandmother traveled all over Europe and parts of Africa and Asia before she married, and sent both her daughters to school abroad—Mom in France and Aunt Lonie in Switzerland. Lonie stayed afterward to travel and learn from famous chefs before coming home. Even Carmen spent a lot of her childhood in New Orleans with her father's family, and then went to France to study. After school she spent a few years working as a chef on private yachts, sailing all over the world.

"I'm like the country cousin, you know? The local yokel, stuck here stagnating, with no experience of the world at all."

Shocked and moved, Rob just stared at him for a moment.

"You've got to be kidding," he finally said. "You don't really feel that way, do you?"

Jonah shrugged, looking away to try to catch the waiter's eye. "Maybe."

"But intellectually you must know that isn't true? That just because you're not as well traveled as some others in your family you're somehow not as good?"

Ignoring the question, Jonah signaled to the waiter for the bill.

"Seriously." Rob persisted, wanting to get to the truth. "You don't think that, do you?"

"No, of course not." Jonah's lips twisted, and he shook his head for good measure. "You make it sound far more intense than it really is. I just want to live a more rounded, interesting life. That's not such a bad ambition, is it?"

"No, it's not." But even as he agreed, and while he was wrangling with Jonah over who would pick up the tab, Rob realized he didn't believe the other man's protestation. Instead, it was as though Jonah's dream was somehow born from a sense of inferiority, rather than desire.

And that knowledge made him incredibly sad.

Jonah left the restaurant feeling like a fool.

He never spoke about such intimate thoughts with anyone. What was it about Rob that made him spill his guts in that way, opening himself up to ridicule?

Clearly Rob thought he was nuts, and Jonah was inclined to agree with him—nuts for having said anything.

They crossed the parking lot in silence, then got into his vehicle without exchanging a word. Rob had a thoughtful expression on his face, and Jonah couldn't help worrying that he was reconsidering…well…everything.

They were driving out of the parking lot before Rob spoke.

"Where are you going to go first?" he asked suddenly, jolting Jonah out of his thoughts.

"What?" he asked, wondering if he'd missed part of the conversation.

"When you start traveling. Where are you going to go first? You must have an idea?"

He didn't know why, but Rob's seemingly honest interest lightened his mood.

"I have a friend from college who's involved with a group that travels to various countries to help organizations that work with endangered species. She's sure she can get me at the very least an interview to join them."

"You'll be a shoo-in." Rob's voice held conviction. "With the work you've done, they'll be salivating to have you."

"I wish I had your confidence," he said, then snapped his mouth shut. Rob really did bring out the honesty in him, and it was disconcerting.

"You should. You have a stellar reputation, a winning personality, and you're damn gorgeous to boot. Who wouldn't want you on their team?"

Jonah was so surprised, he couldn't stop himself from laughing out loud, so hard and long he had to dash tears from his eyes.

"What?" Rob asked. "You don't believe me?"

"Not one word of it," he agreed. "Although I like that you think I'm gorgeous."

"You knew that already," was the sanguine reply.

"Did I?"

"If you didn't, you should've."

Jonah snorted, not knowing what to say to that. He wasn't used to being complimented. Not about his looks anyway.

"What kinds of animals are your favorites?"

The change of subject almost gave him whiplash.

"Sorry, what?"

"What types of animals are your favorite? I'm partial to mammals myself. Never could really get into reptiles, although I treat them when I have to."

Amused by that pronouncement, Jonah was tempted to tell Rob he loved reptiles, but there was something about the other man that demanded honesty.

"Ungulates," he replied. "I've always been fascinated by them."

"You mean horses, in particular?"

"Nope. Cattle, pigs, camels, llamas, alpacas—you name it."

"Interesting…"

He glanced at Rob and found him leaning against the passenger door, gaze trained on Jonah's face. He quickly looked back at the road so as not to get mesmerized by those piercing eyes.

"What's so interesting about that?"

"I'm not sure," Rob said, a hint of laughter in his voice. "I'll need to think about it. I was brought up on a cattle ranch, and the first thing you learn is not to get attached to the steers, so I have a hard time feeling close to cows. I like alpacas and llamas though."

"Have you ever treated one?"

"Nope. Not yet."

Jonah put on his indicator to turn into his driveway. "Then a word to the wise—they can kick sideways, like camels."

"Good to know," Rob said, laughter warm in his voice.

Jonah drove around to the back and used the automatic opener to gain access to the garage. Suddenly nervous, ready to jump out of his skin, he turned to face Rob after turning off his vehicle.

"You'll come in?"

"If you want me to. No pressure."

"None from me, either," he replied, the words wanting to stick in his throat.

"I definitely want to," Rob replied, his tone like warm molasses on a sultry summer day. "But would it sound weird to say I'm nervous?"

And, just like that, Jonah knew it would be okay.

"I am too," he admitted. "But let's see where things go. Come on. I have to take Eunice for a walk, so that'll take some of the edge off. Nothing like a ramble with an elderly dog to show you how to take things slow."

Rob was laughing softly as he got out of the vehicle, and Jonah couldn't resist joining in.

Once inside, they were greeted by Eunice, who looked expectantly between Jonah and the back door.

"Hang on there, sweetheart," Jonah said, before turning to ask Rob, "Do you want a beer?"

"I probably shouldn't, since I still have to get myself back to the hotel. One's my limit when I'm driving."

Without thinking about it, Jonah replied, "Have it, if

you want to. There's plenty of space here. I can definitely find room for you."

Preferably in my bed.

He didn't say it aloud, but perhaps his expression gave him away, because Rob's eyes flared bronze and hot, and Jonah found himself having to look away.

The intensity of desire he felt when Rob looked at him that way was almost frightening, and he was suddenly unsure of how to deal with it.

But he was determined to find out.

CHAPTER THIRTEEN

ROB COULDN'T HELP noticing the aura of suspense and anticipation that surrounded them as Jonah popped the caps on two beers, handing him one, before opening the door to let Eunice out. They followed the golden down the stairs and into the warm, fragrant night at her leisurely pace, walking shoulder to shoulder, brushing against each other with each step. The moon was higher in the sky now, shedding silver light across the plants, creating secretive shadows beneath the trees.

He vaguely noticed the manicured lawn and flower beds, along with the rich scent of still-damp grass, more in tune with Jonah's movements and breathing than his surroundings. Jonah lifted the beer to his mouth, and Rob found himself mirroring the movement, even while thinking how badly he wanted to replace the bottle with his own lips.

He'd been craving a taste of Jonah since the first instant he'd seen him again, and as Eunice snuffled around the base of a hydrangea bush, he knew he didn't want to wait a moment longer.

They'd both stopped walking, and Rob turned to face Jonah, staring at his profile for an instant. His heart was hammering, his body tightened with need, and he swallowed before saying, "Suddenly the thought of kissing you in the moonlight is the most important thing in the world."

Jonah froze, and Rob saw him take a deep breath.

Without moving, Jonah asked, "What are you waiting for, then?"

Rob shifted to stand in front of the other man, so he could look into those sexy eyes, which gleamed beneath their sleepy lids.

"Permission," he replied, so softly the word seemed to disappear into the night.

Jonah stepped closer, so their bodies were just a fraction of an inch apart, and Rob could feel his warmth reaching out to him, and he trembled.

"You have it," Jonah said, equally softly, and Rob rejoiced to hear the tremor in that rumble of words.

But now that the moment was there, Rob found himself wanting to savor it—not rush, although his body clamored for him to do so. Using his free hand, he stroked across one of Jonah's eyebrows, along his cheek, to the corner of that beautifully shaped mouth. Learning the contours of his face, relishing the sensation of warm skin, the slight abrasion of facial hair beneath his fingertips.

Jonah was almost preternaturally still beneath Rob's questing fingers, only the rush of his breath giving an indication of his excitement.

Then, as Rob watched, he licked his bottom lip.

The wave of need that crashed through him made Rob unable to wait a second more, and, cupping the other man's cheek, tilting his head, he bent to cover that luscious mouth with his own.

At the first touch of lips, soft and a little tentative—exploratory—they both groaned, releasing a groundswell of desire that had shimmered just below the surface. Rob inhaled, taking Jonah's scent deep into his lungs, his head swimming with the sheer glory of this first intimacy.

Jonah's arm went around his waist, pulling him near; tightening to tug him even closer yet, if that were possible, and Rob wanted to absorb the other man into himself.

Or be totally absorbed by him.

Tongues tangled and danced together, arms encircled, and there was no mistaking the arousal they shared in equal measure. Rob tilted his hips, rubbing his erection against Jonah's, and the carnality of the sounds that emerged to be lost in each other's mouths was unmistakable.

The sensations threatened to overwhelm him, and Rob broke away. At least fractionally. They were still in each other's arms, but he resisted the draw of Jonah's mouth to rest his forehead against the other man's.

And just that contact still felt right.

"Kiss me again," Jonah growled, his body straining toward Rob's. "Or bring those lips back here so I can kiss you."

How could he resist such a demand?

But when their lips met again, it was with a sort of barely restrained ferocity that threatened to break the chains of his control, and Rob gentled the kiss incrementally, giving himself a chance to regroup as best he could. Sweeping his lips back and forth against Jonah's, he teased the other man before abruptly dropping his mouth to Jonah's neck to lick and suck.

The response was electric. Jonah arched, his head going back, his pelvis tilting forward, his arms tightening so he was hanging on to Rob, as though afraid if he let go, he'd fall.

There.

That spot.

Jonah was shivering, harsh sounds of arousal breaking from his throat, and Rob wanted more. Much more than was achievable in a garden in the middle of the night.

Moving his mouth up to the other man's ear, he growled, "I think we should go inside soon." Swirling his tongue along the edge of Jonah's ear achieved another groan of acquiescence and pushed Rob's desire even higher. "Before I make love to you out here."

"Yes."

It was a deep rasp, and an acknowledgment of mutual need. But Jonah didn't let go, his arms still tight around Rob, his body shivering and straining. Somehow, in that moment, Rob knew not just how badly he wanted Jonah, but also recognized the intensity of emotion building within.

That he wanted not just to make love with him, but show him how much he valued this time together. How much he valued Jonah, just the way he was.

And how much he wanted to give him pleasure—physically, emotionally, mentally.

Any way he could.

Loosening his grip, but putting his arm around Jonah's waist, he turned them back toward the house, calling to Eunice over his shoulder. As though realizing the men weren't really paying her much attention, the golden snorted but obediently trudged along behind them.

They broke apart to go through the door, Jonah waiting for the dog to make her entrance, while Rob took the two almost untouched beers and put them on the counter. Eunice made a beeline for her bed in the corner of the kitchen, and, silently, Jonah walked through to a small staircase at one side of the room and began to climb.

Rob followed, hearing the sound of their footsteps echoing through the enclosed space, slower than his racing heartbeat, as he stared at the broad back and tight ass of the man ahead. The climb felt monumental—not because the staircase was long, but because Rob knew, without a doubt, that his life would never be the same again, once they'd reached the top.

Taking the last two steps in one stride, he caught hold of Jonah's arm just as the other man turned the corner on the landing above. When those dark eyes widened in surprise, and Rob saw they were glazed with desire, he dragged Jonah close to kiss him again, and felt Jonah's body melt into his.

Without conscious thought, he pressed Jonah against the wall, pinning him there, kissing him over and over. Tugging at Jonah's shirt, he freed it from his pants, so as to plunge his hands beneath, letting his fingers race up his taut abs, along his ribs and across the wide chest, finding the tight nipples and lightly pinching.

Jonah was hanging on around Rob's neck, his fingers plunged into Rob's hair, keeping him in place as they kissed and kissed and kissed, breathing into each other with gasps of air and quiet groans. Whereas before Rob had wanted to rush straight to a bedroom, now *this* was all he wanted.

The sensation of mouth on mouth, Jonah's hot satin skin beneath his palms, the sounds of desire stretching out into the darkened corridor.

Then, just as suddenly, it wasn't enough.

Forcing his lips away from Jonah's felt almost impossible, but he somehow achieved it to ask, "Which way?"

Jonah was slow to answer, as though he had to bring himself back to the present to be able to reply, "First room on the left."

Taking his hand, Rob moved swiftly that way, tugging Jonah along behind him.

Jonah stumbled in Rob's wake, his legs weak with desire, his entire body one erotically charged nerve ending. Holding on to Rob's hand provided the only stability he had left to him, so he clutched it tighter.

He'd never been kissed that way before—with such intense mastery—or felt such a rush of desire while being kissed. He could still taste Rob on his tongue, feel the hard length of his body pressed to his, held the scent of him—skin and breath—in his nostrils, and those lingering sensations made him feel high.

If just a few kisses and caresses made him lose himself so completely, what would making love with Rob do to him?

A trickle of fear invaded his brain, but as they entered his bedroom, and Rob searched for then flicked on the light, it floated away.

Rob's eyes were dark, his face tight, his lips—so sinful—were puffy from their kisses, and the sight of him drove Jonah to a new level of lust.

Letting go of his hand, Rob took three steps into the room, then turned to face Jonah, who still stood just inside the doorway, too weak and addled to move.

"Come here."

Rob spoke softly, almost tenderly, but there was an edge of command in the words too, and Jonah's body reacted as though touched.

There was no thought of refusal. No hesitation.

He walked slowly forward, his gaze caught on Rob's. Snagged like a fish firmly on the hook.

"Undress for me," Rob said, still in that soft tone, but making it more of a demand than a request.

Tremors fired along Jonah's spine, and his hands were shaking, but again he didn't hesitate. Something about the situation, the night, made whatever might happen completely right.

Deep inside he knew, with utmost certainty, if he balked at anything Rob wouldn't try to force him into it, and that level of trust was beyond price.

He didn't know just how he was so sure of that, but he was.

Taking off his clothes took only a few moments, and when he straightened from removing his pants and underwear, he froze, transfixed by the expression on Rob's face.

"Damn," Rob groaned. "You're so gorgeous."

Jonah stared in disbelief, and it must have shown on his expression, because Rob stalked closer, slowly, intentionally.

"You don't think I'm telling the truth," he stated, keeping Jonah's gaze captured with his own.

All Jonah could manage was a single shake of his head.

"I'll show you that I mean it," Rob said, and the conviction in his tone made Jonah tremble even more.

Rob pulled off his shirt, then toed off his boots as he was unzipping his jeans. It was torture to watch and wait, but absolutely thrilling at the same time. When Rob was naked, he pulled back his hair and started to secure it at his nape with an elastic band.

"No." Jonah found his voice then. "Leave it loose. Please."

The look Rob sent him was incendiary, as he slipped the band back onto his wrist and said, "For you, anything."

Before Jonah could respond, Rob was right there, pulling him close. And as their bodies collided, all coherent thought left Jonah's brain.

Rob was kissing him, and they were moving in what seemed almost like a slow, inexorable dance toward the bed, before falling together onto it, mouths still locked in kiss after kiss.

Then Rob lifted his head and said, "Let me show you I meant what I said."

Starting at Jonah's head and working his way down, he proceeded to do just that, searching out all the most sensitive erogenous zones, some of which Jonah didn't even know he possessed. Losing all sense of time and space, his world contracting until all that remained were the two of them, and the sublime ecstasy Rob propelled them toward.

All vestiges of control vanished, ceded to Rob in a way Jonah, in the dim recesses of his mind, realized he'd always wanted but had never been able to do with anyone else.

Rob demanded his complete and utter surrender, guiding him into a whole new world of sensual delights, keeping him on the edge of release for what seemed like eons, holding him there effortlessly. In freeing himself from his need to be in charge, losing himself in Rob's concentrated focus and command, Jonah soared to heights of bliss he'd never experienced before.

When his first orgasm crashed through him, he heard himself cry out and, burying his face in a pillow, almost wept with satiation and relief, as Rob found his own release almost simultaneously. Feeling, for the first time in too long to remember, that he was, in that moment, absolutely enough.

CHAPTER FOURTEEN

JONAH WOKE UP the next morning alone in bed, but with the memory of Rob grumbling as he got up to leave in the wee hours of the morning. When he'd sleepily suggested the other man just stay the night, Rob sat down on the side of the bed to put on his boots and shook his head.

"Small towns, man. Your reputation is probably already in jeopardy as it is. Let me at least try to mitigate the fallout by sneaking back into the hotel before anyone's on the road."

It had been on the tip of his tongue to say he didn't care, and that thought was scary enough to keep him silent.

He'd protected himself—his life and desires—from the people around him for so long, the knowledge that he was already willing to throw that away after just one night in Rob's arms was shocking.

So, after a long, sweet kiss that made him want to drag Rob back upstairs, he'd let the other man out and stumbled back to bed, too exhausted to do anything but savor his lingering satisfaction before falling deeply asleep.

Now though, with sunlight trickling into his room, wide awake and with no distractions, it was time to put the sex aside—as difficult as that may be—and seriously consider the ramifications of last night.

It had been amazing. If he were a romantic like Rob, he'd even go so far as to say it had been magical. But he had to remember it wasn't the start of something more. Neither of them, he believed, were destined to remain for any length of time in Butler's Run, and the trajectories of their lives were completely different.

Sooner, rather than later, they'd part ways, and Jonah couldn't afford to get so tangled up with the other man that he'd be hurt. Silly then to feel an ache around his heart at the thought of no longer having Rob in his life.

And remembering the way he'd allowed Rob to take the reins in bed, he had to wonder whether that new power dynamic would threaten to spill over into other parts of their lives. If Rob would feel emboldened to try to boss him around at work.

That thought brought him up and out of bed, scowling, to go take Eunice for her morning walk. It would be a problem he'd face head-on if it came up.

But that eventuality, at least, didn't come to pass.

When he got to work, his stone face firmly in place and determined not to treat Rob any differently than he had before they'd ended up in bed together, it was refreshing to have Rob clearly on the same page.

"Morning," he said, when he strode into the clinic, smiling and sending the greeting out to everyone in general. "What's on the agenda today, boss?"

That was directed to Jonah, but in such a casual way no one would imagine that just a few hours before they'd been rolling around naked together.

"Saturdays are short days," he said, striving for the same sanguinity Rob was displaying, but having to battle with himself to achieve it. Hard to sound unconcerned when his heart was pounding and memories of the night before wanted to flood his head. "We close at three, but we're usually flooded with patients. Mostly pets owned by folks who work and find the weekend the best time to have appointments. Plus, with closing yesterday because of the power outage, we might have to squeeze a few of those patients in too. Inez asked for the day off to go spend some time with her family, since she knew you'd be here, so you'll be running your own exam room today again."

"Sounds good," came the reply, and Rob went off to check on Milo and Ovaltine before getting his room set up, leaving Jonah wishing he'd sent him even some small acknowledgment of what they'd shared. A sly smile maybe, or a wink.

Then he caught himself up, feeling a little silly at his own contrariness.

The day flew by, filled with mostly run-of-the-mill patients, and before he knew it, it was time to clean up the clinic and head home.

Rob came by the office after his last patient, knocking lightly on the open door, standing just inside the room.

"Do you need me for anything?" he asked.

Now, there was a loaded question if ever he'd heard one, and Jonah had to hold back a snort of amusement.

"No, I think everything here is good to go," he replied, trying to keep a straight face.

Rob's eyes darkened, and Jonah's amusement faded.

Clearly the other man had heard the subtle subtext behind his words and he too was thinking about all the things Jonah wanted—needed—from Rob.

"Are you sure?"

The words, and even the tone, were innocuous, but his expression, visible only to Jonah and not the staff members passing back and forth in the corridor, was not.

It sent a tsunami of desire through Jonah's body, so intense that he couldn't break free from Rob's gaze, even if he'd wanted to. And he shook his head, since to say no aloud was out of the question.

"Okay," Rob said, as though Jonah had nodded. "See you later."

When he backed out of the room, Jonah was so surprised he almost called him back, but didn't.

The encounter left him flustered and confused, not knowing how to interpret it, but only a minute later his phone pinged, and it was a text from Rob.

Can I take you for dinner later?

Come by the house. I'll cook.

I'd ask if your cooking is as good as your aunt's, but it doesn't really matter. I'm not that interested in food anyway. Not when you're around.

Thankful that no one could see his face, Jonah spun his chair around, just in case, as he could still hear voices from the rear of the clinic. He was instantly aflame on reading Rob's words.

Hopefully we'll get around to food at some point. Come by in about an hour. Park by the garage and come to the kitchen door.

Putting the phone down after receiving a thumbs-up from Rob, Jonah leaned his head back against the chair and contemplated the ceiling, trying to figure out exactly what he'd gotten himself into.

It felt crazy, this rush of desire, the need. The speed at which they were going didn't faze him, simply because in the past he'd slept with men the same night as meeting them. But he'd never felt as connected to any of them, and he certainly hadn't craved them afterward.

In reality, he'd often felt somehow diminished by the encounters—sad, a bit depressed and lonelier then than before.

He'd been trying to scratch a sexual itch when he'd gone off to Atlanta to the clubs, not looking for someone special or a relationship. What did he know about relationships anyway? His mother had never married again after Daddy's death, and his grandmother had also been a widow. Aunt Lonie's marriage hadn't lasted more than a few years too, before she divorced Carmen's father and he went back to New Orleans. All the most important people in his life had been alone. Independent. Seemingly unwilling to get back into a couple situation. To Jonah, that spoke volumes.

It also left him with a gap in his emotional education. You can't really know how to be if you haven't seen it in practice, can you?

Then he shook his head and tried to put all of those

thoughts out of his head for the simple reason that he wasn't really in a relationship with Rob, and never would be.

Two months, Beeta had said, before Rob got bored and tired of Butler's Run and went somewhere else.

In his mind, the word relationship implied commitment. Long-term.

Whatever this was between him and Rob, it wouldn't last, so there was no use worrying about it.

And he might as well enjoy the thrill, to the max.

The question he asked himself now was: what would be the best way to do that?

Rob got back to his hotel room and took a long, hot shower before heading back to Jonah's, trying to work the kinks out of some sore muscles. But he didn't mind the discomfort, not in the slightest. Especially when he remembered how he'd got it.

He groaned under his breath and stuck his head under the water, but that didn't erase the images his memory conjured up.

Jonah had been so responsive, so receptive to Rob's attentions, it had blown him away. He couldn't remember ever feeling the way he had last night—so completely into the man he was with that nothing else mattered.

Sure, he'd been telling the truth when he told Jonah his greatest pleasure came from giving pleasure to whomever he was with, but last night had gone way beyond that.

There'd been no way to know what Jonah would or wouldn't like, and Rob had gone strictly on instinct. And somehow—by fate or serendipity again—he'd gotten it totally right.

Not just for Jonah, but for himself too.

His easygoing nature and bone-deep desire to make others happy hadn't really given him the opportunity to determine exactly what gave him the ultimate pleasure. He'd always simply taken his cues from the men he'd been with, and been happy enough with that. But with Jonah he'd found his true sexual self, and the result had been explosive.

Mind-blowing.

He'd been a bit worried after he'd left that Jonah would revert to the reticence of before—going back to keeping him at a distance. After all, although he'd known the other man had enjoyed the lovemaking, Jonah had been clear about his habit of seeking out one-night stands and no-strings-attached couplings. He'd also been adamant about keeping his private affairs out of Butler's Run. The combination of those two factors had kept Rob wondering if their first time together would also be their last.

Now he knew that wasn't the case and was thrilled.

Jonah's determination to leave Butler's Run wasn't something he wanted to think about. Not now, with the memories of the night before swirling in his head, arousing and elating.

Instead, he'd concentrate on relishing every moment he could with Jonah, while making plans and preparations for the future.

For the first time in years, he felt at peace with himself and his life, and he wouldn't allow doubts or fears to dull the joy.

Quickly finishing his shower, he rushed to dress, picking out the most casual clothes he had, and making the decision to go online and order some plain T-shirts, casually comfortable pants and shirts. It was freeing to know he could once more dress the way he wanted, and not have to worry at all about his Vet Vic persona ever again.

The relief was palpable.

He had to remind himself not to speed while driving to Jonah's. The urgency he'd felt when deciding whether to tell Jonah he was attracted to him hadn't abated, just morphed into something different—the desperate need to be with the other man as much as possible.

Before Jonah took off to live the life of adventure he'd always wanted.

Driving around to the back of the house, as Jonah had directed, it struck him that doing so meant no one would see his vehicle if they came up the driveway. He understood, of course, but knowing the risk Jonah was taking even by having him here added to his underlying tension.

When he knocked on the back door, Jonah called for him to come in over Eunice's barks, but when Rob opened the door, he saw the golden still lying in her bed, quiet now, but with her tail going a mile a minute.

"Some guard dog," he said with a chuckle. "Didn't even bother to get up."

Jonah laughed. "Eunice knows when to exert herself, and that's only when absolutely necessary."

He was standing by the sink, peeling potatoes, dressed in a loose pair of running shorts and a form-fitting T-shirt, looking so delectable Rob forewent his usual greeting to Eunice. Instead, going straight to Jonah, Rob encircled his waist from behind, bending to kiss the dip just below his ear. Jonah shivered and made a sweet, rough sound in his throat.

"If you keep doing that, you won't get any food tonight," he said in that delicious rough growl his voice became when he was turned on.

Rob pressed closer and murmured into his ear, "You're all the sustenance I need right now. We can always order in."

Jonah shivered again, the potato peeler going lax in his hand. But he made no further protest when Rob insisted they go upstairs.

Later in the evening they finally made it back downstairs to the kitchen and set about cooking together. Rob finished peeling the potatoes while Jonah snapped some beans, after taking the steaks he'd seasoned previously out of the fridge.

As they worked, they talked about a variety of subjects, working their way back to Rob's potential purchase of the clinic.

"I know it'll take a while to figure out the details, if you decide to sell after all," he said, putting the potatoes into the pot Jonah had given him. Setting it on the stove and turning on the burner, he continued, "And in the meantime, I'm going to start looking for an apartment or small house to rent. The hotel is fine, but not an economically sensible choice, over time. I figured the best way to go about it would be to contact a local realtor. You know one?"

Jonah was quiet for so long, Rob wondered if he'd

heard the question, but before he could repeat it, Jonah said quietly, "I think you should move in here."

Stunned, Rob asked, "What?"

"You should move in here, with me." There was no nuance in his tone, nothing to indicate why he was suggesting it. "There's plenty of room. In fact, there's an almost self-contained suite upstairs you could have, which would give you space and privacy."

Still shocked, needing a moment to think, Rob went to the fridge and took out a beer. When he held it up, silently asking if Jonah wanted one as well, the other man nodded. Then, in unison, they both headed to the back door and out onto the porch, Eunice following them.

As the dog made her ponderous way down the steps into the garden, Rob and Jonah sat side by side on the porch glider and each took a sip of beer, as though postponing the upcoming conversation.

In reality, Rob was just trying to wrap his head around what Jonah had suggested. While part of him was absolutely ready to agree to the arrangement, the more cautious part of his nature wanted more information.

"You can say no," Jonah said. "Without hurting my feelings. It's just a suggestion."

"I don't want to say no," Rob confessed. "I just need to understand why you'd be willing to do that."

Jonah snorted. "Is it that preposterous an idea?"

"No. It makes sense on a lot of levels, except one that I can think of."

"Which is?"

"You've made it clear you don't want people knowing about your private life. Even if everyone thinks you're putting me up as a friend, or because you want the rent money, or whatever, eventually there'll be talk. Doesn't that bother you?"

Jonah shook his head. "Maybe you have the wrong idea about me. I'm not in the closet. The entire town knows I'm gay, and has known for years. What I didn't want is people seeing the way I was living—the hookups and such. I'm sure anyone with half a brain and any interest in the subject would guess I was getting me some somewhere, but there was no evidence of it here, which is what I cared about.

"With you, it's different. I won't care if they think you and I are involved."

Rob's heart leaped, excitement and a strange type of hope unfurling in his chest. But he wouldn't—couldn't—allow it to take root.

Wouldn't let himself think that what they had might make Jonah change his mind about leaving. Might make him want to stay.

But he couldn't help it, and that kernel of optimism allowed him to say, "Okay, then. I'll move in…here."

And it was his need to protect his heart that made him hesitate, and say it that way, instead of what he'd really wanted to.

I'll move in with you.

CHAPTER FIFTEEN

THE MONTH FOLLOWING Jonah's invitation to Rob to move in seemed to fly by, and Jonah couldn't believe how happy he was, or that it could last. Even his long-held belief that leaving Butler's Run to see the world was what he needed to do seemed to fade into insignificance when he was with Rob.

It never failed to amaze him—the closeness they'd come to share. Although they both worked and lived together, there was little conflict, and Jonah never tired of being around the other man. They just fit.

Yet, there was a part of him that constantly watched, waiting for the first signs of boredom in Rob. Not even the fact that Rob went out and bought a pickup truck, saying, "I figured I'd need something like this for the rougher farm roads," made Jonah believe he would stay.

Trucks could be sold as easily as they were bought.

Two or three months, Beeta had said, and Jonah had no reason to believe Rob's sister would be wrong.

Which was why whenever Rob asked if he'd contacted the lawyer about the legal paperwork, he kept putting him off. He also made sure to involve Rob in all the farm, livestock and sanctuary visits, making sure he knew what he'd have to do if he stayed. They were invariably messy, sometimes backbreaking, and often futile—like when they spectacularly failed to corner the pig that needed its hooves trimmed, and it took off, busting through a fence to escape.

Jonah had to admit that Rob seemed to take it all in his stride; he even seemed to enjoy himself.

How long that would last was anyone's guess.

In the moments when he allowed himself to think about it, Jonah realized all he wanted was to keep things the way they were until it was over, as he knew it eventually would be. He refused to even contemplate the state of his own heart, which he suspected had given itself, completely, to Rob.

When that thought crept into his head, he reminded himself that he'd survived without the other man in his life, and he could do it again, when necessary.

Nothing lasts forever, as his mother had always said, especially in reference to her husband and the marriage Jonah knew had made her so very happy. Happy enough that no other man ever stood a chance with her, after her husband died.

"My parents got married when they found out Mom was pregnant with me," he told Rob one night, when they were lying in bed together, entwined, talking about their families. "Daddy left college and joined the army, and Mom finished her degree a couple years later. Mom always talked about how they'd planned to travel after college—join an organization like the Peace Corps—and see the world. Daddy was studying to be an engineer, and Mom was studying toward a degree in education, so they'd be a good fit for something like that. She always sounded so wistful when she spoke about it."

Rob was silent for a moment, his long, gentle fingers tracing up and down Jonah's arm, soothing now, rather than arousing, the way they often were.

"So you think they gave up that plan because of you?"

"I know they did. If I hadn't come along, they could have followed their dreams, and maybe…"

He'd never said it out loud before—that secret pain and guilt he felt—and couldn't get the words out now.

"And maybe your father wouldn't have died when he did?"

Jonah froze, the air suspended in his chest to hear his greatest fear spoken out loud in that way. It took an instant to regain his equilibrium, and his first instinct was to deny that was what he'd been thinking.

But, as always, Rob had a way of pulling the truth right out of Jonah's heart.

"Yeah," he admitted softly. "Yeah. I've always wondered…"

"Aww, babe."

Just those softly spoken words and the way Rob tightened his grip, as if to shield Jonah from the hurt, was enough to dull the long-agonizing suspicion. And he appreciated the fact the other man didn't try to tell him it was stupid to hang on to those feelings, which first arose when he was a child, but simply acknowledged his right to have them. Even if, intellectually, they made no sense.

Rob had that effect on him too—making him bring long-hidden emotions out into the open and question them also. Something about Rob's steadying presence brought all kinds of old stories and feelings bubbling to the surface to be examined and somehow mitigated.

There was consolation in the fact that he wasn't the only one opening up.

One evening, sitting on the porch, watching Eunice nose around in the garden, Rob said, "I heard from Beeta today. She's trying to convince me to do another documentary. This one down in Costa Rica."

Jonah's heart sank. *Here it comes.*

Swallowing against the dryness in his throat, he asked, "What did you say?"

Rob shrugged. "I told her no, although it was hard to do. She knows family is my weakness, and always tries to exploit that."

"You said you felt bad because she didn't get the support from your parents when she wanted to go to college, so you helped her. It seems a little…unfair…that she's still pressuring you, when you said you don't want to do the videos anymore."

What he'd really wanted to say was that Beeta was being downright selfish, but he didn't think it was his place.

Rob sent him a sideways glance, his lips lifting in a rueful smile.

"I love her, but I'm not blind. The truth is, Beeta always wanted to get her way, immediately, and had a wicked temper. Abuela never knew how to deal with her, other than to give her whatever she wanted, which made my parents angry when they found out, and then she'd get punished. So, on one hand Beeta was spoiled, and on the other she was almost constantly in trouble.

As her older brother, being closest in age, I felt as though I had to help, somehow. Protect her." He shrugged, and his smile was sad. "Long ago I realized it made me easily manipulated by her, but I didn't have the impetus to make it stop. I do now though."

Jonah wanted to ask what had made the difference, but the words stuck in his throat. Stupid to think maybe it had something to do with their relationship—or whatever the heck to call what they were involved in.

"I'm proud of you," he said, and meant it. "Breaking out of old habits is hard."

Rob smiled, his face lighting up in a way that always made Jonah's heart sing. And when he leaned over for a kiss, there was a sweetness to the meeting of their lips that had little to do with sex, and everything to do with emotion.

And it was almost too much for Jonah to bear.

Rob couldn't remember a time when he'd been happier, or more on edge. The longer he stayed in Butler's Run, and with Jonah, the more confident he became that this was where he belonged. And Jonah, even more than the town, was the reason. Yet, although he thought he and Jonah were perfect for each other, there was a sensation of distance between them sometimes too.

A watchfulness on Jonah's part, that gave Rob pause.

But he didn't know how to broach the subject, or what to do to allay whatever lingering fears the other man had.

He desperately wanted to prove to Jonah that they belonged together but knew it was a fool's errand. The more they spoke about Jonah's family and his past, the easier it was to see why he was desperate to escape his small town and live a life he considered more fulfilling.

It would be easy to point out just how important he was to the town he wanted to leave. Tell him how far he'd come, and how much everyone admired and appreciated him, but Rob knew it wouldn't make any difference.

Just as admitting his love for Jonah wouldn't change anything.

And why should it? Just because he knew what he felt was love, didn't mean it gave him the right to make demands, no matter how much he wanted to.

In bed, he was in charge. In life, they both had to do what was best for themselves, irrespective of whether one or the other of them was going to get hurt.

Best to make the most of the present happiness, right?

Now, if he could just get himself to believe that and put all his trepidation aside.

He had better luck integrating himself into the life of the town, which seemed quite happy to accept him. Sure, there were one or two people who made a point to be unpleasant, but that happened everywhere, and it didn't faze him one bit. What did annoy him were the people who insisted on calling him Vet Vic. That part of his life was well and truly over, but convincing everyone of that fact clearly would take some time.

"What can you expect?" Jonah asked, obviously trying not to laugh at Rob's annoyance after another encounter with the pink-haired Emma Gorman, who not only refused to use his real name, but constantly asked when next he'd be filming. "Obviously she's angling to be featured in your next documentary."

Rob rolled his eyes. "As if that'll happen."

"Which one? The documentary, or Emma being in it?"

"Both," he said, trying to put a snap in his voice but failing in the face of Jonah's amusement.

"But when we went to her farm, you obviously fell for the alpacas. Don't you wanna film them?"

"Now you're just being a brat. Remember how Donny spat in my face?"

They both dissolved into laughter, which was something they did so often, it was hard to remember how solemn Jonah had seemed at first. Even at work he seemed more relaxed, despite the brisk workload. The clinic was thriving, making Rob wonder how he'd be able to keep up, should Jonah decide he was ready to sell.

But that was a topic Jonah seemed unwilling to discuss at any length. Each time Rob asked what the lawyer had said, Jonah had some excuse about why he hadn't contacted her, and Rob let it go. After all, when the paperwork was actually prepared, it would mean the beginning of the end for them as a couple, and Rob didn't want to think about that.

One thing he could say though was that Jonah made sure to show him the full extent of what being a country vet entailed. While Rob was well-versed in dealing with cattle and horses from growing up on the ranch, working with some of the other animals was something he hadn't done since vet school.

Pigs, he discovered, whether pets or farm animals, were especially challenging.

"I dealt with a few potbellied pigs back in LA," he told Jonah. "But never one of that size."

Since Rob happened to be sitting in a mudhole, and the animal in question was halfway across the adjacent field with the owner and Samantha the vet tech chasing after it, Jonah didn't seem inclined to answer.

Or maybe it was because he was laughing too hard. So hard, in fact, that he had to prop himself up on a nearby post to stay on his feet.

Obviously Rob still had a lot to learn, like how to properly use a piece of board to corral a pig in the corner of a pen without getting flattened when the pig broke free.

But he was reveling in all of it.

He hadn't had many doubts about staying in Butler's Run, and with each passing day his decision was confirmed.

This was where he belonged.

The only thing that would make it more perfect was if Jonah and he were planning to build this life together, but Rob accepted that wasn't meant to be. He'd gotten to know Jonah better, recognized the deep-seated need the other man had to venture out into the world. To explore and learn and grow in a way he didn't think he could in his hometown.

Perhaps to live out the life he felt his parents had been deprived of.

It was more than just a dream, and Rob doubted Jonah would ever be truly happy if he didn't experience the life he'd been hoping for all these years. If he were to stay and become bitter and discontented, Rob would be heartbroken.

And more than anything else, he wanted Jonah to be happy.

CHAPTER SIXTEEN

THEY SETTLED INTO a routine of sorts. Work, of course, and making love every night, but Rob also insisted that Jonah show him around the surrounding area, so, on Sundays, they would drive to various places. Hilton Head, Charleston, Savannah, Augusta and the environs. Jonah found himself seeing places he'd known all his life in a whole new way as he absorbed Rob's genuine enjoyment. Whether walking through a historic district, swimming in the ocean or exploring a nature preserve, Rob's natural curiosity made every trip a fun, learning experience. And it didn't matter if they ate at a diner or a five-star restaurant, went to a roadside carnival or aquarium, Rob's cheerful charm turned it into an experience.

They were driving home after one of their jaunts, Jonah at the wheel, singing along to the radio, when his phone rang and he answered it through his vehicle's hands-free capability.

"Cassie," he said, letting his pleasure at hearing from his old friend show in his voice. "Happy to hear from you. Are you back in the States?"

"I am," she replied. "For a short time anyway. I'm hoping to have time to see you. I'll be in Philly for a couple of weeks, then I don't know."

"Maybe I'll take a day off and meet you halfway, unless you want to fly down to Charleston? I want to hear all about your time in Tanzania."

"I'll let you know," she replied. "But either of those would work. We definitely need to catch up. It's been too long. But, in the meantime, I wanted to tell you that the hiring freeze has been lifted, and the organization is taking applications again."

From the corner of his eye, he saw Rob shift in his seat, but Jonah didn't dare look over at him.

"Mmm," he said, his brain churning, not sure how to react.

"I know it's short notice, but it literally just happened. And you said to let you know when it happened. They have some exciting opportunities coming up, including a potential posting in Borneo, and another in Zimbabwe. I think you'd be perfect for either of them."

"Thanks for letting me know," he said, wondering why he felt not one iota of excitement at hearing the news, after champing at the bit for years. "Give me a call when you know how long you'll be here, and whether you have time for us to meet up, okay?"

"Okay," Cassie said, a note of surprised confusion in her voice. No doubt she'd been expecting a far more enthusiastic response to her news, since the hiring freeze had been in effect since the start of the pandemic. "I'll call you again during the week. Get your résumé in order."

"Thanks again. Bye."

The silence in the vehicle after he'd hung up seemed heavy, especially after the fun atmosphere from before.

Jonah wasn't sure what to say, if anything, and eventually it was Rob who spoke first.

"Is that your friend who works with the international organization you want to join?"

"Yeah. She's been in Tanzania for over a year, but she got permission to come back for Mom's funeral. Cassie spent a lot of time with us during holidays and such. She lost her parents in an accident when she was young, and Mom never liked the idea of her spending vacations on her own, so she extended an open-ended invitation to her."

Aware he was babbling, he closed his mouth and kept his eyes on the road, although he really wanted to see Rob's expression.

"Your mom sounds like a really nice lady."

"She was."

He almost added that he wished Rob could have met her, but that sounded somehow too intimate for this particular conversation. So when Rob lapsed into silence and busied himself with apparently trying to find another station to listen to on the radio, Jonah followed suit and shut up too.

When they got home, Rob said he was going to have a shower and went upstairs without inviting Jonah to join him. Just as well, since Jonah felt the need for a little time to himself to think about Cassie's call and what he should do about it. Letting Eunice out into the back garden, he grabbed a bottle of water and went to sit on the porch where he could watch her poke around.

This was an opportunity to follow his dream, finally. Cassie always had the most interesting stories about her travels, not just about the animals and work, but about the local communities too. With the longer postings, sometimes up to two or three years, there was the chance to integrate into the societies she worked with. That was something Jonah found so attractive about the organization she worked for. They believed those long postings created better cooperation between their employees and the people they were assisting and training.

In the past, whenever he thought about getting a two-year job in Africa or Asia or South America, excitement had churned in his belly. Now, though, he felt...

Nothing.

No thrill.

No enthusiasm.

Nothing.

But that wasn't completely true either.

There was a definite emotion building in his chest, and he struggled to ignore it, not wanting to give it a name. No avoiding it though.

It was sadness.

How had things changed so much in such a short period of time?

It was Rob, of course. The way he made Jonah feel. How he'd made life so much brighter and more fun-filled.

How he'd caused Jonah to fall in love with him, and forget everything else that had been so important. Turned his life upside down.

It made him a little angry, and very confused, and he wondered how things would change now. He didn't want things to change. Everything had been...well...perfect over the last couple of months.

Except they'd had the knowledge that their relationship wouldn't last hanging over them. One or the other of them would leave. Maybe both would—going on with their lives alone.

Now that the moment was on them, Jonah was no longer sure of what he wanted for the future.

No, he knew what he wanted.

Rob.

But he wasn't sure the other man wanted him the same way, and he wasn't sure he was strong enough to ask.

Jonah heard Rob coming down the stairs into the kitchen and braced himself, dreading the conversation to come, although he knew it had to happen.

He heard the fridge open and close, then the creak of the screen door as Rob came out onto the porch. Although he was tempted to look at the other man, he kept his gaze trained out into the garden, where Eunice had found a patch of sunlight and settled down to snooze.

"We need to talk." Rob sounded determined, as if he was expecting Jonah to brush him off.

"I know."

The other man exhaled audibly.

"I know that call came out of the blue, and maybe you don't feel ready to apply, but I think you should."

And Jonah thought his heart had just shriveled and died.

Rob watched Jonah's profile, noting that the other man was stone-faced. So different from the smiling, laughing companion of just an hour or so ago.

Not that he blamed him. It was a painful situation, and

he couldn't wrong Jonah for wanting to keep his emotions to himself.

Rob wished he had the same ability, because right now he felt as though he wanted to fall apart and wasn't sure he could hide the agony eating away at him. Yet, he knew he owed it to Jonah not to add more stress to the situation by revealing how hard all this was to him. After all, it wasn't Jonah's fault Rob was in love with him.

"I'm not sure it's the right time," Jonah said, his voice low but steady. "There's the clinic to think about, and Eunice too."

"You know I want to buy the clinic. I haven't changed my mind about that. In fact, I want it more than ever. And I'll take care of Eunice for you. That's not a problem."

"You have it all worked out, huh?"

There was a hint of bitterness in Jonah's tone—or was it hurt? Whatever it was released Rob from the constraints he'd placed on himself, and he knew he had to be completely honest. Even if it meant embarrassing himself.

"No. I don't have it all worked out. This is killing me."

Jonah stiffened, then slowly turned in his seat to face Rob, and the stony mien cracked, ever so slightly. Just enough to give Rob some solace.

"I love you," he said, before Jonah could say anything. "Do you know that I came here to Butler's Run because I saw your name on the proposal the Marsh Tacky people sent to Beeta?" He wanted to get up and pace, energy and fear crackling beneath his skin, but he forced himself to stay where he was, holding Jonah's gaze. "I had a crush on you in college, but by the time I worked up the courage to tell you, you were gone. And since being here with you, I've never been happier.

"If I had my way, you'd stay here with me, forever. But this is too important for you. It's a dream you've had since you were a child, and if you don't take advantage of this opportunity, you'll regret it forever. Maybe become bitter about it. I couldn't stand that."

Jonah was staring at him, eyes not sleepy anymore, but wide with what looked like shock.

"You love me?"

His deep, gravelly tone sent electricity along Rob's spine, but he wouldn't allow himself to hope.

"Yeah, I do. But you can't take that into consideration. I won't let you. You need to think only about what you need to do, to be happy. We can work out the details, whatever they turn out to be, but you have to follow your dream."

"My dream." Jonah said it almost like a question, and then fell silent, his gaze locked on Rob's.

"Yes. That's what's important now."

"No." Jonah shook his head.

"No?"

Instead of elaborating, Jonah stood up and held out his hand to Rob.

"No. What's important right now is that I love you too, and we're here, together. Everything else can wait."

His heart missed a beat, as Jonah's admission rocketed through him like a strike of lightning. And he didn't have the strength to resist when Jonah led him inside and up to their bedroom.

They'd work it out later, he thought, as they came together with a ferocity that not only showed their feelings, but was tinged with desperation.

Waking up later, Rob found himself alone in bed and, rolling free of the tangled sheets, pulled on a pair of shorts and went downstairs in search of Jonah. It was still light out, summer sunshine lingering later and later into the night.

Jonah was at the kitchen table, his laptop open in front of him, an expression of concentration on his face.

"Whatcha doin'?" Rob asked, before yawning his way over to the fridge for a water. Then it struck him that Jonah might be applying to the agency, and his stomach knotted. But he made it a point to cross to the table and kiss the top of Jonah's head, to make sure he knew whatever was to come, Rob was on his side.

"I'm looking at various agency websites," he said. "To see what's available, either for short-term projects or on a volunteer basis."

Knees suddenly weak, Rob plopped down into a chair and stared across at the other man.

"Why?"

"Because you're right. I do want to see more of the world than this little corner, and the way I dreamed of doing it feels right to me, still. What no longer feels right is the thought of leaving Butler's Run and all I've built here forever, especially if I can keep building it with you."

Unsure he was actually hearing him correctly, Rob shook his head, not in negation, but in confusion.

"I don't understand," he said.

Jonah smiled, his eyes gleaming.

"I thought, if I can find an organization that does short

trips for vets to various countries, I could do a trip or two a year. You could run the clinic, and we could get a locum if we need to for while I'm gone, but then I'd be here for most of the time in between." He hesitated for a moment, his gaze sharpening. "If you're in agreement, that is."

The easiest way to answer him was to get up, drag Jonah to his feet and kiss him silly, saying, "Yes, yes, yes," in between each deep, love-filled kiss.

He'd been given a second chance with Jonah Beaumont, and he was grabbing hold of it, with both hands.

And never letting go.

EPILOGUE

ROB SLUNG THE duffel bag onto the back seat of his double cab and slammed the door shut. Then he turned to Jonah and pulled him close, burying his face into the other man's neck for an instant. But because they were in the pickup zone at the airport and it was chaos around them, he let him go quickly, before a cop came to hurry them along.

"Get in," he said, after one last squeeze. "And let's go home."

"Yes," Jonah answered, pulling open the passenger door, relief and love swirling through him in equal parts. "I can hardly wait."

Once Rob had pulled out into the stream of traffic heading away from the airport, he shot Jonah a sideways glance. Jonah watched the other man's profile, drinking it in, unable to tear his gaze away, even if he'd wanted to. Which he didn't.

"That was the longest six weeks of my life," Rob said, checking his mirrors before changing lanes.

"Mine too," Jonah admitted. "Rwanda was amazing, and I learned so much, but damn, I missed you terribly. The next time they ask me to do more than three weeks or a month, tops, I'm saying no."

"Praise the Lord and pass the gravy," Rob replied, which made Jonah sputter with laughter.

"You've been hanging out with Aunt Lonie again, haven't you? She's the only person I know who uses that expression."

"Auntie and Carmen kept me so well fed, I think I put on ten pounds since you were gone. Even if I hadn't been stress eating most of the time, I'd still have been unable to resist their food."

They'd kept in touch as best they could, mostly through email and the occasional video call when Jonah was back at base, so he already knew there'd been some issues with the locum they'd hired to fill in while he was gone.

"How bad was Mitchell, really?" he asked.

"He could have been worse," Rob replied. "But not by much, when it came to customer service. Apparently, he thought working in Butler's Run was the equivalent to being in the middle of nowhere, and everyone there was a total idiot. I had to do some fancy footwork not to lose any clients, and I only saved a couple because I promised them he wouldn't be around for long and that I'd look after their animals myself if necessary."

"Emma Gorman?"

It was Rob's turn to laugh. "How'd you know?"

"Wild guess."

Which made them both snicker, in perfect synchronicity.

When they got home, Jonah got out of the truck and stretched, looking around at the house and garden, smiling. He was home, and he couldn't be happier.

Rob had already retrieved Jonah's bag, and he slung his free arm around Jonah's waist, tugging him close.

"Welcome home, love." Rob sounded as elated as Jonah felt, and they walked side by side up the porch steps, only separating so as to be able to unlock the door.

It was sad not to have Eunice there to greet them, but she'd passed away, peacefully in her sleep, the year before. Instead, it was Rob's two dogs, Skipper and Mary-Ann, that were jumping and prancing around the kitchen, back ends waggling as hard as possible.

Rob dropped the duffel on the floor and turned to yank Jonah into his arms to kiss him, as though he'd never stop.

They'd been together for more than two years, and the love and passion between them never waned. Of course, now it was heightened by their time apart, but Jonah knew that was incidental.

When he was with Rob, he knew he was home.

And that was more than enough.

* * * * *

If you enjoyed this story,
check out these other great reads from
Ann McIntosh

The Vet's Caribbean Fling
The Nurse's Holiday Swap
Twin Babies to Reunite Them
Christmas Miracle on Their Doorstep

All available now!

NURSE'S TWIN PREGNANCY SURPRISE

BECCA McKAY

MILLS & BOON

In loving memory of Nic. A remarkable nurse,
wonderful friend and a brilliant colleague.

You always had a way of making those
long night shifts a little bit brighter,
and it was a real privilege to work alongside you.

PROLOGUE

THE FIRST TIME Hazel saw Garrett Buchanan he was leaning against a tree at the bottom of her friend's garden. She didn't know his name then, of course. Only that he was tall enough for his head to graze the lowest branch, and that the sunlight dappling through the leaves burnished his wavy red hair gold.

His expression was shaded by the branches overhead, but when he caught her eye Hazel felt it like a jolt of electricity to her chest, and she stumbled on the flagstone path, sloshing wine down her new dress.

She swore softly, averting her eyes from the handsome stranger beneath the hawthorn tree and turned her attention to the dark stain against the pale blue satin.

Damn.

At least she was drinking white wine tonight. But still, she'd rather not spend the rest of the party looking as if she was lactating.

Hazel sighed. The only thing for it was to go upstairs and change. Luckily she'd brought a selection of outfits to choose from—mostly at her best friend Libby's insistence that whatever she wore needed to be *perfect*.

'After all, it's not every day you turn thirty,' Libby had said.

Thank God for that, Hazel thought. *Surely it happening once was bad enough?*

She plastered a smile on her face as she passed through the crowded kitchen, but did her best to avoid anyone's eye. The truth was, she didn't know many of the people here tonight. It might be her birthday party, but when it came to drawing up the guest list she'd had to admit she was stumped.

'What do you mean, that's it?' Libby had barely been able to disguise her horror as she'd stared at the hastily scrawled meagre list of names. 'That can't possibly be it!'

But it was.

Somehow, in the nine years since graduating from university as a qualified children's nurse, Hazel had forgotten to make time for almost anything else other than her career. Her social circle had dwindled, becoming ever smaller each year, and short of inviting her buttoned-up retirement age parents, or a couple of cousins she hardly knew, there weren't any others she'd been able to add. It wasn't as though her family would have bolstered the numbers much, even if they'd come.

There'd been Eric, of course, her relationship with him taking up most of her twenties... But then, look how that had turned out.

Hazel pushed the unpleasant thought of her ex from her mind as she made her way up the staircase.

Libby had been very sweet about it all. She always was. Having already offered up her home to host the party, she'd generously supplied two-thirds of the guests too, so that Hazel's birthday shindig appeared to be a roaring success. On the outside, at least. The fact that Hazel herself felt like crawling under a duvet to hide was another matter entirely, and there was really nothing poor Libby could do about that.

The truth was, Hazel was finding turning thirty harder than she'd thought. Only it wasn't the jokes about impending grey hair and wrinkles that were getting her down—it was her own expectations.

She just wasn't where she'd thought she'd be by now. She'd pictured spending her thirtieth birthday with a doting husband and a couple of kids. They'd bring her breakfast in bed—a shambles, of course, but much appreciated all the same. Then they'd picnic by the river and feed the ducks. Later, with the little ones in bed, her handsome husband—decidedly *not* Eric in her more recent imaginings—would pour her a glass of wine and massage her feet and...

'Hello.'

Hazel jumped a mile. She'd been so lost in her fantasy she hadn't realised that she wasn't alone on the upstairs landing.

Oh, God, it was him.

The handsome red-headed stranger from beneath the tree. And he was looking at Hazel in a way that made her insides fizz.

Hazel licked her lips. 'Can I help you?'

'I was going to ask you the same thing.' The stranger gestured to the damp stain across Hazel's chest.

Hazel's face flamed.

'I saw you trip on the path,' the stranger went on. 'I hope you didn't hurt yourself?'

'I'm fine,' Hazel mumbled, mortified.

'You sure? A sprained ankle can be a sneaky thing.'

Hazel raised an eyebrow. 'Quite sure, thanks.'

The stranger shrugged. 'Still, couldn't hurt to take a look, hey?' His smile was shy but his blue eyes twinkled as he held his hand out for her to shake. 'Dr Garrett Buchanan at your service.'

And that was how Hazel came to be sitting on Libby's spare bed, with her foot in Garrett Buchanan's lap.

He turned her foot gently one way then the other. 'Wriggle your toes.'

Hazel obeyed, grateful that she'd remembered to slick on a bit of pink nail polish earlier in the day and half wondering if she'd dozed off before the party and was now dreaming this whole scenario. It certainly felt like something her mind would conjure up. The tall, trim doctor with his burnished hair and ocean-blue eyes, his warm, slender fingers clasped around her ankle...

'All looks to be in order.' He gently lowered her foot to the floor.

Hazel swallowed, though it sounded a little more like a gulp. 'Like I said, I'm fine.'

But it was a lie. Hazel was very much not fine. Her heart was hammering inside her chest, for one thing, and she could still feel the ghost of Garrett Buchanan's touch on her ankle.

What was happening to her?

'Better safe than sorry,' he said. 'Besides, when I saw you out there on the path you looked a little...'

'What?' Hazel prompted.

'Lost, maybe?'

She'd felt it, too. She had ever since the break-up, as much as she hated to admit it to anyone—least of all herself. It had blindsided her, that was all. There she'd been...imagining a rosy future with marriage and babies and a home of their own...and all the while her ex, Eric, had been imagining his own future. Alone. On the other side of the world.

What an idiot she'd been, assuming they wanted the same things. Well, that was a mistake she wouldn't be making again in a hurry.

Hazel shook her head. 'I'm fine—really.'

Garrett Buchanan looked right at her. 'You certainly look it.'

And despite her recent heartbreak, and her angst about turning thirty, and her embarrassment at having tripped over fresh air in front of this ridiculously good-looking man, Hazel laughed.

'That was too corny for words.'

Garrett laughed too. 'Was it? I'm a bit out of practice.'

He scratched the back of his neck, and Hazel noticed that a flush of colour had crept into his pale cheeks.

Was he really trying to flirt with her...?

It had been so long Hazel had almost forgotten what it felt like.

'Don't worry, I won't hold it against you.'

Garrett groaned. 'Oh, please don't set me up for any more terrible chat-up lines.'

Hazel could feel herself blushing madly. She slipped her other foot out of her heeled sandal and stood up. She wasn't sure what she was doing exactly, but sitting on a bed next to Garrett Buchanan was making it hard to think. She crossed the room, the carpet soft under her bare feet, and pretended to look out of the window, down into the garden below, where the party—*her* party—was in full swing.

'It's true, you know.'

Hazel turned to him. 'What is?'

'That you're beautiful.'

Hazel opened her mouth to bat the compliment away, but no sound came out and she closed it again, her teeth crashing together audibly.

Garret Buchanan got to his feet and to Hazel's horror—and delight—began moving towards her. Her stomach suddenly felt like a washing machine on the spin cycle, and she was grateful that she'd only managed a single glass of wine before pouring half the second one down her dress.

Garrett came to a standstill, with barely a foot between them. 'In fact, I think you're the most beautiful woman I've ever seen.'

Hazel stared at him. She might not have had very much to drink tonight but it seemed he had.

'Are you, by any chance, drunk?'

Garrett Buchanan's sandy brows knitted together. 'Not at all.'

Hazel raised herself onto her tiptoes to peer over his shoulder, half expecting to find her best friend giggling in the doorway. It was just the kind of thing she'd do in a misguided attempt to cheer Hazel up—persuade an old friend to flirt with her to boost her confidence.

Maybe she'd even told him to give her a birthday kiss...

Hazel's mouth suddenly felt very dry.

'Did Libby put you up to this?' she croaked.

'Who?'

Hazel gestured vaguely around the room. 'This is her place.'

Garrett Buchanan shook his head. 'I don't know her, sorry. I was invited by my pal, Jake. He said it was someone's birthday and they needed to make up the numbers.'

His throwaway comment hit Hazel like a gut-punch and she took an involuntary step backwards, her hip bumping against the windowsill.

That was her.

So pathetic she couldn't even fill her own birthday party.

But somehow she didn't feel pathetic. Not right now, anyway. Not with the way Garrett Buchanan was looking at her, his blue eyes smouldering.

'You know, you never told me your name,' he said, head tilted.

Maybe this was it. Maybe this was her chance to prove to the universe…to prove to herself…that she wasn't *that* Hazel any more. That she wasn't someone who'd wasted years on a relationship only for it to go up in a puff of smoke—or rather, in the offer of a job overseas. That she wasn't terrified of entering her thirties alone. She was a new Hazel. Someone bolder, braver. Someone who didn't care if her birthday party was filled with strangers—especially not if they were as good-looking as this one.

'Maybe that's for the best,' she said, taking a step forward to meet him. 'In fact, maybe we should stop talking altogether.'

Garrett Buchanan's blue eyes widened as the meaning behind her words became clear.

Before she could second-guess herself, Hazel leaned forward and pressed her lips against his.

If she'd been expecting him to pull back or protest she couldn't have been more wrong. Garrett's eyes stayed open for half a beat, dazzling blue and locked with hers, before falling shut as their kiss deepened.

His lips were soft and firm. He tasted of red wine, heady and delicious, and his light bronze stubble grazed Hazel's chin.

Pretty soon her arms were wrapped around his neck and his hands were in her hair, and it was becoming impossible to tell where she ended and Garrett began as their bodies collided. His torso was firm beneath the crisp cotton of his shirt, and Hazel felt soft and slippery in comparison, beneath the damp satin of her new dress.

She'd never done anything like this before. Not even in her wildest daydreams. But then she'd never felt chemistry like this either… The searing heat between the two of them was like nothing she'd ever imagined.

Suddenly, Garrett pulled away. His chest rose and fell rapidly beneath his shirt and his blue eyes searched hers. 'Are you sure you want this?'

Hazel hesitated. She wasn't the kind of person to have a one-night stand…*or was she?* Just because she'd lived her life one way up to now, it didn't mean it had to be that way forever…

Besides, this feeling was something she'd never experienced before. The air hummed with the electricity that crackled between her and Garrett's bodies.

'Yes.' The word fell from Hazel's lips.

Maybe this magic would only last one night. And if that was true, Hazel was going to savour every single moment.

No sooner had the word left her mouth than the handsome stranger was kissing her again, his hands roaming over her body.

Hazel tried to be quiet, aware that anyone might walk by the door at any minute, but she couldn't help murmuring her appreciation against Garrett's lips as he tugged gently on the straps of her dress. She let them slide from her shoulders, the dress folding to her waist, and she gasped as Garrett's soft hands explored her body before unhooking her bra so that it slipped between them to the floor.

Aware, suddenly, that she was half naked and he was still fully dressed, she began unbuttoning Garrett's shirt. He watched her with hooded eyes before shrugging out of it. She tugged impatiently at his belt and he smiled against her mouth as his hands covered hers, helping her to release the buckle and sliding his jeans down over his hips until there was nothing between them but the slippery satin of Hazel's dress, now bunched around her waist, and bare skin.

Garrett's hand slipped between her thighs and Hazel parted her legs, grasping at the windowsill to steady herself as the handsome doctor brought her to a quick orgasm with his fingers.

She was still seeing stars when she felt him move away, rummaging through their discarded clothing as though searching for something.

Hazel was about to ask him what he'd lost when Garrett turned back to her, and she saw the flash of foil between his fingers and understood. She was relieved that they wouldn't need to have an awkward conversation about protection—that she could lose herself in the moment while still not quite believing that it was really happening.

And then Garrett was lifting her as if she weighed nothing at all, and Hazel was hooking her legs around his waist.

'Is this okay?' Garrett's voice was half-whisper, half-growl.

'Yes…' Hazel breathed.

He pushed into her and Hazel had to press her face into his shoulder to keep herself from crying out. They had to be quiet, she knew—but, *oh, God*, it was almost impossible when it felt so good.

Garrett took his time, even though she knew from the way his pulse bounded in his neck and his eyes smouldered that he didn't want to, that he was holding back for her sake. She climaxed again, her fingers in his hair, and suddenly his pace quickened until she felt his fingers digging into her thighs and he moaned something unintelligible into her hair.

Anyone walking by the door would likely hear them, but in that moment Hazel didn't care. She couldn't believe this was really happening—that she, Hazel Bridges, was having sex with Dr Garrett Buchanan, by far the hottest guy at her birthday party, and that he didn't even know her name, or the fact that it was her party.

They clung to one another, waiting to catch their breath, and then he set her down gently with a shy smile. 'You okay?'

'Never better.' Hazel smiled too, her legs wobbling slightly beneath her.

She couldn't recall a single reason she'd ever thought a one-night stand might be a bad idea. No doubt later it would all come back to her, but for now, as Garrett Buchanan shyly handed back Hazel's underwear, unruly red waves of hair falling forward over his blue eyes as he plucked her bra from where it had landed and held it out to her, Hazel felt on top of the world.

Hazel yanked the sunflower-yellow wrap dress over her head and considered herself in the full-length mirror on the back of the door.

Oh, dear.

The stain-free dress was an improvement from the blue

satin one that now lay crumpled on the floor at her feet, but there was no getting away from how very…*ruffled* she looked.

Her cheeks were scarlet, her carefully applied lipstick was smudged into oblivion, and a pink flush crept across her chest. Her usually smooth bob stuck up at all angles, and she patted at it frantically even as she heard Libby calling her name from the bottom of the staircase.

She turned from her reflection.

She'd have to do.

A moment longer and Libby would probably come storming up here to find her.

Hopefully, Garrett had already made it down the stairs undiscovered and blended back into the party. He'd tried to offer her his number. Standing there, bare-chested, hair rumpled, he'd said maybe they could go for a drink some time… But Hazel had shaken her head.

It would spoil the magic. Stringing it out until he inevitably let her down. She'd much rather keep it at this. One night of pure magic. Never to be repeated.

He'd looked surprised then—but she was certain there'd been a touch of relief in his expression, too. Maybe he had his own reasons for wanting to avoid a relationship right now. Either way, he'd buttoned up his shirt and pecked her on the cheek before disappearing out through the door.

Hazel had stared after him, until a burst of laughter from the party below had reminded her of where she was.

At the thought of facing Garrett after what had just happened Hazel's face grew hotter still, but she forced herself from the room and raced down the staircase, almost crashing into Libby, who was standing at the bottom.

'There you are! Where have you been?' Libby tugged at the fluted sleeves of Hazel's yellow dress. 'Why did you change? The blue looked fantastic on you.' She shook her head. 'Never mind. It's time for the cake!'

She took Hazel by the arm and began pulling her towards the kitchen.

'Oh, no. No, no, no!' Hazel protested. 'I told you I didn't want any fuss!'

She hated being the centre of attention at the best of times, let alone when she was still processing what had just happened... The fact she'd just slept with a total stranger at a party. Her own birthday party, no less.

'Nonsense!' Libby was saying. 'It's your birthday!'

As if she needed the reminder.

It was too late. Already a crowd had gathered around Libby's kitchen island, and there in the centre of it stood a beautifully iced cake, with an oversized, glittery number thirty topper and a staggering number of blazing candles giving off the heat of a small fire.

'Ladies and gentlemen, let's hear it for the birthday girl, Hazel!' Libby lifted the cake and the whole room was filled with singing.

Hazel's toes curled against her sandals and over the flickering flames her eyes searched the crowd of unfamiliar faces for his...

But it was no use. Garrett Buchanan was gone. And he hadn't even waited to say goodbye.

CHAPTER ONE

LANYARD? CHECK. NAME BADGE? Check. Wristwatch off? Check. Shirtsleeves rolled back? Check. Stomach flipping as if he was on a fairground ride? Check.

It didn't matter how many new jobs Garrett started—and he'd had more than his fair share—he still couldn't seem to escape the first-day nerves that came with his first shift at a new hospital.

This was different, though. This was it. The final stepping stone.

But that thought only made his stomach flip faster.

Garrett took a deep breath and tried to clear his mind, but it was impossible. Amongst all the new job jitters and the timetable he'd hastily tried to memorise last night there she was, dancing into the centre of his subconscious.

His mystery woman.

The beautiful woman he'd had sex with four weeks ago at a party only to never see her again. He hadn't been able to stop thinking about it since. Hadn't been able to stop thinking about *her.*

Garrett still couldn't quite believe it had happened the way it had. He'd only followed her into the house wanting to check that she was okay... Yes, admittedly he'd been hoping for a kiss at the bottom of the garden at the end of the night, beneath the midsummer moon. A good omen for this next chapter in his life.

It had been his first day in town, and he'd been grateful for Jake's last-minute invitation, but he had found himself feeling more than a little lost at the party full of strangers. And suddenly there she'd been, looking right at him, seeming a little lost herself, and just for a moment he'd thought...

Well, it didn't matter what he'd thought. Because it was done now, wasn't it? And he was never going to see her again.

Garrett's eyes snagged on the clock above the kitchen counter.

Damn. If he didn't stop daydreaming, he was going to be late.

He grabbed his pager and his keys and dashed out through the door.

Luckily, he didn't have far to go. He'd taken a flat in the staff accommodation on-site at the hospital, meaning his commute was only a ten-minute walk—or a five-minute jog—door to door.

As he joined the throng of people heading towards the hospital's main entrance he thought he caught a glimpse of his mystery woman up ahead. Dark hair swishing above a collared shirt, a yellow lanyard dangling from her neck...

But it wasn't her. Couldn't be her. Besides, he didn't want it to be her, did he? That hadn't been part of the plan.

She'd shaken her head when he'd offered his number and, overwhelmed by the intensity of their connection, he'd been flooded with relief and had scarpered before anything more could be said. Though he'd felt strangely guilty about it ever since. He should at least have said goodbye.

Well, there was nothing to be done about it now.

He needed to stop thinking about it. Stop thinking about her. He had one objective in his life right now—to become a neonatal consultant. A relationship was out of the question. No matter how beautiful she might be—and she was. No matter how powerful their chemistry—and it was.

Garrett Buchanan was a man on a mission and he couldn't afford to forget that.

His footsteps slowed as he reached the rotating doors of the main entrance and he sidestepped out of the flow of bodies so that he could pause for a minute and look up at the sign looming over them, welcoming him to Riverside General Hospital.

This was it. The final step. The last hurdle on his way to

his dream job. To the life he'd promised himself when he was younger. Back when he'd been a scrap of a thing, lying in that narrow bed in his first foster home.

Even then he'd known that he wanted to make a difference to the world. That he wanted to become something more than his backstory.

He'd also promised himself that he'd never rely on anyone else to make his dreams come true, knowing that when it came to it he was the only one who'd always have his back.

No one else could be relied upon. He needed to remember that.

'The usual, love?'

Hazel looked over at the barista, unsure if she should feel grateful at having her order memorised or mortified that she'd become so predictable. Here she was, a new day but the same old routine: arrive early at the hospital, grab a flat white to go from the coffee shop in the foyer, and head up to NICU. It was official. She was thirty years old and stuck in a rut.

When was the last time she'd tried something new? Really pushed herself out of her comfort zone?

But Hazel knew the answer to that, and heat flooded her cheeks at the memory.

Stubble grazing her lips, his hand slipping beneath the hem of her dress, and those eyes—vivid blue and locked with hers...

Hazel shook her head emphatically. Now was neither the time nor the place to be reminiscing about *that* particular experience. It might have been the most sensual night of her life, but it was not something she'd be repeating. Ever. Not least because she had no way of even contacting him...

But then, *she* was the one who'd refused his number...

'You don't want a flat white to take away?'

Hazel jolted back to reality and found the barista staring at her quizzically, one eyebrow raised.

'Oh, no, I didn't mean—' Hazel began to explain herself, and then she stopped abruptly.

If she could share a night of passion with a total stranger, she could change her coffee order.

She smiled broadly at the barista, who looked faintly alarmed at this sudden change in their daily exchange.

'Actually, I think I'll try something new,' Hazel said.

Her eyes flickered over the menu, but before she could make a decision an almighty scream rang out through the foyer.

'Help! Someone, please!'

Hazel spun around. A few feet away a woman was frantically unstrapping a baby from a pushchair. Beside her, a small boy of about three stood clutching a packet of sweets and crying.

Hazel's feet were moving before her brain could catch up. 'What happened?'

'My baby's choking!' The woman was frantic as she pulled a baby of about three months old from the pram. The infant's face was pale, her eyes wide, and her little lips tinged blue.

'Did you see what it is she's choking on?' Hazel asked.

'Her brother—he gave her a sweet. He didn't—he didn't know—'

The little boy began crying louder.

'Here.'

Hazel held her hands out for the baby, and after a second's hesitation the mum handed her over.

'Please!' she said, her eyes filled with tears.

Hazel wasted no time in sliding onto one of the foyer seats and gently flipping the baby girl over onto her front. Laying the baby against her thigh, Hazel administered five back blows, praying silently after each one that the sweet would come flying out.

It didn't.

'I need to do some chest thrusts,' Hazel said, turning the baby onto her back once more and laying her across her lap. Her little face was ghostly white now, her eyes watering and her little mouth puckered as she gasped for air around the sweet her big brother had decided to share with her the moment his mum's back was turned.

Hazel's own heart was pounding as she pushed two fingers into the centre of the baby's chest.

One—two—come on, baby. Three—

The baby gave a weak gurgle.

Yes! It was working. Four—

There was a hoarse cry, and a chewy pink sweet flew from the baby's mouth and landed on the floor at Hazel's feet. Adrenaline coursed through Hazel's veins as she watched pink flood the infant's face before the little girl let out a furious wail.

'Oh, my baby!'

The mother rushed forward, her cheeks stained with tears, and Hazel held the baby out to her with shaking hands.

It was then that Hazel noticed the smartly dressed figure kneeling beside the pushchair.

The dad, perhaps?

But he looked far too composed, given what had just happened, and Hazel caught the flash of yellow around his shirt collar—a hospital lanyard. His rumpled ginger hair brought memories flooding back—memories she'd only pushed to one side moments earlier...

But that was ridiculous—she couldn't go getting hot and bothered over every red-headed male she came across just because of one encounter.

'Didn't mean to,' the little boy sniffed.

'I know you didn't,' the man was reassuring the heartbroken little boy, who was still clutching his paper bag of sweets. 'And your mum knows that too. She was scared, that's all.'

Hazel glanced over to where the mum was pressing her baby daughter to her chest and weeping with obvious relief.

Not a parent herself, Hazel could only imagine the emotions the woman must have gone through in the past few minutes. But even with the terror fresh in the mother's face, Hazel still felt a pang of longing.

Would she ever experience the highs and lows of motherhood for herself, or was she destined to watch from the sidelines every day?

There had been a time not so long ago when she'd thought children were on the horizon—but that had been before her ex had dropped the bombshell that he was leaving...not just her, but the country. As if he'd wanted to put as much distance as possible between himself and the dreams Hazel had for their future.

'Grown-ups don't get scared!' the boy said.

'Sure they do,' Hazel heard the stranger in the blue shirt say. He lowered his voice to an almost whisper. 'I get scared all the time.'

The little boy's brown eyes grew round. 'But you're a *doctor*!' he protested.

Despite her adrenaline-fuelled emotions, Hazel couldn't help but smile. She didn't recognise the mystery doctor—not from this angle anyway—but she'd be willing to bet he was specialising in paediatrics, judging by his easy manner with kids. Already, the terrified sobbing boy from a few minutes ago had been replaced by a calm, curious kid, staring up at the doctor in wide-eyed wonder.

Hazel felt a hand on her shoulder and turned to find the mum standing beside her. 'I can't thank you enough,' she said. She'd stopped crying now, but her face was red and her eyes glittered with emotion.

Hazel squeezed her arm reassuringly. 'Just doing my job.'

'But if you hadn't been here—' A panic-stricken look crossed the woman's face again.

'Then one of our other brilliant members of staff would have done the same thing,' Hazel said soothingly. She gestured to the red-haired doctor kneeling on the floor. 'Like this doctor... I'm sorry I don't know your name...'

He shook hands with the young boy and then stood up. Hazel watched as he unfolded to his full, impressive height.

He must be at least six feet tall...maybe more...

A spark of familiarity fired in Hazel's mind as he slowly turned to face her, and her mouth fell open in shock as his blue eyes met hers.

'Dr Garrett Buchanan,' he said, holding out his hand to her. 'But I believe we've already met.'

CHAPTER TWO

GARRETT WATCHED THE colour drain from her cheeks. Even as pale as a ghost, she was still the most beautiful woman he'd ever laid eyes on.

As it was, he'd laid a lot more than his eyes on her...

But now wasn't a helpful time to remember that.

He shifted uncomfortably and dropped his hand to his side when it became clear that she wasn't going to shake it. He wasn't sure she'd even noticed he was holding it out.

He didn't blame her for her stunned reaction.

After all, what were the chances?

Garrett himself had frozen for a minute inside the busy foyer, when he'd stepped through the doors of his new hospital and found himself watching the woman he'd spent one unforgettable night with four weeks ago saving a baby's life right in front of him.

So he'd been right after all...when he'd thought he'd spotted her in the crowd earlier.

She must work here too.

Right now she was staring at him as if she wasn't sure he was real. Her wide green eyes were locked with his, her full pink lips parted in disbelief. For a brief moment he imagined reaching out and pulling her to him—before remembering where he was, and what he was doing there.

Day one of his new job and late already, probably. Garrett reluctantly tore his eyes away from hers and turned to the mother of the baby she'd just saved.

'Your daughter's had a lucky escape. She'll probably be fine, but I would recommend you nipping round to the paediatric emergency department before you go to get her checked over thoroughly—just in case.'

'Of course.' She began strapping the little one back in her pushchair. 'We'll go right away. Which way is it?'

'Erm…' Garrett scratched his cheek.

He had no clue. He'd been on call in his previous post for orientation day, so had missed the grand tour. Fortunately, Garrett's mystery woman stepped in.

'Take the main corridor as far as you can go, then make a right turn. It's signposted from there; you can't miss it.'

Garrett turned to thank her, hating that he didn't even know her name, but she wasn't looking at him any more. In fact, she seemed to be studiously avoiding his eyes.

He felt a bristle of irritation at the way this was going. Not that he had imagined this would ever happen. He'd thought he'd never see her again.

But he'd hoped…

He pushed the thought away. Whatever he'd hoped, it didn't matter. He was here for six months. To do a job and move on. Onwards and upwards.

Just like always.

As for his mystery woman—he had no idea why she was here. A hospital lanyard hung from her neck, and she obviously knew paediatric first aid, but her smart-casual attire of a sleeveless blouse and tailored black trousers gave nothing away.

Nothing but the shape of her curves anyway.

Damn, he needed to stop thinking like that and concentrate. He was a professional.

'I'm sorry, Mummy.'

Garrett heard the little boy mumble a tearful apology to his mother, and she pulled him in close for a hug.

'I know you are, darling.'

Inexplicably Garrett felt a lump forming in his throat—which was ridiculous. He dealt with emotionally charged situations all the time, but this unexpected encounter had thrown him off, and he couldn't seem to get a grip of himself.

'It was very kind of you to share your sweets with your little sister...'

The mystery woman whose name Garrett still didn't know, but whose voice he definitely remembered, dropped down to the boy's level to speak to him.

'I'm sure you're a very good big brother. Next time, though, make sure you check with your mummy before you give anything to her, okay?'

'Okay.' The boy nodded solemnly.

The mother thanked them both again, and Garrett watched as they were swallowed up in the morning bustle of the hospital.

'You dealt with that fantastically,' Garrett said, as the mysterious woman got to her feet. She was still a good foot shorter than him, even standing.

But he seemed to remember that had worked out rather well when...

'Just doing what I was trained to do,' she said, but she still didn't turn around.

Garrett bit back his frustration. He wanted to see her face, to know her name, to ask her how she'd been, to apologise for dashing off the way he had—

No, wait—not that last part.

He'd never promised to stick around, so he didn't need to apologise... And yet standing here, a month later, it felt as if he should.

'You're a doctor?' he asked.

Finally, she turned, and Garrett was hit by the full force of her beauty all over again. Her high cheekbones had colour once more, her sleek black hair swung around her face, the ends of it grazing her neck. Her green eyes flashed.

'A nurse, actually. And if you'll excuse me? I'm running late.'

Hazel marched away as quickly as she could, trying to disappear into the crowd of staff and patients moving through the main hospital corridor.

Oh, God, that was not the start to the day she'd needed.

Choking babies, frantic mothers, crying toddlers and then *him*. Dr Garrett Buchanan. Standing there in front of her, his copper-coloured hair falling into his face, his blue eyes sparkling and his hand outstretched—as though it was just some happy coincidence, them running into each other, and not Hazel's worst nightmare.

That would teach her to have a moment of madness on her birthday. Now the madness was catching up with her—literally...

'Wait! Please!'

She could hear Garrett Buchanan's voice calling after her, and his footsteps as he jogged to catch up with her as he ducked and weaved through the throngs of people.

Hazel sighed.

Maybe she was being childish.

Maybe it would be better if they faced up to this now and moved on. After all, this was a big hospital—big enough to service the bustling city of York and its surrounding suburbs, and big enough to avoid a one-night fling, surely?

She slowed her steps slightly. Yes, she'd let him say whatever it was he needed to say, wish him well, and then they'd probably never cross paths again.

Although she had just bet on him being a paediatrician...

Hazel's pulse skittered and she briefly considered breaking into a run.

No, that would be ridiculous. She was thirty, for God's sake. She could handle this like the responsible adult she was.

Hazel threw her shoulders back and stepped to one side of the corridor. She caught the obvious look of relief on Dr Garrett Buchanan's face when he realised he wasn't going to have to chase her all the way through the hospital.

As he made his way across the busy corridor Hazel couldn't help but admire how good he looked in his light blue shirt and navy chinos. He was lean, but muscular. Hazel could see the definition of his biceps through his shirt sleeves as he neared her, but even if she hadn't been able to she would have remembered the feel of them as he'd lifted her against—

No! Do not think of that now!

But it was too late. As he came to a standstill before her, all

Hazel could think about was the memory of Garrett Buchanan's body pressing into hers as he'd pushed her against the wall of Libby's spare room, her legs wrapped tightly around his waist. She knew she must be blushing—it was impossible not to be when her mind was filled with images of this tall, handsome doctor in various stages of undress, his hands roaming her body as music had drifted up the stairs from the party below...

But it was one night, she reminded herself.

She hadn't been herself after the break-up, and he'd been there to give her what she needed...or at least what she'd *thought* she needed. But in the weeks since she'd realised that flings were not her style, and she was willing to bet that they very much *were* Dr Garrett Buchanan's style.

Garrett found himself standing across from her once again and he still didn't know her name. He tried, not so subtly, to read her ID badge, but it had spun around—no doubt as she'd been running away from him.

It was clear she didn't want to speak to him—even now she looked as if she'd rather be anywhere else on earth—but he hadn't been able to let her go. Not like that anyway.

'Thank you for waiting.'

She gave a brief, curt nod. Her straight black hair fell forward, and Garrett imagined pushing it away from her face—before imagining the slap he would probably get if he tried it. And deservedly so, too. This was his workplace—and hers, it seemed. Not a bedroom at a house party.

Concentrate!

'I really can't stay. I have a presentation to give in—' she looked at her watch and swore softly '—five minutes.'

She looked ready to bolt again.

'I won't keep you.' Garrett held his hands up in surrender. 'I just wanted to say that—well, I know this is awkward, but I hope that I can—that we can—' He struggled to find the words to express what he wanted to say. The trouble was, he didn't *know* what he wanted to say. He knew what he felt, and he was pretty sure she felt it too. The magnetism between them was like nothing Garrett had ever experienced before.

But you're not staying, he reminded himself. *So what difference does it make?*

Garrett ran a hand through his hair exasperatedly.

This was not in his plans. Not today. Not ever.

'Dr Buchanan.' Her use of his title and her sharp tone cut into his thoughts. 'I have to go. I'm sorry.'

Garrett sighed. 'Then at least tell me your name.'

She hesitated. Only for a second, but Garrett saw it.

Was she really so determined not to have anything more to do with him? After the night they'd shared?

Admittedly it was what they'd agreed they'd both wanted—one night, no commitments—but somehow the thought that she was still willing to leave it at just that, even after running into him here, stung Garrett's pride. He hoped at least she didn't regret it.

Her green eyes met his, warily at first, but then something in her seemed to give way.

'Hazel,' she said. 'Hazel Bridges.'

Garrett found himself smiling. For no reason at all other than that he'd finally learned the name of the woman who had been haunting his every dream this past month—both sleeping and awake.

'Hazel,' he repeated.

It was a pretty name, but strong too. Like her.

Oh, God, he was being ridiculous and he knew it. But he couldn't seem to stop.

'Well, now we know each other's names, perhaps you'll be so kind as to point me on my way?'

Hazel nodded. 'Sure. Where are you heading?'

'It's my first day, and I'm scheduled for my local induction.'

'Which department?'

'NICU.'

Hazel's eyes widened.

'Is there a problem?'

What was so surprising about him working in neonatal medicine?

'No, not at all,' Hazel said, but her voice was high and false. 'Follow me and I'll show you the way.'

She began walking away briskly.

Garrett frowned. 'You really don't have to show me,' he said, jogging after her. 'Just point me in the right direction and I'll take it from there. I don't want you to be late for your presentation.'

She stopped walking and turned to him. 'That's very sweet of you, but I'm going that way anyway. Actually, you're the reason I'm doing the presentation.'

'Huh?'

Hazel sighed heavily. 'If you've read your induction programme—which I'm sure you have—' she raised one eyebrow at him and Garrett smiled sheepishly '—you'll have noticed that the first thing on there is a *Welcome to NICU Talk.*'

'And…?' Garrett still didn't understand. He felt as if he'd left his brain back in the foyer.

Hazel narrowed her eyes at him, clearly wondering just how he'd managed to qualify as a doctor and work his way up to a registrar post when he couldn't even follow a simple conversation.

'*And* I'm the one giving that talk. I do it for all the new NICU staff. I'm a senior neonatal nurse and induction lead. Welcome to the team, Dr Buchanan.'

CHAPTER THREE

'DOES ANYONE HAVE any questions?' Hazel clicked onto the final slide in the presentation and turned to the room expectantly.

There were always questions.

What made today's presentation different from all the others she'd given was that she had questions of her own. Most of them involving a certain doctor who had thankfully chosen a seat in the back corner of the room—otherwise Hazel wasn't sure she'd have been able to follow her own slides.

A smattering of hands was raised and Hazel took the doctors' questions one by one. She remembered her own induction day—the excitement and anticipation at finally landing her dream job as a neonatal nurse laced with a frisson of fear. After all her training she would have the lives of newborn babies in her hands—quite literally. And now here she stood, nine years later, welcoming a room full of doctors to her unit and calming their nerves about what lay ahead.

If only she could get a grip of her own.

It wasn't like her to be so easily rattled, but in her defence she hadn't for one moment expected to be working alongside Dr Garrett Buchanan. He'd been her one moment of madness in an otherwise sensible life. And, yes, she'd thought about him pretty much every day since—but that didn't mean anything. It was the shock of how it had happened, that was all.

She was sure that over time the memory of his mouth on hers and his hands tracing across her body would fade—that in years to come she'd barely think of Dr Garrett Buchanan at all. But for now she had little choice. He wasn't a memory but a very real person, sitting in the corner of the room.

Hazel could feel his eyes on her as she began packing away her things. With their questions all answered, the new doctors were getting to their feet and filing slowly out of the room, ready for the tour of the unit she'd promised. All but one of them.

She heard the approach of his footsteps and an intake of breath but she didn't turn around.

'That was the best induction I've ever had,' Garrett said.

Hazel closed the laptop and looked at him at last, eyebrows raised. 'Having been to a fair few induction days myself, I'm not sure that's the compliment you think it is.'

Garrett grinned, and Hazel felt a flutter of something she shouldn't.

'They're not my favourite way to spend a morning, no. But I think everyone is walking out of here feeling more at ease than when they walked in—which means you did a good job.'

'Thank you.'

Hazel certainly wasn't feeling more at ease as she wound her way through the empty chairs to the door, knowing that Garrett—*Dr Buchanan*—was following.

She led the group of new doctors around the unit, pointing out all the essentials—the storeroom, the staffroom and the blood gas machine. Those would be their three main destinations for the first few days at least.

'This is our special care nursery.'

Hazel waited for everyone to sanitise their hands before pushing open the door.

During her time as a neonatal nurse Hazel had worked in every room on the NICU, from Intensive Care—where the sickest babies were nursed—through to High Dependency and finally to Special Care, where she stood now. Of all of them, this was her favourite. This was the final stepping stone for these babies and their families—one last hurdle before they could be discharged home and begin the rest of their lives.

As much as Hazel loved the buzz of the other two rooms, and the satisfaction of caring for a very sick baby and seeing even the smallest improvement by the end of a shift, it was here where the real magic happened, in Hazel's opinion. It was here that new mums learned to breastfeed, where dads with shaking hands almost cartoonishly large compared to their babies' tiny bodies bathed their sons and daughters for the first time, where babies who'd spent weeks in only a nappy, with wires snaking away from them in all directions, finally got to wear the soft pastel outfits their parents had bought for them before they were born.

Hazel knew that many of these doctors wouldn't see it that way—that they'd be eager to test their knowledge and skills in a faster-paced environment. But she also knew that during their time here many would discover that there was a lot to learn in the nursery too. Not least how to handle and perform basic care on a wriggly newborn—a skill that would put anyone to the test.

'Is this the new lot, then?'

A familiar voice interrupted Hazel's thoughts and she turned to see a fellow nurse, Ciara, bottle-feeding one of their long-stay babies, Harry.

Hazel nodded. 'For better or for worse, they're ours for the next six months.'

She leaned over Ciara's shoulder to get a better look at Harry. 'He looks to be feeding better now?'

Ciara nodded, her face full of pride. 'He's starting to figure out that he needs to breathe now and then, and not just guzzle the entire bottle in one go.'

Hazel laughed. 'That always helps.'

Ciara slipped the bottle from Harry's mouth and gently lifted him into a sitting position on her lap to bring up his wind. No sooner had she got him upright than he let out an almighty belch, followed by a river of milk across the front of Ciara's pale blue scrubs.

'Uh-oh.' Hazel moved to grab a towel for her friend and bumped into someone beside her. 'Oh, sorry, I—' Hazel cut herself off abruptly.

Garrett shook his head. 'Don't worry about it.'

He held out his hand to Ciara and Hazel saw he was already holding a towel.

'Here. Let me take him while you get cleaned up.'

Garrett moved to wash his hands at the nearby sink and Ciara looked over at Hazel, one eyebrow raised. Hazel could tell that her friend was as surprised by the offer as she was, but Ciara handed Harry over to Garrett nonetheless.

'I'd better change my scrub top.' Ciara said. 'I'll only be a minute.'

'Take your time.' Garrett settled into a plastic chair with Harry in his arms. 'Hey, little guy. What do we call you?'

'Harry,' Hazel blurted.

The sight of Garrett holding a newborn was the absolute last thing her ovaries needed, but she found it impossible to look away.

'He was born at twenty-seven weeks.' She heard herself speaking—babbling, actually—to fill the silence. 'He's thirty-eight plus four corrected now…feeding and growing. He's just learning to master the bottle.'

'And suffering from reflux by the look of things,' Garrett said, still looking at Harry.

'He's on medication, but it's not making much of a differ-ence,' Hazel admitted.

Ciara was back, wearing a clean scrub top and no longer smelling like regurgitated milk. 'His weight gain is steady,' she said.

'Does he seem to have any discomfort with the reflux?' Garrett asked.

Ciara shook her head. 'It's effortless—as you saw.'

Garrett nodded thoughtfully, and Hazel found herself re-luctantly impressed. Feeding and elimination were hardly the most glamorous of topics in any field of medicine, but Dr Garrett Buchanan was giving them the consideration they deserved.

'Well, let's keep an eye on it. We can't have you spoiling stylish outfits like this, can we?'

Hazel thought he was making a dig about the shapeless scrubs they were all required to wear on clinical shifts, but then she realised that he was admiring Harry's pastel blue cotton dungarees.

Garrett handed Harry back to Ciara and moved to the sink to wash his hands again.

Hazel watched him for a few seconds, before shaking her head slightly and turning back to the other doctors. 'As you can see, you'll have plenty of opportunities for hands-on baby care here in the nursery. Now, if you'd like to follow me, I'll show you our high dependency room.'

Hazel was just about to bite into her sandwich when the staff room door swung open to reveal the shift co-ordinator, Diane.

'Sorry to disturb you on your break, Hazel, but...'

There it was. The *'but'* that Hazel knew meant she wouldn't be getting lunch after all. She swallowed a small sigh and put her sandwich down.

'What's up?'

Diane's face sagged with relief. 'Delivery suite. Thirty-five plus five, about to deliver. Everything looks good, but they'd like us to send someone just in case.'

'I'll go.' Hazel snapped the lid onto her lunchbox and moved to the sink to wash her hands.

'Brilliant, thanks.' Diane turned to go, but then stuck her head back through the partially open door. 'You don't mind one of the new doctors tagging along, do you?'

'Of course not.' Hazel dried her hands, dropping the used paper towels into the bin.

'I promise not to make a nuisance of myself.'

Hazel's head snapped up so fast she almost gave herself whiplash.

There he was: Dr Garrett Buchanan. Already a nuisance, no matter what he might promise.

'Oh, it's you,' Hazel blurted.

The flicker of a frown passed over his brow. 'Is that a problem?'

Hazel squared her shoulders and lifted her chin. 'Not at all.' *Why would it be?* she reasoned with herself.

This would be a regular occurrence if they were going to

be working together on the unit, so she might as well start getting used to it.

Hazel walked quickly, but of course her pace was no match for Dr Buchanan's long, easy strides. He fell into step beside her as they pushed through the unit doors and out into the corridor.

'Have you attended many births?' Hazel fired the question without looking at him.

'A fair few.'

'Not squeamish, then, I trust?' She paused at the entrance to Delivery Suite, her ID card poised ready to swipe, and turned to him at last.

'Not in the slightest.' He grinned.

Hazel's stomach flipped in spite of herself. She nodded curtly and turned away, busying herself with the entry system and then smothering her hands in sanitiser from the dispenser on the wall. Every little scratch and papercut on her hands screamed in protest.

'Hi, Mandy,' Hazel greeted the receptionist, and was rewarded with a warm smile.

You needed a face like Mandy's in a place like this, Hazel had often thought. In the midst of the organised chaos, with frantic birth partners darting in and out of rooms, along with babies' cries and women's moans mingling together, it was important to have a calm, smiling presence on the front desk.

'Oh, hi, love. It's Room Seven they want you for.'

'Thanks.'

Dr Buchanan extended his arm over the desk. 'Mandy, is it? I'm Dr Garrett Buchanan. One of the new neonatal doctors.'

Mandy's eyes widened a fraction and she shook his hand enthusiastically, glancing over at Hazel as she did so as if to say, *Well, what have we here?*

Hazel resisted the urge to roll her eyes. Instead, she glanced meaningfully towards Room Seven, where grunts of exertion could be heard even from out here.

'We really should get on,' Hazel said pointedly.

'Of course,' Dr Buchanan said. 'Ready when you are.'

'I'm ready,' Hazel said, failing to keep the irritation from her voice. 'You'll need to gel your hands again.'

'I was planning on it,' he said agreeably—which only infuriated her further.

Sure enough, he slathered another layer of sanitiser across his hands as they made their way along the corridor.

Hazel knocked lightly on the door to Room Seven and heard a familiar voice call, 'Come in!' in between some other all too familiar sounds.

Hazel and Dr Buchanan stepped into the dimly lit room, where the mum-to-be was kneeling on all fours on the bed. A wide-eyed man with glasses was tentatively rubbing her lower back. In the corner, a student midwife with long dark hair was busy setting up the Resuscitaire while Libby, a bubbly blonde midwife, who also happened to be Hazel's best friend, stood at the end of the bed smiling.

'The neonatal team is here, Cassandra. And just in time, by the looks of things! This is Cassandra and her husband Ross.'

Hazel was about to introduce herself when Cassandra made an unearthly noise that let her know now definitely wasn't the time.

'Fantastic work,' Libby said with genuine enthusiasm. 'Keep that up and your little one will be here in no time!'

She beckoned Hazel over and began filling her in on the details of Cassandra's pregnancy and labour so far. Meanwhile, Cassandra had fallen quiet, and Hazel guessed she was gathering her strength before another contraction hit. She turned, expecting to see Garrett beside her, but instead he was making his way around the other side of the room, towards the expectant dad.

'Hi, Ross. My name's Dr Garrett Buchanan,' he said. 'And this is my colleague Hazel, a senior neonatal nurse. We're just here to check your baby over, and if all's well we'll clear straight out of your way.'

The dad nodded. 'Thanks.'

'Ask them if he'll be too small,' Cassandra moaned quietly. 'Is he going to be too small?'

Cassandra's husband looked at Dr Buchanan. 'She says...'

'I heard,' Hazel said. 'Not at all, Cassandra. All the measurements suggest that your baby is a good weight. He might have a bit of growing to do before he fits into the lovely outfits you've bought him, but he'll be piling on the pounds in no time.'

A look of relief flooded Ross's face. 'Did you hear that, love?'

Cassandra nodded, but already another contraction was building, preventing her from doing anything but groaning in agreement.

'That's it,' Libby said. 'I can see your baby's head right there, Cassandra.'

The student midwife moved towards the bed with a degree of reluctance.

Nerves, Hazel guessed.

'This is it, Jade—your first catch!'

Hazel felt a flare of pride at Libby's words. She knew how much her best friend loved training new midwives, and what a great mentor she was. Hazel was sure that Jade would remember this first birth as long as she lived. Hazel had never forgotten the first time she saw new life come into the world. The fact that that baby would now be in high school boggled her mind whenever she thought of it.

Hazel positioned herself beside the Resuscitaire, and Garrett stood across from her on the other side. She could feel him looking at her, but she busied herself re-checking everything the student midwife had already done. By the time she'd finished Cassandra was giving her final pushes to bring her baby into the world, and the room was soon filled with the startled cry of a newborn baby.

Hazel couldn't help but smile. As a neonatal nurse, it was always reassuring for her to hear a healthy pair of lungs in action, but more than that, as a *human*, it never ceased to amaze her what that sound could do to her heartstrings.

A new life in the world.

She turned to Dr Garrett Buchanan and found he too was smiling. He caught her eye and she held it for a fraction of a second, allowing the shared moment to pass between them before her professional head took over again.

After the baby had had a brief cuddle with Mum, Libby handed the beautiful bundle of joy to Hazel for a quick examination. Hazel relished the feel of the baby in her arms, before reluctantly placing him onto the warmed Resuscitaire.

She completed the newborn checks with Dr Garrett Buchanan watching from the sidelines. She talked him through every step of the process, even though they both knew he didn't need the walk-through, but Hazel couldn't bear the thought of standing in silence beside him. Not with Libby and Jade the student midwife bustling around behind them, helping Cassandra birth the placenta. No, Hazel was determined to keep things as formal as possible. She couldn't risk emotion taking over as she examined the tiny creases on the baby's palms and felt his minute fingers curl around hers…though her heart stuttered all the same, and that pang of longing stirred somewhere deep inside her, as it always did.

When would it be her turn?

'And that concludes the examination,' she said with forced gaiety. 'All that remains is to weigh him—which I'll leave in your capable hands.'

She watched as Dr Garrett Buchanan carried the swaddled babe over to the scales and gently unwrapped him from his blanket, laying him on the crisp hospital towel that had been spread across the scales.

'Two point nine kilograms!' he announced with obvious delight.

The new dad laughed. 'I've no idea what that means!'

'It means your son is a good, healthy weight and won't need to join us on the neonatal unit,' Hazel clarified. 'In fact, all his observations are good, and his newborn examination hasn't raised any concerns. So provided he's kept warm, and starts feeding well, we shouldn't need to see him again at all.'

'Well, that's fantastic news—isn't it, love?'

Ross squeezed his wife's hand and she gave a tired but elated smile in return. Already she had her arms out, waiting for her baby's return, and her relief when Garrett handed her baby back to her was palpable even from across the room.

There was nothing like the protectiveness of a new mother. It was a fierce, primal thing, and many times over the years Hazel's heart had ached for the mums separated from their babies by corridors and locked doors and incubator walls. It was heartbreaking to witness, even if it was for the very best of reasons.

'We'll leave you to it,' Hazel said.

'Many congratulations to you both,' she heard Dr Garrett Buchanan say, before he followed her out into the corridor.

'You know, it doesn't matter how many births I witness, they never fail to have an effect on me.'

Hazel heard him striding to catch her up.

'Don't you agree?' he prompted as he reached her side.

'Of course,' Hazel said.

She knew she sounded brusque, but the last thing she needed right now was a heart-to-heart—with him of all people. How could she possibly explain how much births affected her? Tell him how much she longed to experience it all for herself without sounding desperate or—worse—bitter?

She collected her paperwork from the front desk, where there was no sign of Mandy.

More's the pity, thought Hazel. She could have used the distraction from this line of conversation.

She tucked the file under her arm and walked more quickly.

'It's not just the babies,' Garrett continued. 'I mean, they're cute enough—don't get me wrong—but it's something about being there at the exact moment a family is made.'

His honesty stopped Hazel in her tracks, and she slowed as they approached the exit and turned to him. 'It sounds like you should have been a midwife, not a doctor,' she teased lightly.

To her surprise, he laughed. 'Perhaps you're right.'

They stepped through the double doors of Delivery Suite into the corridor. It was busier now, with lunchtime over and afternoon visiting just beginning. A bunch of pink balloons bobbed towards them, and Hazel and Garrett stepped away from each other to allow the proud new grandparents through.

They'd just reached the doors to the neonatal unit when a thought popped into Hazel's mind like a missing jigsaw piece sliding into place. She berated herself for not having thought of it before.

Dr Garrett Buchanan obviously had children.

'Do you have kids of your own?' The question spilled from Hazel's lips before she could stop it, and she watched his reaction carefully.

Garrett's eyes widened. 'No. What makes you ask?'

Relief surged through Hazel.

Not that it should matter to her.

After all, having kids didn't necessarily mean being in a relationship, so she didn't need to feel guilty about their time together that night, but still… She would have felt differently about it if she'd discovered he was a dad.

Not for the first time, Hazel found herself questioning the wisdom of having sex with someone she knew nothing at all about.

She realised Garrett was still waiting for an answer. 'You look so comfortable around them,' she said. 'There was that little boy in the foyer earlier, and the way you handle babies… it seems to come naturally to you…' Hazel trailed off.

Garrett scratched the back of his neck. 'Well, thanks, but this isn't my first rodeo. I mean, after six years working in Paediatrics you'd hope I'd be good with kids, right?'

Hazel smiled at his modesty. 'You'd be surprised.'

Garrett smiled back, and Hazel's next question was out of her mouth before her brain could catch up.

'Do you want your own someday?' Hazel cringed inwardly as the words dissipated into the space between them.

What was she thinking…asking something so personal?

She hated it when people asked *her* that, so why was she putting Garrett in that same uncomfortable position?

Because she needed to know, some tiny part of her brain whispered. *She couldn't be caught out by the truth—not again.*

This time Garrett didn't just look mildly surprised—he looked outright shocked.

Hazel felt her embarrassment flaming on her cheeks. 'Sorry, that's none of my business. Forget I asked.'

She swiped her ID card quickly and pushed open the door.

Garrett caught her arm gently, stopping her from striding away. Electricity surged through Hazel's body at Garrett's touch, and she reluctantly turned to look at him.

'No,' he said.

It was one word, and it shouldn't have mattered to Hazel at all. So why, then, did she feel as if the bottom had just dropped out of her stomach and was plummeting towards the floor?

She cleared her throat, but her voice still croaked slightly as she spoke. 'Never?'

Garrett shook his head. 'I love kids—obviously, or I wouldn't do what I do. But I've never wanted that responsibility outside of work. It's one thing to take care of babies professionally, but I couldn't be a parent. That's not what my life is about.'

'I see,' Hazel said.

And she did. For the first time since meeting Dr Garrett Buchanan, she was finally seeing him for who he was, rather than an idea of him that she'd created in her mind, and she realised that she'd been right from the start. They might have shared a moment of passion together, but that was all it would ever be. There could be no future for the two of them, and Hazel's past had taught her that it was better to face that now than to get swept up in something that would never work.

Garrett's eyebrows were knitted into a slight frown. He looked as if he was about to ask her something, and Hazel thought she knew what, and she could think of nothing on earth she wanted to do less than stand there and bare her soul to him, knowing what she now knew.

'Well, these notes aren't going to write themselves.' Hazel waved the file she carried in her hand. 'I'd better get on. Excuse me.'

Hazel rushed into the nursing office before Garrett could repeat her own question back to her. Before she could be forced to confront the truth she carried hidden every day. That she both desperately wanted a child of her own and that she was afraid it might never happen.

Garrett stared at the door he'd just watched Hazel disappear through and replayed their conversation in his mind.

What had he said to make her react like that?

The whole thing had been so unexpected.

Of course he'd had that question before. It was an assumption that came with the job, and maybe for some people it rang true. But not for him.

Being a dad had never been part of Garrett's vision for his life—and not for the reasons people assumed. He'd heard those reasons from the mouths of others, particularly some of the younger guys and girls he'd studied medicine with. They were obvious things—easily named and quantified.

No more lie-ins, no more spontaneous weekends away, no disposable income, no free time...

Sure, they were all good enough reasons to stay childless, if they were important to you, but they were all reasons that could easily be obliterated if you wanted children enough. You could rationalise them away one by one when faced with the innate longing and desire for parenthood that he knew some people possessed. After all, that was how the species survived.

But there were other reasons not to have children. Reasons Garrett knew about only too well. And they weren't the sort of thing that could be waved away or ignored. They were impenetrable and unmoving and, no matter how much Garrett loved his job—loved meeting families, taking care of babies and talking to young kids—he knew those reasons would always be there, like blockades around his heart.

They'd been a part of him for so long that he sometimes forgot about them, but conversations like the one he'd just had with Hazel reminded him of their presence, as solid and unwavering as ever.

Was that why she'd fled? Had she heard that grim resolve, that hardness in him?

Garrett was sorry for the way the conversation had ended, but he wasn't sorry for what he'd said. It was the truth.

Garrett was thirty-five, and some women looking at him might see a man on the verge of settling down, thinking about marriage and babies in his future. But they'd be wrong. Garrett had no intention of putting down roots only to have them wrenched from under him and it was better Hazel knew that now. It was better that he remembered it himself.

It was never going to happen.

CHAPTER FOUR

HAZEL WAS EXHAUSTED. She caught herself yawning as the lift doors slid closed and took another swig of her takeout coffee.

A flat white, of course.

It wasn't unusual for her to finish her working week feeling wiped out and ready for her days off, but it was slightly more unusual for her to *start* the week feeling that way.

Still, here she was, on another Monday morning, and already she was wishing that she was back in her bed.

The lift dinged as it reached the third floor and Hazel stumbled out, wondering what the day would bring as she lifted her ID, ready to swipe her way into NICU. But not without peering through the glass first, to check if a certain someone was waiting beyond the doors.

Okay, so admittedly part of the reason for her fatigue was the amount of energy she was using in avoiding Garrett Buchanan.

Lately, it seemed everywhere she looked there he was. She'd be crouching down to read an incubator temperature and when she stood up there he'd be, on the other side of it, sending her heart leaping into her throat and her stomach fluttering like millions of tiny butterflies taking flight.

Hazel didn't flatter herself that he was deliberately seeking her out. It was just one of the perils of working as part of a close-knit team. She'd be busy performing care on one of her newborns, or checking alarm settings on a monitor, and then the hairs would stand up on the back of her neck and she'd immediately know that he'd walked into the room.

Even if he didn't speak, Hazel could feel his presence. It

was as if every fibre of her being was yelling at her to turn and look at him. But, stubborn as she was, she'd refuse…until the need would feel almost like a palpable physical ache.

And then he'd speak, the low tones of his voice raking through her mind like the wind tossing up autumn leaves. Finally Hazel would hear the doors of the nursery swishing open and softly closing, and then she'd take a gasping breath, as though she needed hooking up to her own CPAP machine.

No wonder she felt she had no energy left.

Hazel shrugged out of her clothes and pulled on her crisp blue scrubs. Shapeless, but comforting in their own way. She knew who she was when she was wearing them—*Hazel Bridges, Registered Nurse.* She had a job to do and clear rules to follow.

Unlike in her love life, where everything was murky and uncertain.

Not that she *had* a love life, per se. After all, her fling with Garrett hardly counted, did it? They hadn't even been on a date.

Still, things couldn't continue the way they were. Hazel knew that. It had only been a week, and already she was running out of ways to avoid him. They were going to be working alongside one another for six whole months. If Hazel had to turn her back or dash to the storeroom every time she saw Garrett Buchanan's red hair appear around a door, or heard his voice from the other side of a room, their colleagues were going to start to notice… Or she was going to lose the plot. She already felt she was halfway there.

But what else could she do?

Just a few minutes in his company had Hazel's mind playing a highlights reel of their moments of passion together, until she could think of little else. And yet she knew they had no future together. They wanted such different things from life that to pretend otherwise would only end in heartache for both of them.

The only way this was going to work was if they both found a way to be sensible about it. To put what had happened between them aside and keep things strictly professional.

Hazel slammed her locker door with more force than strictly necessary.

Now all she had to do was figure out what exactly that would involve...and how to stop her body from reacting every time Garrett Buchanan walked into the room.

Garrett watched Hazel's back disappear through the canteen doors and sighed. The pre-packaged sandwich she'd been deliberating over sat unpaid-for on the counter, where she'd abandoned it the moment she'd spotted him joining the queue.

He'd known that she was avoiding him, of course. It would have been impossible for him not to notice, so dedicated was she to not spending more than a few minutes in his company at any time.

It was making it easier for him, in a way. At least with Hazel darting from the room every time he entered it Garrett didn't have to push away highly unprofessional thoughts whenever he caught a whiff of her shampoo, or the vague outline of her figure beneath the baggy scrubs they were all forced to wear in clinical areas.

But no matter how much he told himself it was for the best, he still found himself drawn to her like a moth to a flame. Or was he the flame? Garrett wasn't sure. He'd never been that great with words, but when he was around Hazel he suddenly found himself a poet. His mind was full of words he'd never spoken out loud and dancing with vivid imagery about the way Hazel looked or moved or the sound of her voice.

It was ridiculous. No, worse than that. It was dangerous.

He'd been honest with her up to now—maybe even brutally so. Letting her know in no uncertain terms that he wasn't *that guy*. That she shouldn't mistake him for someone on the cusp of settling down. Admittedly, he hadn't shared with her why that wouldn't be happening. Why it had never been—would never be—part of his plans. But still, he'd obviously made it clear enough as she'd been avoiding him ever since.

He should be relieved that she'd taken the hint...so why wasn't he?

Why did he get a sinking feeling in the pit of his stomach when Hazel refused to meet his eye? Or when he'd walk through one set of doors just in time to see her disappear through another, her scrubs swishing and her dark hair swaying as she scurried away?

Garrett didn't know. But one thing he did know was that things couldn't continue like this. Sure, it was a large unit, with cot space for thirty-four babies, but regardless, they still needed to work together as part of the team. Sooner or later they were going to have to sit down and talk about what had happened between them like grown-ups.

Garrett just hoped that when they did he'd finally have thought of something to say other than the one thing he knew he shouldn't…which was that all he really wanted was for it to happen all over again.

The beeping hadn't stopped all day, and Hazel knew she'd be hearing it in her dreams later—when she finally made it into bed, that was. Right now, even sleep itself seemed like a distant dream.

It was Tuesday evening and she was ten hours into a twelve-hour shift, during which they'd had three admissions onto NICU, including a set of twins, one of whom Hazel was now looking after. They hadn't been short-staffed at the start of the shift, but with three new babies added to the mix, and one of the nurses having gone home with a migraine, they were certainly overstretched now.

Hazel's own head felt as if it might split open. Intensive Care was a hive of activity, with bright lights and the incessant beeping, as the team tried to stabilise the second Wilson twin, who was struggling to maintain his oxygen levels on CPAP. Hazel knew the next step would be intubation and mechanical ventilation, and she also knew the implications that would have for him moving forward, and they all wanted to avoid that if possible.

She gingerly lifted Baby Boy Wilson from the incubator mattress, one hand cupping his tiny head, the other beneath the miniature nappy she'd put in place. Despite being the smallest available, it looked like a baggy pair of granny pants on him, and would have reached far up past his belly button if she hadn't tucked it down at the front to uncover the plastic clamp where his umbilical cord had been cut.

She turned him gently onto his front. Nursing babies prone almost always improved their oxygen saturations and she hoped this little boy would be no exception. She positioned him carefully, using the bedding nests to help him feel secure, and as though he hadn't left the cosiness of his mother's womb twelve weeks too soon. She was keen to get the overhead lights turned down as soon as possible, but first, she had to be certain he was going to maintain his airway with the CPAP.

'How's he doing?' Anna, one of the staff nurses, stood on the other side of the incubator, peering in at their newest patient. She'd been assigned to take care of his twin sister, who was behaving a great deal better, snoozing peacefully in the incubator next door, with oxygen saturation levels of ninety-seven percent.

Hazel looked dubiously at the monitor beside her. 'I'm not sure he got the memo about sibling rivalry,' she said, not taking her eyes from the screen, as though she could persuade the numbers to rise by sheer force of will. 'I think he's heading for intubation.'

Anna gave her a sympathetic look from over the top of the incubator. 'Boys are always more trouble than girls.'

'I'm not sure I agree.'

The voice belonged to Dr Garrett Buchanan, and Hazel whirled round to find him standing just beside her. His tone was teasing but his expression was serious, his sharp blue eyes focused on the numbers on the monitor behind her, and Hazel saw the concern creasing his brow.

Ordinarily she'd have come up with an excuse to disappear for a few minutes—a last-minute dash to the linen cupboard, or a vague mumbling about needing to check on something in HDU—but right now that wasn't an option. She had a poorly baby to care for, and he was only going to get more poorly still if they didn't act fast.

'Should I set up the intubation trolley?' Hazel asked.

To her surprise, Garrett shook his head.

'But his SaO2 levels…' she began.

'I know.' Garrett's tone was grave. 'I'll prescribe the drugs for intubation and get the trolley.'

Hazel caught the dart of Anna's eyebrows over the top of the incubator, but her friend said nothing. She didn't have to. She knew they were both thinking the same thing. New doctors on NICU typically behaved like a deer in headlights for the first week or two at least. Usually they had to be coaxed and cajoled, with the experienced nurses holding their hands—metaphorically speaking—while they found their feet. Occasionally they'd get a doctor who thought they knew everything, after working a long spell on the children's ward or in adult intensive care, who didn't seem to realise that neonates were neither children nor adults, but a whole separate specialty with rules of their own.

To have a doctor be as confident as Dr Garrett Buchanan, without coming across as cocky, was a refreshing change. Not to mention the fact that he was happy to set up his own trolley, saving Hazel from having to leave the baby's cot side to do it.

It seemed that while she'd been avoiding him Garrett had well and truly made himself at home in NICU. The thought made Hazel feel strangely off-kilter, but she had no time to dwell.

Pretty soon Garrett was back with the equipment and sterile packs, and Anna helpfully drew the screens around their corner of the room, to block the view of other parents visiting their babies. The intensive care unit was exactly that—*intense*. It still caught Hazel off guard sometimes, so she could only imagine what it must feel like as a visitor.

Garrett had no sooner put on his sterile gown than the screen slid to one side and Dr Lee, one of the unit consultants, stepped around it. She was shorter than Hazel, with wide, dark eyes and fine greying hair pulled tightly back from her face, which made her delicate features appear severe. She looked as though a strong wind might sweep her away, but Hazel knew from experience that anyone who underestimated her because of her size would sorely regret it. She had a fierce personality and an incredible reputation in the field of neonatology. As a newly qualified nurse, Hazel had been terrified of Dr Lee, but these days she had nothing but respect for her.

'Dr Buchanan?' Dr Lee spoke quietly, but there was a directness to her words. 'Care to fill me in?'

Hazel half expected Garrett to turn into a flustered bag of nerves, mumbling explanations and apologies. Instead, she listened as he calmly filled his consultant in on the baby's medical history and clinical signs, and the preliminary plan of care he'd devised. It was hard not to be impressed, much as Hazel tried.

Dr Lee waited a moment after he'd finished speaking, then asked, 'Are you confident intubating at twenty-eight weeks?'

'I would like to try,' he said.

Dr Lee's eyes never left his. 'I asked if you were confident.'

Garrett looked down at the tiny baby in the incubator between them and then back at his superior. Hazel thought she could see the flicker of doubt cross his face, but it was there and gone so quickly she wondered if she'd imagined it.

'Yes.'

'Very well.' Dr Lee nodded. 'I'll supervise.'

Hazel and Anna had already drawn up the prescribed sedatives and analgesia to make the procedure easier and more comfortable for the baby, and Garrett administered them via his IV.

Garrett's hands shook lightly as he lifted the laryngoscope, and when Hazel looked over the top of the incubator at him the sheer terror she saw in his eyes made her feel a rush of sympathy towards him. He might have settled in here, and be capable of making clinical decisions and setting up his own equipment, but there were some things that were daunting no matter how experienced you were—and intubating a tiny, premature baby had to be right up there.

'Dr Buchanan, would you like me to assist?' Hazel asked quietly.

His eyes flicked to hers, and the relief in his expression was obvious.

He gave her a grateful nod. 'Thank you.'

Intubations didn't happen every day, which made it difficult for many neonatal doctors—even experienced ones—to practise this essential life-saving skill. Hazel knew that Garrett would want to demonstrate that he was competent at intubation, but she also knew that he'd only get one chance at it. If, after sixty seconds, he hadn't successfully intubated Baby Boy Wilson, then as Garrett's senior Dr Lee would take over.

Hazel provided airway support, keeping the baby's head in a neutral position, with one eye on the monitor above the incubator that displayed his observations and the other on Garrett's hands as he gently inserted the laryngoscope blade over the baby's tongue.

His face was knitted into a tight frown of concentration and Hazel guessed he must be struggling to visualise the baby's vocal cords, which he'd need to pass the endotracheal tube through.

'Thirty seconds,' she said.

He gave the slightest nod and then reached for the endotracheal tube before slowly inserting it into the baby's airway.

Hazel focused her attention on the monitor to her right, her eyes zeroing in on the heart rate as it dipped ever so slightly.

She winced. 'Heart rate one-ten.'

Garrett's Adam's apple bobbed as he swallowed hard, but his hands were steady now, Hazel noticed, and his brow smooth.

'One zero five,' Hazel said quietly.

'It's in,' Garrett said.

They both looked to the monitor. Baby Wilson's heart rate was recovering nicely. From the corner of her eye Hazel saw Garrett's shoulders sag with relief, and she felt her own lowering in unison.

Hazel helped secure the endotracheal tube while Garrett confirmed its position.

It was a relief for everyone when they were able to step back and watch the steady rise and fall of the baby's chest, courtesy of the ventilator beside his incubator.

Dr Lee turned to Hazel. 'Have the parents been informed?'

'No, but I'll tell them now.'

Leaving Baby Boy Wilson under the watchful eye of the

two doctors, Hazel made her way to the nursing station and put a call through to Delivery Suite. She gave up on the tenth ring. Clearly Mandy was on her tea break or had gone to the bathroom. Both things that Hazel hadn't had the luxury of since that morning.

'No answer on DS,' she reported back to Garrett and Dr Lee in the ICU. 'Are you okay here if I nip over to let them know?'

'Of course. Not a problem,' Dr Lee said. 'Dr Buchanan can document the intubation and I'll draw up a plan of care.'

Hazel turned to leave, but halted when she felt the brush of a hand on her bare arm. When she looked up, she found Garrett standing right beside her.

'Thank you,' he said. 'I couldn't have done that without you.'

Hazel tried to hide her surprise. 'Oh. Don't mention it.'

Garrett frowned, and she sensed that there was more he wanted to say, but Hazel wasn't sure she was ready to hear it—especially not here and now.

She forced a smile. 'All part of the job.'

Hazel swept from the ICU room before Garrett could find the words he was looking for.

Out in the corridor, she told herself it was nothing. That he'd only been expressing his gratitude, the way any colleague would. But it hadn't felt that way, and her arm still tingled where he'd laid his hand against her bare skin.

She shook her head, trying to banish thoughts of Garrett and focus on what needed to be done next.

Over on Delivery Suite, she found the reception desk still abandoned. In one of the rooms an emergency buzzer was sounding, and the usual unearthly moans echoed down the empty corridors. Clearly everyone over here had their hands full.

Hazel stepped into the staff room where discarded cups of tea stood on the table, quickly growing cold. She surveyed the whiteboard that took up the majority of one wall, scanning the list of names for the one she needed.

Ali Wilson. Room 11.

Hazel made her way towards the room, preparing herself

for the difficult conversation ahead. The parents would be full of anxiety and questions, and it was her job to reassure and answer them as best as she could.

She found the doors to Room Eleven flung wide open and the bed gone, leaving a gaping space in the centre of the room. By the window, a man in mismatched scrubs and too-small theatre clogs shuffled backwards and forwards, his dark hair partially obscured by a theatre cap.

At Hazel's appearance in the doorway, he stood stock-still. 'Is she okay?'

Hazel faltered, her ready-prepared spiel dying on her lips. 'Who?'

'My wife,' the man answered. 'They took her to Theatre for an emergency C-section…they told me to wait here…but then someone came and said they'd had to do a general anaesthetic so I couldn't go in with her after all…'

Hazel's heart sank. The poor guy was a wreck—that was clear enough. He also had no idea that he was the father of two children, one of whom was now on a ventilator.

'My name is Hazel Bridges,' she said. 'I'm one of the senior nurses on the neonatal unit. I'm looking after your son.'

Tears sprang from the man's eyes instantly. 'I have a son?'

Hazel nodded, swallowing the lump forming in her throat. 'Why don't you take a seat and I'll fill you in on what's happening with both your babies? And then we can find out how your wife is doing. She's probably coming round in Recovery as we speak.'

The man nodded gratefully and fell into the armchair beneath the window. Hazel pushed her emotions to one side and switched back into nurse mode. She had a job to do, and she couldn't do it with tears threatening at the backs of her eyes.

Hazel stripped off her scrubs and dropped them into the laundry bin. It had been a long shift, the hardest she'd worked in a good while, and she felt it in every fibre of her being. Her feet throbbed, her head ached, her stomach was empty and her heart was heavy.

She pulled on her black trousers and pale pink blouse, and

swapped her sensible flat work shoes for the pair of equally sensible flat shoes she wore outside of work.

Who had she been trying to kid?

Her moment of madness with Garrett on her thirtieth hadn't changed a thing. She was still the same old Hazel.

Well and truly stuck.

Sure, she had the job of her dreams, but after a shift like the one she'd just had that felt like scant comfort.

Was this all there was? All there'd ever be for her?

Hazel considered her reflection in the changing room mirror. There were violet smudges below her green eyes. The lick of mascara she'd put on fourteen hours ago had long since worn off, leaving flecks of black below her lash line as the only evidence it had ever existed. Her straight black hair hung flat and limp around her face, and Hazel pushed it back in irritation.

What did it matter anyway?

She'd be going home alone. There was no one to impress… no one waiting up to greet her. The only comfort she'd get tonight would come from a long soak in the bath, a small glass of wine and maybe six hours' sleep—if she was lucky—before coming back tomorrow to do it all again.

With a sigh, she shrugged on her jacket and lifted her bag from its hook. Another day done, and at the very least she could say she'd done her best.

Hazel plodded wearily down the unit corridor towards the double doors and the brightly lit corridor beyond.

On the other side of the doors, leaning against the wall beside the lifts, stood Dr Garrett Buchanan. His copper hair was rumpled and his face was pale under the harsh strip lighting. He was wearing black jeans, and a blue T-shirt the same shade as his eyes. He was probably every bit as tired as she was, Hazel thought. But when he saw her step through the doors and out into the corridor he broke into a lopsided grin that Hazel felt in her chest.

Garrett prised himself away from the wall and stepped towards her. 'I was beginning to think there was some secret exit I didn't know about,' he joked.

Hazel frowned. 'What do you mean?'

'Well, I've been waiting here for you to finish.'

'You have? But…why?'

Garrett rubbed the flat of his palm against the back of his neck. 'I was going to ask if you'd like to join me for a drink?'

'Now?' Hazel couldn't keep the disbelief from her voice.

'Yes. I mean unless you already have plans—which is fine, I just thought maybe we could celebrate…'

'Celebrate what?'

Garrett shrugged, his cheeks reddening under the harsh strip lighting. 'My first successful intubation on a preterm baby. I meant what I said. I really couldn't have done it without you.'

Hazel swallowed hard.

She shouldn't go.

They were supposed to be keeping things strictly professional.

But he'd waited for her, and she was in no hurry to get back to her empty flat. Besides, it was impossible to say no when he was dazzling her with that smile of his, full of hope and promise.

And, really, what harm could one drink do?

'Okay, sure.'

CHAPTER FIVE

THE SUN WAS just creeping below the horizon when Hazel and Garrett stepped out through the main hospital doors and into the summer evening.

'Taxi?' Garrett indicated the rank, where a couple of taxi cabs sat in waiting, engines idling. 'Or would you prefer to walk?'

Hazel looked at him. 'Would you mind? I could use the fresh air after being cooped up all day.'

'Sure.' Garrett smiled. 'I know what you mean.'

They fell into an easy stride together, putting the imposing red-brick hospital at their backs and the York skyline spread out before them.

'You don't drive, then?' Hazel asked.

'Oh, I do—but there's no need. I'm in staff digs.' He gestured to the high-rise building on the far side of the car park.

Hazel tried to hide her surprise. Whenever she'd imagined Garrett outside of work he'd been rambling through the rooms of an old terraced house—the kind with high ceilings to accommodate his lofty height and big bay windows with a view of the river.

She'd never for one moment imagined him in the utilitarian staff accommodation block, sandwiched between the bypass and the hospital car park.

She blinked a few times at the block of flats before turning back to him. 'Is that a temporary thing, while you find somewhere else?'

Garrett shrugged. 'To be honest, there's not much point looking if I'll be moving again in six months.'

'Right. Of course. I guess not.'

They lapsed into silence as Hazel digested this new information. It made sense, of course. Like he said, why waste time house-hunting only to have to do it all again in six months? But still, his nomadic existence made her feel uneasy—as though he might disappear at any minute, leaving no trace of himself behind.

'So…where were you working before?' Hazel forced herself to ask.

'London. And before that Nottingham. Before that Sheffield, and before that Glasgow…'

'Wow. I can't imagine moving around so often,' Hazel said.

Garrett shrugged. 'You get used to it. I've been doing it so long I can't imagine not.'

Hazel nodded, pretending to understand though she didn't really. She'd always known that doctors moved around a lot, of course, but she'd never really dwelled on what that might mean for their personal lives…until now.

'How about you?' he asked. 'Have you always lived in York?'

'I came here to do my nurse training and I loved it so much I stayed.'

'And your family? Do they live nearby?'

'Not far. My parents are about an hour's drive away. They live in a little village in the same house I was born in.'

'Sounds idyllic,' Garrett said.

'Oh, I don't know about that.' Hazel laughed. 'It's a nice place to visit, but it wasn't an easy place to grow up. There were only about six kids in the whole village and not an awful lot for us to do.'

'You're an only child?'

Hazel nodded.

'We have that much in common, at least.'

Hazel frowned at his disclaimer.

How many things didn't they have in common? And had he been counting?

But when she looked up, Garrett was smiling.

'So, where are we going for this drink?'

Hazel thought for a moment. 'I know just the place.'

* * *

The pub was quaint. The kind of quaint that meant Garrett had to stoop to fit through the door and duck under an archway on his way to the bar to avoid hitting his head.

Hazel went to get a table by the window and Garrett ordered the drinks. There was still a voice in the back of his head telling him that this was a very bad idea, but the pub chatter drowned it out nicely.

It was an after-work drink with a colleague, he told himself.

They both had tough jobs and deserved to celebrate small wins where they found them.

Besides, when he glanced over at Hazel as she shrugged her way out of her jacket and draped it over the back of her chair, Garrett felt something like butterflies in his stomach for the first time in a long time.

Or maybe it was just hunger pangs. After all, he had been so busy he'd skipped lunch.

Hazel glanced across and smiled as she caught his eye. Garrett shot a nervous smile in her direction, unsure why he suddenly felt so awkward standing there at the bar.

He looked away.

Why had he invited her out for a drink, anyway?

But he already knew the answer to that. He'd asked her because he couldn't not. Because without her support there was no way he'd have been able to complete that intubation successfully. Because it had only been the knowledge that she was right there beside him that had given him the confidence to step up. And because he wanted her to know that. He wanted to show his appreciation.

Plus, it had been a rough day and he wanted to feel better…and he knew that being around her would make him feel better…

The trouble was, as good as those reasons were, he had some even greater reasons why he should be giving Hazel a wide berth and keeping things professional. He just found it hard to remember that when he was near her.

Besides, it was just a drink. What harm could one drink do?

Garrett carried the glasses over and set them down on the table—a pint of ale for him and a small white wine for her.

'Thanks,' Hazel said. 'So, what do you think of the place?'

Garrett looked around. 'I like it. It's cosy. A bit short on headroom, maybe.'

Hazel laughed. 'That's not a problem for some of us.'

'No, I suppose not.'

'I'm glad you like it. It's one of my favourite pubs.'

'You come here often, then?'

Garrett winced as the words left his mouth, but Hazel only laughed.

'Don't worry, I'll pretend you didn't ask that.'

There was a brief moment when their eyes locked as they remembered that first terrible chat-up line of his at the party. Neither one of them seemed to be breathing…but then someone dropped a glass somewhere in the pub, prompting a collective cheer, and Hazel's gaze slid away, her cheeks pink.

'Not often, no. I'm a bit of a homebody on my days off. But when I do go out for a drink, it's places like this that I like best.'

'I can see why. It suits you,' Garrett said.

He'd meant it as a compliment, but when he looked again at the faded wallpaper, the candles in wine bottles and the rustic furniture, he worried that Hazel might not see it that way. He'd only meant that it came across as warm and genuine—like her.

Hazel smiled. 'Thanks… I think. I mean, the place is over four hundred years old, and they say it's haunted. But then, so is half of the city, if all the tales are to be believed.'

'Is that right?' Garrett raised an eyebrow.

He wasn't one for fairy tales or ghost stories. His childhood had been too visceral to leave much room for imagination. But that didn't mean he didn't believe a place could be haunted. Or a person, for that matter.

'Sure. There are ghost walks around here pretty much every night of the week. You should tag along sometime.'

'Maybe…' Garrett said, trying not to wince at how vague and unconvincing he sounded, even to himself.

Hazel sipped her wine. 'It must make it hard for you to get to know a place when you know you're going to be leaving soon.'

It was a statement, not a question, but Garrett answered anyway. 'I suppose so.'

'And I imagine it's the same for people and relationships…?' Hazel trailed off, but Garrett knew that definitely was a question.

'Of course.' He shrugged. 'It's the same for everyone in this job.'

'But not when you get a consultant post,' Hazel pointed out.

That old familiar knot tightened in Garrett's stomach. 'No,' he conceded.

'You can't be far off now, surely?'

He wasn't. If everything went to plan, this registrar position should be his final stepping stone. But already things weren't going to plan. His plan hadn't included any petite neonatal nurses with glossy black hair and sparkling green eyes, for one thing. Eyes that were assessing him now over the rim of a wine glass as she waited to hear what he had to say about his future.

'That all depends, I suppose.' Garrett looked away, studying the dregs in his pint glass intently.

'Do you know where you want to end up?' Hazel pressed.

Garrett looked up at her. Words bubbled inside him, but he swallowed them down forcibly. 'Neonatology is my passion,' he said. 'But beyond that I haven't given it much thought.'

It was the truth. Or rather, part of it. He wanted a career in neonates, yes. And becoming a consultant had always been the plan. But whenever he tried to imagine what that might look like…where he might be, the people around him, the idea of staying put somewhere long term…the whole image started to blur like a painting left out in the rain.

It was a future he couldn't imagine because it was something he'd never experienced. It was foreign…alien…not for the likes of him. But there was no way he could explain all that to Hazel, with her uncomplicated love for her career and her roots firmly planted beneath her. She didn't wake in the night, heart pounding when she thought about the future—he was sure of it. And he was sure she didn't deserve the burden of hearing about his baggage, either.

'You could do worse than Riverside,' Hazel said. 'It's a good team and a steady workload. Plenty to experience and lots of ways to make a difference.'

'I believe you,' Garrett said. 'It's just not something I've really thought about yet. I find it best to take these things one step at a time.'

Hazel shrugged easily and leant back in her chair. 'Whatever works for you,' she said. 'I'm a planner. The idea of not knowing what I'll be doing beyond the next six months gives me the heebie-jeebies.'

That's where we differ, Garrett thought. *And not just there, either.*

Truth be told, they were like chalk and cheese. Yet another reason to keep things strictly professional.

He drained his pint, ready to make his excuses and leave. It was only meant to be one drink, after all...

'I don't suppose you fancy ordering something to eat?' Hazel said suddenly. 'I'm absolutely starving.'

On that, at least, Garrett could agree.

He grinned in spite of himself. 'All right. What do you recommend?'

They got their order in just before the kitchen closed, and when the food came it was piping hot and delicious. Fish in a crispy, bubbly batter with a heap of golden chunky chips, beside a pot of fresh minted peas.

Hazel's mouth watered at the sight, and Garrett seemed as delighted as she was, splashing vinegar liberally across his plate and tucking in without apology. After a fourteen-hour shift, there was no point in either of them feigning decorum.

They talked some more in between mouthfuls, about work and York. The conversation jumped around quite naturally, but Hazel noticed a reticence to Garrett's tone whenever the topic switched to the future. He seemed happy enough to talk about the here and now, but beyond that was definitely unwelcome territory.

What was that all about? Hazel wondered. *Did he simply not want to jinx himself, talking about making consultant as if it was a done deal? Or was there something else underlying his hesitation?*

She decided not to dwell or to press. At the end of the day, they hardly knew each other, and Hazel had her own sore subjects that she would have shied away from had they come up.

The bell for last orders surprised them both.

'Is it really that time already?' Garrett's eyes widened.

'Time flies.' Hazel reached for her jacket. 'I should get home. I'm back in at seven-thirty tomorrow.'

'Eight for me,' Garrett said.

'Lucky thing.'

Outside, the night was still warm, and alive with chatter as people poured out of the pubs onto the cobbled pavements.

'Taxi?' Garrett asked.

'Oh, you go and grab one while you can.' Hazel gestured. 'I'm not far from here. I can walk.'

Garrett frowned. 'Then at least let me walk you home?'

Hazel was about to protest, but realised she couldn't think of a reason why he shouldn't. He was a concerned colleague, being polite. There was no point reading any more into it than that.

She shrugged. 'If you insist.'

They walked side by side, with a polite distance between them, but the light evening breeze carried Garrett's scent, and despite the fact he'd probably not showered since that morning, and had just sat in a pub for two hours, Hazel found herself inhaling deeply.

Pheromones, she told herself.

Mother Nature was a crafty old thing.

But no matter how good Garrett smelled, Hazel was determined to keep her distance.

The narrow streets widened as they moved out of the city centre and they were soon beside the river, the dark water rippling gently in the moonlight.

'You live on a boat?' Garrett teased.

'Ha! Not quite,' Hazel said. She gestured to a row of Georgian terraced houses up ahead. They would once have been grand family homes, but had long since been divided up into tiny flats, one of which Hazel had been renting for the past year. 'I'm on the first floor, there in the middle.' She pointed. 'My bedroom window looks out over the water.'

'Sounds peaceful,' Garrett remarked.

'Aside from the ducks, quacking at all hours.'

Garrett laughed. 'Hooligans, the lot of 'em.'

They came to a standstill at the front gate. It wasn't much of a garden—just a yard with a few pot plants in need of watering—and there was a cherry-red front door with three brass letter boxes and an intercom to one side.

'Well, thanks for the drink…'

Hazel felt suddenly awkward, like she'd grown extra limbs and she wasn't sure what to do with them. She clasped her hands in front of her, and then thought better of it and let them dangle at her sides.

'And for walking me home,' she added.

'Don't mention it.' Garrett said. 'So this is your place?'

He glanced over her shoulder and Hazel followed his line of sight, her eyes snagging on the summer weeds peeking through the cracks on the front path and the chipped paint on the windowsill of her downstairs neighbour, Mrs Johnson.

'For now,' she said—and then wondered what on earth she'd meant by that.

She had no plans to move…did she?

When she turned back, she found Garrett watching her.

'I like it,' he said, but his eyes never left hers and Hazel was no longer sure that he was talking about the flat.

Her tongue darted nervously across her bottom lip. 'Thanks.'

Garrett took a small half-step forward. He was so close now that Hazel could make out the flecks of navy in his sky-blue eyes and see the pulse bounding in his throat.

Was he…going to kiss her?

Hazel wasn't sure how she felt about that. Her brain told her that it was a terrible idea, but her body seemed to have other feelings entirely. Already she was tipping her weight, rocking forward onto the balls of her feet inside her ballet pumps, closing the distance between them…

Garrett swallowed, and she watched his Adam's apple bob as he leaned towards her.

Hazel's eyelids fluttered.

'Goodnight, Hazel,' Garrett croaked.

She opened her eyes in time to see him walking away.

Hazel watched Garrett until she could no longer make out his silhouette in the shadows of the trees lining the river. Then she turned and walked up the garden path in a daze.

She fumbled with her keys, eventually slipping the right one into the lock, and stepped out of the warm night into the cool, dark hallway. She paused there a moment, in an attempt to gather her thoughts.

There could be no future for her with Garrett Buchanan. He'd told her as much himself. But even as she crept up the stairs to her flat, mentally listing all the reasons it could never work between them, Hazel's stomach continued to somersault as she imagined what might have happened if he'd kissed her.

CHAPTER SIX

HAZEL WOKE UP feeling a little queasy.

Was it the food?

But she'd eaten at The Red Lion many times, and the food last night had been so hot and fresh. On the other hand, she couldn't believe that two small glasses of wine had given her a hangover...

Maybe she was coming down with something.

She'd ask Garrett today how he was feeling.

Hazel's stomach flipped again—only this time it was for an altogether different reason...one she knew only too well.

She'd been so sure that Garrett was about to kiss her... Had she misread the signs or had he changed his mind at the last minute?

Hazel knew it shouldn't matter either way. That she should just be grateful he hadn't complicated things between them further. But she couldn't shake the nagging disappointment she felt whenever she remembered the way the night had ended.

She threw back the covers with a groan.

She was being ridiculous.

She had a job to do, and she couldn't let some handsome red-haired doctor with a commitment phobia distract from that. He'd be gone in six months anyway, onto the next city and the next woman who fell into his arms, no doubt. Until then, Hazel needed to focus on what mattered. The only thing she seemed to have any success with.

Her career.

* * *

'You're shift co-ordinator today, Hazel.' Bree, the deputy ward manager, handed Hazel a handover sheet and a crash bleep the minute she saw Hazel step out of the ward kitchen, coffee in hand.

Bree looked like a woman who desperately needed her bed.

'Rough night?' Hazel clipped the pager to the pocket of her scrub top and started scanning the sheet.

'You could say that...' Bree drawled. 'Is everyone else here?'

Hazel nodded. 'All waiting in the staff room. Oh, and there's a new student nurse too—Jessica. Seems no one knew she was starting today. She looks like a rabbit caught in headlights.'

'Lord help her,' Bree said. 'I hope this isn't her first placement?'

'No, she said she's done a few weeks down on Starling, and a placement out in the community.'

Starling was the general children's ward, which meant the student would know the basics at the very least.

'Let's just hope we don't put her off,' Bree muttered as they made their way to the staff room for handover. 'I've never known it so busy. And we're short, as usual. They promised me an agency nurse overnight, but of course one never materialised.'

Hazel clutched her coffee cup a little tighter. Her shift hadn't even officially started yet, and already she felt apprehensive about what lay ahead. Normally a busy shift or an understaffed one didn't faze her, but she wasn't firing on all cylinders today as it was. She'd felt queasy for the entire bus journey into work, and despite the cup of very strong coffee her eyelids still felt heavy. Not ideal if Bree's gloomy outlook about the day was to be believed.

They reached the staff room door. Hazel heard the chatter and clatter of mugs beyond, and was grateful that no matter what the shift held she'd have her team around her.

Bree pushed open the door and the voices died down. Hazel slid into a chair by the door, still feeling a little woozy, and tried to concentrate on the handover sheet in her hand.

She had a feeling it was going to be a long day.

* * *

Hazel slipped her feet from her work shoes with a sigh of relief.
She'd made it.

Bree had been right about the shift. It had been one of the busiest Hazel had worked in a long time. Between caring for two babies in High Dependency, teaching the new student, Jessica, and co-ordinating the shift, Hazel had barely stopped.

She'd been so busy she'd barely had a chance to look up, but on the few occasions she had Garrett had been looking her way.

Just a coincidence, she told herself. But it had been nice to work alongside him today, rather than feel she had to dart out of the way whenever he came near. Maybe things would work out after all, and they could keep things professional and friendly...

Hazel got to her feet, turning to her locker just as the changing room door opened behind her.

She knew it was him even before she looked around. The tiny hairs on the back of her neck rose and she swallowed hard.

'Hey.'

Hazel turned to where Garrett was standing, still half in, half out of the doorway.

'Hey, yourself,' she replied, working hard to keep her tone and expression casual.

'You done for the day?'

She nodded. 'You?'

Garrett pulled a face. 'I'll be another couple of hours at least.' He stepped into the changing room fully, letting the door fall closed behind him. 'Listen, Hazel. About last night...'

Hazel's pulse leapt. What was he about to say? That it couldn't happen again? That it hadn't meant anything? She knew all that, anyway. Besides, it had only been a drink...it wasn't as if anything had happened.

Garrett sat down on one of the benches in the centre of the room, then seemed to think better of it and got to his feet.

Hazel blinked up at him. He seemed even taller now she was barefoot.

'I just wanted you to know… Well…' Garrett trailed off, rubbing one hand across the back of his neck. 'The thing is…'

Hazel waited for him to go on, trying not to let her impatience show.

'I had a good time.'

Hazel stared at him.

Was that it?

'Yeah…me too,' she said warily.

Garrett took a step forward, closing the distance between them to barely anything.

'But there's something I should have done.'

Without warning, his lips were on hers, and Hazel's mind emptied as Garrett Buchanan kissed her.

Hazel kissed him back, relishing the feel of Garrett's mouth moving against hers. She'd forgotten what a good kisser he was, and just how right it felt to be close to him like this.

She lifted her hands, resting them lightly against his shoulders, but just as the kiss was deepening, and the space between their bodies reduced to zero, Garrett's pager sounded, sending the two of them flying apart.

Garrett looked down at his pager and swore softly.

'Sorry, I have to—'

'I know,' Hazel said softly. 'It's okay. Go.'

Garrett hesitated half a second, his warring emotions playing out across his face, and then he rushed from the changing room, leaving Hazel staring after him, her heart pounding and her lips still tingling from his kiss.

CHAPTER SEVEN

HAZEL PAUSED AT the main doors of the neonatal unit.

*Had that really just happened? Had she kissed Garrett...
again?*

She shook her head and stepped out into the corridor. She
needed a lie-down—and time to process things. Fortunately,
tomorrow was her day off, so she'd get both.

Her stomach rolled and she vowed to book an appointment with her GP if she still felt this rough in the morning.
Working in a busy hospital, she was used to picking up the
odd virus now and again, but she'd never had anything quite
like this before.

Hazel's mind was spinning, both metaphorically and literally, and she paused, pressing her hand to the cool wall of the
corridor, swaying a little on her feet.

'Hazel?'

Hazel opened her eyes to find Libby standing in front of
her. Her friend's face was creased with concern.

'What's wrong?'

'Nothing,' Hazel lied, but she knew even as she said it that
it wouldn't wash with her best friend.

As predicted, Libby folded her arms across her chest. 'Nothing? Hazel, you look dreadful...'

'Thanks.' Hazel rolled her eyes and immediately wished
she hadn't, as it made her feel dizzier than ever.

'Rough shift?' Libby prompted.

'You could say that.'

Though it still didn't explain why she felt so terrible.

'Come on—you're coming with me...' Libby hooked her arm around Hazel's.

'No, honestly, it's fine, Lib. I'm heading home now, anyway. I'll call my GP tomorrow...'

Libby snorted. 'They'll only tell you it's a virus. That is if you can even get an appointment.'

Libby was probably right. Community services were even more stretched than hospital services, if that was possible. Still, she hated to be fussed over.

'Really, I'm fine—'

'Well, you don't look fine,' Libby said. 'Come on through to Delivery Suite and I'll run some tests.'

'No, no, no.' Hazel waved a hand. 'There's no need.'

'Hazel, you look *green*.'

Hazel relented. 'Honestly? I feel it.'

Libby led her through the double doors and along the Delivery Suite corridor to one of the waiting rooms that was currently empty.

'I'll grab a sphyg,' she said. 'And in the meantime, you fill this.' She plonked an empty urine specimen container on the table beside Hazel. 'I trust you know where the bathroom is?' She winked.

'But I don't need—'

Libby held up a hand to stop her. 'I'll be the judge of what you need, thank you very much. You may be the expert on babies, but half of my patients are grown women, and urine samples are the bread and butter of this job. So just skip along to the toilet and meet me back here in five minutes.'

Hazel thought better of arguing. Besides, she did need the bathroom—she always did by the end of a shift, but she'd been in such a daze after what had happened with Garrett her whole routine had been well and truly thrown off.

Ten minutes later, Hazel had a blood pressure cuff around one arm and an adult-sized oxygen saturation probe on her finger.

'Your blood pressure is a little on the low side,' Libby said. 'But not dangerously so. I take it you haven't had much to drink today?'

'When do we ever get the chance?' Hazel shrugged.

'Everything else seems normal…even your temperature.' Libby unhooked Hazel from the monitor. 'I'll take that sample off you now and do a quick dipstick in the clinic…see if anything comes up. Maybe you've got a UTI brewing.'

'I've probably just eaten something dodgy,' Hazel said. 'It's really not worth all this bother.'

But Libby was already halfway out through the door.

Hazel sighed and slumped back in the vinyl-upholstered chair. As uncomfortable as it was, she felt as if she could fall asleep right there and then. Thankfully, Libby reappeared before she could accidentally doze off.

Hazel struggled to her feet as her friend came through the door.

'See? I told you nothing would come up,' she told her. 'Thanks for checking anyway, though.'

Libby didn't say anything. She was standing stock-still in the doorway, with a strange expression on her face.

Hazel frowned. 'Lib? What is it? Have I got a UTI?'

Libby shook her head. 'I think you'd better see this…'

Hazel's heart leapt into her throat. Those were not words you wanted to hear from a healthcare professional. Her pulse raced as she followed Libby into the midwives' clinic room, and she was glad that no one was taking her observations now. Based on the way Hazel's heart was galloping in her chest, she felt sure they'd probably be calling the crash team.

'It's just routine,' Libby was saying. 'I went onto autopilot. And then, when I realised what I was doing, I thought, *Oh, what the hell…* I figured we'd have a laugh when I told you that you weren't… But it turns out…you are!'

'What are you talking about?' Hazel asked.

But as she neared the urine specimen container, set neatly on the side alongside two testing strips, understanding quickly began to dawn on her.

One strip to test her urine for blood, glucose, ketones…all the usual suspects.

The other strip to test for a very specific suspect. The kind of suspect that Libby dealt with day in, day out.

Pregnancy.

Hazel was hardly breathing as she approached the testing strip, but even from a foot away she knew the result. She could see the two pink lines as clear as day.

'Libby is this a joke? Because…'

But Hazel couldn't finish, and from Libby's expression, and the vehement shake of her head, she knew this wasn't the kind of prank her friend would pull.

Hazel picked up the pregnancy test with shaking hands and tilted it towards the light, as though that might change the result somehow. But of course it didn't. Nothing would.

Because Hazel was pregnant.

And when it came to the father, there was only one possibility.

Dr Garrett Buchanan.

'You have to tell him.'

Hazel blinked a few more times, convinced the line would disappear while her eyelids were closed. Then she looked up at Libby, dazedly.

'Who?'

'The father, of course!' Libby said. 'From your reaction, I'm guessing it wasn't planned?'

Hazel shook her head. This had never been part of any plan. But Libby was right, of course, Hazel would need to tell Garrett. Regardless of the circumstances, she was pregnant—and it was his baby too. She felt a stab of fear, remembering their conversation about parenthood. He couldn't have made it any clearer if he'd tried that this wouldn't be welcome news, but she'd still have to tell him all the same.

'It's the new doctor, isn't it?'

Hazel felt her eyes widening. She gaped at her friend. 'How did you…?'

Libby shrugged. 'The chemistry between you two is obvious.'

Hazel hid her face in her hands and peeked out at her friend from between her fingers. 'Do you think everyone knows?'

'A few people might suspect, but not everyone's as observant as me.' Libby winked. 'So how long have you been together? And why didn't you tell me?'

She didn't think now was the time to tell Libby that this baby had been conceived in her spare room.

Oh, God, a baby!

The truth hit Hazel all over again.

She dropped her hands from her face. 'Well…we're not exactly *together*, as such.' Hazel winced and her cheeks flamed. 'I mean, we're not officially a couple…'

Libby held her hands aloft in surrender. 'Hey, you'll get no judgement from me. I'm a midwife, remember? There's no place for it in this job—and trust me, I've seen and heard it all. But he seems like a nice guy. How do you think he'll react to this?'

'Honestly?' Hazel shook her head. 'Not very well.'

Libby touched a hand to Hazel's arm. 'You know I'm always here if you need to chat…or talk through your options.'

Hazel felt a wrench in her gut at the hidden meaning behind Libby's words, but she knew her friend meant well.

After all, hadn't she just basically told her she wasn't with the baby's father and that he wouldn't be happy to learn she was pregnant?

No wonder Libby was reminding her that she didn't have to go through with the pregnancy. But Hazel knew herself well enough to be sure that wasn't an option she could consider. Not after wanting this for so long… Though never in her wildest imaginings would it happen under these circumstances.

But it had.

Somehow, despite the fact they'd used protection on that balmy summer evening, Garrett and Hazel had made a baby together. And now she would have to tell him that their one night of passion would have consequences for both of them…forever.

CHAPTER EIGHT

THE RIVER WAS STILL, and even the ducks were quiet this morning. Hazel scattered a handful of breadcrumbs across the surface of the water and the ducks began paddling over.

After her shock discovery, Hazel was grateful for a day off from work to get her head together. She couldn't have imagined facing Garrett this morning, with all her surprise, anguish and uncertainty written across her face. Instead, she'd had a long lie-in and woken up feeling marginally less queasy.

That had to be a good sign, she decided.

Or was it a bad sign?

For all her experience of babies and birth, Hazel had really no clue about early pregnancy.

She smiled at an elderly couple walking in the opposite direction beside the river and they said good morning. She saw them along here often, always together, always with one hand in each other's and the other on their walking sticks.

The kind of love that lasts a lifetime.

It was something Hazel had hoped to find, but was looking increasingly unlikely. Why did she keep picking the wrong men? Men who were afraid to commit…who didn't want to be tied down…who didn't want the same things as her?

She'd downloaded a tracker onto her phone last night and entered the relevant dates, cursing herself that she hadn't noticed her missing period sooner. But she'd never been one of those women who could set her watch by her cycle. Her period tended to turn up when it wanted to, and then Hazel would rifle through her bag for supplies, dutifully note it in her diary and assume another would follow in around a month or so. And it always had...until now.

The tracker told her she was already six weeks pregnant, and that her baby was the size of a baked bean. Hazel tried to imagine it, but she couldn't quite believe any of it was real.

For so long she'd wanted to be a mum—to experience the highs and lows that she'd seen played out in front of her for years.

She'd planned to start trying as soon as she got her senior nursing post, but then her ex had dropped his bombshell, packing his bags and moving out—and halfway across the world—just a few weeks later, leaving Hazel reeling.

An angry quack from one of the ducks brought Hazel back to the present day, and she absent-mindedly scattered the remaining bread across the water and watched the flurry of activity that followed.

And now here she was, not a year later—pregnant! The thing she'd wanted for so long was finally happening. But in all the wrong circumstances. She was carrying the baby of a man she hardly knew, and what she did know told her that he wouldn't be overjoyed to learn of his impending fatherhood, or keen to be involved once the baby arrived.

It was a tale as old as time, and a situation she'd watched unfold from the sidelines many times throughout her career in neonates but not one she'd ever for one minute imagined herself in. But then she supposed probably no one did...until it happened to them.

One thing Hazel knew for certain was that she would be keeping her baby, regardless of what Garrett Buchanan might say. She would tell him tomorrow, but no matter what his reaction was she was prepared to do this alone if she had to.

She just hoped it wouldn't come to that.

Hazel had been bracing herself for another wild shift, but when she walked onto the neonatal unit all was calm—or at least it appeared to be.

She found Ciara in the break room, eating her packed

lunch and flipping through one of the magazines that had been stacked on the table.

'How is it?' Hazel asked.

Ciara looked up. 'Better than yesterday. Look—I'm even eating my lunch at lunchtime!'

'Now that *is* a miracle,' Hazel agreed.

She flicked the kettle on, then thought better of it. Hot drinks tasted weird, and she could no longer go on blaming the milk. Not now that she knew the truth.

I'm pregnant.

The words were still pinballing around her skull, and she was afraid she might accidentally blurt them out at any minute.

'Hi…'

Jessica peered around the door tentatively and Hazel felt a rush of relief. She was glad to see that they hadn't put the poor girl off.

'Jessica! Good to see you back!'

After she'd polished off her sandwich, Ciara relayed the shift's handover to Hazel, Jessica and the rest of the afternoon staff.

Hazel had been allocated three babies in the Special Care nursery, which would make a nice change of pace after the intensity of her last few shifts. Not that the nursery was always the easiest room to work in. There was a lot of parentcraft involved and, unlike the very premature and sick babies in the Intensive Care and High Dependency rooms, the babies in the nursery had learnt how to demand attention—and they weren't shy about letting the nurses know when they weren't happy.

Hazel might not have as many lines to worry about, or medications to administer, but she was sure that her three little ones would keep her busy for the next eight hours and she was grateful to have Jessica's help.

Having a student to teach would help keep her mind occupied too—and far away from the conversation she'd need to have with Garrett later.

Hazel began her routine checks of the nursery safety equipment and crash trolley, running through the procedure with Jessica.

She'd deal with that when she came to it.

For now, she needed to push her own worries to the back of her mind and concentrate on her job.

There she was.

When Garrett hadn't seen Hazel in either ICU or HDU he'd panicked, thinking maybe she was avoiding him after their kiss...or, worse, that she was sick. He remembered that she hadn't seemed quite herself last time they'd worked together.

But when he'd stepped into the Special Care nursery he'd spotted her right away. She looked beautiful, as always. A little paler than usual, maybe, but her hair and eyes were shining.

How did she make standard-issue hospital scrubs look so good?

She had a baby in her arms and she was swaying to and fro as she talked to one of the staff nurses. But Garrett's mind needed to be on his ward round, not on the way Hazel looked as she rocked the baby to sleep or how the sight made him feel.

'Dr Buchanan?' Dr Lee was asking him something about home oxygen policy and Garrett, only half listening, turned quickly and mumbled his apologies.

When the ward round reached Hazel's side of the nursery, she was just placing the baby down to sleep in one of the plastic cribs. Garrett watched her attach a blue wire to one of the apnoea alarms and tuck the sheets in softly around the sleeping baby.

'And who do we have here?' Dr Lee checked her notes. 'Ah, yes... Bella, isn't it?'

Hazel nodded. 'Feeding well. Due to be weighed again tomorrow morning. Foster parents are visiting today, to spend some time with her before hopefully taking her home next week.'

Garrett's heart felt as if it stopped before it began hammering against his ribs at double-time.

Dr Lee frowned. 'Remind me again of Mum's circumstances?'

'She's from HMP Branlow,' Hazel prompted.

'Oh, yes,' Dr Lee said. 'A very sad case.'

'Mum's still over on the postnatal ward. She's been expressing milk for Bella, but she's due to return to prison any day now.'

Garrett had been silent, but now he managed to croak out a few words. 'What's her sentence for?'

Hazel looked at him in surprise. 'Something drugs-related, I think. I know Mum was on methadone during pregnancy. But this isn't her first offence, and Bella's not her first baby...' She trailed off.

'No, that's right. She had a boy, if I recall correctly,' Dr Lee said. 'Three or four years ago, it must have been. He was premature too, and showed signs of Neonatal Abstinence Syndrome.'

Garrett swallowed hard. 'Where is he now?'

'I'm afraid I couldn't tell you,' Dr Lee confessed. 'We don't often get to know in these cases. He was discharged directly into foster care—as little Bella here will be in the next few days. Unless there are any concerns?'

She directed her question at Hazel.

Hazel shook her head. 'She's doing great. She's weaned off morphine now, and shows no signs of NAS. Her blood sugars are stable and she feeds like a dream.'

'Well, then, let's plan for discharge by the end of the week, providing she continues to feed well and gain weight. Have the foster parents had resuscitation training, do you know?'

'I'll check,' Hazel said.

Dr Lee nodded and moved over to the next cot. Hazel followed. They began discussing the baby boy there, whose parents were sitting beside him, eager to discover when he might be able to join them at home.

Garrett didn't move. He knew he ought to. He knew that if he didn't someone was bound to notice and wonder what was wrong. But he couldn't bring himself to. Not yet. He stared down into the little plastic cot and the tiny bundle beneath the hospital sheets. Baby Bella's eyes flickered beneath her paper-thin lids as she slept, and Garrett wondered what babies dreamt of and if she knew what lay ahead of her. Knew the struggles she'd face when she found out where she'd come from and the circumstances of her birth. If she, like him, would find herself constantly moving, never still, never quite trusting what she had in case one day she woke up and found it gone.

He moved to Hazel's side. 'Can we talk?' The words were out of Garrett's mouth before he even realised he'd thought them.

Hazel looked as surprised at the question as he felt.

'Sure,' she said, with a meaningful glance over his shoulder at their colleagues. 'Later?'

'How about lunchtime, in the canteen?' Garrett suggested.

'Okay. I'll meet you there.'

It was a risk. Neither one of them was guaranteed a lunch break, but there were things he needed to say—things Hazel needed to hear. He couldn't be sure how she'd react, but Garrett knew he had to tell her either way.

Can we talk?

Three little words with a very big meaning.

Hazel was no expert in dating and relationships, but even she knew that was never a good sign.

In all likelihood Garrett wanted to reiterate what Hazel already knew—that he wasn't looking for anything serious and that he wouldn't be sticking around for long. Information she'd had at her disposal before their kiss in the changing room but that she'd chosen to ignore.

She should have been more sensible—she usually was—but when it came to Dr Garrett Buchanan she couldn't seem to get her head straight.

Hazel's stomach was rolling like it was at sea.

What would he say when she dropped her own bombshell?

When he learned that, whether he liked it or not, a part of him would be sticking around much longer than either of them had anticipated...that in less than eight months she'd be having his baby?

The sudden beeping of an oxygen saturation monitor brought Hazel crashing back to reality. She moved across to Kayden's cot and found that he'd kicked his SaO2 probe off his foot. She taped it back in place and watched his oxygen levels and heart rate return to a more respectable figure on the monitor.

Hazel only wished her own heart, pounding beneath her scrubs, would do the same.

The staff canteen was busy, and Hazel couldn't see a free table anywhere.

Was Garrett already here somewhere?

Her eyes roved over the sea of blue and green scrubs until she spotted his unruly red hair at a table by the window.

Here goes.

Hazel approached the table the way she might a sleeping tiger, her footsteps slowing more the closer she got.

Was she really going to go through with this? Was she really going to tell the father of her child that she was pregnant *here*, of all places?

She glanced around her, suddenly uncertain if she was doing the right thing.

'Hazel! Hey.' Garrett waved her over.

Hazel slid into the seat opposite him with a smile that she feared was more like a grimace.

How was she even supposed to begin?

She thought of all the cute announcements she'd seen on social media over the years—the friends of hers who'd wrapped up positive pregnancy tests as Father's Day gifts, or thought of cute, quirky ways to break the news to their other halves. She couldn't recall a single announcement that had happened in a workplace canteen.

Would he even hear her over the hubbub?

Hazel was quickly beginning to think this was a terrible idea. That she should have put Garrett off a little longer. At least until she knew what she was going to say.

'Are you okay? Only, you look a bit…distracted.'

If he only knew.

Distracted was the least of it.

'I'm fine,' Hazel lied. 'So, you wanted to talk…?'

She wanted to hear what he was going to say first. It might help her to handle what came next…and if not, at least it would buy her some time to figure out exactly how she was going to tell him.

Garrett set down the sandwich he'd been holding and stared at it a moment, as though it held all the answers.

If only, Hazel thought.

'Actually, there's something I want to tell you,' he said. 'Something about me that I think you should know.'

Oh, God. That had to be right up there with all those phrases Hazel dreaded but kept hearing lately…

We need to talk. I think you should see this. And now, *There's something you should know…*

She swallowed audibly. 'Okay.' She nodded, waiting for Garrett to go on as her mind began conjuring a million dreadful possibilities.

He was secretly married…he had a terminal illness…or perhaps he wasn't really a doctor at all.

Hazel cupped her hands around her untouched cardboard cup of tea to stop them from trembling in anticipation of what Garrett was about to tell her.

It couldn't be more shocking than what she had to tell him, surely?

Hazel braced herself for whatever it might be.

Garrett sighed. There was no easy way to begin, so he was just going to have to jump right in.

'The thing is… Well, I didn't exactly have the easiest time as a kid.'

Hazel tilted her head and her brow creased, as though she'd been expecting him to say something else. 'I'm…sorry to hear that,' she said.

'Thanks. But I'm not telling you so you'll feel sorry for me. I'm just trying to explain why I am the way I am.'

Hazel frowned. 'You don't have to explain yourself to me.'

'Yes, but…' Garrett shook his head, glancing away into the crowded canteen before turning back to Hazel. 'I'd like to try.'

Hazel held his gaze a moment before looking down into her cup of tea.

'Look, you may as well know… I was in foster care.'

Hazel's head snapped up and he saw her eyes widen.

'Like Bella?'

Garrett nodded, but he pressed on, knowing that if he stopped he might never get it all out.

'I never knew my dad. I asked a couple of times, of course, but my mum—' He broke off, shaking his head. 'It was obvious she didn't want to talk about him. She told me that my life would be better without him in it and I believed her.'

He shrugged.

'We seemed to be getting along just fine without him. At least as far as I was concerned, anyway. But, looking back, I can see how tough it must have been for my mum. Louise— that was her name—had me when she was young. She was a single parent, working two jobs at minimum wage to put food on the table. She did a brilliant job, but then...'

He took a deep breath, readying himself for what he had to say next—what he needed to get out.

'She died suddenly when I was six.'

'Oh, Garrett,' Hazel said. 'I'm so sorry.'

Garrett swallowed the lump forming in his throat. 'I was the one who found her. She'd come home to switch her uniform between jobs and collapsed on the bedroom floor. I got home from school and—'

Garrett had to stop as he relived the moment all over again. Even all these years later it still took his breath away, remembering the moment his world had come crashing down.

He shook his head to clear the images away. 'She'd had a cardiac arrest. One minute she was fine, and then...she wasn't. SADS, they call it now, but back then no one had any answers for a six-year-old boy who couldn't understand what had happened or why his world had been torn apart.'

'Is that why you went into medicine?' Hazel's voice was soft.

'I wanted to be the one with the answers. I wanted to prevent others from going through the agony of not knowing why or if there was anything that could have been done.'

'And here you are,' Hazel said.

'Here I am,' Garrett repeated.

He took a deep, shaky breath.

Nearly there. He'd nearly done it. Nearly got out what he'd been holding in all this time.

'When my mum died there were no grandparents or aunts and uncles to take me in. It had always just been the two of us. So I ended up in the care system...' He trailed off, unsure how to finish what he'd started, not certain it was enough to help her understand.

Hazel was looking at him now, head tilted, her mouth curved down at one side and her eyes full of sympathy. 'I'm so sorry, Garrett. I had no idea.'

'I got bounced around. You know the way it is...' Garrett paused, shrugging.

Hazel might not have experienced the care system for herself, but he knew she'd have dealt with it plenty as a children's nurse. She'd have sat through all the same safeguarding training sessions he had and heard about the experiences of kids like him. Not that they ever truly captured how it felt to be on the other side of it all.

She nodded. 'That must have been tough.'

Garrett nodded. There was no use lying. It *had* been tough. The constant moves...never knowing when it might be time to pack up and go. At first he'd tried to get to know the people he was living with—his foster carers, the other kids, his classmates... But pretty soon he'd learned it was a waste of time and so he'd stopped bothering.

What was the point when he'd be moving on again before long?

And so the pattern for the rest of his life had been set.

'I got used to it,' he said now. 'The way any kid does. You have to adapt to survive. The trouble is...'

'You're still doing it?' Hazel finished softly.

Garrett nodded. 'You have to understand... For so many years I was the only person I could rely on. Nothing else was certain. I couldn't bear the thought of putting down roots somewhere or getting attached to someone when there was no guarantee it would last.'

'I guess that makes sense,' Hazel said quietly.

'I don't want to be one of those people who uses their past as an excuse,' Garrett said. 'I've worked hard not to let my past define me. But I can't sit here and pretend it hasn't had an impact—because it has.'

'It would be strange if it hadn't,' Hazel said. 'We're all shaped by our early experiences.'

'Of course,' Garrett agreed. 'But I think for some of us it leaves a deeper mark than for others. You seemed so shocked when I said I don't want kids…when I told you I didn't want to settle down. I guess I just wanted to explain why it's such a big deal for me. Why it's not something I've ever wanted or planned for.'

Garrett risked a glance at Hazel, but immediately wished he hadn't. She looked positively stricken. Her face was pale and she was on the edge of her seat. She reminded Garrett of a wild animal—frozen, but about to bolt at any moment.

'Garrett, I—'

He shook his head quickly. 'It's fine,' he said, shutting the conversation down—shutting himself down with abrupt finality. 'I don't expect you to understand. I mean, how could you? No one can.'

Hazel winced. 'Actually, Garrett, there's something—'

'Oh, thank God! You don't mind, do you?'

They both blinked up at Aasiyah, one of the NICU junior doctors, who was hovering beside the table with a tray in her hands.

'Only there's nowhere else to sit…' She gestured around the canteen.

'Right. No, of course, not.'

Garrett slid across to the next seat so Aasiyah could sit down with her lunch.

'At least we're getting a break, hey?' she said, cheerfully oblivious to the tension she was cutting through with her chatter.

Hazel got to her feet abruptly, still clutching her tea. 'Actually, I'd better get back.' She held Garrett's gaze a moment longer. 'Catch you later, maybe?'

He nodded, suddenly sure that there'd been something she

was about to say before Aasiyah had sat down—perhaps even before he'd blurted out his life story. Something crucial.

But it was too late. Hazel was already at the canteen doors, dropping her untouched cup of tea into the bin before she pushed through them, stepping out into the corridor and disappearing from view.

Garrett sat back in his chair and let Aasiyah's chatter wash over him.

Why did he feel as if he'd missed something vitally important?

CHAPTER NINE

SHE SHOULD HAVE told him.

But how could she have when he'd opened up like that? Baring his soul to her and underlining what she already knew to be true—that he didn't want to be a father.

Only it was much too late. He already was. He just didn't know it yet.

And then Aasiyah had turned up, nattering away, and Hazel's chance to break the big news had evaporated right before her eyes.

Hazel knew she'd have to tell Garrett, and soon... But how or where or when, she had no idea.

Today. She'd tell Garrett today for definite, she resolved.

And hopefully, unlike yesterday, there wouldn't be any more revelations or interruptions to derail her.

'Hazel, are you busy?' Ciara popped her head round the door.

Hazel looked over at the three cots nearest to her. All the babies were fast asleep, and likely would be until their next feed or nappy-change.

'Not at the minute.'

'There's been a stock delivery and the storeroom is crammed with boxes. Any chance either you or Miriam could spare twenty minutes to sort through it and put a few things away?'

'Sure, I'll ask Miriam to hold the fort.'

Miriam was a staff nurse about three months away from retirement. She'd been doing the job longer than Hazel had been alive, and what she didn't know about neonatal nursing wasn't worth knowing. Hazel knew that the Special Care nursery would be in more than capable hands under her supervision, and also that Miriam and her creaky knees would rather be sitting down bottle-feeding a baby than kneeling on the hard floor of the stock room.

'Thanks. You're a star,' Ciara said. 'I'd do it myself, but it's non-stop in HDU today.'

'Don't mention it,' Hazel said.

At least in the peace and quiet of the stock room she could plan how to break the news of her pregnancy to Garrett. The man who'd already told her in no uncertain terms—twice—that he didn't want to be a dad.

Garrett arrived early for his shift and pulled on his scrubs. His mind was preoccupied, as it so often was these days.

What had Hazel been about to say yesterday?

The more he'd thought about it, the more he'd become sure she'd been about to tell him something important before Aasiyah had interrupted.

Garrett pushed his backpack into his locker and pulled his lanyard over his head.

Well, there was only one way to find out.

There was a strange atmosphere on the neonatal unit. Nurses were standing off to one side, whispering amongst themselves, and a sombre mood hung over the Special Care nursery, where a nurse who looked though she should have been drawing her pension long ago was bottle-feeding a baby.

'Sorry to interrupt, but have you seen Hazel?'

The grey-haired nurse looked up from the baby she was feeding and blinked at Garrett through her glasses.

'Oh, pet… You mean you haven't heard?'

Garrett's stomach suddenly felt as if he'd swallowed led.

'Heard what?'

Ciara, one of the other nurses, appeared beside him, worrying at her bottom lip with her teeth. 'Hazel collapsed.'

A ringing filled Garrett's ears and he looked about in wild panic, as though Hazel was about to spring from behind one of the cots and tell him it was all a joke.

'When? How? Where?' He could hear the panic in his own voice.

Ciara looked at him, her expression curious. 'In the store-room…about an hour ago. Liam heard a clatter, rushed in, and found her keeled over in a pile of feeding syringes. She must have been trying to reach the top shelf to put them away—' Ciara broke off with a sniff. 'It's all my fault. I'm the one who asked her to help out…'

'There, there, pet. You can't blame yourself,' the older nurse soothed.

Garrett looked between them both, feeling like he was losing the plot. He was trying to stay calm, but his mind and his heart were racing.

'Where is she now?'

At this, Ciara shrugged. 'Liam brought her round and Dr Lee bundled her into a wheelchair and took her to the ED.'

'Thanks,' Garrett called over his shoulder, his feet already moving.

The Emergency Department was on the other side of the hospital, and Garrett ran there as if he was responding to a crash bleep.

He arrived sweaty and out of breath, and had to take a minute before he could speak to the receptionist—a young lad of about twenty, who was chewing gum and looking like he'd rather be anywhere else on earth.

You and me both, thought Garrett.

'I'm looking for a patient—Hazel Bridges.'

The lad looked him up and down.

'ID?'

Surely the green scrubs were enough?

Garrett yanked his lanyard from where he'd tucked into his scrub top to stop it swinging during his sprint through the corridors.

'Dr Garrett Buchanan,' he said, flashing his ID.

'Neonates?' The lad raised an eyebrow.

'Is she here or not?' Garrett was trying to be polite, but impatience was getting the better of him.

The lad sighed. 'Hold on. I'll check. What's the patient's date of birth?'

Damn. They hadn't got round to discussing birthdays. 'I don't…uh…'

The lad rolled his eyes. 'Hospital ID number?'

'Um…'

The receptionist sighed with the bone-weary heaviness of someone seventy years older. 'Never mind,' he said, while intoning that he very much *did* mind. 'Bridges… Hazel… Here we go…' He studied the screen in front of him. 'That patient has been transferred.'

Garrett's pulse leapt.

Transferred—not discharged. That wasn't a good sign.

'Where?'

'Let's see…um… EPU.'

'EPU?' Garrett repeated, frowning.

The receptionist stopped chewing his gum just long enough to shoot Garrett a death stare. 'Early. Pregnancy. Unit,' he said, enunciating each word carefully, as if he thought Garrett might not understand.

Which, to be fair, he didn't.

Why would they take Hazel to EPU when she wasn't…?

'But that isn't—I mean, I don't—' Garrett stammered.

The receptionist sighed heavily again, misunderstanding Garrett's confusion. 'Left out of the double doors, up the main corridor, turn right in the purple zone and take the lift up to the second floor…'

'Right. Thanks…' Garrett muttered, backing away from the reception desk in a daze, not having heard a single thing the lad had said after the words *'Early Pregnancy Unit'*.

Garrett's feet were moving on autopilot, but his mind was frozen in place.

Hazel was pregnant?

'How are you feeling now?'

Hazel's eyes flickered from the smiling midwife to the needle in her left arm, and then to the bag of IV fluids hanging from the drip stand beside the bed.

'A bit strange,' she admitted. 'I'm used to being the nurse, not the patient.'

The midwife, Jenny, smiled sympathetically. 'It can't be easy, being pregnant and doing what you do…knowing what you know…'

Hazel hadn't really thought of it that way. She'd barely had a chance to think about it at all, truth be told. She'd been so focused on telling Garrett that she wasn't sure she'd fully processed it herself yet.

'I guess…' She pointed to the medical records that Jenny was holding. 'So, what's the verdict?'

'Low blood sugar and low blood pressure. Not a great combination—especially not in early pregnancy. You need to take better care of yourself.'

Hazel winced. The young midwife was right.

Why did she need someone else to tell her that?

She'd been bustling around, skipping meals, hardly sleeping, hardly stopping…no wonder she'd passed out in the storeroom.

God, what a sight she must have been, sprawled across the floor. And what a fright she must have given everyone…

The door flew open, startling both her and Jenny, who spun on her heels to see who had burst in.

Hazel, however, remained motionless, frozen in place by Garrett's gaze, which seemed to be pinning her to the bed. His blue eyes were wide and clear and fixed on hers, and without him saying a single word Hazel knew.

He knew.

CHAPTER TEN

'AND YOU ARE…?' The midwife, Jenny put one hand on her hip, glowering at Garrett, who was still standing stock-still in the doorway.

'It's okay,' Hazel said, finally tearing her eyes from Garrett's. 'He's…a friend.'

From the corner of her eye she saw Garrett's eyebrows rise at her choice of words.

'Hmph…' Jenny said, clearly unimpressed. 'Well, you can stay for now, but I'll be back to do your observations just as soon as that's finished.' She pointed to the bag of IV dextrose currently being pumped into Hazel's veins.

'Right. Thanks.'

Hazel waited for her to leave before turning to Garrett.

Hazel licked her lips. 'Take a seat.'

She gestured to the chair beside the bed, but Garrett didn't move.

'Garrett, I—'

'You're pregnant.'

It wasn't a question.

Hazel nodded.

'Is it mine?'

Hazel swallowed hard and nodded again. 'Yes,' she whispered.

Garrett's chest rose as he inhaled sharply. 'Are you sure?'

She tried not to be offended. After all, as far as Garrett Buchanan knew Hazel might have wild, one-night stands with new doctors all the time.

Her cheeks flamed. 'Yes, I'm sure. There hasn't been any-one else.'

Garrett nodded slowly. 'How long have you known?'

'Two days. I'm sorry. I tried to tell you—'

Garrett nodded. 'Yesterday. I knew there was something, but I never for one moment—' He broke off and ran a hand through his hair, leaving it sticking upon end. 'Do you want to…? Are you going to…?'

He couldn't seem to finish his sentence, but he didn't need to. Hazel knew what he was trying to ask.

'I'm keeping the baby,' she said quietly.

He stared at her then, for what felt like an eternity, his expression unreadable.

'You are?'

'Yes. I know it's not ideal, but…' Hazel trailed off.

But what? What exactly was she trying to say?

'But I'll make it work,' she finished. 'Obviously, I'd like you to be involved…'

Garrett's eyes widened. 'Hazel, I—'

Neither of them seemed capable of finishing their sentences any more, but really, was it any wonder? The situation was totally surreal. She couldn't believe it was actually happening to her and that this was really her life.

She was pregnant. With Garrett's baby.

And here they were, gawping at each other like two lemons, not knowing what to say or how to act.

She took a deep breath. 'I understand it's a shock, so if you need time…' Hazel trailed off once more, hesitant to point out how little time they really had to get used to all this. Already the clock was ticking.

'Time?' Garrett repeated, as if he was on autopilot. Then he seemed to snap to attention, his eyes flicking up to the clock on the wall. 'Time!' He swore softly. 'My shift started twenty minutes ago. I'm sorry, Hazel, I have to—'

There was a knock on the door and Jenny strode in. 'How are we doing? Oh, good—your IV is finished.'

She began bustling about, disconnecting the IV from Hazel's arm and taking her blood pressure and blood sugar readings. Either she was oblivious to the strained atmosphere in the room, or she'd become an expert at ignoring tension between couples.

'Much better,' she declared. 'Now, remind me again of your dates—how far along are you?'

'Um…' Hazel glanced at Garrett and he caught her eye. 'Nearly seven weeks, or thereabouts.'

Jenny jotted it down. 'Great. We should be able to see something at this point—to put your mind at rest.'

'See something…?' Hazel struggled to keep up.

'On a scan,' Jenny said. 'By around six to seven weeks we can usually measure the baby, check everything's where it should be, and sometimes we can even see the heartbeat.'

Hazel's own heart started pounding. 'I'm having a scan?'

Jenny hesitated. 'The doctor has ordered one, yes. What with you taking a bit of a funny turn, they'll want to rule out anything untoward…'

'Such as…?' Garrett prompted.

Hazel turned to him in surprise. His glazed expression was gone. He was Dr Garrett Buchanan once more. Focused and in control.

Jenny shifted her weight from one leg to the other and looked down at the chart in her hands as though she didn't really want to answer his question. 'Well, there's always a worry that the baby might not be in the right place… Dizziness and fainting spells can sometimes be a sign of ectopic pregnancy.'

Hazel's stomach lurched. All this time she'd thought her biggest worries would be Garrett's reaction, and how she'd manage to bring up a baby alone, but suddenly she felt foolish for even assuming she'd get to that point. All sorts of things could go wrong between now and then—she should know; she'd seen it for herself enough times.

'When's the scan?' Hazel croaked.

'If you're feeling okay now we can take you round to the ultrasound room right away.'

'Of course.' Hazel shuffled herself upright.

'Slowly does it,' Garrett said gently.

Hazel suddenly felt like crying. She wasn't used to feeling

fragile, or being taken care of, and she wasn't sure she liked it. Part of her was glad that Garrett was here, but another part of her knew it would make it worse, somehow, when he left.

Hadn't she better get used to that? After all, he was hardly going to be accompanying her to her appointments, was he?

Hazel tried to push the thought away and focus on what was about to happen here and now. This was it. The moment she would see her baby for the first time. She wasn't sure how she should be feeling, but her legs felt like jelly as they entered the scanning room.

'If you pop yourself onto the couch,' Jenny said, 'I'll get Ruth, the senior midwife who'll be doing your scan.'

Hazel stood up slowly and eased herself onto the narrow bed lined with a strip of blue paper.

'Do you want me to stay?' Garrett asked.

Hazel tried to hide her surprise. 'But your shift... I thought—'

'I'll call Dr Lee and explain. That is...if you want me to?'

'Do you want to stay?' Hazel held her breath, waiting for his answer.

'I want to know that you're okay,' he said eventually.

Hazel's stomach fluttered, and she wasn't sure if it was Garrett's words, a pregnancy symptom, or her nerves about the scan.

'Of course you can stay,' she said quietly.

What else could she say?

It was his baby too. Besides, she didn't want to be on her own if it turned out to be bad news.

She tried to swallow the lump she felt forming in her throat.

Garrett nodded. 'I'll be right back.'

Hazel stared up at the ceiling, trying to process everything that had happened since the start of her shift that morning. It felt as if she'd stumbled into a play, somehow, and was acting a part she'd never for one minute imagined playing.

Garrett stepped back into the room. 'Dr Lee is covering for me. I explained the situation to her.'

Hazel raised herself onto her elbows. 'You *told* her?' She couldn't keep the disbelief from her voice.

'I told her you were having an ultrasound,' Garrett said. 'I didn't tell her anything else.'

Hazel lowered herself back onto the couch. No doubt Dr Lee would have her suspicions, but there were plenty of reasons a person might need an urgent ultrasound—and besides, Hazel knew the consultant well enough to know that she would be discreet.

Hazel should probably feel relieved that Garrett hadn't announced her pregnancy to their colleague. After all, she didn't want everyone knowing her private business, did she? But there was a small part of her that felt disappointed, somehow. As though she and the baby were something shameful that Garrett didn't want to acknowledge.

There was a soft knock on the door and a middle-aged woman in a navy tunic stepped into the room. Hazel vaguely recognised her, but probably only because they'd likely passed one another in the hospital corridors at some point. The staff from EPU and NICU rarely crossed paths, working, as they did, at opposite ends of the pregnancy spectrum.

'Hi, Hazel. I'm Ruth, one of the senior midwives, and I'll be scanning you today. Can you just confirm some details for me?'

Hazel confirmed her date of birth, and the date of her last period, and the fact that this was her first pregnancy.

'And you are…?' Ruth turned to Garrett.

'Dr Buchanan. Garrett. I mean… I work with Hazel and I… I mean we…' He looked at Hazel helplessly.

'He's the dad,' Hazel said.

What was the use of pretending?

Everyone would guess sooner or later anyway, and it wasn't as though Ruth was going to go blabbing it all over the hospital. She was a professional. They all were. Only this time Hazel was on the other side of it all, and struggling to acclimatise.

Garrett's eyes were like saucers, but Ruth only smiled.

'Okay. Well, let's see what we can see, then, shall we?'

She dimmed the lights and got Hazel to lift her scrub top and ease down her drawstring trousers slightly.

'This is a bit cold, sorry.'

Ruth squirted freezing cold gel onto Hazel's lower abdomen and she gasped. 'You weren't kidding.'

But Ruth was quiet now, concentrating on the screen as she ran the probe over Hazel's pelvis, left to right and back again, slower now and pressing in, so that Hazel was reminded that she hadn't been to the bathroom in a while.

Hazel looked at Garrett, but he was frowning over at Ruth, as though trying to read her expression and guess what she might be looking at on the screen.

'Is everything okay?' Hazel's voice cracked.

Ruth didn't answer at first, but rolled the ultrasound wand in a different direction. She clicked on something on the screen.

'I need to take a good look around before I can confirm anything,' Ruth said vaguely.

Hazel's nausea came flooding back with a vengeance.

Confirm what, exactly?

'Is it ectopic?' Garrett piped up. 'Will she need surgery?'

Surgery?

Hazel looked at him in alarm, and then back to Ruth. This was all happening too fast. She couldn't take it in.

Finally Ruth turned the screen so that both Hazel and Garrett could see what she was looking at. 'Not ectopic, no,' she said with a smile.

Hazel exhaled, and realised she hadn't done so for quite some time. She felt woozy all over again.

'Oh, thank God.' Garrett fell back in his chair as if the air had been let out of him, but then he sat forward again just as quickly, squinting at the screen. 'So everything is okay?'

'It sure is. Here is your baby—' Ruth gestured to the screen '—nestled in the right spot and measuring six weeks and six days.'

On the screen, a little white blob the shape of a kidney bean floated in a pool of black space. A little pixel in the centre of the blob flickered.

'And that is baby's heartbeat,' Ruth added.

Hazel's cheeks felt wet, and when she lifted a hand to her face she realised she was crying.

Then Ruth swirled the ultrasound probe across Hazel's abdomen, pointing it in the opposite direction and increasing the pressure ever so slightly.

'And here is baby number two—also looking good and measuring exactly the same.'

Hazel stared at this second little bean and its flickering heartbeat and tried to compute what she was being told.

'Baby number two?' Garrett repeated. 'So…?'

'There are two of them?' Hazel gaped at the monitor.

Ruth smiled. 'Congratulations—you're having twins!'

CHAPTER ELEVEN

'TWINS? ARE YOU SURE?' Hazel couldn't stop staring at the two flickering dots on the screen.

Two heartbeats. Two babies. Twins!

She turned to Garrett. Now he looked like the one in need of IV fluids and a hospital bed.

He wasn't going to faint, was he?

Hazel's brow furrowed and Garrett seemed to suddenly snap back to reality.

'That's…' He looked from Hazel to Ruth, clearly grasping for a word…any word. 'That's…great.'

Hazel's eyebrows lifted. 'It is?'

'Of course,' Garrett said. 'I mean…what a relief, the pregnancy isn't ectopic…' He trailed off.

Hazel swallowed her disappointment. 'Right.'

Ruth gently removed the probe from Hazel's abdomen. 'I'll print you out a picture.'

She excused herself from the room, and the minute she left Garrett got to his feet.

'I have to go. I'm sorry—'

'It's okay,' Hazel lied. It wasn't okay—none of it was—but what else could she say? He was on shift, and this had not been in either of their plans. 'At least you were here for the scan.'

'Right…' He walked to the door, turning at the last minute. 'We should talk.'

Hazel nodded, mute.

'About this…' He gestured to the blank monitor, and then between the two of them. 'And…us.'

'Later, then,' Hazel said.

'Later,' Garrett agreed.

'Here we go!' Ruth was back, waving a small black and white image in one hand.

'Sorry—got to dash,' Garrett said, practically running from the room.

The midwife frowned after him. 'Everything okay?' she asked Hazel, clearly sensing that she was on the verge of tears.

'Fine…fine.' Hazel sniffed. 'It's just a bit of a shock for us both, I think.'

'Bad timing?' Ruth guessed.

Hazel smiled, blinking back her tears. 'You could say that.'

Babies. His babies.

Garrett couldn't believe it. They'd used protection—he was sure of it. He remembered the pause, their shy laughter, the rummage for his wallet.

But then these things sometimes failed, didn't they?

He'd just never imagined it happening to him. He was a doctor, for crying out loud, he was supposed to know about this sort of thing. But here he was, being told he was going to be a dad. Him! Garrett Buchanan. Of all people.

It was impossible.

He'd sworn to himself all those years ago, lying awake in that narrow single bed beneath a narrow window that looked out over a narrow street, listening to strangers talking about him in hushed whispers outside the door. That first night, in his first ever foster home, he'd made a promise to himself that he would never, *ever* have a child of his own. It was too risky. No one could guarantee being around forever.

Even his mum had let him down in the end. It hadn't been her fault—he was old enough to know that—but still, the result was the same. With no family to take him in, he'd been alone in the world from that moment on, entering the system, where he'd stayed until he started medical school.

What if he said he'd stick by Hazel but later down the line it turned out they didn't like each other as much as they'd thought and they split? Then what? He'd be in and out of the children's lives, letting them down every time he couldn't make a visit because he was on call. Or what if something terrible happened? Men his age had heart attacks all the time. He felt fit as a fiddle, true, but that didn't mean he could guarantee he'd be around for the next eighteen years to raise two children.

No. It was out of the question.

Better he be out of the picture right from the start like his own dad—an unknown quantity in his life that he couldn't miss because he'd never known him.

Though that didn't seem fair on Hazel, he had to admit...

Garrett was so wrapped up in his thoughts he was stunned to find himself outside the doors to the neonatal unit, his feet having carried him there on autopilot.

'Dr Buchanan. Is everything okay?' Dr Lee's sharp gaze assessed Garrett as he entered the Intensive Care nursery.

He nodded, unsure what he could say—what Hazel would feel comfortable with him sharing.

'Hazel's...fine,' he said. 'Feeling much better already.'

Dr Lee nodded, though he caught the quirk of her eyebrows. 'I'm glad to hear it.' She indicated Aasiyah, standing next to her. 'Now, I was just saying to Dr Malik—'

But she was cut off by a sound that made Garrett's heart sink and his stomach drop to the floor—the emergency bleep tone from the pager at his waist. Dr Lee's own bleep was chiming in alongside it, and Aasiyah's eyes grew as round as saucers.

'Is it a test?' she asked.

Garrett shook his head.

This was the real thing.

As Garrett ran, his mind raced along with him.

Thank God Hazel wasn't carrying a crash bleep today, or she'd be running alongside him. He hated the thought of her racing about in her condition. But he supposed his pregnant colleagues did it every day, so why should Hazel be any different?

Because he cared for her? Because she was carrying his babies?

Garrett shook the thought away. This was no time for navel-gazing and self-reflection. He had a job to do, and if he was going to do it well he needed to focus.

As they approached Obstetric Theatres, the corridor was eerily quiet.

Then a midwife Garrett vaguely recognised rushed past him. 'Placental abruption,' she said. 'They've just taken her through to Theatre Three.'

Garrett's stomach dropped. The last placental abruption he'd attended had been back when he was a junior doctor, and it hadn't ended well.

He shook the thought away.

That was then—this is now.

No two clinical scenarios were exactly alike, and there was no use jumping to conclusions without knowing the facts.

Entering the theatre, Garrett suddenly understood why the corridor had been so quiet—all the staff were in here.

One of the midwives filled him in, her voice low behind her surgical mask. 'Thirty weeks. Placental abruption following a road traffic collision. The adult trauma team will be taking over after the section.' She nodded her head towards a handful of faces on the other side of the theatre that Garrett didn't recognise.

'Any stats on the baby?'

The midwife's eyes met his over the top of her mask. 'CTG on arrival showed a sinusoidal foetal heart rate…'

Garrett's own heart rate was racing, but he knew he needed to remain calm if they were going to have any chance of resuscitating this very premature, possibly very sick newborn.

He busied himself setting up the Resuscitaire alongside Aasiyah, under Dr Lee's watchful eye.

Within minutes, the consultant obstetrician had delivered the baby. But rather than the hearty cries of an indignant baby pulled from the warmth of its mother's womb, a tense silence filled the theatre.

'Baby girl. Born fourteen thirty-five,' one of the midwives announced.

The baby was rushed over to where Garrett and Aasiyah were waiting, and Garrett began working his way through the resuscitation flow chart ingrained in his mind, quickly moving through the steps as the baby failed to respond to his efforts.

'I think we need to intubate,' Garrett told Dr Lee.

'I agree.'

Garrett looked at Aasiyah. He wanted to give her the opportunity to step up, as others had done for him, but she gave the slightest shake of her head.

Not here, her expression said. *Not now.*

Garrett didn't blame her. He wouldn't want his skills put to the test under these circumstances either.

He took a deep breath, and then his hands were moving of their own accord.

He grasped the laryngoscope in his left hand. 'We need a size three ETT.'

Aasiyah held out the endotracheal tube, ready.

Garrett gently inserted his fingers into the baby's mouth, followed by the laryngoscope blade. She was so tiny, and his hands seemed absurdly large in comparison to her head, but they were steady as he guided the tube to where it needed to be. There was no way he could have done that if he hadn't already successfully intubated a preterm baby in the relative calm of the neonatal unit. No way he could have done it without remembering the way Hazel had stepped in to support him with her steady calm and her confidence in him.

Aasiyah immediately began the process of three compressions to one ventilation breath.

'What's our next step?' Dr Lee's voice had a quiet urgency to it, and Garrett looked over at her in surprise. She was asking him? And then he realised she wasn't asking him at all— she was giving him the opportunity to step up. Just as he'd tried to do for Aasiyah. She wanted to show that she trusted his clinical judgement. She wanted him to know that he could do this. He could lead an emergency resuscitation.

'I think we should commence a blood transfusion.' Garrett tried to sound more confident than he felt. 'With the placental abruption, it's possible that she's hypovolaemic. A transfusion could improve circulating volume and oxygenation to aid our resuscitation efforts.'

Dr Lee nodded, seemingly satisfied with his answer, and turned to speak to the midwife in charge. Within minutes, a unit of emergency blood was in the theatre and ready for use.

Garrett knew that if they could increase the baby's blood volume she'd have a better chance of survival, but first they'd need to gain vascular access—something that was notoriously tricky in preterm babies at the best of times.

'We'll need UVC access,' Dr Lee said.

Garrett swallowed. 'Right.'

The procedure involved inserting a catheter into the vein of the baby's umbilical cord, so they could use it to administer the blood transfusion and any other drugs or fluids she might need. It would get the blood circulating quicker, but it was hard to achieve.

'Would you like me to take over?' Dr Lee offered.

Garrett hesitated for a moment, sweat pooling in his lower back. Then he shook his head. 'I can do it.'

He prayed that was true as Aasiyah pre-flushed the line and he readied forceps to stabilise the baby's umbilical cord while he carefully inserted the catheter, aware that one wrong move on his part could be disastrous for the tiny baby lying before him.

When he felt it was in the right place Garrett drew back on the syringe, exhaling at the sight of blood. That was a good sign. He flushed the line once more, and advanced it another centimetre to be sure.

Already the midwives were beside him, performing the rigorous checks needed to ensure that the blood transfusion was the right one for this baby.

After what felt like a lifetime the transfusion was underway, and when Garrett glanced up at the clock on the Resuscitaire, to note the time, he couldn't believe his eyes. Fourteen-fifty. She'd only been born fifteen minutes ago, and yet it felt like hours had passed since then.

He, Aasiyah and Dr Lee were taking it in turns to perform CPR and maintain the baby's airway.

Garrett held his stethoscope to her chest.

Please...

'I've got a heartbeat.'

'Rate?'

Garrett held his breath, counting. 'Eighty.'

Dr Lee nodded. 'Discontinue compressions.'

Relief surged through Garrett's veins as he watched the tiny baby in front of him becoming visibly pinker as the blood transfusion and resuscitation efforts worked their magic.

'Let's get her over to the unit.' Dr Lee's tone was business-like, but Garrett could see the relief in her expression, and Aasiyah's eyes were losing that deer-in-headlights look he recognised so well.

They weren't out of the woods yet, but they had restored a heartbeat in a premature baby who, fifteen minutes ago, hadn't had a discernible one, and that was something to be grateful for.

'You did fantastically well today.'

Garrett looked up from the computer and found Dr Lee standing in the doorway.

'Thank you.'

'We'll debrief tomorrow, but for now you should go home and get some rest.'

In the changing room, Aasiyah was pulling on her coat. She looked pretty miserable, and Garrett felt he should say something encouraging, to let her know she'd done well in a high-pressure situation.

'Thanks for all your help today. You were great.'

She pulled a face. 'I froze.'

'It happens.'

'It shouldn't. What if it happens when I'm on my own?'

'We work as a team—you know that. There'll always be someone to support you in an emergency. You shouldn't be so hard on yourself.'

Aasiyah exhaled. 'Thanks. I mean… I'll try. But you know how it is.'

Garrett did know. He knew that no matter how hard he worked, or what he was able to accomplish, there'd always be a little voice in his head questioning if he'd done everything possible, if there wasn't something else he could have tried or done better to improve a baby's outcome. It was the nature of the job, and anyone who said otherwise was either lying or not doing it right.

He gave Aasiyah's arm a friendly squeeze. 'You're a good doctor, Aasiyah. I'm glad you're on my team.'

As Garrett stepped out of the hospital into the summer evening the daylight and fresh air hit him like a ton of bricks, and the day's events sent him reeling.

Garrett stumbled to a bench in a shaded corner of the hospital grounds and almost fell onto it.

He'd led a resuscitation today—a complex one at that—with very little intervention from his consultant. He'd saved a baby's life. Or at least he hoped he had. He was humble and experienced enough to know that a successful resuscitation was only a fraction of the equation. The baby's outcome was still very much unknown.

And on top of all that he'd found out he was going to be a dad.

Garrett's insides felt as if they were at war, and it was all he could do to drop his head into his hands and focus on one breath after another.

To his surprise, the only person he wanted to speak to about all of it was Hazel. After all these years of building up barriers around his heart, she was the one person who had started dismantling them, piece by piece. But of course he couldn't speak to her. Not about this or anything else. Not after the way he'd left her, with everything hanging unresolved between them.

CHAPTER TWELVE

HAZEL KICKED OFF her shoes and flopped down onto the sofa.

She'd been discharged from EPU following the scan, when her blood results had come back clear—though she'd still had a stern telling-off from the midwife, Jenny, with a reminder to start taking things easy.

She'd gone back to the unit, but had been instructed to take the rest of the day off. She'd been half hoping she might bump into Garrett, so they could resume their conversation, or at least make a plan for when exactly they were going to discuss the fact she was carrying his babies.

But then Ciara had filled her in about the crash call, and Hazel had known there would be no point sticking around. Who knew how long it might take the team to stabilise the baby? And even then Garrett's mind would be fully on his work—as it should be.

So Hazel had taken a taxi home, no closer to knowing what the future held for the two of them other than the fact they were going to be parents either way.

Hazel placed a hand to her abdomen. It was still as flat as ever, but it wouldn't be long before she'd be showing. Even in baggy scrubs, a twin pregnancy would make itself known, and then the curious glances and questions from colleagues would start.

She only hoped she'd have some answers by then.

It was nearly lunchtime, and little baby Bella was ready. Hazel, on the other hand, was not. She still had paperwork to complete, and notes to write, and every time the nursery door swung open she was convinced it would be Garrett and that their shared secret would be written all over her face.

Hazel tried to concentrate on filling in the discharge paperwork. Bella's foster carers would be coming to collect her in a couple of hours, so she needed to make sure everything was in order. No one wanted to be the reason a family couldn't take their baby home on the day they'd planned—not after the long and gruelling journey most of them had been on to get to that point.

The nursery door opened a fraction and Hazel's heart leapt. But it was only a tired-looking young woman accompanied by a support worker in a uniform Hazel didn't recognise. *Agency staff perhaps?* They must have lost their way, looking for a newly admitted baby.

'Can I help you?' Hazel asked. 'Are you looking for your baby?'

The woman nodded, biting her lip with worry. 'I don't know which cot she's in...'

Hazel smiled. 'What's her name?'

'Bella,' the woman said quietly.

The support worker gave Hazel a pointed look, and all at once Hazel realised her mistake. That wasn't an agency uniform, it was a prison guard uniform, and this wasn't a new mum who had come to meet her baby...she was a new mum who'd come to say goodbye.

'Of course,' Hazel said, recovering herself. 'I'm Hazel, I'm looking after Bella today. If you follow me, I'll show you to her cot.'

She led the two of them over to where Bella lay dressed in her nicest pink-and-white-striped Babygro. Her belongings were already packed into a holdall at the cot side.

Hazel noticed Bella's mum's swift, sorrowful glance at it and felt a wrench in her own gut. It must be so hard...knowing she was going home with someone else.

'Can I get you a glass of water? Or a cup of tea, perhaps?' It wouldn't help, Hazel knew, but she didn't know what else to offer.

The young woman shook her head.

'Can I get you anything?' Hazel turned to the guard, who flashed her a grateful smile but shook her head.

'Don't worry about me, love, I'm sure you've got enough to be doing. I'm Helen, by the way, and this is Jodie.'

Hazel smiled. 'Nice to meet you.'

But Jodie was busy gazing at her baby. She slid into the seat at Bella's cot side and peered over the plastic sides at her daughter. 'She's so beautiful.'

'She is,' Hazel agreed. 'Takes after her mum, I suppose.'

Jodie smiled sadly at the compliment, probably thinking of the bags under her eyes and her unwashed hair. But it was true, Hazel thought. Beyond the obvious new mum tiredness, and a deeper world-weariness, she could see that the young woman in front of her would once have been stunningly beautiful. Not that it seemed to have done her any favours...

'Do you think I could hold her?'

'Of course.'

Hazel lifted Bella from the cot and placed her into her mum's arms. Then she fetched a soft fleece blanket from the laundry cupboard to drape over the two of them.

'There you go.'

Jodie didn't say anything. She just stared at her daughter, clearly mesmerised.

Hazel and the guard looked at each other.

After a couple of minutes Jodie looked up. 'I think I'll just sit here for a bit, if that's okay?'

'Of course.' Hazel nodded.

'Fine by me.' The guard pulled up a chair and sat down on the other side of the cot.

'You can give Bella her bottle in half an hour—if you like?' Hazel asked.

Jodie nodded enthusiastically—then stopped suddenly, her face falling. 'But...won't her foster mum be doing that?'

A lump formed in Hazel's throat, but she swallowed hard. 'Not today, no. The carers aren't coming to pick her up for another couple of hours, so you have a bit of time to spend with her, if you'd like?'

'Yes,' Jodie said quietly. 'I'd like that...thanks.'

Hazel went back to the nursing station on the far side of the nursery to finish her paperwork, but every few minutes she found herself glancing up in their direction. There was something so heart-wrenching about the situation. Jodie gazing down at a sleeping Bella, and Helen, the prison guard looking on.

Jodie sat stock-still, watching little Bella sleeping soundly in her arms, and every minute that ticked away on the big standard-issue NHS clock on the wall behind Hazel felt like a cruel blow against this mother and daughter who already had so much stacked against them.

Hazel wasn't naive—she knew Jodie was no angel, and that she must have made some bad decisions, and broken the law more than once to end up where she had. But Hazel had seen enough of these cases to know that, for the most part, these women from the local prison were usually continuing a legacy that had started well before they were born.

Brought up in less than ideal circumstances, with few chances, and little support, most of them turned to crime as a means of survival or a means of escape. And those who fell pregnant paid the heaviest price when their babies were removed to foster care.

It was a broken system, but Hazel had no idea how it could begin to change or if it ever would.

As she prepared a bottle of milk for baby Bella she thought about Garrett, wrenched from the only family he had at such a young age, entirely at the mercy of strangers, and her heart ached. Her childhood might have had its challenges, but they paled in comparison to what Garrett had been through. No wonder he couldn't get his head around the idea of becoming a parent himself.

Not that it made it any easier for her. After all, these weren't hypothetical babies—they were coming into the world whether Hazel and Garrett were ready or not.

Hazel warmed the bottle and held it out to Jodie. 'Have you fed her before?'

Jodie shook her head. 'I haven't dared to visit until now... I didn't want to see her in case I fell in love with her. I thought it would be easier if I stayed away... But I couldn't manage it. I had to see her.'

Tears pricked the backs of Hazel's eyes. 'I can only imagine,' she said.

Jodie held a hand out for the bottle. 'I fed her brother, though. They let me do it before he...' She trailed off. 'I remember what to do.'

Hazel passed her the bottle and turned away quickly, before the building tears could escape. She was a professional with a job to do. The decisions in Jodie and Bella's case weren't up to her. Jodie had a sentence to serve, and little Bella deserved the best possible start in life with trained foster carers who could nurture her and give her the best possible start in life.

Still, that didn't make it any easier, somehow, to watch these precious moments between mother and daughter that Bella wouldn't even remember.

Would she ever know they'd taken place? Who would tell her?

Hazel busied herself feeding Henry, who was almost ready for home himself, now his reflux was under control. As Henry glugged away on his bottle Hazel felt her own stomach rumble. The piece of plain toast she'd forced down before work felt like a long time ago, and Hazel knew she'd need to eat something soon if she wanted to keep the nausea at bay.

At the sound of voices beyond the nursery door Hazel looked up, just in time to see Dr Lee pushing her way through. Trailing behind her came a gaggle of other doctors. Ward round.

Hazel's heart thumped. At the back of the group was Garrett. He was frowning at a piece of paper in his hand, then he tucked it away in his scrubs pocket and looked up, catching her eye.

Hazel looked away, directing her attention back to little Henry in her arms. She listened as the doctors began their round and placed Henry on her shoulder to get his wind up. He let out an almighty belch and the doctors all turned at once.

Dr Lee laughed. 'Better out than in!'

'Unless it's followed by a trail of sick down my back,' Hazel muttered, but thankfully Henry's reflux medications were still working, and her shoulder stayed dry.

She tucked him back into his cot, reattaching his apnoea monitor.

'Anything I need to know about in here today?' Dr Lee asked.

'Bella Ritchie is being discharged home this afternoon,' Hazel said.

'Ah, yes.' Dr Lee nodded. 'And is everything ready?'

Hazel nodded. 'Everything aside from the discharge summary. That will need completing before her foster parents arrive in an hour or so.'

'I can do that,' Garrett offered.

Hazel still couldn't meet his eye.

'Thank you, Dr Buchanan,' Dr Lee said. 'And is that Mum with her now?'

Hazel nodded. She caught Garrett's sharp glance in Jodie and Bella's direction and saw a strange expression settle across his features, making him look so much younger and more vulnerable than he usually did.

It must be so difficult for him to remain professional despite his personal experiences, Hazel realised. Not to feel invested in this case because of his own background.

'Let's go and say hello,' Dr Lee suggested.

Jodie had just set the empty bottle down, and was rubbing Bella's back in circular motions. 'This is how you do it, isn't it?' She looked up at Hazel as they approached. 'I'm not doing it wrong?'

'No, you're not doing it wrong,' Hazel reassured her. 'That's fine. You can rub or pat. A combination of both usually works best.'

Jodie began patting Bella's back, and Bella let out a polite little belch.

The guard, Helen chuckled.

'Jodie, isn't it?' Dr Lee said.

Jodie nodded.

'You know Bella is being discharged today?'

Jodie nodded again. 'They told me,' she said, obviously referring to the midwives. 'I wasn't going to come but I couldn't stop myself. I had to see her.'

Hazel glanced in Garrett's direction and saw his Adam's apple bobbing. She wanted to reach out a hand to comfort him, but how could she under the circumstances?

'That's understandable,' Dr Lee said. 'Is there anything you'd like to ask us at all, about Bella's condition or her care?'

Jodie looked from her daughter up to Dr Lee and back down again. 'I just want to know if she'll be okay,' she whispered. 'If she'll be happy.'

Dr Lee gave her a sympathetic smile. 'I can't predict the future, but I can tell you she's a perfectly healthy baby girl, and I know she'll be well taken care of.'

'And loved?' Jodie asked, her voice cracking.

Hazel's hand moved to her abdomen automatically. She pressed her palm over her flat stomach. *Love*. That was all a baby really needed. Anything else was a bonus.

She looked up at Garrett again, but he was studying Bella's observations chart intently, a tic working in his jaw.

'Of course,' Dr Lee confirmed.

'That's all I need to know,' Jodie said.

She placed Bella in the cot and began tucking her in carefully. She rested her palm lightly on top of the hospital blankets.

'Bye-bye little one.'

Hazel swallowed hard and blinked back tears.

Jodie looked at Helen. 'I'm ready to go.'

Helen nodded, and got to her feet. 'Alright, love.' Her voice was softer now. 'If you're sure?'

Jodie nodded. 'I am.' She turned to Hazel. 'Thank you for looking after her, and for letting me feed her.'

'Of course.' Hazel didn't know what else to say. She could feel the lump in her throat growing thicker and the hot tears pressing against the backs of her eyes as she watched Jodie and Helen leave the Special Care Nursery.

Dr Lee was now checking some blood results on the computer for another baby, and divvying up tasks between the junior doctors, but Garrett stood a little way to one side. He caught Hazel's eye and then he looked down, slowly and deliberately. Hazel realised she still had a protective hand over her stomach, and dropped it immediately to her side.

As the doctors moved along to the next cot Garrett hung back. 'Are you okay?' he murmured.

How could he ask her that under the circumstances? And how on earth could she answer?

Hazel gave a silent nod, but Garrett held her gaze as though he didn't quite believe her.

'Dr Buchanan?' Dr Lee called over her shoulder, and Garrett tore his gaze from Hazel's and turned away.

Hazel felt her breath leave her in a whoosh and tears needled the backs of her eyes.

Not here, she told herself, *not now.*

She blinked them away and turned her attention to Bella's discharge paperwork. She could cry over Garrett Buchanan later, but right now she had a job to do.

CHAPTER THIRTEEN

'So, HOW ARE YOU finding it here?' Dr Lee leant back in her chair, her cool grey eyes assessing Garrett keenly. He felt like a sample under a microscope.

'Yeah, it's great.' He winced internally.

Was that really the best he could come up with?

This was his first supervision session with his consultant, the formidable Dr Lee. This meeting was supposed to be a review, of sorts—a chance to bring up any issues or reflect on things that had gone well during his first few weeks on the team.

Garrett cleared his throat and tried again. 'I feel like I'm consolidating my skills and growing in confidence.'

Dr Lee gave a small smile. 'Based on your performance, I'd have to agree. You really stepped up yesterday—you hardly needed me at all.'

'Thank you,' Garrett said. 'But I couldn't have done it without your support.'

'Oh, I think you could. In fact, I'm certain of it.' Dr Lee tilted her head. 'So what is it that's holding you back, do you think?'

'I… I don't understand. What do you mean?'

'Well, it's clear to me that you'll be ready for a consultant post any day now—perhaps you already are—and yet I sense you're not keen to progress…that there's something keeping you where you are.'

Garrett shook his head. 'No, that's not true… I definitely want to progress. Becoming a consultant has always been my end goal.'

Dr Lee raised a dark eyebrow in his direction. 'Are you sure? Because it seems to me you're quite happy as you are. You could have taken the leap before now—your previous supervisor told me she was surprised you didn't stay on for an upcoming consultant vacancy there.'

'I wasn't ready.' Garrett shrugged. 'I needed more time.'

'Hmm…' Dr Lee tapped a pen against the sheet of paper. 'Dr Buchanan, none of us are ever ready to step into the unknown, but we do it anyway because the alternative is staying stuck where we are. You seem to be in a holding pattern of sorts. Is it the security of having a superior to double-check your clinical decision-making? Because you know, even if you do become a consultant, you'll still have your colleagues to support you…'

'It's not that.' Garrett said.

'Then what is it?'

'I just…need more time.' It sounded lame and false, even to him.

Dr Lee sighed. She scribbled something on the piece of paper. 'Well, hopefully your time with us will be sufficient. I'm sure you'll make an excellent consultant when you're finally ready to step up.'

'What if I don't?'

Dr Lee looked up sharply and Garrett realised, too late, that he'd spoken out loud, voicing the worry swirling in his head.

'Excuse me?' Dr Lee said.

Garrett sighed and leant forward, his elbows on his knees. 'Ever since I was a kid, this is all I've ever wanted. To be at the top of my game…helping families, saving lives, making a difference. I've focused on it exclusively, to the detriment of… well…everything else.' Garrett threw his hands up in the air.

Dr Lee nodded in understanding. 'Many of us do the same. It isn't easy to strike a work-life balance when the job demands so much of you. Please, go on.'

'Well, what if, after all that, it's not enough? What if I let someone down? Or make a mistake?'

Dr Lee looked sympathetic. 'We all have those fears. It's only natural when we have so much responsibility on our shoulders.'

Garrett sighed. 'I suppose so... But what if *this* is a mistake? What if a consultant post isn't what I want, after all? What if I finally achieve what I've had my heart set on all these years and discover it isn't for me? I've never stayed in one place longer than a few months... I'm not even sure that I can.'

Dr Lee smiled. 'I think we're getting to the real heart of the problem now, aren't we? You're afraid to put down roots. To say *This is it* and be satisfied with your lot.'

'Something like that,' Garrett said quietly.

He was afraid to let people down or to be let down. He was afraid to get comfortable in case it was all yanked away the minute he relaxed.

'So you start to self-sabotage? To end things prematurely on your own terms rather than see them through to their logical conclusion? Up sticks and go on to the next job or hospital or town...? Is that it?'

Garrett sat stunned for a moment at how incredibly perceptive Dr Lee was. 'I... I suppose so,' he said, eventually.

Dr Lee tilted her head. 'But either way you're the one who is affected—having to leave everything behind and start over. It may be your choice rather than someone else's, but the end result is the same.'

All the while Garrett had been thinking of himself, but suddenly the image in his mind was of Hazel, her belly swollen and eyes sad.

'The end result is the same.'

Dr Lee's words rattled around his head. Whether he let Hazel and their babies down now, by failing to step up, or later, after he'd tried and failed to be a dad, the end result would be the same. Only his way he'd be letting them down sooner... quitting before he'd even tried.

What kind of doctor did that? What kind of man did that? Not one he wanted to be. Whether he was ready or not, he was going to be a dad. And unless he stepped up right now he was going to forfeit his right to even try.

'I think...just maybe you're on to something there,' he said.

Dr Lee smiled. 'I suspected as much. Is there anything you'd like to add? A comment for the appraisal form, perhaps?' She held it out to him.

Garrett took it and glanced over the notes she'd made about his capabilities, his triumphs, the challenges he'd faced in his short time here and her suggestions for moving forward.

Needs more conviction!

He smiled and added his own sentence below, then signed his name with a flourish on the dotted line at the bottom of the page.

Dr Lee took the form back and read his comment out loud. *"'I'm ready to step up.'"* She laughed. 'Let's hope so!'

Garrett wasn't sure if that applied to being a father too, but he knew one thing for sure: he was going to beg Hazel for the chance.

Hazel jerked awake with a start.

Blinking through bleary eyes, she realised she'd fallen asleep in front of the TV. Her eyes felt puffy and her throat hoarse.

From all the crying, she remembered, as she reached for the TV remote.

The intercom buzzed and Hazel started.

So that was what had woken her! But who could be calling so late?

'Hello?'

'Hazel, it's me.'

Hazel stared at the intercom as though it might be lying. 'Garrett?'

'Please tell me you weren't asleep?'

'No. I mean, yes. I was. But it's fine. Did you want to come up?'

What was Garrett Buchanan doing at her door? Had he walked all the way from the hospital when his shift ended?

Hazel glanced up at the clock. It certainly seemed that way. 'If that's okay?'

Hazel glanced around the flat frantically, her eyes snagging on the plate of half-eaten toast she'd abandoned earlier and the row of incredibly practical and dreadfully unsexy knickers drying on the radiator.

'Um...sure. I'm on the first floor. Come on up.'

She buzzed Garrett in and raced across the room, scooping up the laundry and the plate.

In the kitchen, she chucked her underwear in the dryer, set the plate by the sink, and hastily splashed water on her splotchy, tear-stained face.

This was it.

Garrett was here and they were going to talk. She'd finally get the answers she'd been waiting for...

But suddenly Hazel wasn't sure she wanted to know.

What if he was coming to confirm what she already knew— that children weren't part of his plan? What if he was only here to let her down gently? To offer some token financial support, maybe, but to tell her that he wouldn't be part of their lives?

She placed a palm flat against her stomach, as though that might ease the sudden swell of nausea.

One thing at a time.

Hazel considered her pale, tired reflection in the hall mirror, her eyes still rimmed with pink. Through the door, she could hear Garrett's footsteps on the stairs.

Oh, well, there's nothing to be done for it now.

She fluffed up her flattened hair, rubbed the sleep from her eyes and pulled open the door to greet him. 'Hey.'

'Hi.'

Garrett's cheeks were pink, and Hazel wasn't sure if it was from the walk across town or embarrassment at having turned up at her door unannounced.

He rubbed a hand over the back of his neck. 'Listen, I know it's late, but—'

'It's fine, honestly. Come in.' Hazel opened the door wider and stepped aside, gesturing him in.

As he stepped through the door Hazel noticed that he was holding a bunch of pink roses at his side. He saw her looking and held them out to her.

'They're for you.'

Hazel felt her eyes widening. She knew she should reach

out and take the flowers, that she should thank him, excuse herself to grab a vase…anything. But all she could manage was to stare at him slack-jawed.

'I should never have run off the way I did. I'm sorry. I guess I just panicked. But still, that's no excuse. I mean, you must be as shocked about all this as I am, but you don't have the option to run away.'

Hazel swallowed the lump forming in her throat. 'Apology accepted.'

She took the flowers from him and showed him through to the living room.

'Take a seat. I'll make some tea.'

When she returned with the drinks she found Garrett perched awkwardly on the sofa, the cushions still indented from where she'd been sleeping. Hazel winced and hoped she hadn't left a patch of drool behind as well.

'So…' She sat down on the armchair opposite, her hands clasped together in her lap.

This was awkward.

'Nice place,' Garrett said, glancing around.

Hazel followed his gaze, seeing only the imperfections—the coffee-stained rug, the sagging bookshelves, the houseplants in desperate need of a little TLC.

'Thanks,' she said. 'It was only meant to be temporary. After my ex and I split—' She broke off suddenly.

What was she thinking? He'd come here to discuss their future and she was bringing up the past!

Garrett tilted his head. 'You were saying?' he prompted.

She waved a hand. 'It doesn't matter.'

'No, go on. Please.'

She sighed. 'We'd been living together for three years. I thought everything was going great. And then one day, out of the blue, Eric—that was his name—told me he'd been offered a new job. He hadn't mentioned that he was even applying, so I was stunned—but delighted for him, obviously. *"Great,"* I said. *"Where?"* And that's when he told me—Australia.'

Garrett spluttered and set down his tea on the coffee table. 'Australia?' he repeated. 'As in—?'

'The other side of the world,' Hazel confirmed. 'Apparently it was something he'd been thinking about for a while, but he knew I wouldn't approve so he'd kept it to himself until the last possible minute. By the time he told me he'd already accepted the offer and completed all the paperwork.' Hazel shrugged. 'As far as he was concerned there was nothing left to discuss.'

'And he didn't even think to ask you if you wanted to go with him?'

Hazel shook her head. 'I guess he knew I would say no, so he figured by not saying anything he could avoid all the tears and arguments—or at least put them off as long as possible.'

'Jesus… I don't even know what to say.'

Hazel waved a hand. 'It's fine, honestly. I mean, what *is* there to say? It was just such a shock, you know? There I was, merrily going about my life, with no idea about this big bomb that was about to go off and blow the whole thing to smithereens. Anyway, he flew out two weeks later, leaving me to deal with everything. I couldn't afford the house on my own, so I had to find somewhere else fast, and this was the only place that came up within my budget.' She gestured around her.

'Well, I like it,' Garrett said. 'I think you've done a great job with the place.'

Hazel smiled. The compliment sounded genuine, so she accepted it rather than batting it away as she normally would.

'Thanks. I've done my best, but it was a real wrench leaving the old place. It was this pretty little cottage on the outskirts of the city, and I'd put my heart and soul into decorating it. I bawled my eyes out when it was sold. Sometimes I think maybe I was more upset to lose the house than to lose him…' She trailed off, suddenly embarrassed at having opened up, at having said more than she'd meant to.

But Garrett was nodding, his expression full of sympathy. 'I get it. I felt the same about my first foster home. When my mum was alive we lived in a council flat, so when I turned up at the Joneses place it was like walking onto a film set. They had this big old place, and all this land. Looking back, it was probably only a couple of acres, but I'd never seen so much open space. On my first day there one of the hens escaped and chased me down the garden path. I cried, thinking it was going to bite me.'

Hazel laughed before clapping a hand to her mouth. 'Sorry, that's not funny.'

Garrett laughed too. 'That's okay. It really is. Anyway, I soon got used to them. There was this old one with a broken wing… I'd carry it around under my arm, showing it all the different parts of the garden, telling it about my mum…' He trailed off, his grin fading.

'Why did you have to leave?' she asked.

Garrett sighed. 'It was no one's fault. The Joneses wanted to retire… *"We can't keep doing this forever."* That's what they said when they sat the four of us foster kids down at the table to tell us. Mr Jones had had a health scare, I think. Angina, maybe. I remember him suddenly looking frailer, and my foster mum looking anxious, reminding him about pills, nagging him about cutting the fat off his bacon. Thinking about it now, I can't blame them for putting his health first, but of course I did at the time. It all felt so unfair.'

Hazel reached for his hand without thinking. 'It *was* unfair. I'm sorry.'

He looked at her hand on his and then up at her face. He seemed almost startled, as if he'd forgotten where he was… who she was.

'Anyway, what you were saying about your ex, about the house…it reminded me of that chicken. I loved the Joneses, I suppose, and their place. Not in the way I'd loved my mum, of course, but I was grateful to them for opening up their home and their lives to me…for taking a chance on an unknown kid. But that chicken—' He shook his head. 'I couldn't get over it, somehow. I must have cried over it every night for a month.'

He sighed, and placed his other hand over hers, sandwiching it between his.

'I don't know how to do this, Hazel. I don't know how to be someone who stays still, in one place, and commits to something not knowing how it might turn out.'

Hazel could feel the tears pooling in her eyes and willed

them not to spill down her cheeks. It was what she'd already known, after all.

So why did it feel like such a blow?

Garrett looked up from their hands to her face. 'But if you'll let me, I want to try.'

Hazel frowned, her tears halting. 'You mean…?'

Garrett nodded. 'I think we owe it to ourselves—and to those two little ones.' He gestured to her middle. 'Don't you?'

Hazel nodded slowly, still not quite trusting what she was hearing.

Was he really saying he wanted to stick around and be involved? To be a father to their babies?

'What about us?' she murmured.

'You mean are we a couple?'

Hazel nodded.

'Do you want us to be?'

Hazel squirmed. 'I mean…we hardly know each other…'

'Hmm… I guess that's true.' Garrett's brow creased.

'We haven't even been on a date,' Hazel pointed out.

Garrett smiled. 'Then maybe we should do something about that.'

CHAPTER FOURTEEN

HAZEL TWISTED ONE way and then the other, trying to see what she looked like from the back in her full-length mirror.

It was no use. The dress was far too tight.

'Urgh.'

She yanked it up over her head and tossed it onto the discarded pile building up on her bed.

'Back to the drawing board,' she muttered to herself.

Hazel had known her body would change during pregnancy, but she hadn't expected it to start happening so quickly. She glanced at the clock on her bedside table. She had just half an hour to get ready before she was due to meet Garrett in town.

They'd booked onto one of the city's most popular ghost walks—a walking tour of York's most haunted spots. Part of her was glad that they'd be among a crowd of tourists, because it made it seem infinitely less daunting than a real date, but she had to admit that part of her was disappointed too. That deep down she wanted Garrett Buchanan all to herself.

She rifled through her increasingly empty wardrobe, eventually settling on a vest top, a floral maxi skirt and sandals, in a nod to the balmy summer evening.

Now, if only she could settle her nerves...

'And they say she still haunts the cellar to this very day. In fact, if you take a deep breath, you might even catch a whiff of smoke from the great fire...'

The tour guide inhaled deeply and looked around to check that his audience were doing the same.

Hazel obliged, but the only thing she could smell was Garrett—though the effect was just as dizzying as if she had seen a ghost.

'You know, I feel like this would be a lot spookier if it wasn't a glorious summer's evening,' Garrett whispered.

Hazel laughed. 'I think you might be right.'

Garrett leaned in, his breath tickling her neck. 'Maybe we should do it again at Halloween?'

A shiver snaked down Hazel's spine, and it had nothing to do with ghosts and everything to do with how close Garrett was standing.

Halloween. She'd be five months pregnant by then and the whole world would be able to tell. Would she and Garrett officially be a couple? Or would their chemistry have petered out, leaving two people tethered by a pregnancy neither one of them had expected...?

Hazel's smile faltered. 'Maybe.'

'I'm sorry, we've no tables free this evening.'

'No worries,' Hazel said, though her stomach grumbled in disagreement.

They stepped back out of the restaurant—the fourth they'd tried so far, with no luck, and glanced up and down the street.

Garrett swiped a hand through his hair. 'I'm sorry. I should have thought to book in advance.'

Hazel shrugged. 'You weren't to know how busy it gets.'

Garrett pulled a face. 'I mean, it's Saturday night. I probably could have figured it out. I guess I'm a little—uh—out of practice.'

Perhaps he didn't date as often as Hazel had imagined. Or, if he did, they weren't the kind of dates where he went out for dinner.

Hazel's stomach rumbled again, and this time they both heard it.

Garrett groaned and apologised again. 'This must be the worst date you've ever been on.'

Hazel laughed. 'Not by a long shot. Listen, why don't we go back to my place and order a takeaway?'

'Are you sure?'

Hazel's stomach growled and Garrett laughed.

'I'll take that as a yes.'

Garrett Buchanan was in her flat. Again. He was sitting in her living room right now, waiting for her to bring the drink she'd offered him.

What were they going to talk about other than the obvious? Had she done the right thing, inviting him back, or were things moving too fast? But they were meant to be getting to know one another, weren't they?

Hazel's thoughts raced as she uncorked the wine, sloshing it unceremoniously into two glasses before reality hit.

She clapped a hand to her forehead.

What was she thinking?

For half a second there she'd almost forgotten…

She tipped the second glass down the sink, and poured herself an orange juice instead.

Hazel took another deep breath.

She could do this. It was a date—that was all.

Her hand moved automatically to her abdomen.

But it felt like so much more.

After ordering the food, they chatted about work, which turned into tales about their training, and finally moved on to themselves, swapping favourite films and most memorable holidays, both of them laughing when it turned out the last book they'd read was the same neonatal textbook.

'We're such clichés,' Hazel said.

'Oh, I don't know about that,' Garrett said with a smile. 'I don't remember any clichés about this.'

He gestured between the two of them, and Hazel's stomach fluttered.

'I guess you're right.'

There was a brief interruption when the food arrived, and Hazel bustled about getting plates and cutlery, but once they began tucking in the conversation continued to flow.

Hazel had expected it to be a little awkward—given the fact that they'd already slept together—and the fact she was pregnant—but it actually felt strangely normal. Or as normal as a date with the father of your unplanned twins could feel.

When Hazel glanced out of the window, the sun had set and the street lamps were lit.

Garrett got to his feet abruptly. 'I should be going. It's late and you need your sleep.'

'Right...of course.'

Ordinarily, Hazel would have been dozing off already, her eyelids drooping as she tried to concentrate on some TV show or other, but tonight was different. She was wide awake. Every fibre of her being on high alert as Garrett leaned in to kiss her goodnight.

His lips landed on her cheek, soft and warm, his stubble gently grazing her skin. 'Thank you,' he said.

'For what?'

'Giving me a chance.'

Hazel swallowed hard, her heart suddenly pounding. Every time she told herself that it was only a date, that they were just two strangers getting to know one another, she was hit by another reminder that it wasn't quite true. No matter what happened between them, Garrett was the father of her children. She could tell herself it didn't matter how things worked out, but in reality it did.

'I know I messed up, not booking a table—'

Hazel opened her mouth to protest, but Garrett rushed on.

'But, even so, this is the best first date I've ever had.'

Hazel smiled. 'Me too.'

'Though technically we cheated the system by hooking up first.'

'Right...'

'Not that I regret it.' Garrett's eyes searched her face. 'Do you?'

Hazel bit her lip, shook her head. Things might not have turned out the way she'd imagined, but she still didn't regret what had happened between them on her birthday.

How could she when it had been one of the most sensual experiences of her life?

'Good,' Garrett said softly. 'I'm glad.' He took a step closer. 'But I'm guessing it would be a bad idea if we were to repeat it.'

'Right...' Hazel said, her voice cracking.

'I mean, it would probably complicate things...'

And things were definitely complicated enough already. But that didn't stop Hazel wanting it...wanting him. Her stomach danced with butterflies as Garrett's hand cupped her jaw, his fingers sliding into her hair. Her mind knew this was indeed a bad idea, but her body didn't care, and she let out a sigh as Garrett kissed her—on the lips this time.

Why was it so difficult for her to be sensible when it came to Dr Garrett Buchanan?

She'd never had this kind of chemistry with anyone before, and it made it impossible to think clearly. Her senses were swamped by the proximity of his body, just millimetres away from her own, by his soft mouth against hers, the light brush of his stubble, the heady smell of him...

His fingertips grazed her scalp and tiny shockwaves rippled down Hazel's neck, raising the fine hairs on her arms and making her shiver with anticipation.

Garrett drew back with a sigh of his own. 'I'm sorry. I know we're meant to be getting to know each other. Not—' he gestured between them '—this.'

Hazel wanted to argue with him—wanted to list all the reasons they should give in and just allow this to happen, but deep down she knew he was right. They already knew they were compatible in the bedroom. The question was whether or not this intense physical connection translated into anything deeper.

As if reading her mind, Garrett took a small step backwards, increasing the distance between them. 'I should probably go...'

'Right.' Hazel nodded, swallowing her disappointment.

'Goodnight, Hazel.'

Hazel waited until she heard the front door downstairs close with a soft thud and then let out her breath in a long whoosh.

She knew pregnancy came with a whole host of weird and wonderful symptoms, but she didn't recall ever having been warned about this insatiable desire. Though she suspected that had less to do with her hormones and more to do with the electrifying chemistry she and Garrett seemed to have.

She only hoped they could build it into something more. Something that would last.

CHAPTER FIFTEEN

'MORNING, HAZEL.'

Anna had been on the night shift, and yet somehow she looked chirpier than Hazel felt after ten hours of sleep.

Why had no one ever told her just how rough early pregnancy felt?

'Morning...'

Hazel tried to sound more enthusiastic than she was. It wasn't that she didn't love her job—but, *man*, she could have used an extra couple of hours of sleep. Besides, work meant seeing Garrett, and she wasn't sure how they were supposed to act around one another—given they were now dating and she was carrying his babies.

Hazel's hand fluttered towards her abdomen instinctively, but she jammed it into the pocket of her scrub top at the last minute and pulled out a pen.

'Ready for handover when you are.'

Hazel slotted the capillary sample tube into the blood gas machine and waited for the results to print.

'Hey.'

She turned to find Garrett standing behind her. His hair was even more rumpled than usual, and she had to resist the urge to reach up and straighten it out.

'Hey.'

Turned out Hazel needn't have worried about how to act around him. The shift had been so busy they hadn't had a chance to speak until now.

'I just wanted to say thanks again for last night,' Garrett said.

The blood gas machine whirred as it began printing out the results Hazel was waiting for.

'No problem. I had a great time.'

Garrett rubbed the back of his neck. 'I was wondering if you'd like to do it again sometime?'

Hazel's stomach flipped, but she tried to act casual, reaching for the blood gas results. 'Sure, I'd love to.'

Garrett beamed. 'Great.'

Hazel smiled in return, but when she glanced down at the results in her hand her expression fell, her brow creasing as she tried to make sense of the numbers.

'Is there a problem?'

'It's baby Max. His pH is low and his PCO2 is high.'

'Here.' Garrett held out his hand. 'Let me take a look.'

Hazel's palm tingled as his fingers brushed against hers.

'Hmm… Maybe we should try CPAP?' he suggested.

It wasn't until much later, when Max was finally settled on his CPAP machine and her shift was nearing its end, that Hazel realised they hadn't actually set a date after all.

Garrett straightened the tablecloth for what must have been the twentieth time and stood back to assess the scene.

The empty wine bottle doubling as a candle holder was a nice touch, but he wished he had matching plates. It wasn't something he'd ever considered before, but now, with Hazel coming round for a romantic dinner for two, it suddenly seemed essential.

Garrett glanced at the clock on the wall. There was no time for a last-minute dash to the shops now. Her shift was due to finish in half an hour, although in reality that meant it would probably be at least an hour before she arrived…

Garrett adjusted the tablecloth again.

It wasn't that he was nervous, exactly, but… Well, he was nervous.

He and Hazel had been working opposite shifts for a couple of weeks now, so it had taken longer than he'd expected for them to find an evening when they were both free. In the end he'd suggested that she come round to his place after work and he'd cook her a meal. It wouldn't quite be the five-star fine dining experience he'd hoped to give her, to make up for last time, but who knew when they might next both be free?

The truth was, Garrett didn't want to wait any longer. Already his gut was needling with anticipation at seeing her. They'd barely crossed paths at work for a fortnight, and their snatched conversations and stolen glances had only fuelled his desire to see her again, to talk to her, to have her all to himself.

It was unexpected—and a little alarming. They were meant to be getting to know one another for the sake of the pregnancy, to see if they were compatible enough to raise kids together. But this felt like so much more, somehow. Like nothing Garrett had ever experienced.

He wanted tonight to be special. He wanted to show Hazel that he appreciated being given a chance to prove himself— to show that he could be relied upon to do right by her and their unborn children.

Children.

The thought of it still knocked the breath from his lungs every time.

Twins.

As if the idea of becoming a parent wasn't mind-blowing enough.

Garrett shook his head and turned his attention to the oven, where his homemade lasagne was bubbling away nicely. He turned down the heat and decided on a last-minute shower to cool off.

Though he had a feeling that once Hazel arrived, it wouldn't make a difference. She had a way of raising his temperature just by looking at him.

'That was delicious.' Hazel set her cutlery down on her plate with a satisfied sigh. 'Thanks for going to so much trouble.'

'It was no trouble at all.'

But Hazel knew that wasn't true. She could see the effort Garrett had gone to to make his staff accommodation look homely and inviting. To make the tiny fold-down table and chairs look like a cosy table for two at a bistro. He'd even laid a tablecloth and lit a candle, and she was fairly certain neither of those were a regular feature in Garrett Buchanan's kitchenette as he wolfed down a microwave meal for one after a busy shift.

'Well, thanks all the same.'

He shooed away her offer to help clear away the dishes, leaving her to wander around the tiny flat, taking it all in. Not that there was much to see. Aside from a stack of textbooks and a lone plant on the coffee table, there were very few personal touches. There was a desk in one corner that held a laptop and a stained coffee mug. Above it hung a cork noticeboard, peppered with notes and flyers—mainly takeaway menus, Hazel noted as she stepped closer, and handwritten reminders in Garrett's familiar scrawl.

Bin day Tuesday one read.

Another note had the standard drug calculation formula nurses used written in red capitals:

WHAT YOU WANT X WHAT IT'S IN DIVIDED BY WHAT YOU'VE GOT.

Hazel smiled, remembering how long it had taken her to memorise that when she'd first started working with neonates.

Behind it, she caught a glimpse of something else. Not a handwritten note, and not a takeaway menu either.

She lifted the scrap of paper and there, beneath it, was a sun-faded photo of a small red-headed boy, clutching a scruffy-looking hen under one arm and squinting warily into the camera.

Hazel's heart swelled and tears needled the backs of her eyes.

He must have kept this picture safe all these years…through all those house moves.

She peered closely at the small boy in the photograph, and with a jolt realised that she was catching a glimpse of what her children might look like as they grew up.

She stepped back from the photo. Whatever happened between her and Garrett tonight—or tomorrow, or next month—they would be inextricably linked forever.

The realisation made her chest feel tight and she struggled to catch her breath. There was so much riding on this date…

on this relationship. And not just for the babies, but for her too. She could feel herself falling for Garrett more with each passing day.

Hazel turned from the faded photograph and made her way into the kitchen, where Garrett was pouring alcohol-free wine into two glasses.

'Hey, just in time.' He held out a glass to her. 'Is this stuff any good?' Garrett sniffed his glass and wrinkled his nose.

Hazel laughed. 'You get used to it.'

Garrett lifted his glass and tapped it against hers. 'Well, then—cheers.'

'Cheers.'

'I know it wasn't exactly haute cuisine—' Garrett began.

'It was delicious.' Hazel cut him off. 'And you need to stop apologising. I've had a lovely evening.'

Garrett smiled. 'I'm glad. Me too.' He set his wine glass down on the side. 'There's something I've been meaning to ask you...'

Hazel's heart sped up. 'Oh?'

'When's your birthday?'

A mix of relief and disappointment surged through Hazel. 'Why do you ask?'

Garrett shrugged. 'It's the kind of thing people ask on a date, isn't it? And that day when I came to find you, the receptionist in ED asked, and I realised I didn't know.'

Hazel smiled. 'You do know. You were at my party.'

Garrett's brow creased. 'Your...?'

Hazel laughed as realisation dawned on Garrett's features.

'That was *your* party?'

Hazel nodded.

'You mean, when we—? That was your birthday?'

Hazel nodded again, her face heating at the memory.

'I had no idea.'

Hazel shrugged. 'It was my big three-oh and I was freaking out a bit.'

'Well, you were hiding it very well,' Garrett said. 'I'm only sorry I didn't know or I'd have got you a gift.'

Hazel looked down at her stomach and Garrett followed her gaze. They both laughed.

'Right…' Garrett said.

'You know, I'd never done anything like that before,' Hazel admitted.

'Me neither.'

Hazel's stomach danced with butterflies as Garrett took a step closer, sandwiching her between the kitchen sink and his tall, lean body, just inches away from hers.

'I know we said it would complicate things, but I'd really like to kiss you right now.'

Hazel swallowed. 'I'd like that too.'

Garrett dipped his head towards her. 'So maybe it doesn't have to complicate things…?'

Hazel's brain was firing warning signals to her heart, but it was difficult to pay attention when Garrett's mouth was so close and her senses were swamped by the dazzling blue of his eyes and the heady scent of his skin.

Hazel leaned in, closing the distance between them. 'I mean, really, how much more complicated could they get?' she murmured.

Then she pressed her lips to his and uttered a silent apology to her heart.

Garrett hadn't been sure if Hazel would want a repeat of what had happened between them at the party, but when he felt the heat, the need behind her kiss, he knew.

She wanted him as much as he wanted her.

He plunged one hand into the silk of her hair and pulled her into him, needing her closer, wanting nothing between them.

But then he forced himself to stop. To pull back and take a breath.

Hazel blinked up at him, her expression wary. 'Something wrong?'

'No—God, no. You're amazing…'

'But?' Hazel prompted.

Garrett wasn't sure how to say what he wanted to say. The first time they'd had sex it had been a wordless, breathless affair, in the upstairs bedroom at a house party. He'd taken her against the wall, her beautiful summer dress hiked up around her waist. And it had been wonderful. Better than wonderful, even. Incredible…amazing…the best night of his life. But how could he explain that he wanted—no, *needed* to slow things down? To really appreciate what was happening between them?

He scratched the back of his neck. 'I just thought…maybe we could go somewhere more comfortable?'

Hazel looked around the tiny kitchen and laughed. 'I guess you're right.'

She kissed him softly on the lips, and Garrett took her hand and led her to his bedroom.

This is unexpected.

Hazel had been ready for Garrett to take her then and there, against the kitchen counter, with the dishes draining on the side, half in and half out of their clothes. She'd wanted him to… Or at least she'd thought she had.

But now, with the sun setting through the bedroom curtains, the summer breeze drifting in through the open window and her desire mounting with every second that passed, Hazel wasn't sure.

Maybe Garrett had been right. Maybe this way was better.

'Let me see you,' he said.

Hazel removed her clothing piece by piece. It was the closest she'd ever come to a striptease, and the way his eyes lingered over every single reveal of skin made her feel as if she was under a spotlight. The heat rose in her with every item she shed, until Hazel's skin felt like it was on fire beneath Garrett's gaze.

Just as she was about to make a joke about first trimester bloating, to break the almost unbearable tension that was building, Garrett began his own striptease of sorts, unbuttoning his shirt with a deliberate slowness, his eyes never leaving hers. Hazel fell silent…waiting, wanting.

When, at last, they were both naked, the air around them

felt statically charged. Hazel licked her lips, resisting the urge to squirm, and tried to keep her eyes on Garrett's.

'You're perfect,' Garrett said.

For once, Hazel didn't feel like arguing.

They both stepped forward in unison and then Garrett's hands were on her. She let her own hands stray across his body, murmuring appreciation against his lips.

Garrett walked her backwards to the edge of the bed and then lowered her gently down, kneeling between her legs. Hazel felt a flicker of anxiety, but then he was raining kisses over her thighs as his fingers explored her, and Hazel forgot to feel shy, or to wonder when her last bikini wax had been. All she could focus on was Garrett's touch, gentle and insistent, and then his mouth, hot and wanting against her.

A moan escaped Hazel's lips, and before long there was nothing but the rhythm of Garrett's tongue and his fingers, and the slippery heat building between Hazel's thighs. Her orgasm was swift and noisy. But unlike at the party she didn't have to worry about who might hear, or what anyone might think, leaving her free to surrender to the ripples of pleasure flooding her body.

Garrett trailed kisses up her body. 'You're a goddess…'

And right then, with the candlelight flickering around them and Garrett worshipping her on his knees, Hazel felt like one.

She only hoped it wouldn't hurt too much when she finally came crashing down to earth.

'Good morning.'

Hazel nearly jumped out of her skin. She sat bolt-upright, almost headbutting Garrett, who was perched on the side of the bed and had to dive backwards to avoid getting knocked out.

He winced. 'Sorry.'

'Oh, my God. I'm so sorry. I didn't realise—Wait, what time is it?'

Garrett looked decidedly sheepish. 'Six-thirty. I've got work at seven, so…'

She'd stayed the night.

They hadn't spoken about it. It had just happened.

Lying there in each other's arms, talking in quiet murmurs, it had seemed the most natural thing in the world to allow herself to drift off to sleep. But now, waking up naked in Garrett's bed, Hazel felt strangely exposed and vulnerable. As if she'd been caught doing something she shouldn't.

Hazel tried to rub the sleep out of her eyes—and then remembered she hadn't removed her make-up last night, so was probably making the situation even worse.

God, she must look terrible.

Garrett, on the other hand, looked as fresh as a daisy.

Damn him.

'Right,' she mumbled. 'Work.'

'I didn't want to just leave without saying goodbye,' Garrett said. 'I made you a coffee.' He gestured to the bedside table. 'Don't worry, it's decaf.'

Hazel looked from Garrett to the oversized *Trust Me, I'm a Doctor* mug.

'You got decaf in, just for me?'

He shrugged. 'I noticed you don't bring coffee to work any more. I figured it must be a craving thing.'

It was a tiny thing. A silly thing. Hazel knew that, but just the fact that he'd noticed, and had gone to the trouble of buying a jar of decaf, made her smile and the buzzing in her head quieten just a little.

'Thanks.'

'No problem.' Garrett checked his watch. 'I'd better go if I'm going to grab a coffee before handover.'

Hazel shuffled upright. 'Of course. I'll get dressed and order a taxi.'

Garrett frowned, and touched a hand to her bare shoulder. 'Hey. No need to rush. You're on the late shift today, right?'

Hazel looked at him dubiously. 'Right...'

Garrett shrugged. 'So take your time. I'll leave the spare key on the table and you can lock up when you leave.'

'Are you sure?'

'Of course I'm sure.' He planted a kiss on her forehead. 'I'll see you later.'

Hazel listened for the click of the front door and then fell back against Garrett's pillows with a groan.

Oh, God, what had she done?

She gingerly sipped the coffee he'd left her, but it was no use. Her stomach was churning almost as fast as her mind.

She'd committed the ultimate act of self-betrayal and now her heart would pay the price. After all, it was one thing to sleep with a handsome but highly unavailable doctor—it was quite another to accidentally fall in love with him.

And last night Hazel had done both.

CHAPTER SIXTEEN

GARRETT COULDN'T STOP smiling as he waited in line for his morning coffee. He knew that if he kept it up someone was sure to comment, and then what would he say? But right now he didn't care.

Last night with Hazel had been amazing. It had been every bit as good as he'd remembered and more.

He knew she'd disagree if he told her, but already she was glowing, her body softening and rounding at the edges, igniting something primal in Garrett. She was carrying his children, and for once the thought hadn't sent ripples of anxiety through him, but a surge of fierce protectiveness.

They'd fallen asleep in one another's arms, and when he'd woken to find her at his side it had felt like the most natural thing in the world.

It was only after he'd left, setting his spare key on the coffee table before he went, that he'd stopped to wonder if they were moving too fast.

Should they have waited longer before sleeping together? Spent more time getting to know one another?

His smile faltered now as he moved forward in the queue. The electrifying chemistry they had made it nearly impossible to think clearly when Hazel was near him, but he knew he had to try. He wanted to get this right. There was so much riding on it.

Garrett stepped forward to give his coffee order and tried to ignore the slither of fear lurking at the base of his skull. The one that had been with him since his days in foster care. The voice that told him to be careful. Not to get too comfortable. That nothing this good could ever last. That it would soon be time to move on.

Shift work made any kind of routine impossible, but they'd fallen into a rhythm of sorts. Snatching conversations and lunches together in the canteen at work, spending two or three nights together each week, staying over at one another's places...

It was still early days, but Hazel felt hopeful. The more she got to know Garrett, the more she wanted to get to know him. And the more time she spent around him, the more she wanted to spend time with him. She was wary of letting herself fall in too deep, but part of her knew it was a little late for that.

He'd held her hand at her dating scan, leaning into the side of the narrow examination table and letting out a whoosh of breath onto her neck when they'd been given the news that both twins were measuring perfectly and everything looked as it should.

Now, in her second trimester, Hazel was beginning to feel more like herself again—albeit a slightly more round version. Her baggy work scrubs were helping to keep their secret under wraps, but Hazel knew that even they couldn't conceal a twin pregnancy for much longer.

She tugged her scrubs top down as she reached for the suction tubing on the wall and tried not to think about the fact that Garrett and the other doctors were at the next incubator along, doing a ward round, or about how much longer the two of them could keep up this charade.

When the doctors reached the baby she was caring for Hazel took a step back to allow them to perform their examinations, and so she could keep busy charting observations rather than trying to avoid catching Garrett's eye.

'We're going to need an X-ray here,' Dr Lee said.

'Right.' Hazel nodded. 'Wait! What?'

Her head snapped up and her eyes met Garrett's over the top of the incubator.

She couldn't assist with an X-ray when she was pregnant! But of course Dr Lee didn't know that. No one did.

Hazel looked wildly around the Intensive Care nursery, but aside from the doctors there was only Ciara, and she was busy helping one of the new mums set up a breast pump beside her baby's incubator.

'Uh…an X-ray…right,' Hazel repeated slowly, her brain working at a million miles per hour.

'Is there a problem?'

Hazel turned back and found Dr Lee watching her.

'Um…no. No problem. I just…' Hazel threw a desperate glance in Garrett's direction, but if it was possible for a person to shrug with their eyeballs, that was what he was doing.

Hazel sighed. There was nothing for it. She was going to have to come clean. 'Actually, Dr Lee… I'm pregnant.'

It had to come out sooner or later. Admittedly, she'd have preferred to do it on her terms, but she couldn't compromise the safety of her unborn babies just to avoid the awkward questions she was sure would be coming any minute now.

'Oh, my goodness—congratulations!' Dr Lee said. If she'd suspected it, she certainly wasn't letting on as she beamed at Hazel.

Aasiyah clapped her hands together. 'Congratulations!' she chorused.

Garrett dropped his gaze from Hazel's to the floor and rubbed the back of his neck.

Hazel's face felt as if it was on fire. 'Thanks,' she mumbled.

Ciara appeared, seemingly from nowhere. 'What are we congratulating?'

Hazel sighed.

'Hazel's pregnant,' Garrett said quietly.

'Oh, wow! That's fantastic news. Congratulations!' She grinned. 'Finally one of your own, after working with babies for—how long now?' Ciara prompted.

'Nine years,' Hazel said automatically. 'And actually…it isn't just one.'

Ciara's eyes grew wide. 'Twins?'

Hazel nodded, biting her lip.

She waited for her colleagues to begin warning her of all the added risks and complications, but Dr Lee only smiled.

'Wonderful,' she said. 'Just wonderful. I'm so pleased for you, Hazel.'

Ciara pulled her into a hug. 'Me too, you sly fox! I didn't even know you were seeing anyone...'

'Yeah, well it's fairly new, and it was all a bit...unexpected,' Hazel admitted, still blushing.

'So, when do we get to meet the father?'

Hazel's eyes slid automatically to Garrett, and he gave the briefest of nods.

Or perhaps she'd imagined it? Was he really ready for their relationship to become public knowledge? Was she?

Dr Lee, Aasiyah and Ciara were all looking at her now, expectantly.

'Um...actually, you've already met him,' Hazel said.

Ciara frowned. 'We have?'

Garrett cleared his throat and they all turned to him.

Realisation dawned on Ciara's face. 'Wait...are you telling me...?'

Dr Lee smiled again, and nudged her shoulder against Aasiyah, whose round eyes told Hazel that she'd worked it out too.

Tension rippled through Hazel's body and her fists clenched automatically at her sides. It was all so awkward. What must they think? But then she felt the warmth of Garrett's hand as it took hold of hers and squeezed.

'It's true. Hazel and I are a couple.'

She looked up at him in surprise, and then back to their colleagues, who were all clearly as stunned as she was, but smiling all the same.

'Well, then, congratulations to you both,' Dr Lee said. 'Now, about that X-ray...'

'Of course.' Garrett gave Hazel's hand one last squeeze before he let go.

'I'll take care of the X-ray.' Ciara winked. 'If you can show my baby's mum where she can store the breast milk she's expressed for him?'

'No problem,' Hazel said, her feet moving on autopilot while her mind spun like a broken record, going over and over what had just happened.

There it was.

There was no going back now. Not only had she announced her pregnancy, but she and Garrett were officially a couple.

Hazel's eyes fluttered open at the sound of the front door closing. She wriggled herself upright on the sofa and rolled her neck.

Damn it.

She hadn't meant to fall asleep.

She swiped the back of her hand across her mouth in case she'd been drooling.

Jeez, pregnancy was attractive.

Garrett stepped into the living room. 'Sorry,' he whispered. 'I didn't mean to wake you.'

'I needed waking,' Hazel mumbled. 'What time is it anyway?'

'Eleven.'

Hazel rubbed her eyes with the heels of her palms—then remembered that she'd applied mascara earlier, which would now be smudged around her eyes, making her look like a raccoon, no doubt.

'Finished late?' she murmured.

'Yeah.' Garrett dumped his backpack and joined her on the sofa. 'By the time I'd written up my notes, had a quick shower and ordered a taxi it was ten-thirty.'

'It's no good,' Hazel said. 'We can't keep doing this.'

Garrett hung his head. 'I know. I'm sorry. Next time I get held up I'll spend the night at my own place.'

Suddenly Hazel was wide awake. 'No, Garrett, that's not what I meant.'

Garrett frowned. 'It isn't?'

Hazel shook her head. 'I meant maybe there's another solution that wouldn't have you traipsing backwards and forwards across the city.'

'Such as?'

Hazel hesitated. She wasn't sure how he was going to respond to what she was about to say, but it had been on her mind for a few weeks now, and of all the solutions she'd come up with it was the one that made the most sense, long term.

She took a deep breath. 'Maybe we should look for a place together?'

Move in together?

Garrett opened his mouth to speak, then closed it again, frowning.

Was she serious? Or was she just half-asleep and sick of sitting up waiting for him when he was late night after night?

'Are you sure?' he asked.

Hazel shrugged. 'I mean, why not? All being well, there'll be four of us come March, and we won't all fit here.' She gestured around her.

Garrett looked at the cosy living room. He loved Hazel's place. It was warm and inviting, and so very her, with the mismatched plant pots and brightly patterned rugs, but she was right, of course. It was a generously sized, nicely decorated one-bedroom flat, but totally impractical for a family of four.

A part of him had known they'd have to have this conversation sooner or later. After all, it wasn't as though his bachelor pad in the hospital digs was a more suitable place to raise twins, so clearly they were going to have to find somewhere ahead of Hazel's due date. But… He'd never lived with anyone before. Not since his early days at medical school, anyway, and even then he'd got out of shared housing as soon as he could.

Not that he'd disliked his fellow students—it was just that after so many years in foster care he'd been desperate for four walls he could call his own. Somewhere he could close the door and be alone.

If he moved in with Hazel there'd be none of that. She'd be there all the time—and so would he. There'd be no escaping one another. They'd be together at work and at home.

What if, after spending all that time together, they realised they didn't like one another so much after all?

'Garrett?'

Hazel's voice brought him back to reality.

She placed a hand on his arm. 'Look, we're both exhausted.

This probably wasn't the best moment to bring this up. Why don't we talk about it another time?'

Her make-up was smudged around her eyes but they still sparkled, filling him with the same warmth he felt emanating from this flat. It wasn't about where they were—it was about her. Wherever she was felt like home to him.

'Let's do it,' he said.

'Really?'

Garrett could hear the doubt in her voice but he nodded. 'Let's find a place together. Somewhere with fewer stairs and a doorway wide enough for a double buggy. Near enough to the hospital that we can both get to work easily, but without being right on the doorstep. Somewhere we both love.'

'Not asking for much, then?' Hazel teased.

Garrett pulled her towards him. 'Honestly? If you're there it will be perfect.'

Hazel rolled her eyes. 'That was too corny for words.'

But she was grinning all the same.

Garrett couldn't help but grin back, and at that moment he decided to do something he hadn't done in a very long time and trust his feelings—trust that what he and Hazel were building was real, and that if they got it right it might just have a chance of lasting.

CHAPTER SEVENTEEN

'I'VE GOT GENTAMICIN due at six,' Ciara said. 'Any chance you can check it with me?'

'Sure.'

Hazel peeled off her gloves and apron and washed her hands, then quickly jotted down baby Max's hourly observations before she joined Ciara to check the medication.

They ran through the prescription chart together, and Hazel watched as Ciara drew up the correct dosage before accompanying her to the baby's incubator, where they checked the number on baby Sasha's ID band against the number on the prescription.

Neither was in any doubt that the tiny twenty-four weeker lying prone in her nest was Sasha, but it was standard protocol for any medication, and these safeguards existed for a reason. So, as tempting as it was sometimes to skip them, Hazel never did.

Her lower back twinged and she pressed a hand to it. Being on her feet all day was getting tougher with each passing week of her pregnancy.

Ciara caught her wince. 'Take a break,' Ciara said. 'Honestly. I can hold the fort here.'

'Are you sure?'

Ciara nodded. 'Absolutely.'

In the break room Hazel made herself soup in a mug and a slice of buttered toast and sat down heavily on a chair. The further along she got in pregnancy, the harder it was to keep doing her job the way she wanted. Now in her third trimester, her expanding stomach strained against the extra-large scrubs she'd managed to dig out of the linen room.

Her feet were expanding too, from her being on them all day without a break, and she'd given up trying to squash them into anything other than the widest-fitting rubber clogs.

All in all, she was feeling highly unattractive and pretty damn fed up.

So of course that was when Garrett strolled in.

Hazel dashed a hand hastily across her chin, pretty sure she'd dribbled some tomato soup there.

'Hey,' Garrett said. 'Good to see you taking a break.'

Hazel didn't mention that this was the first time she'd sat down since she'd gone to the bathroom about three hours ago.

'How's it going in there?' He slid into the seat opposite.

Hazel shrugged. 'Not too bad.' She rapped her knuckles against the tabletop. 'Touch wood.'

'Good soup?'

Hazel pulled a face. 'Not particularly. But it's quick and I'm starving.'

'We can get a takeaway after the house-viewing if you're still hungry later.'

'Sounds good.'

This was the most promising viewing they'd arranged so far. After weeks of traipsing around too-small, too-damp, too-expensive properties, they'd finally landed on one they were both excited about. A three-bed cottage just a short drive from the hospital and with a garden!

Hazel could just picture it now—her and Garrett pushing the babies on swings, or helping them navigate a little plastic slide in the sunshine.

'Well, I'm just about finished, so shall I meet you there?'

Hazel had assumed they'd be going to the house viewing together, and swallowed her surprise along with the horrid soup. 'Oh…sure.'

'You have the address, right?'

Hazel nodded. 'It's in the email from Lorna—the estate agent.'

Garrett stood and gave her a quick kiss.

On her forehead, Hazel noted. *Not her lips.*

Mind you, he probably didn't want to taste the remnants of this disgusting soup…

'Great. Let's hope this is the one!' Garrett said, but he was already halfway out the door.

Hazel rinsed the remaining soup down the sink and washed up the bowl and spoon, trying to ignore the gnawing in her gut. She told herself it was hunger. She was growing two babies, and had barely eaten all day, but deep down she knew that wasn't the reason.

Something was off.

Garrett had seemed distracted for a couple of weeks now— ever since the anomaly scan. After his initial relief at the news that their babies were healthy and growing well he'd seemed distant, somehow. It was as though reality had finally hit.

Was he getting cold feet? Did he not fancy her now she was huge?

Hazel could understand that. She hardly recognised herself any more. But it still hurt.

Weren't men supposed to find their pregnant partners irresistible?

Mind you, even if Garrett did miraculously find her attractive, she'd been so exhausted lately, and their shifts had clashed so much, they'd barely had a night off together for him to act on it.

Shouldn't she be glowing around about now?

Hazel had never felt less glowing in her life as she yanked open the door of the breakroom.

'Aasiyah, have you seen Garrett?'

Aasiyah looked up from the notes she was writing. 'He's in the resource room.'

'Great—thanks.'

She was going to try and catch Garrett before he left. Ask him what was wrong. Suggest that they spent their one evening off together doing something more enjoyable—and romantic—than yet another house-viewing.

But the resource room was empty. The glowing computer screen was the only sign that someone had recently been in there.

Hazel lowered herself into the desk chair with a sigh.

She'd just have to speak to him later. Maybe if this house really was the one they could celebrate with a drink afterwards, and then Garrett might be tempted to open up and say what was on his mind.

Hazel's arm nudged the mouse and the computer screen flickered into life. Her eyes skimmed over the words in front of her, confusion giving way to dismay as she began to understand what she was seeing.

It was a job advert for a neonatal registrar at Shoreside Hospital…in Devon.

But surely he wouldn't…?

They were moving in together. They were going to be parents. He'd promised to stick around… So why was he looking at an advert for a job three hundred miles away?

Hazel skimmed the ad again. The closing date was tomorrow, so if he had applied it must have been a last-minute decision.

Did that make it better, or worse?

She swallowed the lump forming in her throat and took a deep breath. It wasn't that she didn't trust him…but she had to know.

She clicked into the browser history and there it was. With a time stamp of just ten minutes ago, it was the evidence that she'd hoped not to find.

Thank you for your application.

Reference number 307501

Tears sprang to Hazel's eyes. This was why Garrett had been so distant. He had no intention of sticking around after all.

He was leaving her.

Hazel asked the taxi to drop her at the end of the street. It was raining hard, but she needed time to compose herself before she saw Garrett. She needed to be able to hold it together at least until they'd got through this house-viewing.

Then she could confront him.

Then she could finally let him see her broken heart.

The estate agent's car was just pulling up outside the house and already Hazel loved the place. The cul-de-sac was quiet, and the cottage itself was set back from the road with a sweet little front garden.

When Hazel reached the garden gate she saw that Garrett was already waiting beneath the front porch, sheltering from the driving rain.

Hazel pushed the gate and it creaked. Garrett's smile when he turned sent another fault line tearing through Hazel's heart.

How could he look at her like that? How could he keep up this charade when he was planning to leave her?

Hazel tried to smile back, but she felt her eyes filling with tears and hoped she could pass off her smudged mascara as being a result of the rain.

'So glad you could both make it,' Lorna the estate agent was saying as she bustled up the path, holding a folder over her head. 'I think this one is going to be perfect for you. It ticks all your boxes.'

Garrett took Hazel's hand and gave it a squeeze. 'You okay?'

Hazel nodded. She couldn't bring herself to speak or to look at him.

The estate agent threw open the yellow front door and stepped inside, scooping up a handful of unopened mail as she went. 'Come on in and see what you think.'

What Hazel thought was that this was going to be much harder than she'd anticipated. Garrett might be a master at pretending everything was fine, but it turned out Hazel wasn't. If the house itself had been awful, that might have made it easier—but it wasn't. Just as Lorna had promised, it was perfect.

There was a living room with a log burner, a second room that would make an excellent playroom, and a kitchen with enough space for a table. The garden was mostly overgrown lawn, but there were secure fences on all sides, and at the bottom an old tyre swing hung from the thick branch of an oak tree.

Hazel hoped that upstairs might reveal some black mould, or perhaps asbestos ceiling tiles in the bathroom. Something that would rule it irrevocably out of the equation so that she

and Garrett could get out of here and get to the business of
breaking up.

No such luck.

There were three good-sized bedrooms and a family bathroom, with a separate bathtub and shower cubicle.

'That looks big enough for two,' Garrett whispered with
a wink.

Hazel's heart stuttered.

Was he really making a sex joke right now?

She turned to the estate agent and began asking questions
that she didn't really want the answers to. Questions about the
neighbourhood, about the price, about schools... Garrett interjected with a few questions of his own and Lorna obligingly
answered them all—not that Hazel was paying the slightest
bit of attention.

*How could he stand there and fake it, knowing that just a
few hours ago he'd applied for a job hundreds of miles away
without even mentioning it to her?*

Finally Lorna seemed to register that Hazel wasn't really
listening to her waffle about low crime rates and onward
chains—or maybe she was just running out of things to say.
Either way, she stopped talking and smiled.

'Why don't I leave you to have another wander around by
yourselves? That way you can get a proper feel for the place
without me crowding you.'

Hazel moved to the bedroom window and stared out through
the rain-streaked glass at the perfectly imperfect back garden,
with its impossibly tall dandelions peeking up through the
grass and a view of the open fields beyond. She waited for
the estate agent's footsteps to recede down the staircase before finally allowing the hot tears to spill down her cheeks.

Garrett moved to stand beside her. 'Well, what do you
think?'

Hazel turned to him, making no effort to hide her sadness now.

After all, what was the point?

'Hazel? What's wrong? Don't you like it?'

'I love it...' She sniffed.

'Then what is it? Why are you crying? Did something happen at work?'

'I *know*, Garrett.'

His brow creased. 'Know what?'

Hazel swiped at her cheeks, though it was pointless really, when the tears kept coming and she couldn't seem to stop them. 'I know why you've been so distracted lately.'

Garrett's blue eyes widened. 'You do?'

It was true, then.

Hazel nodded.

Garrett exhaled. 'I'm sorry. I should have told you. But I couldn't find the right time.'

'The right time?' A spark of fury surged through Hazel, momentarily interrupting her grief. 'Before putting your application in might have been a start!'

Garrett frowned. 'Application? Hazel, what are you talking about?'

The anger was making itself at home inside Hazel now, and she let it.

How dared he?

'Don't pretend you don't know.'

Garrett swiped a hand across his face. 'I'm not pretending. I genuinely have no idea.'

'I saw the job advert!' Hazel snapped.

'Whoa…hold on.' Garrett held up his hands. 'You mean the registrar post?'

Hazel folded her arms across her chest, half in anger and half in an attempt to soothe herself. 'Why? Was there more than one?'

'What? No! Hazel, that application wasn't mine.'

Hazel had been ready with a scathing retort, but at that her mouth snapped shut.

Garrett's eyes grew wide. 'Wait a minute… Did you seriously think…?' He trailed off, shaking his head.

Hazel's heart had been in her throat, and now it plummeted. She had thought he was leaving her. She hadn't even stopped to think that there might be an alternative explanation.

How could she have jumped to that conclusion so quickly? Without even asking him?

But she knew the answer to that. Because it had happened to her before, and her heart was still on guard, waiting to make sure it didn't happen again.

Garrett swiped a hand through his hair. 'I was proofreading it for Aasiyah. She told me that if it all looked okay I should just hit send or she'd be dithering over it all evening.' He looked around the empty room and back at Hazel. 'I can't believe you'd even think…'

A sob burst from Hazel's chest. 'I didn't want to believe it,' she said between tears. 'But it all made sense. You've seemed so distracted lately… And then I saw the application confirmation—'

'And you assumed I was abandoning you? Hazel, how could you believe that?'

He was right. How could she?

Hazel was a swirling mess of emotions. Relief, anger, embarrassment, confusion and guilt.

How could she have been so quick to think the worst of him?

The man she'd fallen in love with…the father of her unborn children…

'I'm sorry. It's just that you've been so distant. I knew something was on your mind. When I saw the job advert I just figured that was the reason. That it was all too much for you and you wanted a way out.'

'Hazel, I would never do that to you. *Never.* You know that, right?'

She did know that, Hazel realised. On some level she'd known it couldn't be true, but instead of listening to her instinct she'd panicked and assumed the worst. Assumed that, just like in her last relationship, her partner was hiding his true feelings and desires and there was no way they could both want the same future. No way that she'd finally get everything she longed for.

'I'm sorry,' she said again.

'No, *I'm* sorry.' Garrett took a step back. 'I should have told you what was going on sooner, then maybe it wouldn't have come to this…' He shook his head. 'The day of the anomaly scan…it was the anniversary of my mum's death.'

Hazel inhaled sharply. 'Oh, Garrett, why didn't you say?'

'It didn't seem fair, somehow, to burden you when you already had so much on your mind. I thought that seeing the twins, hearing that they were healthy, would be enough of a distraction that it wouldn't affect me…but I guess I was wrong.'

Hazel placed a hand on his arm awkwardly and they both looked down at it.

She let her arm fall back to her side. 'I'm sorry.'

'So am I.'

The estate agent walked back into the room. 'So, any thoughts on the house?'

Garret glanced over at her, and then back to Hazel. Their eyes met, and when he spoke Hazel could feel the sorrow behind his words.

'I think we need more time.'

CHAPTER EIGHTEEN

OUTSIDE THE RAIN had stopped and the air was thick with the smell of damp earth.

Hazel watched the estate agent's car pull away from the kerb and turned back to Garrett, who stood looking at her from beneath the porch of their dream house.

Lorna had been right after all. It was everything they'd been looking for and it was theirs for the taking. All they had to do was put in an offer. But how could they after what had just happened between them?

Garrett should be smiling…she should be happy. But instead Hazel felt as if her heart was breaking.

How could it have gone so wrong, so quickly?

She couldn't help but blame herself for jumping to conclusions…for thinking the worst of the man she was supposed to be moving in with, the father of her unborn children. But she couldn't deny that there was some small part of her that wondered if it wasn't better this way—if it would have come to this anyway.

True, Garrett hadn't let her down yet. But he would eventually, wouldn't he?

'I don't understand how you could think that I'd betray you like that…that I'd sneak away, abandoning you and the babies…'

Garrett's voice cracked and Hazel knew he must be hurting as much as she was right now. She longed to reach for him, but felt rooted to the spot somehow.

If only she could explain… But she couldn't. She had no idea what had come over her—only that when she'd seen the job application, there on the screen, a primal urge to shut down and protect herself had come over her in an instant.

Now she'd learned the truth about her mistake she should be overjoyed, but she mostly felt a deep sense of shame and sadness that she could have thought Garrett capable of such a thing—that despite wanting to trust him she somehow didn't... perhaps couldn't.

'I'm sorry,' she said, knowing it wasn't enough.

It was too late and the damage was already done.

'Do you really think I'm that kind of guy?' Garrett pressed.

Hazel shook her head. 'No, of course not.' But she bit her lip to keep herself from saying the rest of her sentence out loud—*but how would I know?*

Their relationship had been a whirlwind, propelled along at breakneck speed to keep up with the progression of her pregnancy. There'd barely been time to get to know one another as people. Instead the focus had been on building something stable enough to welcome children, on preparing for the fact they were about to become parents.

Perhaps that was why it had been so easy for her to assume the worst—because she had so little evidence to assure herself that Garrett was different. That he wouldn't do that. That he wasn't like her ex.

That was what it came down to at the end of the day, Hazel knew. She hated to admit it, but how could she pretend otherwise? The way her last relationship had imploded, leaving her scrabbling about in the ruins of her life, was a memory so fresh and vivid it still hurt to think about. What had she been thinking, letting herself be swept up in a romance so soon, and with such shaky foundations? It was only ever meant to be a one time thing! Had she really believed they could so easily turn that into forever?

'I'm sorry, Garrett,' Hazel heard herself say. 'I really am. It's just—'

'We barely know one another?' Garrett finished.

Hazel nodded miserably. 'It's all happened so quickly, and there's so much riding on it...' She looked down at her bump.

'It's hard to keep perspective. But I still should have given you the benefit of the doubt.'

'Yes, you should have.'

Garrett didn't sound angry, just sad. He looked as miserable as she felt.

'Maybe you're right. Maybe it is all happening too fast. Perhaps we should slow things down...' He swallowed audibly. 'Take some time apart?'

The words felt like a physical blow to Hazel's already tender heart, but how could she argue? After all, hadn't she just said it was all too much too soon? Wasn't she the one who'd started this, in her eagerness to think the worst?

She looked down at the rain-speckled path and nodded. 'That would probably be for the best.'

Garrett sighed heavily. 'I'll call us a taxi.'

When the cab pulled up at the kerb Garrett opened the door for Hazel, but he remained standing on the dark grey pavement.

'You're not coming?'

He shook his head. 'I'm going to walk around for a bit. I need to clear my head.'

Hazel nodded. 'Okay.'

Garrett leaned in, planting the softest of kisses onto her forehead before closing the car door gently.

As the taxi pulled away Hazel twisted in her seat to look out of the rear window, but Garrett had already turned from her and was walking away.

He didn't understand how Hazel could think so little of him.

Or maybe he did. After all, wasn't that how he saw others too? Unreliable. Likely to let you down without warning. Not to be trusted.

He'd lived most of his life believing that, so was it really so surprising that Hazel would assume the worst of him? Especially after what her ex had put her through.

The idea that he'd abandon her, though... Abandon their children...abandon his responsibilities...

He'd done everything he could to show her that he wasn't

that kind of guy. It cut him deep. Did she really think so badly of him? Or was it simply that they didn't really know one another well enough? Their relationship had been a race against the ticking clock of Hazel's pregnancy.

He knew how bad she must feel at accusing him of something so terrible, and she'd apologised immediately, but she hadn't been able to explain to him why she'd leapt to the worst possible conclusion without even pausing to consider an alternative.

He'd felt terrible, suggesting time apart, especially as they'd stood there beneath the porch of the perfect house. The one they should have been putting in an offer for, would have been moving into, had Hazel's discovery not upended everything, throwing their relationship into an entirely new light.

Garrett knew Hazel was hurting, but the truth was so was he. The thing he'd been most afraid of—losing the promise of another family—seemed to be happening already, and the worst of it was there didn't seem to be anything he could do about it.

It wasn't as though either one of them had done something wrong, so they could atone and be forgiven. It seemed they were both just stuck in the past, dragging their hurts along with them. Garrett was afraid to commit fully, and Hazel expected to be abandoned at a moment's notice.

Between them they'd created a pressure pot, where even the slightest thing could be seen as evidence that the other wasn't all in—that it was all about to crumble around them at any moment. That was no way to live...no situation to bring children into.

Garrett had seen enough in foster care to know that hurt people could hurt others, often without even meaning to. He didn't want that for him and Hazel...for their children. He hoped that, with time, they could leave their pasts behind and find a way forward, but they'd need space to do that.

Space that they wouldn't be able to get if they were working together every day.

There was only one thing Garrett could think of to do. He

didn't like the idea, but he didn't see what choice he had—it was clear they couldn't go on as they were.

Tomorrow he would request a temporary transfer to Starling Ward. That way he'd no longer be Hazel's colleague on the neonatal unit. Instead he'd be working on the children's ward, at the other side of the hospital. Maybe then they would both get the space they so desperately needed to figure things out.

The nursery doors swung open and Hazel's heart leapt as she glanced across, but of course it wasn't him.

Wouldn't ever be him, she reminded herself.

Not now that he'd transferred.

It was for the best—Hazel knew that. It would have been impossible for either one of them to gain any perspective or heal from what had happened if they were constantly working alongside one another. But that didn't make it any easier. It didn't stop her holding her breath in anticipation whenever a tall doctor in green scrubs walked into the room.

But none of them had his red hair, his blue eyes, that lazy grin...that way of making her feel.

Hazel swallowed the lump forming in her throat and swiped a hand across her eyes, batting away any stray tears.

It was getting harder and harder to keep her emotions in check at work these days. It was getting harder to be here at all, if she was honest. Now thirty-four weeks pregnant, she was counting down the days until her maternity leave would start. She'd planned to work up until her thirty-sixth week of pregnancy, knowing there was a chance she might be induced not long after.

She got to her feet with a groan.

Just under two weeks to go. And then what? she asked herself as she lumbered into the linen store. *Would she and Garrett finally be ready to talk? To make a plan for what would happen after their babies arrived? Would he be there for the birth?*

Every morning she woke up with more and more questions swirling in her mind, and right now she had answers for none of them.

She just wanted someone to hold her, to tell her it was all going to be all right.

But how could she expect Garrett to do that after what had happened?

After the assumptions she'd made about him.

The way she'd jumped to conclusions, painting him in the same light as her spineless ex…

It was all too awful.

Hazel let the tears fall unchecked now she was in the safety of the linen cupboard.

How would they ever move on from it all? Her past, his past…everything that had happened between them…

The door creaked open behind her.

'Oh! Hazel. I didn't know you were in here. I just came to borrow—' Libby broke off, frowning. 'Hey, what's wrong?'

Hazel sniffed and shook her head. 'Nothing. Ignore me. I was just restocking the linen in Special Care.'

'I didn't realise it was such a distressing task,' Libby said, one eyebrow raised.

Hazel half sobbed, half laughed, before sitting down heavily on the step stool they kept on hand for reaching the higher shelves.

'It's all such a mess!' she groaned, dropping her head into her hands.

'I assume we're not talking about the linen cupboard now?' Libby said gently.

Hazel looked up. 'Garrett and I had a falling out.'

Libby's eyes grew round. 'Is that why he transferred?'

Hazel nodded miserably. 'I guess he thought it would make things awkward if we were working together every day.'

'What happened?'

Hazel shook her head. 'That's the thing… I don't really know. It was all going so well, but then I messed it up without meaning to.'

She explained to her best friend about the job application and her confrontation with Garrett.

'Oh, Hazel,' Libby said softly. 'But you must have known he wouldn't do something like that, surely?'

'I should have, I know. But when I saw the application—' She broke off, shaking her head. 'I don't know…it will probably sound crazy to you, but there was a tiny part of me that almost felt validated. As though I'd been waiting for it…expecting it. As though I'd never really believed it would work out and we would actually live happily ever after.'

She sniffed again, the tears flowing freely again now.

'It doesn't sound crazy,' Libby said softly. 'In fact, it sounds pretty logical. I mean, your ex left you without warning, right? Just upped sticks and flew to the other side of the world?'

Hazel winced and nodded. 'Right.'

As her best friend, Libby had been a rock for Hazel in those early days after Eric had packed his bags and left. In fact, Hazel suspected Libby probably bore more of a grudge against Hazel's ex than she did.

'So then this perfect guy comes along, and the two of you are planning for this wonderful future…' Libby gestured to where Hazel's bump was straining against her cotton scrubs top. 'And your brain panics! It thinks, *Oh, no, not this again. We won't survive another betrayal!* And so it's looking for a way out…a reason not to trust…and then there it is. The job application. As though history is repeating itself all over again. No wonder you assumed the worst!'

'I guess…' Hazel said slowly. She turned Libby's explanation over in her mind. 'But how do I move past it? How do I learn to trust again?'

'How do any of us learn anything?' Libby said. 'By doing. Just like when we were students, remember? We didn't have a clue! We were eager to know it all, but terrified of messing up. Keen to be doing the job, but afraid we weren't up to the task. It's just the same with relationships. There's no rule book, no guarantees, but we keep trying anyway, figuring it out as we go. We keep putting our trust in people, even after others have hurt us, because what's the alternative?'

Hazel blinked up at her. 'Um…sitting in a linen cupboard crying at thirty-four weeks pregnant?'

'Exactly!' Libby said, triumphant.

'But how do I explain all that to Garrett? How do I help

him understand that I'm trying my best? That I want to trust him? That I know he isn't my ex?'

Libby smiled. 'You'll find a way. You'll have to, Hazel. Soon it won't just be you two that all this affects.'

Hazel laid a hand on her bump, protectively, and felt one of the twins squirm beneath her palm. She smiled through her tears. 'You're right,' she said. 'Of course you're right. This is a conversation I need to have with Garrett.'

Libby nodded. 'I mean, preferably not in a linen cupboard...'

Hazel laughed and got to her feet. 'All right—if you insist. I'll invite him over to my place this weekend and we can talk it through. Who knows? Maybe he's feeling the same.'

She reached up to grab a pile of cot sheets from one of the higher shelves.

'Here, let me,' Libby said.

'It's fine, really—'

Only at that exact moment Hazel's stomach tightened and she felt a curious popping sensation, followed by the trickle of warm liquid down her inner thigh.

She looked down in horror. 'Oh, my God.'

'What?'

Hazel turned to her best friend slowly, her heart hammering against her ribs. 'I think my waters just broke.'

Hazel felt another tightening. Mild, but unmistakable.

There was no doubt about it. She was in labour.

It was still six weeks until their due date, but Hazel and Garrett's babies were on their way.

CHAPTER NINETEEN

'THAT'S A NICE bear you've got there.'

The preschooler shot Garrett a wary scowl and hugged the teddy tighter.

Garrett didn't blame him. This was the third day in a row he'd needed to take little Arlo's bloods, and the toddler was quickly getting wise to the fact that Garrett's appearance meant something unpleasant was about to happen.

'I'm sorry, buddy,' he said, 'but it's that time again. There's a sticker in it if you sit super-still, though.'

Garrett lifted the sticker sheet from his scrubs pocket and little Arlo's expression temporarily brightened.

Garrett couldn't say he wasn't enjoying working on Starling. It had been a challenge to brush up on skills he hadn't used in a while—like persuading stubborn three-year-olds to let him take a blood sample—but the change was doing him good, keeping him busy and his mind well occupied, so that it didn't stray into painful territory—or at least that was the theory, anyway.

The truth was, barely an hour went by when he didn't think about Hazel. When he didn't wonder what she was up to and how she was doing. When he didn't worry about the babies. He knew they would be making their way into this world likely sooner rather than later.

He'd thought about calling Hazel a few times. He'd even set out along the corridor one day, with a vague plan to drop into the neonatal unit on his break. But in the end he'd turned around and come back, afraid to make the situation worse, afraid to apply pressure where there was already so much. Afraid to make a mistake that might mean losing her for good.

Garrett pushed Hazel out of his mind as he took Arlo's blood sample as gently as possible, and explained when the results would be available to his anxious parents.

At the nursing station his colleagues were discussing a recent admission, and Garrett half listened as he processed the paperwork for Arlo's blood tests.

They were a nice bunch of people down here, but he missed the pace of NICU and his colleagues there… And one in particular, who he couldn't seem to keep out of his mind for more than a few minutes today.

'Have you met the parents?' one of the nurses was asking another. 'They're the nicest couple.'

The other nurse made a general noise of agreement as she typed up her notes.

'After everything they've been through you'd think it might have worn them down, or torn them apart, but no matter what life throws at them they stick together, through thick and thin.'

'I know. The way they're there for one another is an inspiration.'

Garrett set Arlo's blood samples in the collection box—and then froze as something clicked into place in his mind.

These last few weeks he'd seen parents supporting each other through one of the toughest things he figured any parent could go through—their child being ill. He'd seen terrible things happening to wonderful people, and difficult situations taking their toll on the staff. And throughout it all his mind had kept coming back to Hazel and their babies.

After all, they were a family, weren't they?

His family. His future.

And he'd been wasting time worrying about having his heart broken when he could have been at Hazel's side, supporting her. It hit him now that instead of stepping back when things got difficult, and allowing the complications of their pasts to get in the way, he should have stepped up.

She and the babies were worth the risk of heartache. They were worth everything to him. And he should have told her as much—should have done all he could to make her believe it, even when she was struggling to…perhaps *especially* when she was struggling to.

Well, he would.

Just as soon as he could get away from the ward today he'd find Hazel and tell her everything.

'Dr Buchanan?' A nurse whose name Garrett didn't yet know held a telephone receiver across the top of the nursing station. 'There's someone on the line for you.'

Garrett frowned. 'Did they say who?'

'No, but I think she said she was a midwife.'

The nurse shrugged and Garrett's stomach plummeted all the way to the floor.

That could mean only one thing…

But it was way, way too soon for that, surely?

It was all he could do not to snatch the phone from the nurse's grasp.

'Hello?'

'Garrett? It's Libby.'

The bubbly midwife. Hazel's best friend.

Oh, God.

'What is it? What's happened?'

The line crackled and Garrett's gut lurched.

'You'd better hurry. Hazel's in labour. Your babies are on their way.'

As Garrett ran, his stomach and his mind churned in unison.

Hazel was in labour.

But the babies weren't due for another six weeks yet—the date was marked in red on his phone calendar.

Sure, the doctor in him knew babies came when they wanted—that twins, especially, were more likely to arrive early—but as he sprinted along the busy corridors he realised he hadn't ever fully prepared himself for the possibility that it might happen to them.

That his and Hazel's babies would be early.

That they'd be NICU parents themselves.

And now it was happening. And Hazel was on her own.

I should have been there with her, Garrett berated himself. *How advanced was her labour? Was she coping? Were the babies coping? Would she need a caesarean?*

His medical knowledge seemed to worsen his fears rather than allay them, and he forcibly shoved his anxieties to one side. He couldn't think about that right now, or he'd be no use to Hazel when he finally did arrive. He needed to keep his head. He needed to be strong, the way he'd so often seen other fathers be.

Yes, he was scared, but he was realising that the only thing that would have been more painful than losing his mum as a young boy would have been never having had her in the first place. It had been her strength and love and support in his early years that had kept him going through the difficult times that followed.

By letting his fears get the better of him, Garrett was letting his past dictate his future. He saw that now. And the only thing worse than risking another heartbreak would be not telling Hazel how much he loved her and wanted to spend his life with her and their children.

He loved Hazel.

He didn't know why he hadn't seen it before—why he hadn't been able to admit it, even to himself— but Garrett was overcome with a sudden urge to tell anyone who'd listen, to shout it out in the corridor. But what he wanted most of all was to tell Hazel herself.

He wanted to tell her how he loved the way her wide smile lit up her whole face…how he loved the smattering of freckles across her nose and cheekbones, and the way her glossy black hair swished as she walked. That he loved how she made him feel right from the very first moment he'd seen her on that garden path, the way she made him believe a different future was possible. He loved how easy she was to talk to…how he could make her laugh without really trying, although he did try. How much he loved seeing her in action on the neonatal unit, and how dedicated she was to her job, to the babies in her care. And how proud it made him feel to see how tenderly she cared for them and their families.

He knew she'd make an incredible mother, and he only hoped he'd be at her side to witness her nurture their own children the way she had so many hundreds of others.

He knew that she was just as scared as he was to make the leap after so much heartache and disappointment, but between them he believed they could find the strength to move forward and face whatever lay ahead. He wanted to be there with her for all of it—the good and the bad. He only hoped she'd let him.

Garrett skidded around a corner and raced up a flight of stairs.

One thing was certain. If he ever got to hold Hazel again, he was never going to let go.

CHAPTER TWENTY

HAZEL COULD FEEL another contraction building and she braced herself for it.

'That's it…just breathe,' Libby soothed.

Breathing was easier said than done when it felt like her entire body was caught in a vice, but Hazel tried to focus on her friend's voice, since it was the only thing keeping the panic at bay.

It was all happening so fast. Too fast.

Would Garrett even make it in time?

Hazel knew she should be focusing on what was happening in her body, and on the fact her babies would soon be here, but she didn't want to do this without him. No matter how complicated things had become, she wanted him at her side for this. She wanted Garrett to see their children come into the world.

If only she'd had a chance to speak to him before her waters had broken…to tell him how sorry she was for doubting him and to figure out a way forward for the four of them.

She only hoped they hadn't left it too late.

The contraction eased and she fell back against the bed, panting.

'They're coming much closer together,' Libby said, jotting something down on the notes in front of her. 'It won't be long now.'

'How long?' Hazel couldn't keep the fear from her voice.

Libby's expression softened. 'He'll be here, Hazel.'

Tears pooled in Hazel's eyes. 'What if he isn't? What if he misses it?'

'Why don't I go and call Starling again? See if there's been a hold-up.'

Libby got to her feet.

There were shouts in the corridor.

'You can't just barge in—'

The door flew open and there he was, his cheeks pink and his blue eyes wide, his chest rising and falling rapidly beneath his scrubs top. Garrett's expression was wild, but it eased slightly when his eyes landed on Hazel, who immediately burst into tears at the sight of him.

A horrified student midwife tugged at Garrett's arm. 'I'm so sorry! He insisted—'

'It's okay,' Libby reassured her. 'He's the father.'

'Oh!' The student midwife looked even more horrified now. She gestured to his scrubs, and the ID badge swinging from his neck. 'I just assumed—'

'Dr Garrett Buchanan,' he said, holding up the badge for her to read. 'Neonatologist and father-to-be. Now, if you'll excuse me…?'

He gestured to where Hazel sat sniffling on the bed, hooked up to various wires and machines.

'Of course. I'm so sorry…' The student midwife scuttled away.

Garrett stepped into the room, closing the door behind him. 'Hazel, I—'

He shook his head and glanced over at Libby, as though only just realising she was there.

Libby raised her eyebrows. 'I'll give you two minutes,' she said. 'But not a moment longer. These babies of yours aren't hanging around.'

When she'd left, they both started to speak at once.

'Hazel, I'm so sorry—'

'No, *I'm* sorry. I should never—'

They both broke off, and Hazel gave a nervous laugh.

'I should have been there for you.' Garrett's expression was pained.

'And I should have let you.'

'I've been going crazy these past few weeks…trying to stay

away from you, telling myself it's the right thing to do, that we both need time to heal… But when I heard you'd gone into labour all I could think was that I wasn't there when you needed me. That you might have brought our babies into the world not knowing how much I love them…how much I love *you*.'

Hazel's heart seemed to stutter in her chest as she absorbed Garrett's words and the raw emotion behind them. 'Garrett—'

'I'm sorry. I know it's probably too soon, or too late, or not the right time at all, but I need you to know that.'

Hazel's cheeks were wet, and when she raised a hand to her face she felt the tears streaming down them, although she hadn't even realised she was crying again.

'I love you too.'

'You do?'

Hazel nodded. 'I have for a long time. But it seemed so hard to admit it, somehow. Like it was too much of a risk to trust someone again. But I don't care any more. I just want you to know.'

Garrett pulled her into a gentle hug, being careful of the wires and tubes snaking away from her in every direction.

When he let go, Hazel laughed through her tears. 'We seem to be doing everything in the wrong order, don't we?'

Garrett squeezed her hand tight. 'Just so long as we're doing it together.'

'That's it. You're doing so well.'

Garrett pushed Hazel's hair back from her face and she tried to focus on his voice and his eyes, rather than the pain that shuddered through her body as another contraction began to build.

'Garrett—'

'I'm here.'

Hazel nodded and took another deep breath as she rode the wave.

'Excellent,' Libby said. 'I think you're almost ready to push.'

Hazel should have been pleased. It had been a relatively quick labour, by all accounts, but she had felt every one of the eight hours. Pushing meant it was almost over, but any relief she felt about being fully dilated was overshadowed by the inescapable fact that everything was happening too fast. Her babies were supposed to stay put for another six weeks.

Of course she'd known there was a chance of them coming sooner, and she'd mentally prepared herself for the possibility of giving birth at perhaps thirty-seven or thirty-eight weeks pregnant, but this? This was way too soon.

'Here comes another contraction,' Libby said. 'Do you want to try to push with this one?'

Hazel shook her head, but her body took over regardless, and at the end of her contraction she found herself grunting and bearing down. It seemed she had little choice in the matter. These babies were coming out whether she was ready for them or not.

'It's going to be okay,' Garrett told her. His voice was gentle but firm. 'You can do this.'

'But what if—?'

'They're going to be fine,' Garrett said.

'How do you know?'

Garrett pressed his lips to her forehead. 'I just do.'

Garrett had been scared many, many times before in his life, but never had he experienced such sheer terror as now, during Hazel's labour.

He'd attended so many births in his time as a neonatal doctor, and he'd always felt sympathetic towards the women and their birth partners, but he'd never for one minute imagined himself in their shoes. He'd never expected to find himself the dad-to-be, equal parts excited and terrified, wishing he could do something—anything—to lessen the pain for the woman he loved and hoping and praying to anyone who might listen that both she and their babies would be okay.

The difference was that, unlike most dads-to-be, Garrett had an excellent understanding of all the things that could possibly go wrong and what the potential outcomes might be for their premature twins.

He'd heard people say a little knowledge could be a bad thing, but in this case Garrett felt sure that far too much knowledge wasn't great either. Every time the CTG trace shifted, or the midwife frowned, or Hazel's grip tightened on his hand, he imagined a hundred different scenarios all at once.

It was all he could do to push them away long enough to reassure Hazel, to hold a cool flannel against her forehead and make promises that he had no business making when the truth was that no one could possibly know if it was going to be okay or not—least of all him.

Still, this was neither the time nor the place to admit that to Hazel.

She let out a roar now, as yet another contraction built.

'That's it!' Libby said. 'Get angry with it. Push like you mean it, Hazel.'

Hazel nodded, gritted her teeth and bore down with all her might.

Garrett wished he could do something. He'd never felt so useless.

Hazel let out her breath as the contraction faded.

'You're amazing,' Garrett told her.

In a matter of seconds another contraction was building. Garrett watched Hazel's abdomen tighten, and her face crease as the pain took over.

Please let it nearly be over.

'Fantastic. Here we go,' Libby said. 'Gently, now, Hazel. Breathe through this one, okay? Your first baby's head is almost out.'

Hazel's eyes flew open and locked with Garrett's.

He gave her a nod. 'You can do this.'

Hazel panted, blowing away her contraction as she brought their first baby into the world.

'It's a girl!' Libby cried.

She lifted the baby and both Garrett and Hazel stared in amazement at their daughter, with her smattering of red hair, her scrawny limbs and little shoulders furred with lanugo. Then Libby handed her to the second midwife and the baby was swiftly carried to the other side of the room to undergo the checks that would usually be Hazel and Garrett's domain.

'Go,' Hazel said to him.

Garrett felt torn. He knew the hard part wasn't yet over for Hazel. The second twin would be following any minute. But he also knew that Hazel needed to know how their daughter was doing. That she was going to be okay.

Garrett moved across to the Resuscitaire. He tried not to crowd the team but stood back a little, craning to see over their shoulders. Fortunately Dr Lee was at the baby's airway, which not only filled Garrett with relief, but also meant he got a good view of what was happening.

His training and experience allowed him to fill in the blanks.

Their daughter was gasping. She was making efforts to breathe on her own, but tiring herself out in the process, and since she was so early, and didn't have the fat reserves of a full-term baby, the team would need to take over.

'Dad?' Libby said. 'Do you want to see your second baby being born?'

It took Garrett a moment to realise she was talking to him.

Dad? Oh, God, he was a parent now. A father of one and another on the way—any minute now!

He returned to Hazel's side. 'She's perfect,' he murmured. 'Grunting a little, but they've stabilised her.' He held out his hand for Hazel to grip. 'You ready for round two?'

Hazel shook her head, but then she was pushing with all her might.

Twin number two was born crying.

'Another little girl!' Libby declared. 'And a feisty one at that!'

She laid the second twin on Hazel's chest for a couple of minutes and Garrett marvelled at their youngest daughter's wrinkled pink skin and jerky movements as she mewled her discontent at this cold, bright world she'd been born into.

When the second midwife apologetically swooped her away Garrett realised his cheeks were wet with tears, as were Hazel's. He took her in his arms and they sobbed onto each other's shoulders.

Their twins were both here. Yes, they were early, but they

were pink, and they were breathing—hell, one of them was currently filling the room with her furious newborn cries.

It was the absolute best they could have hoped for under the circumstances.

'I can't believe they're here,' Garrett said. 'I can't believe they're ours.'

'They're ours.'

Garrett's words broke through Hazel's pain and exhaustion. *The twins are here, and we're parents at last.*

It was something Hazel had always wanted, but never expected. Something she'd almost given up hope of ever happening. She was a mother to two beautiful baby girls and their father was squeezing her hand now, his eyes shining.

'You were incredible. I'm so proud of you.'

Hazel smiled. She felt as if she'd been turned inside out and might never be quite the same again, but she supposed that was how all new mums felt. And if her nine years as a neonatal nurse had taught her anything, it was that it was all worth it once you got to hold your baby in your arms.

Only, Hazel was going to have to wait for that experience.

As she watched her twins being wheeled out of the delivery room Hazel's heart ached and her arms felt empty.

'Go with them,' she told Garrett.

She didn't want him to leave her side, but she needed to know that he was with them. That her daughters wouldn't be on their own for even a second. That their dad would be watching over them until she could.

CHAPTER TWENTY-ONE

IT HAD BEEN the longest three hours of Hazel's life. The seconds stretching into minutes and the minutes into hours as she'd waited for the all-clear to visit her babies over in the neonatal unit. Now, finally, with a clean bill of health and both twins stabilised and ready for visitors, Garrett was wheeling her round to NICU.

'I'm sure I could walk.'

'Hazel, you just gave birth—to twins, no less. Just sit back and enjoy the ride, okay?'

'All right,' Hazel muttered.

She felt weak and vulnerable, as though everyone was looking at her—though of course they weren't. She'd spent her entire pregnancy feeling over-emotional, and had assumed that once the babies were born she'd feel more level-headed. But it clearly didn't work that way, and the kindly smile of an elderly gentleman passing them in the corridor almost set her off crying again.

'Here we are.'

Garrett swiped his ID badge and navigated the hospital wheelchair through the doors of the neonatal unit, albeit with some difficulty.

Anna came forward to meet them. 'They're both in HDU,' she said. 'Twin One is fast asleep and Twin Two is wrestling her oxygen off. Come on through and you can meet them.'

As Garrett wheeled her between the two incubators the tears that had been filling Hazel's eyes on the journey from Delivery Suite finally spilled over, running down her cheeks. Garrett kissed her forehead, and Anna wordlessly handed Hazel a tissue.

Just as Anna had said, the smaller of the two, the first to be born, was snoozing peacefully on her front. A CPAP mask covered most of her tiny face, but Hazel drank in every other detail that she could, from the fair, downy hair covering her little shoulders and scalp to the minute foot peeking from beneath a lemon-yellow blanket.

To her right, the second and slightly bigger of their daughters was lying on her back, her oxygen tubing askew, her tiny brow furrowed and her blue eyes blinking up at Garrett, as though she was demanding to know who he was and what was going on here.

A laugh fought its way through Hazel's tears. 'Like chalk and cheese already.'

Anna nodded in agreement. 'I think you'll have your hands full with this one.'

'Oh, I don't know...' Garrett looked from one baby to the other. 'It's sometimes the quiet ones you have to watch out for.'

Anna gave them a full update. Twin One was on CPAP to help her maintain her airway pressures, but she wasn't requiring oxygen and her observations were all stable. Twin Two had been prescribed low-flow oxygen, but based on the fact that she was currently wearing her oxygen prongs on her cheek rather than in her nostrils, she clearly wasn't a fan and didn't seem to be struggling without it.

'We can start feeds as soon as you're ready to express,' Anna said.

'Already on it.'

Hazel handed over the two tiny syringes of colostrum she'd managed to express back in Delivery Suite. *Liquid gold*, they all called it. Full of the specific nutrients and antibodies the twins needed to grow and develop now they were no longer inside her.

Hazel touched a hand to her slightly deflated bump. It felt so strange that her womb was empty now. That those same babies she'd carried all these months were now lying here in front of her, out in the big world, their own little people, separate from her and one another.

'I wonder if they miss each other,' she murmured.

'I'm sure they do,' Garrett said. 'Do you think—?'

Anna nodded, answering his question before he had asked it. 'Of course,' she said. 'Let me get some screens.'

And there, ensconced behind the pastel-coloured screens, in one corner of the High Dependency unit, Hazel finally got to hold her babies.

The feeling when Anna handed them to her was indescribable. Hazel felt grounded for the first time since giving birth. As though at last things made sense.

She'd been afraid that the unexpected pregnancy and the whirlwind birth might affect the bond she felt. That being separated from her babies for a few hours might mean she'd miss out on that rush of love everyone spoke about. But she needn't have worried. The moment she felt their skin on hers, and pressed her nose to their tiny heads, something primal was activated in her and Hazel felt, deep in her bones, that these were her babies, and that she would lay down her life for them over and over, no matter how big they grew or whatever happened in the future.

They were her children and she loved them.

When Hazel looked up she found Garrett brushing away a stray tear with his thumb.

'I can't believe we have twins!' he said.

'I know,' Hazel whispered. She felt the rise and fall of their tiny chests against hers. 'Would you like to hold them?'

Garrett's eyes widened. 'I don't… I mean…are you sure…? What if I…?'

'Garrett,' Hazel said. 'You must have held a million babies before! You'll be fine.'

'Yes, but those weren't… I mean, these are *our* babies.' Garrett's voice was filled with awe.

'Exactly. And you're their dad. You'll know what to do.'

Anna joined them behind the screens and helped Hazel pass the girls across to Garrett, who sat waiting in a chair beside her, his arms out and his eyes wide.

'Relax,' Anna told him before she left them alone again.

Once both babies were positioned in his arms Garrett's shoulders fell and he began to breathe once more. He stared down at the twins in wonder. 'Well, hello, little ones…' He shook his head and looked up at Hazel with a frown. 'This is no good.'

'You're not comfortable?'

'No, I don't mean that. I mean *little ones*, *girls*, *Twin One*, *Twin Two*… It's no good. We have to name them.'

Hazel laughed. 'I suppose so.'

They'd talked about names briefly, but that had been before the misunderstanding with the job application…before their time apart. Hazel had pushed the topic to the back of her mind in recent weeks.

She'd expected to have so much more time…

'Do you still—?' Hazel began.

'What do you think of—?' Garrett said at the same time.

The two of them laughed.

'I think this one is Hope.' Hazel touched a finger to Twin One's tiny nose. 'And her sister here…' Hazel stroked twin two's cheek '…is Faith.'

Garrett nodded. 'Hope and Faith. Perfect.'

'Hope Elizabeth,' Hazel said. Elizabeth was her mum's name, and she knew how much it would mean to her to have one of her granddaughters share it. 'And Faith Louise.'

Garrett looked up, his eyes catching hers. She saw his Adam's apple bobbing as he swallowed hard.

'Are you sure?'

Hazel nodded. 'That way she'll always have a connection to her.'

A connection. Between Garrett's past and his future. A name shared by his late mum and his new daughter. His worlds colliding…before and after.

It was almost too much to take in. It *was* too much to take in. But he tried anyway, as he breathed in the new baby scent of his daughters and his girlfriend's smile as she looked on.

Anna took photos of the four of them and later, when the

twins were sleeping and he and Hazel were back on Delivery Suite, Garrett marvelled over the images, reliving the rush of emotion all over again.

'I'm a dad…' he murmured.

Hazel smiled at him from the bed. She looked exhausted, but radiant.

'How does it feel?'

Garrett tried to narrow down the hundreds of thoughts and emotions swirling through him, grasping on to any he could identify.

'Incredible…but also slightly surreal.'

Hazel laughed. 'Tell me about it.'

'I mean, I'm a parent. Me! Dr Garrett Buchanan. A dad!' He shook his head. 'I just hope I'll be a good one.'

'You will,' Hazel said.

'But what if I'm not? I never had a father figure myself. How will I know what to do?'

Hazel shrugged. 'You'll figure it out. You'll learn as you go. The same way you learned how to be a doctor.'

'That's different,' Garrett protested. 'I studied at university. It's not like there are courses on how to be a good parent.'

'University isn't what makes you a good doctor,' Hazel said. 'That comes from the hours you put in and the effort you make to get it right, from learning when you don't. Being a good doctor is about more than your qualifications, it's about your heart. That's why you'll be a good dad, Garrett, because you're a good man, with a good heart.'

She looped her fingers between his and brought the back of his hand to her mouth.

'And if you ever doubt yourself you'll have three strong women by your side to remind you.'

'I still can't believe I'm a mum,' Hazel murmured.

The twins were settled in their incubators and sleeping soundly. Hazel pressed her forehead against the side of baby Hope's incubator, drinking in every detail, before turning to do the same with Faith.

'Garrett…?'

Garrett was down on one knee on the floor between the two incubators, looking intently at the foot in front of him.

'Did you drop something?'

He turned his head up to her and Hazel could see unshed tears shining in his eyes. He shook his head and held out his hand, grasping one of hers.

'Hazel Bridges, will you marry me?'

Hazel's hands flew up to her face and she wobbled slightly.

'Whoa!' Garrett jumped to his feet and lowered Hazel gently into the wheelchair behind her. 'Too much, too soon?'

Hazel shook her head and burst into tears. 'Yes, of course I'll marry you!' she choked out between sobs.

'You will?'

Hazel nodded, and Garrett blinked a couple of times, as if to make sure he wasn't imagining her response, before breaking into a grin.

He leant down, kissing her gently, but when he broke away his grin faltered. 'I haven't got a ring.'

Hazel laughed. 'It's fine.'

'No, no…' Garrett looked around them, rummaging in the pocket of his scrubs. 'There must be something…'

He pulled out a roll of surgical tape.

'Aha!' He dropped to one knee once more, this time holding out the tape. 'Will you do me the honour of being my wife?'

Hazel laughed, nodding, and Garrett wound the tape around her ring finger, snipping it off with a pair of medical scissors.

Hazel looked down at the tape ring, and then up at the man she loved. Either side of her their newborn twins slept soundly, unaware of the drama her parents were creating at their cot side.

Hazel's eyes were swimming with tears, but her heart was full. She had everything she'd ever wanted, and even though it looked nothing like she'd imagined, it felt exactly right.

CHAPTER TWENTY-TWO

IT WAS THE big day.

Truth be told, they'd had a few big days since they'd met. The day Hazel had found out she was pregnant...the day she'd told Garrett...the day they'd discovered they were having twins... the day their girls had been born...

But now they were facing another major milestone.

After six weeks of visiting their twins on the neonatal unit Hazel and Garrett were finally taking their babies home. Like so many other NICU parents they'd been counting the days until this moment. Hazel had hardly slept last night, and had been up at the crack of dawn making sure everything was ready.

'You're like a little kid at Christmas,' Garrett said, with a yawn.

Hazel turned to see him leaning against the doorframe of the nursery, rubbing sleep from his eyes. They'd moved in together a month ago, but Hazel still wasn't used to having him around twenty-four-seven, and her pulse skittered as it always did at the sight of him. Her handsome fiancé.

'I can't help it,' she said. 'I can't believe it's finally here. That we're bringing them home at last.'

She turned back to the room, with its side-by-side cribs, pale grey walls and lemon-yellow curtains. Garrett had worked so hard to get it ready. Between visiting the girls at the hospital, and starting his new post as a neonatal consultant, he'd been busy building flatpack furniture and painting the nursery walls, while Hazel expressed milk and read every parenting book she could find.

'Don't we know all this stuff already?' Garrett had frowned

over her shoulder as she'd read aloud the safe sleeping guidelines for what must have been the fiftieth time.

'Yes, but you can never be too prepared,' she'd said.

And now they *were* prepared, everything was finally ready, and Hazel's stomach was dancing a jig.

As if he could sense it, Garrett came up behind her and wrapped his arms around her. 'It's perfect,' he said. 'And you're going to be the perfect mum.'

Hazel considered arguing. After all, how would he know? Just because she was a neonatal nurse, it didn't mean she knew how to be a parent. But instead she let her shoulders drop and leaned back into Garrett's embrace.

'I hope so.'

Garrett kissed the top of her head. 'I know it.'

The unit was busy, but a few familiar faces stopped to say hi, or to wave as Hazel and Garrett made their way to the Special Care nursery, where their girls were waiting.

'How are they today?' Hazel asked Miriam.

'Like chalk and cheese, as usual.'

Hazel peered into their cots. Faith was wide awake, staring up at them with round blue eyes. Hope, on the other hand, was asleep, and had a little patch of milk drool at the corner of her mouth.

Hazel laughed. 'I see what you mean.'

'They were fed an hour ago, and Dr Lee handled the discharge paperwork herself, so they're ready when you are.'

Hazel's stomach flipped.

This was it.

At last. After forty days in the NICU they were taking their babies home. It felt wonderful, terrifying and surreal, all at the same time.

It was still cold outside, but after wrestling the twins into their matching coats, hats and booties, Hazel was sweating lightly.

'They look so tiny,' Garrett said.

Next to some of their NICU roommates Faith and Hope had appeared huge, but now, in their car seats, they were suddenly fragile newborns all over again.

Hazel's heart constricted. 'They do.'

'All right—let's have a photo of the four of you,' Miriam said.

She used the unit's Polaroid camera, and when the photo developed she wrote the date beneath the image in black marker pen.

'One for the memory box.' She winked at Hazel and Garrett. 'In a few years you'll never believe they were once so small.'

Hazel both could and couldn't believe it. She hadn't been sure this day would ever come, but now here she was—a mum. She struggled to imagine a time when her daughters would be walking and talking, starting school, or slamming doors and rolling their eyes at her. But she knew that those days would come, and she couldn't wait to experience them all. To treasure every single minute.

The entire unit congregated to wave them off, and the cheers and cries of 'Good luck!' were only just dying down as they stepped off the unit and out into the hospital corridor beyond.

Down in the foyer they passed the coffee shop where Hazel had dithered over her order just months ago, wondering if she was capable of changing something so small about her life. Now here she was, carrying her baby daughter in a car seat as her tall, handsome red-headed doctor partner walked beside her, carrying their other daughter.

As if reading her mind, Garrett grinned sideways at her, making her stomach flip with his hooded gaze. 'You remember that first day we met?'

He gestured to the seating area, where Hazel had saved the life of the choking baby.

'That wasn't the first time we met,' she reminded him.

'Oh, I remember.' Garrett winked and Hazel laughed.

The automatic doors opened as they approached, and together they stepped out of the hospital into the crisp March sunshine, ready to face their future.

Hazel didn't know what it held. No one could. But she knew that no matter what it might bring they would be in it together. That what had started as one moment of passion had turned into forever.

EPILOGUE

One year later...

THE COBBLESTONED COURTYARD glittered with frost and the sky above matched the shade of Hazel's dress.

'You know, they say snow on your wedding day is a sign of fertility.' Libby wiggled her eyebrows.

Hazel laughed. 'Don't you think I have my hands full as it is?'

They both looked down to where Hazel was grasping her twins' hands. Little Faith and Hope were wearing mini bridesmaids' dresses to match the grown-up version Libby was sporting. Not that either one of them seemed very impressed. Faith was already tugging at the bow on the front of her dress with a scowl.

Libby touched Hazel's arm, her expression suddenly serious. 'Are you nervous?'

Hazel glanced up at the glass doors ahead, both thrown open despite the frigid March air. Beyond them, she knew Garrett would be waiting, along with her family and their friends and colleagues.

Butterflies danced and somersaulted in Hazel's stomach, but when she looked down at her daughters at her side her nerves eased. She and Garrett were already tied to one another forever by their beautiful girls. Today was about celebrating that and making it official.

What was there to be anxious about?

Hazel shook her head and Libby smiled.

'There you are—my three best girls.'

Hazel's dad pulled her into an embrace and beamed down at his granddaughters. Behind him, Hazel's mum stood, hands clasped and tears glistening in her eyes.

'Oh, darling, you look wonderful.'

'Thanks, Mum,' Hazel whispered, her own voice thick with unshed tears.

They might not have been close when she was growing up, but ever since she'd announced her surprise pregnancy and—not long after that—the twins' early arrival, her parents had set everything aside to be there for Hazel, and they had embraced becoming grandparents in a way she'd never imagined. They also loved their new son-in-law-to-be almost as much as Hazel did.

Watching them delight in her twin daughters had healed Hazel in ways she hadn't even realised she needed, and it had brought her closer to her parents than she'd ever been. She was beginning to realise that while they might have made mistakes, and while her childhood might have lacked in some ways, they'd only ever been trying their best—just as she and Garrett were doing now.

'Ready?' her dad asked, holding out one arm for Hazel and a hand for one of his granddaughters.

Hazel nodded and took his arm as Libby stepped into position behind them, and inside the register office music began to play.

It was time.

At the very first note Garrett's heart leapt into his throat. He could feel his pulse bounding there, and the urge to turn around, to glimpse his bride-to-be, was overwhelming.

His best man leaned in. 'Not yet.'

Garrett nodded.

It had been an easy decision, in the end, who to ask. If it hadn't been for Jake's last-minute party invitation Garrett might never have met Hazel that fateful night...

'She's here.'

Jake's words brought Garrett back to the here and now.

He glanced over his shoulder and his chest swelled with

pride at the sight of Hazel walking towards him. Her green eyes sparkled beneath her long lashes and her skin glowed. She smiled when she caught him looking, and Garrett couldn't help but grin back at her. She looked stunning, and the sight of their daughters, tottering along in their matching dresses, only melted his heart even more.

Finally the trio reached him, coming to a standstill at his side.

'You look incredible,' he whispered.

'You don't look so bad yourself,' Hazel murmured.

Garrett dropped into a crouch. 'And you two are as beautiful as ever.'

Faith scowled and Hope poked her dad in the cheek before Libby led them away to sit—or at least wriggle around—on the front row.

The registrar welcomed everyone and ran through the order of service.

Garrett had expected to feel more nervous—hell, he *had* felt more nervous. All morning he'd been a jittering mess of nerves. But right now, standing next to Hazel, waiting to say his vows in front of the people they knew and loved, it suddenly felt like the most natural thing in the world.

What was there to be nervous about?

She loved him and he loved her—with all his heart. The four of them were a family. And although Garrett couldn't predict the future, he could promise that he'd never stop loving Hazel and their children, no matter what it might hold.

When the registrar asked him to make his vows Garrett's voice was clear and steady, but thick with the swirling mix of emotions he was feeling

'I call upon these persons, here present, to witness that I, Garrett David Buchanan, do take thee, Hazel Marie Bridges, to be my lawful wedded wife.'

Hazel made her vows to him, eyes shining, and then the registrar was declaring them husband and wife.

'You may kiss the bride.'

Garrett didn't need telling twice. He gently swept Hazel into his arms, pressing his mouth to hers, and he felt her smile beneath his lips, her cheeks wet with happy tears.

'I love you, Mrs Buchanan.'

'And I love *you*, Mr Buchanan.'

Around them, the room burst into applause.

The ting of a fork against crystal hushed the chatter in the room, and Jake got to his feet.

'Ladies and gentlemen… If you'll allow me a few minutes, I have some words I'd like to share with you about my friend Garrett.'

Hazel tensed.

The best man's speech.

It was the only part of the day she hadn't been looking forward to. In fact, it was fair to say she'd been dreading it. It was silly, she knew, but she couldn't help but worry about what Jake might have to say.

After all, he'd known Garrett far longer than she had, and they'd been medical students together. Who knew what wild antics they might have got up to? And now Jake was about to share that knowledge with a room full of people…

Hazel lifted her glass of bubbly and knocked it back in one. Garrett raised one eyebrow and squeezed her hand beneath the table.

'I know you'll all be dying to hear what Garrett and I got up to as med students,' Jake said, 'and that you can't wait for me to dish the dirt on Dr Garrett Buchanan.'

A few cheers went up and Hazel winced.

'But I'm afraid I'm going to have to disappoint you all.'

There was a collective groan.

'Not because of any sense of propriety, you understand,' Jake continued. 'But because there isn't any.' He shrugged. 'The truth is, Garrett Buchanan is an all-round top bloke— almost annoyingly so. It's made writing this speech a bit of a nightmare, actually.'

There were a few laughs around the room and Hazel exhaled.

'When I was trying to come up with funny stories to tell they all seemed to end with Garrett as the hero. Like the time we all went to a festival together and got separated, and we found Garrett volunteering in the first-aid tent. Or when we entered him into a drag contest for a laugh and he ended up donating his pink stilettos to another contestant whose heel had snapped.'

Hazel looked to Garrett, her eyes shining, and saw he'd ducked his head in embarrassment.

'The guy's not a bore—don't get me wrong. He was always the first to get a round in at uni, and when we passed our final exams he drank so much champagne that he passed out. We all took photos of him in compromising positions with Geoff the skeleton from the clinical skills lab.'

Hazel laughed out loud.

'I thought about incorporating them as a slideshow here for you today, in fact, but weirdly I couldn't find the files...'

Jake raised an eyebrow at Garrett, and Garrett held up his hands as if to say, *Not guilty.*

'Anyway, my point is, you've got yourself a good man, Hazel.'

Hazel nodded in agreement. She already knew that.

'And Garrett? You once told me the reason you went into medicine was to make your mum proud of you. Well, I don't think there's any doubt that you have. I know that, wherever she is, Louise Buchanan will be looking down on her son today with as much pride in her heart as I have. Congratulations, my friend.' Jake raised his glass. 'Please join me in a toast to the happy couple.'

There were cries of 'Cheers!' and a deafening round of applause.

Garrett swiped a hand across his eyes and Hazel leaned in and planted a kiss on his cheek.

After the cheers had died down, the DJ announced that it was time for the first dance.

Hazel frowned as Garrett lifted her to her feet and led her to the dance floor.

'A first dance? I didn't know we'd chosen one.'

The song started and her eyes widened.

'You remember?' Garrett asked.

'Of course I remember.'

As the first notes played, memories flooded Hazel's mind of the first time she'd spotted Garrett Buchanan, leaning against a tree at the bottom of her friend's garden, sunlight burnishing his red hair and his expression shaded by the branches above. She remembered how he'd caught her eye then, and again later, in an upstairs corridor with music floating up the staircase…

It was supposed to have been for one night only. And yet here she was, safe in his arms, swaying to the very same song that had been playing when they'd first met. His wedding ring on her finger, and his promises of forever ringing clear and true in her mind.

Hazel looked up into Garrett's eyes and saw the same war of emotions she felt playing out on his face. They'd been through so much in such a short space of time. Going from literal strangers to parents in a matter of months. And now here they were, husband and wife.

There were no words that Hazel could find to describe how that felt, or how much meeting Garrett Buchanan had changed her entire life for the better.

As if reading her mind, Garret spoke. 'I didn't know it then, but that was the best night of my life,' he said, eyes shining.

'The best night of your life *so far*,' Hazel teased.

Garrett laughed. 'True.'

He pulled her to him and they kissed as though they weren't in the middle of a room full of people.

'Now, about that honeymoon…' Garrett murmured as Hazel pulled away.

She laughed, but her cheeks blazed and the butterflies in her stomach took flight at the mere suggestion of a honeymoon with her incredibly hot husband.

Her husband!

How long would it be until she got used to that word?

The song that Hazel would forever think of as 'theirs' came to a close, and over the music came a chorus of toddler chatter. They both turned to find the twins tottering towards them across the dance floor.

'I think maybe the honeymoon will have to wait,' Hazel said.

Garrett grinned. 'Then it's a good thing we have forever.'

* * * * *

MILLS & BOON®

Coming next month

NURSE'S DUBAI TEMPTATION
Scarlet Wilson

Theo's presence in the room made her catch her breath. She tried not to notice how handsome he was, or the way her body reacted to the smell of his aftershave.

He looked up in surprise at Addy. 'What are you doing here?'

She raised her eyebrows. 'You mean you aren't part of the plot to destroy me?'

He sagged down into a seat with a look of bewilderment.

'I've not been here long enough to plot anything,' he said easily. 'And I'm not important enough, and I don't have enough hours in the day. But—' he took a breath and looked amused '—I might be up to plotting some kind of coup at a later date.'

She leaned forward. 'And why would that be?'

He sat back and folded his arms. 'Let's just say I'm watching and waiting. Biding my time.'

'Are you planning on becoming leader of the world?'

He shook his head and grinned at her. 'You forget I have a three-year-old. Leader of the world is tame. He'd expect me to be leader of the universe.'

Continue reading

NURSE'S DUBAI TEMPTATION
Scarlet Wilson

Available next month
millsandboon.co.uk

COMING SOON!

We really hope you enjoyed reading this book.
If you're looking for more romance
be sure to head to the shops when
new books are available on

Thursday 24th
April

To see which titles are coming soon, please visit
millsandboon.co.uk/nextmonth

LET'S TALK

Romance

For exclusive extracts, competitions and special offers, find us online:

- 🅕 MillsandBoon
- 𝕏 @MillsandBoon
- 📷 @MillsandBoonUK
- ♪ @MillsandBoonUK

Get in touch on 01413 063 232

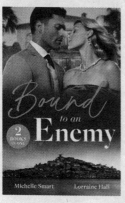
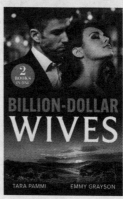

Afterglow Books is a trend-led, trope-filled list of books with diverse, authentic and relatable characters, a wide array of voices and representations, plus real world trials and tribulations. Featuring all the tropes you could possibly want (think small-town settings, fake relationships, grumpy vs sunshine, enemies to lovers) and all with a generous dose of spice in every story.

♪ @millsandboonuk
📷 @millsandboonuk
afterglowbooks.co.uk

#AfterglowBooks

For all the latest book news, exclusive content and giveaways scan the QR code below to sign up to the Afterglow newsletter:

SCAN ME

afterglow BOOKS

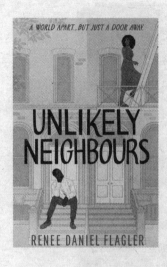

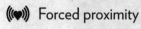

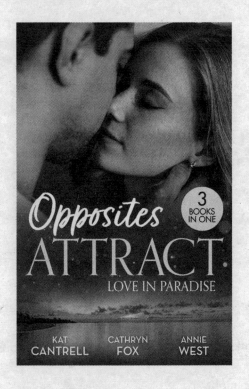